THE DRUPERMAN TAPES

THE

DRUPERMAN

TAPES

John Goodger

 St. Martin's Minotaur ❧ New York

www.minotaurbooks.com

Library of Congress Cataloging-in-Publication Data

Goodger, John.
    The Druperman tapes / John Goodger.—1st ed.
       p. cm.
    ISBN 0-312-32199-6
    EAN 978-0312-32199-4
    1. Casinos—Fiction. 2. Extortion—Fiction. 3. Security consultants—
Fiction. 4. Ex-police officers—Fiction. 5. Las Vegas (Nev.)—Fiction.
I. Title.

PR9199.4.G665D78 2004
813'.6—dc22   2004050803

First Edition: January 2005

10   9   8   7   6   5   4   3   2   1

To Carol, *with love and appreciation*

Acknowledgments

To all the people who so generously gave of their time, talent, and expertise to help a fledgling writer get his first book off the ground, sincere thanks: to Brendan Pierce for introducing me to the people, places, and customs of South Boston; to Lieutenant Robert O'Toole of the Boston Police for sharing his encyclopedic knowledge of the department; to Robert Johnson-Lally, archivist of the Roman Catholic Archdiocese of Boston, for information about the parochial school system of the sixties and seventies; to Bill Lessley of Everett, Washington, for guidance to the streets and sights of the Olympia-Everett corridor; to Margaret Kurtz of Caesars Palace for a fascinating glimpse into the infrastructure of the casino world; to Sergeant Greg McCurdy of the Las Vegas Metropolitan Police Department for his patience on a busy day; to Mike Donahue of the Las Vegas News Bureau for a wealth of information about the world's premier entertainment destination; to Captain R. L. Sgrignoli of the U.S. Marines for her comprehensive insights into the Corps; to Doug Shaddock of Nortel for his help with cellular telephone technology; to Robert Nagy of Voyageur Colonial for showing me around intercity buses; to Peter Constantine, Jean Ledoux, David Goodger, and especially Shelley Grandy for their invaluable suggestions; to Eddie Kritzer for believing in the book; to Jessica Kaye, my perspicacious agent, for proposing changes that greatly improved the story; and to Linda McFall, my editor at St. Martin's Minotaur, for her expert guidance.

—John Goodger, Montreal, August 2004

LAS VEGAS,
OCTOBER

PART I

1 **Even before the envelope** containing the tape and the threatening letter landed on his desk, a series of minor annoyances had upgraded Emmett Druperman's disposition from everyday irascible to red-flag aggravated.

For starters, early-morning pickets were teeming around the Galaxy like ants at a picnic, discouraging walk-in traffic and reducing the casino drop alarmingly.

Then there was this message on his machine from Tony Francisco's agent, suggesting that unless the hotel upped the ante, the singer might be "forced" to cancel an appearance on whose promotion Druperman had just invested well over half a million dollars.

And just to finish things off nicely, his hemorrhoids were on fire.

Preoccupied with these fiscal and physical irritants, Druperman came close to consigning the envelope to the trash along with the few other pieces of junk mail that had escaped Edith's steely eye. Only the envelope's very *plainness* saved it. The padded brown nine-by-twelve envelope bore neither postage stamp nor metered imprint; no courier slip was attached; it had no markings except for a neatly printed address label.

Which was the other funny thing. EMMETT DRUPERMAN, PRESIDENT OF LVCA, CONFIDENTIAL, the label read. Druperman never got mail in his capacity as head of the Las Vegas Casino Association. Few people knew that the LVCA even existed, fewer still that he was its president. Secrecy had always been the association's watchword. Its members, powerful men who ran most of the casinos in Las Vegas, frequently bent the law to suit their own purposes, rarely committing anything to paper. Certainly they never *wrote* to one another. Most of Druperman's everyday correspondents addressed him by his far better known title of Chief Executive Officer, Galaxy Hotel and Casino.

For a fleeting instant, he considered the possibility of a letter bomb. Before corporate respectability had become the norm in Vegas, the CEO had acquired his share of enemies. But just as quickly, he banished the notion—after all, this was the twenty-first century and the town had long since outgrown its gangster heritage. Besides, Edith had already slit the envelope open and survived. Druperman imagined his secretary blown to pieces, bits of her scrawny body pasted to the ceiling, those goddamn pearls she always wore embedded in the walls like bullets at a crime scene. He enjoyed the thought briefly, then put it out of his mind.

Druperman tipped the contents of the envelope onto the polished mahogany surface of his desk, noting three items: a laser-printed letter on a single unfolded sheet of white paper, a VHS tape in a generic cardboard sleeve, and a red five-dollar chip from the Dunes Hotel and Casino.

His curiosity aroused, the CEO examined the red chip. Nothing unusual about it; chips from defunct casinos were a dime a dozen in Vegas. He rolled it between thumb and forefinger absently while straightening his bifocals, then picked up the letter.

As he read, it dawned upon Emmett Druperman that he might now have a real problem on his hands, a potentially deadly one that could cause his current concerns with hard-ass unions and hemorrhoids and double-dealing entertainers to pale by comparison. With a deepening frown, he inserted the tape into one of the VCR units in his media wall. Returning to his desk, he picked up the remote and pushed PLAY. He stared at the TV in disbelief, his normally sanguine countenance darkening several shades as the message on the big screen became clear.

The CEO pushed a button on his speakerphone and barked into it. "Edith? Call Steve Forrester."

After thirty seconds, his secretary's voice came back, "He's not in yet, Mr. D."

"Well, find him. And get him in here—now."

Emmett Druperman released the speakerphone button, ending the discussion. Where the hell was his Vice President of Security when he needed him? He squirmed in his plush leather chair, trying unsuccessfully to promote a little relief from the burning pain in his ass.

2 **After years** of paying rent on a series of tacky bachelor apartments, interrupted only by a brief stay in married quarters, Steve Forrester had finally scraped up the cash and the courage to buy into the luxury Conquistador Trail development. He had felt some obligation to live up to his newfound prosperity as Vice President of Security of the Galaxy Hotel and Casino, Las Vegas's premier megaresort. He also realized that with land values soaring, virtually any investment in Vegas real estate was a solid bet.

Located three miles west of Las Vegas Boulevard, the Conquistador Trail Country Club consisted of an upscale cluster of Spanish-tiled condominiums nestled around a lush private golf course. Access was through wrought-iron gates, where a cascading tiered waterfall welcomed owners and their guests. Conquistador Trail provided its residents all the amenities of estate living with none of the petty annoyances that plagued the middle class. Everything from grass cutting to pool maintenance was transparently provided; private cops patrolled the grounds; Avon ladies, Jehovah's Witnesses, and other uninvited callers were politely but efficiently shooed away by twenty-four-hour security. The quiet, civilized luxury of the development suited both *arrivé* and upwardly mobile, the latter a class in which Steve Forrester definitely qualified for membership.

On the morning Forrester got the call from Druperman's secretary, the day had dawned clear and bright at Conquistador Trail. While Steve dreamt fitfully, an enterprising foursome below his bedroom window cast long shadows across the dewy grass as they prepared to tee off. It was the best time of day to play golf in Vegas. Even now, at 8:15 on a fine October morning, the thermometer outside was nudging seventy degrees Fahrenheit. By eleven o'clock the temperature would be over eighty; by two it would be pushing ninety.

Forrester stirred. The dream was beginning to lose its form, but his body wasn't quite ready to burst the cocoon of sleep. Then the phone rang, reducing the dream to forgotten shreds.

Disoriented, he kicked off the covers and scrabbled for the phone.

"Hello," he croaked into the wrong end of the receiver.

"It's Edith." In the voice of Emmett Druperman's secretary there was a distinct note of triumph at having woken Forrester, modulated by an undertone of accusation that he was still at home—and sleeping, to boot. "Did I wake you?"

He ignored the rhetorical question, righted the receiver, and forced himself to focus. "What time is it?"

"Eight-seventeen."

"Jesus Christ, Edith." Had he forgotten some appointment, missed some early meeting? "What's up?"

"*Mister* Druperman wants to see you on the Bridge. Now."

"Any idea why?"

"He sounded mad."

"At me?"

She pressed her advantage relentlessly. "I think so. You'd better not keep him waiting."

"All right. Tell Emmett half an hour."

She hung up.

"Douche bag," Forrester muttered as he clattered the phone back into its cradle and reached for the pack of Vantage 100s he kept on the bedside table. Then as the last wisps of sleep evaporated, he remembered—the cigarettes weren't there anymore. He'd quit. God, had it actually been two days? Could he make it through another day without a smoke? Another hour? At that moment, he had his doubts.

With an effort, he rolled out of bed and stumbled into the bathroom. He lathered his face for shaving and winced at the reflection. Dark smudges under his eyes and a throbbing vein in his temple bespoke too much Jack Daniel's the previous evening. Otherwise, it was a not-unpleasant mug: only a slightly off-center nose, memento of his high-school wrestling days, marred its symmetry. It featured hazel eyes— at this moment somewhat bloodshot—a strong chin, and a firm mouth. A sprinkle of gray appeared to have taken a foothold just above the ears, and the small laugh lines at the corners of the eyes were becoming a little more permanent, but these things did not bother Forrester. Below the neck he was still in reasonable shape, never more than two or three pounds over his high-school wrestling team weight—thanks more to heredity than to any conscious effort at exercise on his part.

Showered and shaven, Forrester plugged in the electric kettle and popped a Nicorette. Instead of chewing it slowly as the package instructed, he bit down hard and swallowed the bitter juice. The nicotine rush felt so good that he immediately crunched down again. Maybe he *could* make it through the day. If he could just get past the goddamn 7-Eleven on the way to the Galaxy, he'd be too busy working to think about smoking. As far as he could remember, he hadn't touched a cigarette last night. Which was something to be proud of. From three packs a day to none, cold turkey.

That just left the drinking; the insistent pounding in his skull was a painful reminder of that. Once he had the cigarettes beaten, really beaten, no bullshit, no bumming OPs, then maybe he'd start working on the booze. Not that it was a serious problem for him; unlike many of his colleagues in the high-pressure gaming industry, he wasn't *hooked* on the stuff. It was just that he'd always had this tendency to overindulge. And at age thirty-eight, his body was starting to tell him: hey, pal, the party's over, time to be healthy. For one thing, he had noticed that the hangovers with which he frequently paid for his alcoholic excesses, once minor annoyances to be shrugged off within minutes of rising, were becoming noticeably more uncomfortable—while lasting considerably longer into the day. And right now, he had to shake this one.

Caffeine, and lots of it, sometimes did the trick.

Optimistically, he dumped a heaping teaspoonful of Folgers Crystals into the cleanest mug he could find, slopped in the hot water, and slurped the pungent brew. Coffee and a Nicorette. Not exactly breakfast at Tiffany's, Forrester rationalized, but it would help steel him against the wrath of Emmett Druperman. Whether or not that wrath, as Edith Frick hoped, really was directed at him.

The drive to the Galaxy was short, hardly more than ten minutes, but to Steve Forrester it was the best part of the day. He always looked forward to it during top-down weather; there was a fresh, cleansing quality to the early-morning desert air that magically absolved yesterday's excesses, somehow wiped the grubbiest slate clean. Even after a rough night, the glorious sunrises airbrushed on the clear canvas of the desert sky never failed to arouse his admiration. Compared with nature's awesome displays, the glitzy monoliths along the Strip were nothing more than children's building blocks, the neon spectaculars mere tinsel. In an uncharacteristic moment of insight, despite the dull ache that had now migrated to the back of his head, Forrester reflected upon the insignificance of himself in particular and of mankind in general. Yet as if to immediately discredit this notion, the Galaxy's giant electronic billboard looming a hundred feet over his head shouted down in dancing red letters: TONY FRANCISCO. LIVE THE LEGEND.

Forrester noted that the picketers were already out, already circling in a prison-yard shuffle on the concrete sidewalks just beyond casino property. WE DEMAND A LIVING WAGE, one of their cardboard placards stated. UNFAIR LABOR PRACTICES, complained another. THE GALAXY REFUSES TO NEGOTIATE, a third sign accused. The strikers, many of whom Forrester knew personally, made no attempt to hinder his progress, but neither was his halfhearted wave returned.

Nodding at the two security guards, he wheeled the silver Mercedes-Benz SL 500 convertible down the ramp toward his reserved parking space in the Galaxy's cavernous garage. Aside from Conquistador Trail, which he considered more an investment than a luxury, Forrester's only real indulgence was the car. It had cost him half a year's salary (and his ex-wife more than one late alimony payment), but he had never regretted the purchase.

At the barrier he stopped the big car and fumbled for his magnetic pass card.

One of the valet parking attendants, a Hispanic youth, compliantly attired in the Galaxy's regulation starship-officer uniform, ambled up to the car and leaned irreverently on the windshield frame. "Morny, boss. Jew luke like *sheet*."

Forrester raised an eyebrow and regarded his young critic with a bleary eye. "Thanks for noticing, Ramon. I *feel* like shit."

The attendant feigned concern. "Better lemme park it, my frien'. Jew gone scratch thees baby agay joss li' jew deed las' mont'."

These guys were never short of excuses to burn rubber in his SL 500. At least today's excuse incorporated a suggestion of concern for the welfare of his car. Anyway, the kid was probably right: there was a good chance that in his present condition he might indeed damage the Mercedes again. With a sigh, he capitulated and stepped out.

The attendant slid behind the wheel with thinly concealed glee. Forrester pushed the door closed with his fingertips, the solid, reassuring *thunk* he normally relished causing his hangover-sensitized ears to ring in discomfort. "Leave the keys in the office, okay? And keep it under warp speed."

"Jew got it, Cap'n Kirk."

The young man jammed the big sports car into gear and roared away in a haze of blue smoke.

"I said, keep it under—," Forrester called out, but his voice was drowned by the thunder of the SL 500's twin exhausts. In spite of the headache, he smiled faintly as he turned toward the elevators. At least he'd provided one wannabe Indy racer with a little excitement during an otherwise boring day of squealing tires and two-dollar tips.

Steve secretly felt a trifle embarrassed for the people like Ramon who had to wear Galaxy uniforms—perhaps *costumes* was a more accurate description—although many of them admitted that they enjoyed working in the outfits. They make us feel *special,* they'd say.

For the Galaxy—like New York–New York, the Excalibur, the reincarnated MGM Grand—was one of the new Las Vegas breed of themed megaresorts, a mixture of Disneyland and casino gambling designed to attract the high-volume family trade with its something-for-everyone philosophy. The line staff was obliged to embody the Galaxy's particular metaphor of intergalactic-life-sometime-in-the-future by wearing costumes that were clearly inspired by the popular TV and Hollywood space blockbusters. Unlike the old-style casinos, which had been conceived and operated by gangsters, the Las Vegas of the millennium was designed and run by lawyers and marketing men. Forrester appreciated that the Galaxy concept represented a triumph of marketing genius, attracting two generations of Trekkies and their families by the thousands.

The hotel-casino complex was built to resemble a giant space station. It consisted of a massive doughnut-shaped wheel invisibly suspended around a four-hundred-foot-tall central tower, much like a colossal gyroscope. The base of the tower around which the wheel hung was clad with millions of matte-black obsidian tiles, their nonreflecting surfaces adding to the illusion of the wheel's "floating on air." Within the tower, which tapered gracefully skyward from a base diameter of over five hundred feet to an apex of two hundred feet, four thousand guest rooms were accessed from circular balconies ringing an enormous atrium above the main casino floor. The wheel structure housed additional gaming areas, showrooms, lounges, bars, convention rooms, theme restaurants, and offices.

Within the central gaming area, rising almost to the peak of the atrium, stood the Galaxy's most flamboyant crowd-pleaser: a towering 365-foot replica of NASA's venerable Saturn rocket. In a city founded on superlatives, where the Mirage boasted a simulated volcano and Treasure Island offered hearty pirate-ship battles, nothing quite topped the sheer pulse-quickening spectacle of the Galaxy's star attraction. Every hour on the hour it "blasted off" among a maelstrom of colored lights and artificial smoke and rumbling THX sound. In a simulation that would have done David Copperfield proud, three-dimensional projections on the smoke caused the mighty rocket to seem to magically lift skyward on its five thundering F-1 engines. From any viewing angle in the main casino, a holographic clone of the Saturn rose smoothly and majestically on a realistic column of "fire," masking the actual structure of the rocket as it appeared to vanish among the stars.

The first and second stages of the rocket contained a bank of elevators, connected by gantrylike Plexiglas-railed walkways radiating out to the circular balconies fronting the guest rooms. Above the rocket, the domed ceiling of the atrium, actually a highly sophisticated planetarium, featured a constantly changing panorama of stars generated by a Digistar II projector hidden in the "command module" of the rocket.

"Satellites" and "asteroids" were hung from invisible wires over the casino area to heighten the cosmic illusion, devices which doubled as housings for the high-definition video cameras that enabled security personnel to monitor and videotape the various games. Most casinos had years ago replaced, or augmented, the traditional peephole system hidden in false ceilings with video technology, but the name "eye in the sky," or just plain "eye" in casino jargon, had stuck.

Backing on the main hotel-casino complex, the Galaxy's domed Final Frontier Amusement Center occupied another fifty acres of prime Strip real estate. It enticed visitors with an imaginative escape from the bounds of Earth into the farthest reaches of interstellar space. For just a few dollars, enthralled guests could experience "weightlessness" as roaring jets of forced air floated them aloft in the Zero Gravity ride. Parents and kids could thrill to the 3-D simulation of a meteor shower on the Voyage to Venus. Or spin wildly in the cylinder of Galileo's Black Hole as centrifugal force glued them to the padded wall like human flies. They could scream in delighted terror on the giant Wormhole Roller Coaster or battle indigenous monsters in virtual reality on Planet X, a 3-D first-person multiplayer "visit to a strange world."

When the kids finally tired of the rides, a brilliantly lit, wonderfully noisy video arcade kept them occupied for hours, zapping aliens and saving Earth while moms and dads from all over America compliantly exchanged their spare cash for casino chips and slot tokens and impossible dreams.

Since its creation, the Galaxy's unique motif had attracted visitors in ever-increasing numbers, with almost every month setting a new attendance record.

This month would be an exception, Steve Forrester knew, because of the strike.

But the long-term financial outlook for the Galaxy couldn't be brighter. He could not imagine any shadow casting serious doubt upon the casino's future.

3 **Emmett Druperman's office** was known familiarly to the staff as "the Bridge" in recognition of his post as de facto captain of the Galaxy Hotel and Casino. The sixty-three-year-old chief executive officer presided over a staff of four thousand people, most of whom wholeheartedly agreed with his flagrant self-characterization as the toughest son of a bitch in Vegas.

Behind his back he had been nicknamed Droopy, a sobriquet reflecting as much his personal appearance as his surname. Everything about Emmett Druperman *drooped*. A single black eyebrow set in a disapproving V flopped like hairy Spanish moss above his eyes, while sets of concentric bags the color of ripe eggplant hung below them. Druperman's face resembled that of an angry bloodhound—a resemblance reinforced by a pair of elongated ears that ended in rubbery half-dollar-size earlobes. Nor was the CEO's drooping confined to his face—his shoulders slumped, his stomach sagged, and his suits, to the despair of his tailors, invariably bagged at elbows, waist, and knees. Yet regardless of this excessive droopiness, he commanded the respect, if not the affection, of his employees and the grudging admiration of his competitors in the industry.

He had been shrewd enough to publicly dissociate himself from the mob influences that dominated the Las Vegas of a generation ago—although it was rumored that his private address book still included the coordinates of certain individuals not unknown to federal law enforcement agencies—and had managed to effect a seamless transition to the lily-white corporate propriety into which his industry had metamorphosed.

Now, at the dawn of the twenty-first century, Druperman reported only to the board of directors of Summit Enterprises, the giant conglomerate that counted among its assets more than a hundred subsidiaries, including cable networks, movie theater chains, car-rental companies, and resort hotels. Among all its investments, the most productive cash cow was the Galaxy, and in deference to his successful track record, the board had handed Emmett Druperman virtual carte blanche. Their only criterion was a steady growth in the bottom line, which Druperman had consistently delivered.

The speakerphone buzzed.

"Mr. D?" Edith asked.

"What?" he snapped impatiently, annoyed at this distraction from his tenth reading of the letter.

"Mr. Hooper from the United Hotel Workers is here."

Druperman put down the letter and unwrapped a fifteen-dollar cigar, the first of three he allowed himself daily. "I'm busy. Tell that fat prick to go shake down some bellboys for tips."

"He says it's important."

"Important to who?" the CEO asked rhetorically as he bit off the cigar's tip and spat the plug onto the broadloom. "Just tell Hooper he's had my last offer. I don't want to see or hear from him or his goddamn union again until they're ready to say uncle." Druperman pushed the speakerphone button, lit a match, and raised it to his cigar.

Suddenly, a wild thought struck him. Or maybe not so wild. He pushed the button again. "Wait a minute, Edith." He shook the match out, his cigar unlit. "Is Hooper still there?"

"Yes, Mr. D."

"Send him in."

Five seconds later the door opened and an overweight, sweating man in a wrinkled tan suit waddled into Druperman's office. Forcing a toothy smile, the union negotiator extended his hand. Druperman ignored it and impatiently waved him to a seat.

"Good to see you, Emmett," Hooper began. "I trust—"

"Shut up, Hooper." Druperman half rose and without preamble flourished the brown envelope in his visitor's face. "Are you and your goons responsible for this crap?"

The smile faded from Hooper's florid countenance. "I don't know what you're—"

"Because if you are, I'll arrange a little visit from a couple of my friends. From the old days."

The fat man paled at the mention of his host's legendary mob connections. "Honest to God, Emmett, I have no idea what you're talking about."

Druperman eyed his visitor skeptically. He extracted the letter, videotape, and Dunes chip from the brown envelope. "You had nothing to do with this . . . this shakedown, this threat?"

Hooper reached for the letter, but Druperman pulled it back and laid it on the desk in front of his visitor.

"Don't touch it; just read it."

Hooper's eyes widened as he scanned the letter. "Christ, no. We may not be choirboys, but we don't do stuff like this."

"I've heard otherwise."

"My mother's grave, Emmett."

"I'd better not find out different, Hooper."

"Come on, Emmett. You don't really think it was us. I never even *heard* of this Las Vegas Casino Association outfit," he said nervously. "Besides, what good would . . . *threatening* you guys do?"

The CEO considered this for a moment, then fixed Hooper with an icy stare. "You know what, my fat friend? You're right. Threatening me and . . . my associates—what, to screw concessions out of us?—*would* be pretty fucking stupid, even for you guys."

"We'd never—"

"Matter of fact, if there's any threatening to be done around here, *I'll* be the one doing it."

The union man forced a smile and faked a chuckle. "What a sense of humor you got, Emmett—"

"You think I'm kidding, Hooper? I say the word, you'll be sharing accommodations with Jimmy Hoffa, permanently."

"Jesus Christ, Emmett, I come in to see you with the best of intentions, and all's you do is treat me like shit."

Druperman picked up his unlit cigar and reached for the matches. "Well, I'm real sorry if I overestimated you."

The negotiator considered Druperman's last remark and frowned briefly, unsure whether he'd been further insulted. "No offense taken," he said, pasting the smile back on. "Now, there's just a couple of outstanding contract items I'm sure you and me can—"

"I told you last time, Hooper, no more contract talk." Druperman consulted his desk calendar. "You've got exactly six days before I start firing.

And by the way, don't breathe a word about this letter to anybody, understand? If it gets around, I'll know it was you."

The CEO stared stonily at his visitor, who gathered himself up and prepared to leave, another skirmish lost to this hard-nosed son of a bitch.

"Oh, and Hooper . . ."

Halfway to the door, the union man turned, his eyebrows raised hopefully.

"I do believe you about the letter."

Hooper nodded and smiled. "Thank you, Emmett. You know we'd certainly—"

"You wouldn't have the balls." Druperman puffed his cigar alight. "Don't slam the door."

Diplomacy was foreign to Emmett Druperman's nature; he subscribed to an unbending policy of survival of the strongest. It was a tactic that had generally served the company's—and his own—interests well. Right now, with the Detroit boys testing the waters by attempting to gain job security, pay raises, and whatever fringe benefits they could dream up for the Galaxy's service personnel, he was adamantly refusing to knuckle under, thereby incurring the wrath of the unions and of the affected employees—along with the gratitude of his competitors. The other owners were relieved that the union had targeted the Galaxy for this latest test of nerves. Most of them would have given in, sacrificed a little of their bottom line for labor peace. But not Druperman. His competitors knew he'd fight the union to his last breath. And probably win. Like his hero, Dean Rusk of Cuban missile crisis fame, Emmett Druperman would stand eyeball-to-eyeball with his adversaries until either they blinked or he dropped dead.

Druperman's legendary toughness and his leadership ability were undoubtedly the reasons for his ascent to the presidency of the Las Vegas Casino Association. The LVCA was a highly secretive, high-powered group that included the heads of all the Strip casinos and many of the larger downtown establishments. It held a scheduled meeting once a month, more often if circumstances required. Each casino owner took a turn hosting the meeting, and until Druperman took over the position of president, it was a matter of pride to these wealthy men that each gathering should eclipse the previous one in luxury and splendor. Showgirls, expensive wines, charter flights to exotic locales—the sky was the limit. Upon his election, however,

Druperman quickly put an end to this practice, pointing out to his colleagues that it was stupid to waste money impressing each other—money that could be better spent where it would do some good, such as battling unions or bribing Gaming Commission officials.

Emmett Druperman glanced once again at the ominous brown envelope, and then at his watch. Almost nine. Where the fuck was his Vice President of Security?

At that moment, a somewhat haggard Steve Forrester cracked Druperman's double doors and popped his head through. "Morning, Emmett," he ventured warily.

"Closer to afternoon," the CEO scowled. "Anyway, you're here. Come in. Sit down. We've got a problem."

Forrester was relieved to note that his boss's anger appeared to be focused more on a certain padded brown envelope than on himself. "What's wrong, Emmett?"

"What's wrong? My hemorrhoids are killing me, that's what's wrong," the CEO rasped. "The fucking unions won't back down. That show business dago and his shyster agent are trying to screw me. And now *this*." He slid the envelope across the polished desktop to his Vice President of Security. "I put the stuff back inside. This is just the way it came." A rectangular address label on the outside bore the printed words, EMMETT DRUPERMAN, PRESIDENT OF LVCA, CONFIDENTIAL.

Forrester refrained from asking questions. Instead, he carefully emptied the envelope.

The computer-printed letter, the videotape, and the red five-dollar Dunes chip slid out.

The younger man read from the letter aloud: "'ATTENTION LAS VEGAS CASINO ASSOCIATION! WE WILL THIS WEEK STRIKE YOU HARD. WHAT WILL HAPPEN IS ON THE VIDEOTAPE HEREWITH SHOWN. THIS IS NOT A TRICK. WE HAVE THE KNOWLEDGE AND THE POWER TO TAKE THIS ACTION. AGAINST US THERE IS NO DEFENSE. A LARGE SUM OF MONEY MUST BE PAID TO STOP MORE ACTIONS. UNLESS YOU PAY WE WILL INCREASE THE STAKE. YOUR ORDERS WILL FOLLOW.' IT'S SIGNED 'THANATOS.'"

Having scanned the letter silently at least a dozen times, Druperman had virtually memorized its contents. But it was only when he actually heard his vice president of security read the letter aloud that he noticed the awkward English. Whoever wrote the letter was not only a criminal but a foreigner, too, a combination that did not sit well with the CEO. He drummed the desk, angry to have been forced into a situation over which he had no control. It was a position Emmett Druperman hated. He believed that knowledge was strength and that knowledge of your adversary was the key to successfully resolving any situation. But unlike his traditional opponents, bureaucrats and union organizers and entertainers' agents, this enemy was faceless. Who were they and how dare they threaten him? Finally Druperman said, "Well?"

"We could have a serious problem, Emmett. Or it could be nothing."

Druperman raised a bushy eyebrow and twisted uncomfortably in his chair. "For insight like this we pay you, what, two hundred large a year?"

Steve ignored the sarcasm, correctly assuming that it was mostly Emmett's hemorrhoids doing the talking. "Any idea who or what Thanatos is?"

"Never heard the name before."

"What's on the tape?"

"Some kind of fucking movie. Put it in the machine and I'll show you." Forrester did as he was told; Druperman thumbed a remote control and the TV screen in the wall came to life.

After a few seconds of snow, the image of a grossly obese man slumped facedown in a plate of food appeared on the screen. The setting was a dark room. Somber mood music played in the background; it was obviously a clip from a movie. A black man who appeared to be playing the part of a detective entered the frame and shone a flashlight over the victim. Another man carrying a medical bag came into the room. A third man—young, white, handsome—asked the detective, "You thinkin' it's poison?" At that point the clip ended and the screen went blue. Forrester had vaguely recognized both the young white actor and the detective but was unable to come up with names.

"I fast-forwarded right to the end of the tape. There's nothing else on it," said Druperman. "So, Mr. Security. What do you make of it?"

"It's pretty obvious. I don't know what the name of the movie is but I don't think it matters. The implication is clear."

"It doesn't take a genius. They're going to poison somebody."

Over the years, Steve Forrester had intercepted a number of threatening letters, both at the Galaxy and in his previous life as a detective in the Las Vegas Metropolitan Police Department. None of the threats had ever materialized. But he had a funny feeling about this one.

"Sounds that way, Emmett. But at least the threat is directed against the association generally, not the Galaxy specifically."

"What's the difference? Whoever threatens the association threatens everybody in it. And everybody includes us."

"Let's analyze what we've got here." Forrester forced himself to concentrate. "First, they're smart enough not to use handwriting. There's no postage stamp or courier slip, so they must have slipped it into the mailroom themselves or through an accomplice. They know your name and your position in the association." He scanned the letter again, careful not to get any more fingerprints on it. "They've obviously done their homework—"

"Well, the fuckers sure got my attention," Emmett snapped. "Not many people know the association even exists, let alone that I'm president of it."

"These guys obviously do. They know that the association controls most of the money in this town, which, of course, is why they've targeted it. But the funny thing is, they haven't told you how or when to pay the money. Or even how much they want."

"You keep saying 'they.' What makes you think this is more than one guy? Maybe it's just some crazy *momser* acting alone."

"Could be, Emmett. Anything's possible. The letter said 'we' and 'us.' I just have a feeling."

"A feeling?"

"You know, cop's instinct. Or ex-cop."

The CEO raised a skeptical eyebrow. "And what does your ex-cop's instinct tell you about this Dunes chip?"

Forrester carefully picked it up, using his handkerchief.

"I already touched it," Druperman said unrepentantly.

"Probably doesn't matter." Mercifully, the Folgers was kicking in and Forrester's hangover headache was beginning to subside. "The chip most likely has some weird significance, but right now I have no idea what."

"And why the movie clip? Why go to all that trouble?"

"You mean, why not just write, 'We're going to poison somebody to prove how vulnerable you are,' in the letter?"

"Yeah."

"My best guess is that they wanted to . . . *dramatize* their threat. To make sure they had our attention."

"Well, they got my attention. But I'll tell you, Steve, that's all the fuck they're gonna get."

"Emmett, quite frankly I'd be surprised—*and* disappointed—if you said anything else!"

"My friend, I've been shook down by the best in the business." The CEO's facial creases angled slightly upward and his drooping eyes displayed a hint of a twinkle. "They all rolled the dice with Emmett Druperman, and they all crapped out."

"It wouldn't be those redneck union boys trying to soften you up?"

"I already thought of that. I talked to Hooper. I don't think they've got the balls *or* the brains."

"You're probably right. This isn't their style." Forrester surveyed the ceiling thoughtfully.

"So, what the hell do we do?" Druperman asked finally. "You think these *ganifs* are for real—or is this just some sick joke?"

"Well, I wouldn't treat it lightly. It sounds like these people are laying the groundwork for some future extortion. But will they really follow through? And if so, who are they going to poison? And when? And where? And after that, what the hell happens? I'm wondering whether maybe you should alert the other members of the association."

"They're busy men. They don't need this shit any more than I do."

"Well, that's up to you, boss. But I'd better get Metro in on it right away."

"All right. But tell them to keep it unofficial. I don't want this splashed across the front pages. It could be a fucking disaster."

"I've still got contacts on the force. We can trust them to keep a lid on it. I'll talk to Frank Marshall off the record—"

"Who's Frank Marshall?"

"He was my partner when I was on the job. We're not exactly bosom buddies anymore, but he's a good cop. He can run all this stuff through the lab. I'll check the mailroom myself to see if anybody saw the envelope delivered. But somehow I doubt if we'll find anything significant."

"I'll tell you one thing," said Druperman.

"What's that?"

"These bloodsuckers are not squeezing one lousy nickel from the Galaxy or from anybody else in the association as long as I'm president. Poison or no poison."

At that moment, the CEO was totally unaware that his reaction not only had been anticipated but actually constituted the cornerstone of a plan that had begun to crystallize six months earlier. . . .

LAS VEGAS,
THE PREVIOUS APRIL

PART II

4 **Even after a decade** behind the wheel, the Starlight dealer still marveled at the incredible stupidity of roulette players.

Long-term, none of them had a prayer of winning; their only hope was to get lucky fast and get out. But few did. Most believed in some ridiculous system or other. Against all logic, they wrote down past winning numbers and studied them carefully, imagining patterns and trends. Then they used this meaningless information to project future winning numbers. As if the wheel had a memory. Or the little white ball realized that double zero was overdue. Or that it was red's turn to win because black had been coming up just a *little* too often.

The Starlight Hotel and Casino encouraged this nonsense by obligingly providing system players with preprinted cards and pencils for the purpose of writing down the winning numbers. Lately they'd even added electronic scoreboards showing the results of the past twenty spins so these pseudo-theoreticians could save themselves the trouble.

For the dealer, the most galling aspect of the whole charade was having to humor his players—to congratulate them on their wins, to sympathize with them on their losses, to gravely nod his head while they spewed their moronic theories. Because the plain fact was, these retards were his lifeblood. Hustling tokes was the real name of the game as far as he was concerned— the casino paid dick and you survived on your tips. All tips were divided equally among all dealers on all games, so it didn't matter whether you were dealing fifty-cent roulette or five-thousand-dollar craps, you still got your share. For which he thanked God because right now, seven hours into his shift, there wasn't even a lousy quarter in the toke box.

Wearily, he thumb-squirted the white ball and launched it upon its familiar orbit. Once more, the ivory sphere whizzed smoothly around its varnished oak path. Again, comet tails of reflected light scintillated upon the counterspinning brass hub, mesmerizing the gullible, seducing neophytes with the promise of easy wealth. Step right up, folks, the wheel hummed alluringly, get thirty-five to one on your investment! Divine the right number and you'll be in the chips!

"No more bets," intoned the dealer, his carny rasp as always dissolving the spell like a hypnotist's finger snap.

Gradually, the ball slowed in preparation for reentry as centrifugal force surrendered its early lead to gravity. Inexorably, the ball's orbit decayed. It clattered over the diamond stops and tumbled into the counterrevolving spokes of the wheel, rattling and bouncing indecisively, in one pocket and out again, up the bowl and down, losing energy, finally settling into its temporary home and dashing the prospects of the sparse crop of brightly colored chips seeded optimistically on the neighboring field of green felt.

"Thirty-two red," the dealer droned mechanically. "No winner." He set the Lucite marker on thirty-two, raked the losing chips into the mucker, and sighed audibly.

He was bored to distraction. Only two players had shown up during his entire shift: a couple of chatty elderly women—from Kansas, they told him—who had arrived half an hour ago. They said they were *actually* slot players (no shit, Sherlock, the dealer thought) and they were excited because this was their *first time ever* at a roulette wheel. The old broads were betting chump change: fifty-cent chips, straight up, the table minimum for inside bets. And despite the croupier's unsubtle hints, they weren't tipping.

He scanned the casino floor hopefully; there was still an hour left on his shift, still time for the action to pick up. Maybe some crazy Arabs would show up—they usually tipped big. Or drunken conventioneers determined to piss away their money. Just to break the monotony, he'd even settle for a table full of Chinamen with their noisy, excited jabbering. In the dealer's private opinion, the only situation more mind-numbing than just standing behind your table doing absolutely nothing and trying to stay awake was dealing to cheapskate penny-ante players. His sole consolation during such sessions was an ability to titillate himself by fantasizing about the parade of drop-dead gorgeous chicks who regularly sashayed past his table. As a result of which, he was not concentrating terribly hard on the game.

The roulette floorman wasn't exactly into the game, either. He trusted his dealers to make the correct payoffs and watch the tables, especially when there were only a few players in action.

Neither the dealer nor the floorman paid much attention to the well-dressed, nicely tanned gentleman who sat down at the other end of the table from the two ladies.

Like the two women from Kansas, the new arrival was playing the inside—betting the numbers straight up and sometimes splitting his bets between several numbers. And, of course, *he* wasn't tipping, either; once again the dealer glumly wondered how these pikers always managed to find *his* table. The man was making five- and ten-dollar bets, higher than the ladies but still low enough to warrant no more than an occasional cursory glance from the floorman.

Although a casual observer would never suspect it, judging by the ladies' squeals of delight whenever one of their bets was successful, none of the three players was really making much headway. Even at thirty-five to one for a direct hit on a straight-up number, the house edge of over 5 percent was grinding out its toll.

Then it happened. The dealer spun the wheel and the ball bounced around as usual and settled into a slot. "Four, black," he intoned as he turned to place the Lucite marker on the winning number.

And right there, square on number four, sat a gleaming black hundred-dollar chip.

"Hey, wait a minute," said the dealer loudly, his libidinous fantasies abruptly vaporized. "That check wasn't there before."

The well-dressed man appeared taken aback. "I beg your pardon," he said. "That black check was not on the table when I closed the betting."

"Well, I definitely put it there *before* you said, 'No more bets.'"

The croupier frowned. "Absolutely no way. I would have noticed a hundred-dollar bet."

"Let's just say you missed this one—an honest mistake." The player smiled conspiratorially. "So. Here we are. I guess you owe me, what, thirty-six hundred dollars? My original bet plus thirty-five hundred?" The man paused, seemingly puzzled at the dealer's slowness in paying off the bet. Then he grinned and winked. "Of course—stupid of me! Better throw four greens into the payoff so I can look after you—"

"Sorry, sir." The dealer bit his lip, frustrated at losing out on his only toke of the shift but correctly reasoning that no tip was better than no job. "I'm going to have to call the floorman."

But that wasn't necessary. Attracted by the discussion, the dealer's boss was already on his way to the table. "What's the problem?" he asked his subordinate.

"This gentleman says he bet the black check on four. But it wasn't there when I closed the betting."

"Sir, we can't pay off on that," said the floorman firmly. "You past-posted the bet."

The man pushed back his stool and stood up, apparently perplexed. "Past-posted?"

"You know what I mean. You bet the hundred after the four came up."

The player looked hurt. "Are you accusing me of cheating?"

"Take it any way you want. Maybe you didn't understand the rules. But we're not paying."

The would-be winner extended his arms, palms up. "Is this the way you treat winners at the Starlight?"

"It's the way we treat grifters."

"You've made a big mistake. Please call your supervisor."

"I'm not calling anybody. I *am* the supervisor."

"If your dealer had been paying attention—"

"Never mind the dealer. You've been betting red checks since you sat down, and now all of a sudden you're betting a black? And it just happens to win? That's quite a stretch."

"I have a system. Look at the board. Four was overdue—"

"Bullshit. You were past-posting. Take that check and get your ass out of here."

"Hey, there's no need to be rude. I won the bet fair and square. Maybe the dealer didn't notice my bet. You know, black on black? Easy to miss—"

"Listen, mister, I'm getting tired of this crap. And I'm not buying your act. Now, are you leaving, or do I have to call Security. . . ?" He left the threat hanging.

For a moment, the two men eyed each other in silence, the floorman angrily defiant, the player evidently puzzled and hurt. The ball continued to spin silently in its black pocket; the hundred-dollar chip remained on number four.

Realizing that the player was not about to abandon his claim, the floorman turned away and reached for a phone . . . when he was interrupted by a small, quavery voice from the end of the table: "Excuse me—sir? Sir?" It was one of the Kansas ladies.

"Are you speaking to me, ma'am?" Receiver in hand, he spun impatiently to face her.

"Yes, sir. Well . . . this may be none of our business?" she ventured, timidly inflecting the statement into a question.

"Ma'am?"

The woman hesitated. Her friend nudged her. "Go ahead, Ada," the other lady whispered encouragingly. "Tell him."

"Yes. Well, that gentleman really *did* bet the hundred dollars before the dealer closed the betting? My friend and I both noticed it and we even said, wow, that's a lot of money to bet on one number?"

"And you'll forgive me for saying this, sir," added the other lady, "but the dealer wasn't really watching the game. He seemed to be more interested in admiring the girls walking by than watching our bets."

"We thought it was kind of *rude* of him?" inflected the first Kansas lady. "To tell you the truth."

Faced with this unexpected testimony, the floorman hesitated. Maybe he shouldn't call Security just yet. Just to make 100 percent sure of his position, maybe he'd better check with the eye. "Let me call the camera people and see what they say." He punched in a different extension.

In a remote office behind the casino, the Starlight's daytime eye-in-the-sky operator depressed a flashing button and picked up his phone. "Video Surveillance."

The floorman identified himself and continued, "Roulette three. I need you to look at the last few minutes on the tape."

The operator glanced at his bank of monitors. "I have you on camera, but we weren't recording. I thought you guys knew we changed tapes at eleven." At the eye, the practice was to change tapes three times every twenty-four hours: at eleven A.M., seven P.M., and three A.M. The eight-hour tapes were archived for a month, then reused.

The floorman glanced at his watch. Eleven-oh-two. "Shit, shit, shit," he muttered into the phone.

"What happened?"

"Ah, we've got a past-poster. I'm sure of it. But the other players here back him up. Anyway, if you've got no tape, I've got no choice. I have to pay the schmuck."

"Sorry about that, man. Do you want us to start taping right now?"

"Don't bother. This guy is not playing here anymore. I don't care if he's got Mother Teresa and the Virgin Mary for witnesses—he's history."

Cradling the phone, the floorman turned to the dealer and curtly instructed him to pay the man his $3,600. Then he leaned over the table so that his face was inches from the player's. "Funny how you timed your action for just when we were changing tapes in the eye," he said intensely. "I don't know how you did it, but I do know you screwed us. Unfortunately, we have to pay you."

The player said nothing, but for just an instant the merest shadow of a triumphant smile flickered across his lips. The floorman caught the look, and his face darkened. The dealer had started to slide two tall stacks of black chips across the table, but the floorman held his hand out over the stacks, palm down, blocking the player from reaching them. "If I ever— ever—see you in here again," he breathed, "I'll make sure you leave in a goddamn basket. Understand?"

The man flicked an imaginary speck of dust from an immaculate lapel, raised an eyebrow, and said, "I hear you."

The floorman lifted his hand from the chips and shoved them roughly toward the player, knocking the stacks askew. "Then take your money and fuck off."

Dan Shiller calmly gathered his chips and walked away.

He was very good at his job.

In the Starlight coffee shop, Ada and Maud, the two ladies from Kansas, were excitedly discussing their adventures at the roulette table.

"What a nice man he was?" inflected Ada. "Giving us all that money to play roulette with?"

"And all *we* had to do was tell a little white lie about his black chip," Maud giggled.

5 A fiery sun crested the night-purple mountains ringing Las Vegas, silhouetting the Galaxy's massive electronic billboard at the edge of the Strip and creating long shadows inside the front doors of the gigantic casino. Jurgen Voss blinked and squinted as a horizontal flash of sunlight swept across his field of vision. Maybe it was a sign that he was pushing his luck. He'd been counting down blackjack shoes at the Galaxy for over two hours, well beyond his usual self-imposed time limit. It was a dangerous game. But this was the last hour and a half of the graveyard shift, when the pit crew was tired and typically least watchful. Plus the cards were running well, the dealer was cold as penguin *scheisse,* and he was already up over two thousand. It was his most profitable session in ten years of card counting.

For Voss, in addition to possessing a photographic memory, was a mathematical genius.

Of course, there was more to professional card counting than mere brains. You had to be intelligent, but more important you had to be *smart.* Early on in Jurgen's casino career he had learned the hard way that even a two-hundred-plus IQ was not enough. You could play *totally perfect* precision blackjack, but if they discovered that you were counting, it was game over. He'd been caught only once, just after he'd embarked on his card-counting career. It had happened at Harry's in Reno and it was an ordeal he never wanted to reexperience. He'd remained too long at the same table, allowing the pit personnel time to evaluate his playing technique and betting strategies and to mark him as a card counter—an enemy of the house. Two large men had seized him and unceremoniously dragged him to a back room—casino storm troopers with pea-size brains who had shown absolutely no respect for his intelligence. He'd been photographed, ID'd, punched in the belly, and rudely ejected with dire warnings never to return.

After the event Voss had consoled himself with the notion that a major casino was actually *scared* of him or, more specifically, of his mental abilities. He had always harbored a deep-seated pride in those abilities, and the roughing up had vindicated that pride with at least some recognition, however painfully delivered. It was at once the highlight and the low point of his career. Difficult as it was to hide his light under a barrel, to assume a mantle of stupidity like some gold-digging bimbo in a May-December marriage, he had vowed from that moment on to keep his bets more conservative, to limit his table time to no more than an hour at a stretch, and to act *dumber*.

In fact, card counters were the bane of any casino's existence. Short of out-and-out cheating, Jurgen knew, there was no way a player could consistently prevail over the casino edge at craps, roulette, baccarat, or any other table game with a fixed house percentage. Only at blackjack did a skilled player have a mathematical chance of beating the house. By mentally keeping track of the cards that had been dealt, a card counter could calculate the general composition of the cards that remained. If these remaining cards favored the counter—if there were more tens, jacks, queens, kings, and aces than average left—then the shoe was "positive" and the counter would increase his bets and take more chances on doubling down and splitting pairs. Conversely, if the remaining cards favored the house—if the small cards outweighed the big ones and the shoe was "negative"—then the counter would reduce his bets and take fewer chances on splits and doubles. Expressed as a percentage, a good card counter's advantage over the casino might average only one or two points, but Jurgen Voss knew that this seemingly insignificant edge was all you really needed to realize a decent return for your efforts at the tables. Huge casino empires had been founded on tiny advantages.

Like any business, casinos hated to lose money. For that reason, most Nevada casinos had an unwritten policy of barring successful card counters from the blackjack tables. Technically, the counters weren't *cheating*. They didn't touch the cards or practice any physical flimflammery—they simply used their eyes and their brains to take advantage of information available to anybody who knew how to use it. Voss resented the fact that people like him, people with superior intelligence, were constrained from freely demonstrating that intelligence to beat the house at its own game. But as a realist, he recognized the industry sine qua non that if too many players won, there'd be no industry. So he suppressed his ego and resigned himself to obeying the professional card counter's Ten Commandments of Casino Camouflage:

1. *Emulate typical tourist behavior by acting "dumb."*
2. *Hesitate on "difficult" hands.*
3. *Don't act guilty or nervous.*
4. *Interact pleasantly with the dealers and the pit personnel.*
5. *Don't move your lips or your head while you're counting.*
6. *Don't jump your bets suddenly when the cards turn positive.*
7. *Don't drop your bets suddenly when the cards turn negative.*
8. *Don't make expert plays, like doubling down on soft eighteen.*
9. *Don't handle your chips expertly—be a klutz.*
10. *Don't play too long at one table or in one casino.*

In Nevada (unlike Atlantic City, where the courts had ruled in favor of card counters, albeit with some restrictions) the law stated that any player could be expelled from any game solely at the casino's discretion. Even so, most Nevada casinos tolerated limited card counting because they had learned that incompetent card counters often dropped more money at the tables than good basic-strategy players. In cases of semicompetent counting, they would sometimes adopt countermeasures such as shuffling up early to wipe out the counter's advantage. Only in very unusual circumstances—if the counter was exceptionally adept, betting and winning big—did they take more drastic action.

For Jurgen, that meant the high-rolling lifestyle was too risky. Augmenting his own bitter experience, he had observed other unfrocked counters barred or, like himself, physically abused by casino knuckle draggers. So he kept a low profile and bet small enough to remain unnoticed among the hordes of dummkopfs swarming the blackjack tables.

The card counter's unusual outward appearance had oddly enough turned out to be an asset to his business: it helped distract the casino watchers from his forbidden activities. He was a short, scrawny man with a large head perched precariously on a skinny neck, forming the cranial silhouette of a Ping-Pong paddle. His white-blond hair was combed back severely from a sharp widow's peak, which, combined with wire-rimmed Coke-bottle glasses, lent his pale, pinched features an owlish aspect. Voss's nervous habit of chewing his fingernails had eroded them to a bleeding rawness; defensively, he tried to conceal his mutilated fingertips from the view of others, even going so far as to signal for hitting and standing at the blackjack table with a partially closed fist, fingers bent and thumbs tucked in. Aside from this one quirk, he attempted to act as "average" as possible.

The deception irritated him. With an ego that was inversely proportional to his physical size, he desperately longed to flaunt his talents, to display his remarkable abilities for the world to admire, to show the casino big shots that their precious game could be beaten.

But subterfuge was necessary to reduce the risk of exposure. By swallowing his pride and meekly following the Ten Commandments, he could usually clear a few hundred dollars a week after expenses.

Thanks to the dozens of new casinos and riverboats springing out of nowhere like mushrooms on a wet lawn, Voss could have eked out an existence in any of the American states or Canadian provinces where gambling was now legal. But he had always preferred Vegas. The blackjack house rules were generally more favorable for card counters, and the hot weather suited him fine.

It was not a great life, but it was a living. Most important, the revenue from card counting provided Jurgen with the means to buy the special equipment he needed to keep the shameful secret hidden and to satisfy his private needs.

As usual, the computer in Voss's mind was on autopilot. Windows projected upon this mental screen effortlessly and precisely calculated the variable factors affecting his playing and betting strategies. His phenomenal multi-tasking capabilities allowed another part of his brain simultaneously to carry on easy conversations with dealers, cocktail waitresses, and other players— without ever missing a card.

Plus twenty-two, read the Running Count window in his head.

Five point five, said the True Count Adjustment window, modifying the Running Count to compensate for the number of decks remaining in the shoe.

Hard nine against the dealer's seven, his eyes told him. Most blackjack players would merely hit this hand, but the Hard Doubling Point Count Numbers Matrix required him to double his bet.

Ace Adjustment Factor: *Plus three—*

"Can I get you anything, sir?" asked a cocktail waitress who had suddenly materialized beside him.

"Maybe a coffee," Jurgen replied with an apologetic smile, sliding another forty dollars next to his original bet. He never drank alcohol at the blackjack table although sometimes he pretended to in order to reinforce the typical-tourist image he was careful to project. "Black, please."

The dealer gave him an ace and flipped herself a queen, making hard seventeen and losing to Voss's soft twenty.

Up two thousand and eighty-seven fifty, said the Win Tally window in Jurgen Voss's head.

As far as Voss could determine, there was no heat whatsoever from the pit: the young floorwoman was talking on the phone, tapping on her computer keyboard; nothing appeared to be out of the ordinary. She seemed to be totally uninterested in his relatively modest twenty-to-eighty-dollar spread. After all, bettors of his caliber were small fry in a *verschwenderisch* carpet joint like this. Maybe he'd count down one more shoe and then clear out.

During the shuffle, the attractive brunette floorwoman walked casually over to his table. To avoid "fitting the profile," Jurgen had selected the middle seat of the table—instead of the card counter's traditional third base position—because he'd mostly been going head-to-head against the dealer and there were no other players' cards to count.

She introduced herself with a smile. "Good morning, sir, I'm Lucy Baker. You're doing very well. I don't believe I've seen you at the Galaxy before, Mr. . . . ?"

"Jackson," he lied smoothly. "Harry Jackson. It is my first time in your casino. I am here on a convention."

"Is there anything we can do for you, Mr. Jackson? Breakfast, perhaps?"

For some reason, instinct maybe, certainly not because of anything the lady had actually *said,* a small alarm bell sounded in the back of Voss's head. "Thank you, but I shall be soon leaving," he replied.

6 **It has been said** that the 315,000-candlepower pencil of light shooting photons into space from the apex of the Luxor pyramid is one of the few works of man that could theoretically be discerned with the naked eye by a person standing on the moon. This hypothesis has never been tested. In 1972, the last time our satellite was visited by humans, the Luxor was but a scribble upon the back of a napkin, a gleam in the eye of architect Veldon Simpson.

In that year of Apollo 17, the closest candidate for celestial visibility would have been the midnight-sun spectacular of downtown Las Vegas, five miles to the north.

Concentrated mainly in just four city blocks on Fremont Street, uncounted millions of candlepower blazed relentlessly, creating concentrated sunlight twenty-four hours a day. Miles of garish neon tubing buzzed and hummed while myriad colored bulbs pulsated and flashed in rainbow rivalry, enticing bedazzled and bewildered visitors into this or that palace of pleasure. The Golden Nugget. The Four Queens. Binion's Horseshoe. Diamond Lil's.

Unfortunately for our lunar observer, the radiance of downtown Vegas has largely been obscured by the recent construction of the Fremont Street Experience, a multimillion-dollar light canopy that effectively screens most of the street's glare from overhead viewing. The Experience soars ninety feet into the air, roofing the neon jungle from Main to Fourth Streets with a gigantic awning studded with 2.1 million bulbs, which come to life each night, creating a massive video screen four and a half football fields in length. In this unsubtle attempt to lure America back to the heart of Vegas, away from the megaresorts of the Strip, more than two hundred speakers blast out half a million watts of sound, combining with the video to produce a spectacular light-and-sound show every hour on the hour from dusk to midnight.

Between the casinos, the air on that early-spring evening was unnaturally warm, even for southern Nevada. The tightly packed buildings and acres of pavement had acted as a massive heat sink, absorbing the fierce desert sun all day long and only now releasing its stored energy. It was almost sinfully pleasurable to be greeted by the refreshing curtains of cool air at the doorless casino entrances.

But bright lights and cool air were not uppermost in the mind of one Mr. Dan Shiller, professional casino cheat. Stepping inside the Golden Nugget, fresh from two successful implementations of the roulette scam, Shiller's thoughts as always were focused on his next score. He was the archetypal con man, the consummate scoundrel for whom concepts such as honesty and rectitude were simply the purview of suckers. In Mr. Shiller's private code of ethics, cheating was synonymous with success, deception with winning, thievery with prosperity. Anyone who stood in his way was quite simply *dispensable.*

His appearance belied his profession. In fact, Dan Shiller's carefully cultivated image constituted his most important attribute. Prematurely gray hair complemented by a prosperous tan lent him a distinguished air. His clear blue eyes exuded trustworthiness, his well shaped eyebrows bespoke sincerity, his firm chin suggested integrity.

To round out the package, Shiller always dressed immaculately. On this warm evening he had selected a lightweight beige Armani sports jacket, crisply pressed gray slacks, and brown Gucci loafers. A Hathaway sports shirt, open at the collar to reveal a tasteful gold chain, completed Dan's ensemble. He was the very model of a Fortune 500 CEO, a successful banker, a lawyer, a stockbroker. Had he actually chosen any of these legitimate career paths, Shiller would no doubt have risen to the top, as he had in his current profession.

But his success was empty. He lived well, he traveled in style, he had endured relatively little jail time. However, there was always the big problem, the problem of what happens next month, next year, next decade. In the grifting game, you couldn't stay ahead of the posse forever—you got older, you got sloppier, and your concentration slipped. He'd seen it happen to the best in the business. Unfortunately, Dan Shiller couldn't afford to quit. Despite his best intentions, he had never quite managed to amass a nest egg sizable enough to retire on in the style he fancied. In reality, he could no more hold on to his ill-gotten gains than he could grasp a fistful of water. A taste for the good life inevitably caused his fortunes to ebb as fast as they flowed.

As the years wore on, this problem weighed increasingly on his mind. Shiller was not getting younger; he was closer to fifty than forty. What he needed was the one substantial score, the one elusive hit that would set him up for life. Not for Dan Shiller the tedious 5 percent solution at the savings and loan; no way did his patience extend to the hypopraxia of the mutual fund. He fantasized about a luxurious retirement on some Caribbean island, preferably one of the more remote ones, but at this very moment could hardly afford a month of it, let alone a lifetime.

But that was a problem for later. This was now, and Dan was very much a man of the moment. Constantly attuned to opportunity's knock, he did not restrict his clandestine practices to cheating at casino games. He would seize upon any chance for larceny as a matter of course. As long as the risk was commensurate with the reward, Dan Shiller was compelled to *take* that risk. The practicality of a scam was his only consideration, the morality or immorality of a deed never entering the equation. Dan was purely and simply amoral.

Fine dining was one of Shiller's passions, but the trickster saw no reason to pay for it, especially in hotel-casino restaurants. Dan wisely avoided drawing attention to himself by *never* asking pit bosses for complimentary meals—instead, he took the liberty of arranging his own comps via an ingenious swindle he had personally developed and perfected over the years. Generally it took less than five minutes to set up, well worth the substantial fiscal saving in restaurant checks and virtually risk-free.

Shiller looked at his watch, surveyed the hotel directory and decided on Stefano's for dinner. The fact that he had never been seen in the restaurant before was a prerequisite to the success of the operation.

He walked purposefully to a bank of house phones in the lobby of the Nugget and picked up the handset.

"Operator. May I help you?" said a tinny female voice.

"Please connect me with Mr. Johnson's room." Nine times out of ten he hit the jackpot immediately with Johnson, Smith, or Brown.

"One moment, please." Pause. "I have two Johnsons listed, sir. Lawrence or Arthur?"

"Lawrence."

"Thank you. I'll connect you now."

After a few seconds, Dan heard a phone ring. A sleepy voice answered, "Hello?"

A bull's-eye on the first try! "Hello," said Shiller in his modulated baritone. "Bill?"

"There's no Bill here. You've got the wrong room."

"Isn't this seventeen forty-two?"

"Not even close. It's thirty-eight eleven."

"Sorry." The con man smiled to himself, hung up, and jotted the room number on a scrap of paper.

Dinner in Stefano's was superb. After lubricating his palette with a double dry martini, Shiller started with the Fiori di Carciofi. He followed it with a magnificent veal Marsala, and capped the dining experience with a perfectly frozen spumoni. The meal was accompanied by a splendid (and very expensive) 1998 Querciabella Orvieto.

"Will this be a room charge, sir?" asked the waiter as Dan Shiller helped himself to an after-dinner mint.

"Yes."

"May I have your name and room number?"

"Lawrence Johnson. Thirty-eight eleven. Oh, and bring me an Italian cigar when you come back."

"Yes, sir." The waiter bustled away to confirm the validity of his customer's name and room number. He returned in a few minutes, satisfied that a Mr. Lawrence Johnson actually did occupy thirty-eight eleven, with a hand-rolled Toscani cigar on a silver tray accompanied by a computer-printed bill for a shade over three hundred dollars. "If you'll just sign here, sir. . . ."

Shiller ignored the proffered Bic and extracted a gold Cross pen from the inside pocket of his Armani jacket. He scribbled Lawrence Johnson's name rapidly on the bill and replaced it on the tray, slipping the cigar into his breast pocket.

"Thank *you,* sir," said the waiter, noting the generous tip his customer had added to the total before signing the check. "I hope we'll see you again before you leave the hotel, Mr. Johnson."

"I'm sure you will." *In your dreams, asshole.*

Dan knew that the cost of his meal would probably come out of the waiter's pocket, but that wasn't *his* concern.

He had other business to take care of.

The roulette scam had pretty well exhausted its potential for a while in this town. Having successfully perpetrated it at the Starlight with the help of the old bags from Kansas and at the Four Queens with the assistance of an attractive but flat-broke honeymoon couple, he had a feeling that it would be tempting fate to play it any further. Shiller knew that the casinos, while competing fiercely among themselves for players, shared information freely about flimflam men like himself.

Fortunately, he was a resourceful man who had other swindles to fall back on, including the fine art of hand mucking at blackjack. A hand mucker is a card sharp, a sleight-of-hand artist who specializes in "holding out" cards—cleverly concealing them and reintroducing them into the game at an opportune moment. Shiller might hold out an ace, wait for a ten-value card to be dealt to him, and combine the two to produce a natural twenty-one or "blackjack," which was an unbeatable hand.

The deceit could not be perpetrated when blackjack was dealt faceup from a shoe; in this type of game, players were not allowed to touch their cards. However, in many casinos, particularly in downtown Las Vegas, blackjack is hand dealt from a single or double deck and the player's first two cards are delivered *facedown,* requiring him or her to pick them up in order to see them and complete the hand. Additional cards, if the player needs any, are dealt faceup.

Through countless hours of practice, Dan Shiller had perfected the technique of holding out cards in hand-dealt games. The casinos, of course, attempted to protect themselves from this type of chicanery by establishing certain rules—for example, the cards could be picked up with one hand only, and the player was required to keep them over the table at all times— but these rules were no deterrent to a highly skilled hand mucker. The fact that exactly two cards were dealt to the player—and hence exactly two cards had to be returned to the game—presented no problem for Shiller. He would simply wait until he was dealt a standing hand made up of four or five cards, then distract the dealer with some question or comment while he leaned forward to block the overhead camera's view and surreptitiously palmed a card from among the pile in front of him. The value of this purloined card did not matter; once he had three cards to work with—the two he was dealt each time plus the extra one —he would simply mix and match them to suit his purposes.

It was a dangerous game, especially in some of the smaller establishments around Nevada where security harbored no compunction about administering severe beatings to exposed cheats. One of Dan's colleagues, an older man well beyond his best game, had suffered the misfortune of having been caught hand mucking in Tahoe, and his captors had broken every finger on his right hand. For the hundredth time, the grifter thought, *One day that'll be me. I need to get out of this racket before they get me, too.*

Maybe it was time to concentrate seriously on his retirement plan.

He'd been working *on this scheme for years but, despite a growing sense of urgency about his career, had yet to actually implement it.*

The original inspiration for Shiller's plan had been the Chicago Tylenol poisonings—the grandfather of all the product-tampering cases. "What kind of human being could conceive such a scheme, carefully open the capsules and pour in cyanide, then see to it that the product was placed among rows of similar medicine on the shelves of drugstores?" asked a newspaper editorial.

"An idiot," answered Dan Shiller, scornfully noting that the poisoner had never asked for anything by way of extortion, never squeezed a cent from the manufacturers of Tylenol—even though the death toll in the case finally reached seven. In Dan's world, the only logical motive for such actions was money. Revenge, power, a flaunting of intellectual superiority—these were not reasons to run such schemes. Despite his contempt for the poisoner, however, Shiller could not help but admire the simplicity and relative safety of the operation. With the inclusion of a payoff, it would have been perfect.

But perhaps that was the fly in the Tylenol poisoner's ointment. Maybe he could conceive no foolproof payoff plan, no way to actually pick up the extortion money without risking capture. Dan mulled over this aspect of such crimes for some time before what he believed to be a practical solution—simple and relatively safe—came to him one day while he was glancing through the financial section of the Las Vegas Review-Journal.

The months and years passed, and Shiller continued to ply his trade, practicing his black art at the gaming tables of Nevada and anywhere else he could promote a dishonest dollar. Life was good for the swindler. He owned a BMW 760Li sedan for which he'd paid cash. He lived well in a series of small hotels, furnished apartments, and boardinghouses, registering under assumed names and moving frequently. He had a small but expensive wardrobe and the resources to freely indulge his tastes for fancy women and recreational drugs.

Like many of his kind, Dan Shiller was simply continuing a tradition. His father had been a tin man—a swindler who sold nonexistent aluminum siding and shoddy repairs to unsuspecting homeowners. One of his brothers ran a telemarketing scam; the other was an accomplished stock swindler. Even Dan's mother had been involved in the family business: she specialized in bad checks.

But nobody in the Shiller family shared; there was no family fortune to fall back on when the clandestine skills deteriorated and the concentration began to slip, as Shiller knew they would in time. So he spent much of his free time thinking about the plan. As the scheme grew in magnitude and complexity, the con man realized that it would be extremely difficult to organize and execute by himself. For one thing, it involved violence—a level of violence far beyond a "mere" poisoning. Dan Shiller was not himself a violent man, although he had absolutely no reservations about using others for that purpose. For another thing, it required at least two accomplices, and he had yet to come across the right people. For this kind of work you couldn't just run an ad in the classified section of the local paper.

Consequently, Dan Shiller's plan remained on hold.

So far in his career, Shiller had been relatively lucky. Apart from a couple of arrests over twenty years ago, he had managed to avoid capture, no small accomplishment in his line of work. Dan's constant watchfulness usually enabled him to sense casino heat and slip away before it turned into trouble. He was keenly attuned to the danger signals: whispered consultations among the floorpeople, with furtive glances in his direction; hostility on the part of the dealer, who might start flinging the cards at his knuckles rather than dealing them flat on the table; the sudden materialization of one, or worse, several security guards for no apparent reason. Whenever he felt the slightest heat, Dan would get up and leave the casino immediately, not even stopping to cash in his chips. He knew he could always return later, during another shift, and exchange them with impunity.

Dan Shiller was not a blackjack card counter, but he had adopted some of the guiding principles of that profession. In particular, he utilized the "paper route" technique, never lingering more than a short period of time in any one casino during any one shift and rotating his visits over several days or even weeks. It was the reason he had never become known to casino personnel—his was just another anonymous face among the thousands who thronged the tables.

Checking his watch, the swindler casually stood up to leave the blackjack game at the Golden Nugget. He had managed to take them for a few hundred without attracting the slightest suspicion. He decided to hit one more joint before calling it a night. Maybe the Fremont, maybe Diamond Lil's.

There were plenty of casinos to be fleeced, and Shiller believed in spreading his business around.

7 **Francis Marion "Buster" Malloy** occupied the post of security guard at the Galaxy. Second-generation Irish, he was a neckless, pork-bellied block of a man of fifty-four with thinning red hair, a pink boozer's face, and a penchant for violence. The black patch over his left eye—courtesy of a Vietcong sniper—lent his countenance a not-undeserved air of toughness. The injury had provided Buster with an honorable discharge, a Purple Heart, and an abiding hatred of Asians. Any distinction between Vietnamese, Japanese, Chinese, and other Orientals was lost on the burly ex-Marine, who detested them all equally.

His position at the giant hotel-casino–amusement park complex was relatively undemanding, and Malloy tolerated it, despite the stupid cybercop uniform he was obliged to wear. Back in South Boston he'd held a lot worse jobs than this one. Mostly in quasi–law enforcement—mall cop, security guard, armored-car attendant—because despite the lousy pay, he enjoyed the heady feeling of power that a uniform bestowed, along with the chance to indulge his proclivity for beating up the occasional drunk or transient whenever the opportunity arose. But that was then, back in the rough-and-tumble neighborhood of Southie. These days, whenever he was obliged to use force, as in breaking up fights or evicting undesirables from the premises, Buster usually disciplined himself to accomplish the task with restraint. Management at the Galaxy, despite CEO Emmett Druperman's legendary toughness, frowned upon excessive violence.

Money fascinated Malloy—and he handled plenty of it at the Galaxy. More accurately, he handled plenty of *containers* that held money. His duties included collecting filled casino drop boxes—the locked metal containers secured under each of the tables into which dealers dropped gamblers' cash and markers through slots in the tabletops—and replacing them with empty ones at the end of each shift. The boxes were loaded onto rolling cages—wheeled metal carts that Buster, another guard, and an executive delivered to the counting room. Casinos never permitted anybody to be alone with their money, even when it was locked inside metal boxes.

Slot machines were emptied differently. Their contents were dumped into open buckets, right there on the casino floor, in plain view of anybody who happened to be walking by. This operation was performed only once a day, during the small hours of the morning—a timetable that Malloy reasoned quite correctly was adopted because the Galaxy desired as few witnesses as possible to the staggering tonnage of coins excavated daily from its one-armed gold mines.

The other requirements of Buster's job included patrolling the grounds, checking the hotel corridors, and occasionally escorting a cash-laden high roller to his suite after a winning session. Malloy resented this last duty and seethed inwardly at the unfairness of a system that often saw gamblers wagering as much on one roll of the dice or flip of the cards as he himself earned in a year.

Usually these winners would tip him quite generously—twenty-five, fifty dollars, sometimes even more—depending on the degree of their alcohol-induced bonhomie. The big Irishman would swallow his pride and accept the handouts, stoically suppressing the urge to beat the shit out of his charges and abscond with the rest of their money.

Despite a lack of formal education, Buster Malloy possessed a shrewd, street-smart intelligence and made it his business to learn as much as he could about the inner workings of the megaresort that employed him. He memorized the security codes that provided access to all but the sanctum sanctorum of Executive Row. He familiarized himself with the labyrinth of corridors and stairways and loading docks, the mailroom, and other service areas. He knew most of the employees by sight, if not always by name. Because, he figured, you never knew when that kind of information might come in handy.

The longer Malloy lived in Las Vegas, the more he liked it. Its weather was kinder to his Irish bones than Southie's, its people were more laid-back, and you could get anything you wanted, from booze to pussy to cheap food, twenty-four hours a day.

For beyond the buck-ninety-five buffets, the blackjack tables, and the blazing neon there was another Las Vegas that the average tourist rarely saw and generally couldn't care less about.

Over a million ordinary people with wives and husbands and kids and desires and dreams made their homes in and around this other Las Vegas. Beyond the Strip and the downtown casino core there existed a city much like any other in the Sun Belt, with schools, office buildings, parks, museums, a zoo, shopping malls, and thousands of homes. And just as in all the other cities and towns of America, the caliber of these homes reflected the circumstances of their occupants.

Atop the real-estate pyramid sat the mansions of the entertainers who had settled permanently in America's glitziest show town. At the corner of Pecos and Sunset, Wayne Newton, possibly the best known of all the resident Vegas stars, raised Arabian horses and other exotic animals on fifty-two very expensive walled acres, behind an ornate wrought-iron gate ostentatiously flanked by a pair of prancing bronze stallions. On Vegas Drive, Siegfried and Roy, Masters of the Impossible, shared an equally magnificent home. A veritable phalanx of white lions guarded their gates, a white wall circumscribed their property, and a forest of white palm trees could be glimpsed within the compound. A brass *SR* monogram on the gates left no doubt as to the identity of the occupants of this particular Las Vegas estate.

The next level of residential splendor comprised the comfortable upscale ranch houses and condos of the city's businesspeople, professionals, and casino executives.

Somewhat lower down the Las Vegas real-estate pyramid were the modest bungalows, town houses, and apartments of the casino dealers, cocktail waitresses, taxi drivers, valet parking attendants, construction workers, and all the other honest, hardworking folk who constituted the backbone of Las Vegas's population.

The base of the pyramid consisted of the run-down shanties and mobile-home parks of the shoestring retirees, the poor, and the unemployed who eked out a marginal existence under the desert sun. In the meanest of these parks on Miller Avenue just outside the Las Vegas city limits, Buster Malloy had purchased a secondhand mobile home. It was more of a converted travel trailer, really; the previous owner had added an aluminum screened porch and, ostensibly to impart an air of permanence, had enclosed the underside of the trailer with plywood panels, now badly delaminating. In the dirt around Malloy's trailer sat a rusted satellite dish surrounded by clumps of sagebrush and unkempt patches of Indian rice-grass. The fact that the park was strewn with junked cars, festooned with clotheslines, and littered with garbage irritated Malloy, but it was cheap living and all he could afford.

Buster bitterly resented the casual abandon with which gamblers at the Galaxy, especially the Asian ones, pissed away small fortunes. He'd personally witnessed those goddamn slopes blow the price of a fucking *mansion* on one flip of the cards at baccarat—while he was obliged to wear a Mickey Mouse outfit and kiss serious ass just to keep a crummy tin roof over his head.

Filled with envy, prone to violence, Buster Malloy was not an easy man to like. He had acquired a few drinking buddies, mostly local ex-leathernecks at the First Marine Division Association who tolerated him more for their mutual military background than for his good fellowship. There was something *ominous* about the one-eyed man; even these battle-toughened Vietnam vets recognized the latent danger and afforded him plenty of space. He was rarely invited to their homes.

The person closest to Buster was Helga Johanssen, a hooker in the twilight of her career who shared the big Irishman's mobile home on a semiregular basis.

Prostitution was one of the facts of Vegas life. Unofficial policy regarding prostitutes at the Galaxy inclined toward tolerance. As long as the women conducted their affairs in a reasonably discreet manner, nobody bothered them. The hookers furnished a necessary service for some of the guests, and it would have been foolish to force those guests to seek that service elsewhere. While the managers of the Galaxy knew full well that many of these women were "represented" by certain hotel employees, they reasoned that the extra income the employees derived from such activities was income that the hotel would not have to provide.

Helga was a big, buxom Swedish blonde of somewhere between thirty-five and forty-five—Malloy had never bothered to ascertain her precise age—whose Las Vegas "business" career had begun two decades earlier in the wide-open pre-AIDS era.

She'd been a waitress at a second-class steak joint in Long Beach, struggling to bring home $150 a week, when a coworker had invited her to drive to Vegas for the weekend. Helga, who hadn't ventured east of Los

Angeles's city limits since emigrating from Europe with her parents, had never dreamed there was such a place! She was enchanted by the bright lights, swept up by the excitement—and totally mesmerized by the money. She had never seen so much of it in her life. To the teenage waitress, it seemed to flow as freely as the waters out of the marble fountains at the Roman Palladium. Finally, *this* was the American dream. Helga vowed then and there that she was going to get her share of it.

Helga Johanssen became a weekend warrior, one of the legion of young women—housewives and waitresses and secretaries, mostly from L.A.—who had discovered that they could make more money turning tricks in Vegas in a single weekend than they could working forty hours a week for an entire month back home. After a few profitable weekends of commuting to Las Vegas, Helga decided to take the plunge and move to Glitzville permanently.

In the beginning, she hustled business anywhere and any way she could. She'd hang around bars or cruise the streets in her old car, soliciting "dates" from solitary male strollers. As she became more familiar with the Vegas scene, she realized there were easier ways to ply your trade—as long as you knew the right people. And the right people were the bell captains, the bartenders, and the pit bosses of the big hotels. Naturally, you had to look after them—either in cash or in trade—but that was simply a business expense.

Over the next twenty years, Helga Johanssen established a comfortable, expensive lifestyle for herself. But with time, her freelance business diminished and she signed on with an escort service—actually a thinly disguised pimping operation—that for the past few years had provided most of her clients. She had somehow managed to avoid drugs, the downfall of many of her colleagues. But lately she'd begun to face the fact that she really had nothing to show for her two decades of self-employment, apart from a luxury sports car, a closet full of beautiful clothes, and some good jewelry.

As Helga approached forty, the customers grew scarcer. Aside from a generalized slowdown of activity in her field due to the onset of AIDS, Helga no longer fit the current preferred-prostitute profile. She was tall, where petite was the style; she was pushing middle age, where the Lolita types were fashionable.

When Buster Malloy met Helga Johanssen, she was a no-longer-young hooker, still reasonably attractive but desperately aware that her remaining years in the business were limited. She'd been fired from the escort ser-vice. Her hotel contacts were beginning to look elsewhere for talent. Most of the money she'd earned in two decades of hooking had somehow slipped through her fingers. *Twenty years older,* she thought ruefully, *twenty years wiser, but right back where I started.* Well, there was nothing for it but to cruise the bars again.

Helga Johanssen had always prospered at Halley's Comet, a piano lounge at the Galaxy, rarely leaving unaccompanied. She smiled at Charlie, the portly greeter, as she ascended the steps to the bar, surreptitiously slipping him a folded twenty in passing.

"Thanks, Helga," said the tuxedo-clad doorkeeper as he smoothly pocketed the bill. "Haven't seen you for ages. Where've you been?"

"Oh, around. Those bastards at the service let me go. I'm on my own again."

"That's a bummer, Helga," Charlie replied sympathetically. "But you still look super. As a matter of fact—"

A great crash inside the bar followed by angry shouts distracted Char-lie from his chat with Helga. Seconds later a harried-looking bartender ran out and whispered urgently in the greeter's ear.

"Better stay out here for a few minutes, Helga," Charlie said. "Prob-lems . . ." He reached for a phone, then hesitated as he spotted the familiar cybercop uniform of a Galaxy security guard striding past the bottom of the stairs. He recognized the burly Irishman immediately. "Malloy!" he called out. "Can you give us a hand here?"

Buster Malloy instinctively felt for his billy club as he ran to answer Charlie's summons. "What's the problem?"

"The usual. Some drunk is trying to redecorate the joint."

"I'll take care of it."

Malloy plunged into the darkness of Halley's Comet and emerged mo-ments later triumphantly supporting a sheepish-looking man by the back collar of his jacket as if he were displaying the prize catch in a fishing derby. The hulking one-eyed security guard dragged his trophy down the stairs, propped him against a pillar, and spoke intensely for a moment to the offender. The man blanched, nodded vigorously, and staggered off as fast as his rubbery legs could carry him.

Helga Johanssen watched in fascination. She was intrigued by the big security guard with the eye patch—mesmerized like a rabbit by a rattlesnake. There was definitely something *evil* about the man, something cruel. Yet for no logical reason at all, she felt a strange need to meet him, to talk to him, to find out what made him tick.

She casually strolled over to Buster. "What did you say to that man?" she asked, quietly so that Charlie wouldn't hear. But Charlie was already back on the phone, the incident with the drunk forgotten. Helga was alone with Buster—as alone as any two people could be outside a popular piano bar in a crowded casino.

Malloy sized her up. Big blond woman, good-looking—but no spring chicken. Nice figure, sexy black dress, expensive-looking jewelry. A hooker, for sure. The Irishman had no moral objection to prostitutes. In his opinion, everybody was entitled to make a living; he himself had engaged their services on numerous occasions. Buster answered with a twisted smile: "I told 'im if 'e ever come back, I'd take 'im in the back room an' cut off 'is balls with me Swiss Army knife."

"And he believed you?" she whispered wonderingly.

Malloy grinned crookedly. "Maybe I wasn't kiddin'."

"My God, you weren't, were you?"

The one-eyed man said nothing.

"My name's Helga," she offered, then added the mandatory Vegas corollary: "I'm from L.A. And Sweden before that."

"Buster. Buster Malloy. From South Boston." There was an awkward pause, during which Malloy merely stared down in amusement at the big Swedish hooker. If this bimbo was looking for witty conversation, she was barking up the wrong tree. The silence lengthened.

"Well, Buster, nice to have met you," she said finally, nervously turning to ascend the steps to the bar and explore its commercial possibilities. "Maybe we'll see each other another—"

"Wait a minute." Malloy sensed that this woman *liked* him; he hated to pass up a potential freebie. "Do you wanna . . . would you like to maybe get together later?"

Helga ignored the small warning bell that was ringing in her subconscious. "Yes," she replied simply.

That first night, Malloy resisted his natural impulses by forcing himself to be as gentle as possible. But she sensed his repression and said, "Don't be afraid to get tough with me, Buster—just no bruises, please," and Malloy was glad to oblige. From then on, he'd knock her around a little before they got it on. Both enjoyed the rougher aspects of sex.

Sometimes the fun went too far. He'd had to take her to the Sunrise ER on more than a couple of occasions after getting a little too enthusiastic with his fists. Yet she stayed with him, for reasons even she didn't understand, or want to.

As the years passed, Malloy recognized that for him, with an aging hooker for company and a beat-up trailer to live in and twelve bucks an hour at the Galaxy, this was probably as good as it was ever going to get. He'd never make the kind of money those fucking slopes threw around the tables like confetti. There'd be no fine house with in-ground pool, no fancy car, no lavish vacations. The more the specter of personal failure clouded the big Irishman's soul, the more he felt like hurting somebody.

Near the end of a particularly brutal shift at the Galaxy—the crowds were fierce and security guard Buster Malloy had been nursing the mother of all hangovers—he overheard a commotion in the baccarat pit.

Square foot for square foot, baccarat was by far the casino's biggest moneymaker. The game attracted the highest of the high rollers, mostly Japanese, Chinese, and Taiwanese businessmen, many of them with seven-figure credit lines. The Galaxy spared no effort to create a cachet of sophisticated opulence for these premium baccarat players. The pit area was set down three steps and segregated from the rest of the casino by an oak railing; it was elegantly draped in red velvet and carpeted with inch-thick broadloom.

A carefully selected buffet of Oriental delicacies was laid out for the convenience of the players so that they might remain at the table for hours, leaving only to obey the occasional call of nature. The idea of providing restroom facilities in the baccarat pit, something of a deluxe Johnny-on-the-spot, had been suggested by some Galaxy executives but ultimately abandoned as perhaps a little too predatory even for Vegas.

The caller and the dealers were attired in formal eveningwear, while beautiful young ladies in gorgeous gowns, actually shills in the employ of the casino, pretended to play the game. The Asian gamblers appreciated this American arm candy, habituated as they were to the ubiquitous hostesses of Tokyo or Hong Kong or Taipei.

The noise grew louder as Malloy approached the pit.

"I no pay you shit commission! You bastard take enough money from me al'eady!" a middle-aged, somewhat inebriated Hong Kong Chinese player was shouting angrily at Al Mitchell, the caller.

In the game of baccarat, gamblers could wager either on "bank" or "player." Winning bets on either side were paid off at even money, except that winning bank bets carried a 5 percent house commission, usually collected by the dealers only *after* the eight-deck shoe had been completely dealt out. It was possible, therefore, that a player who had lost money during a particular shoe, despite winning some bank bets, would be obliged to pay the house an amount additional to what he had already lost. This was evidently the case here, Malloy saw.

"Sir, you know the rules," the caller protested. "We have to collect the comm—"

"I say fuck you rules. You not make me pay one more dollah. I go now."

Malloy stumped into the area. "Need any help here, Al?" he asked the caller.

"I think we're okay, Buster. I'm sure Mr. Ling will reconsider his position—"

But the player refused to be mollified. "Mistah Ling not reconsidah. Mistah Ling go *now*. Tell you shithead security guard *back off*," he added, his voice rising in that supercilious mixture of anger and disdain with which the Chinese address their social inferiors.

Malloy laid a big hand lightly on the player's shoulder. "Sir," he began, attempting to disguise the contempt he felt for the little yellow scumbag. All Orientals were scum to his way of thinking, whether you found them in the jungles of Vietnam or the casinos of Las Vegas. "Please keep your voice—"

Without warning, Ling responded by picking up his drink from the table and hurling the contents in Buster's face. "No touch!" he hissed.

Buster Malloy fought to control his temper—and lost. Stung more by the insult than the alcohol, his normally pink face darkened several shades to the hue of a beefsteak tomato. Throbbing purple veins on his neck threatened to pop his uniform collar. Buster's hands shook with fury and tightened into ham-size fists. Bitter memories of 'Nam came flooding back, filling his heart with rage. He grasped the little man's shirtfront with one hand and drew back a huge fist. . . .

Alarmed, Mitchell stepped between the two men referee-style, some-how managing to separate the big Irish security guard and the diminutive Asian gambler. "Cool it, Buster," he snapped. "Mr. Ling is one of our best cust—"

"I don't give a shite," Malloy shouted, attempting to reach past the caller and get his hands on the now-fearful player. "'E ain't got no right doin' what 'e did."

"*Malloy!* You take this any further and I guarantee you'll be out of a job in five minutes," Mitchell panted as he struggled to protect his customer from the larger man. "Is that what you want?"

Enraged, Malloy ignored the caller's warning and continued to press forward. "I'll kill the yellow motherfucker," he roared.

Mitchell looked around in desperation. "Give me a hand here, guys," he called out to his associates in the baccarat room.

Defiantly, Buster shouted, "Let me at that little zipperhead!" Only with the belated assistance of the two male baccarat dealers was Mitchell able to keep Malloy from assaulting a thoroughly shaken Ling. Stymied, the big man ceased his struggling.

The caller straightened his tie, brushed off his jacket, and scowled at the furious security guard. "I'm going to have to report this, Malloy."

"It just ain't fuckin' *fair,* Al," Buster growled in frustration, wiping the liquid from his face with a soiled handkerchief. "If this was Vietnam, I'd know what to do," he added grimly. "But this is America an' a man's gotta eat shit just to make a crummy livin'. An' I guess *that* ain't never gonna change."

"You know what, Malloy? I think you've got a real problem. I don't want to see you in here again. Ever. And I'll make goddamn sure Steve Forrester hears about this."

Buster Malloy stomped out of the baccarat room, muttering about his lousy luck.

The big Irishman never suspected that within six months he would finally get his one and only shot at the brass ring.

8 "**Good morning, Steve,**" said Suzanne Hughes, Steve Forrester's British executive assistant. "Lovely spring day. Coffee's on. Al Mitchell's waiting in your office. And Thurman has a card counter; he needs to see you s.a.p. in the eye."

"Take a number, folks." Steve poured himself a mug of steaming Blue Mountain coffee and lit his tenth Vantage 100 of the day. "What does Mitchell want?"

"Something about a punch-up in the baccarat room."

Freshly summoned to the carpet in Vice President Steve Forrester's office, Buster Malloy stood rigidly at attention, clenching and unclenching his huge fists. His face was still flushed, the result of his outburst in the baccarat room an hour earlier.

"So that was it? You grabbed Mr. Ling?"

Malloy set his jaw resolutely. "I didn't *grab* 'im, Mr. Forrester. I jus' touched 'im politely on the shoulder to kinda get 'is attention."

"Al Mitchell says you attacked him."

"Only after 'e threw 'is drink in me face. Before that, I was jus' doin' me job."

"It isn't your job to beat up the customers."

" 'Specially not the high rollers," Buster muttered bitterly.

"I don't care whether they're high rollers or nickel slot players. You know the policy here: no physical contact unless security is threatened." Forrester lit a cigarette. "As it happens, you attacked one of our biggest clients. He has a million-dollar credit line, and we sure as hell don't need *you* to collect his markers."

"The little zipperhead 'ad no call doin' what 'e did."

"Zipperhead? What kind of racist remark is that?" demanded Forrester.

"Shit, I spent me best years zappin' monkeys like 'im. That's what Vietnam was all about—protectin' people like *you* from—"

"For your information, the gentleman was Chinese, not Vietnamese—"

"There ain't no difference. A slope is a slope."

"Look, Malloy, this discussion is pointless. The Galaxy will not tolerate that kind of vicious retaliation."

"'E still didn't have no right to do what 'e did," Malloy repeated sullenly.

"Maybe. But neither did you. And the difference is, he's the customer."

Malloy hated the position he was in. Why the fuck did he have to explain his actions to this bollixing bastard? Only because he *needed* the goddamn job. He struggled to control his temper. "All right, then, Mr. Forrester." He swallowed hard. "I'll say I'm sorry. It's me only slipup in t'ree years on the job—"

"Is that a fact?" Forrester picked up a file folder from his desk and thumbed through the contents. Acting as judge and jury in matters like this was a duty he disliked intensely, but it was one that went with the territory. *God knows, I probably would have done the same thing in Malloy's position,* he thought. "Yes. I see that your performance reviews have been satisfactory." He sighed and closed the folder. "Okay, Malloy, I guess under the circumstances—look, man, nobody's perfect. And I can see you *were* provoked. Everybody deserves a second chance. As Mr. Ling isn't pressing charges, I'm willing to overlook the incident. This time. But, goddamn it, Buster, if anything like this ever happens again . . ."

Buster Malloy bit his lip, clenched his fists, and stifled the urge to beat the shit out of this arrogant prick. "Understood," he mumbled.

"Then let's say no more about it."

"Yes, sir." Malloy remained livid, an emotion tempered only slightly by the knowledge that he hadn't lost his job.

For his part, Steve Forrester had never believed in holding grudges or remaining angry. Once a situation had been resolved, you put it behind you. Life was too short. Remembering what Suzy had said when he arrived, he thought for a moment and addressed Malloy in a matter-of-fact, business-as-usual tone: "As long as you're here, Buster, there's something you can help me with right now. It appears we've got a blackjack card counter downstairs. Why don't you come along with me for backup?"

"Yes, sir. We goin' down now?"

"In a few minutes. I just want to check it out with Thurman Washington first. Walk with me to the eye, then we'll go down together."

Unlocking an unmarked door on level two, Steve Forrester and Buster Malloy stepped into the eerie half-world of the catwalks hidden above a false ceiling over the casino. The central section of the Galaxy's main gaming area was open to the top of the atrium in order to accommodate the Saturn rocket and was spied upon by suspended, retractable cameras that were concealed in simulated satellites and asteroids. The catwalk area covered the rest of the casino; here, Plexiglas bubbles and one-way mirrors (strategically placed to afford a direct overview of the baccarat pit and the higher-stakes blackjack tables) complemented the video cameras. Despite the electronic surveillance, it was still desirable on occasion to observe the games directly. The catwalks also provided a means for technicians to service the cameras.

Forrester strode purposefully along the railed walkways while Buster Malloy followed a few paces behind, fists clenched and jaw set in an angry line. Only with the greatest restraint did the recently chastised security guard resist the impulse to shove his superior over the rail and send him crashing through the ceiling to the casino floor forty feet below.

Unaware of the fury seething within Malloy, Steve Forrester glanced down at the games in progress below. It was totally illogical, but in the catwalks he often felt a slight twinge of voyeuristic guilt. Keyhole peeking had never been his sport. In any event, there didn't seem to be too much happening; early morning was always the slowest time of day at the Galaxy. Without incident, the two men reached the eye-in-the-sky office, located at the intersection of two catwalks, and stepped inside. Both needed a moment for their vision to adjust to the near darkness within.

Aside from two low-voltage spotlights in the black acoustic-tile ceiling, the only illumination in the room came from a wall of softly glowing video monitors and from the green, red, and white LED readouts on the control console. A bank of VCRs hummed quietly, recording every moment of every table game as well as the higher-denomination slot machines.

Steve rolled up a chair next to Thurman Washington, his graveyard eye-in-the-sky operator, and sat down. Malloy remained standing stiffly.

"Hey, Thurm. What's so important, I couldn't even finish my morning coffee in peace?"

"Sorry about that, Steve. But I'm pretty sure we got us a counter on thirty-six." The reference was to blackjack table thirty-six, located in pit four.

"How much is he up?"

"Not much. A couple of thousand, maybe."

"What's he betting?"

"Lucy says twenty to eighty."

"Lucy?"

"Lucy Baker, the floor supe."

"For this you dragged me all the way up here?"

"Only following your instructions, boss. Remember the memo you sent out last month? How we're cracking down on cheaters? You said, and I quote, all incidents of suspected card counting are to be brought to your attention?"

Forrester did remember the memo. The Vegas Strip had recently been plagued by a team of card counters from Atlantic City, and he was determined that they'd never make a dime at the Galaxy. Normally, he wouldn't involve himself personally in situations that could easily be handled by the floor people. But under these circumstances he felt that his personal intervention was warranted. Besides, it didn't hurt his tough-guy reputation amongst the grifters of Las Vegas to show the flag from time to time. Secretly, Steve was pleased that his instructions were being followed. But he couldn't resist the urge to gripe.

"I should have my head read. Who is this guy, anyway?"

"He says his name is Harry Jackson. Lucy thinks it's a phony."

"Let's see the tape."

Washington pressed a button, and the thirty-five-inch screen directly in front of him lit up. The crisp full-color image displayed an overhead view of a blackjack table, with a skinny, owlish fellow perched on the middle seat, nursing a few small stacks of five-, twenty-five-, and hundred-dollar chips. The man did not look like any of the Atlantic City team members they'd identified so far.

"That's our boy," said Thurman.

"Fast-forward to the beginning of the next shoe, please, Thurm." At high speed, the three men watched as the six decks were shuffled, reinserted in the shoe, and redealt. Then Washington slowed the tape down to normal speed. "I'm going to count this shoe down along with our friend," Forrester said.

During the video replay, the player started with a twenty-dollar bet—four red chips. For the next six or seven hands, according to Steve's calculations, the deck remained *neutral*—neither positive nor negative. And the man's bet remained at twenty dollars. He won a few hands and lost a few.

The swing happened very quickly, and it was what Forrester had been waiting for. A series of small cards raised the true count to *plus eight,* a very advantageous situation for a card counter. And just like clockwork, the suspect raised his bet—to thirty-five, then fifty dollars.

"Look, Thurm, the son of a bitch won," he exclaimed, unable to disguise a note of reluctant admiration in his voice. "Let's give him a little more rope."

Gradually, while the count remained positive, the player raised his bet to sixty, to seventy, to eighty dollars, splitting a pair of kings against the dealer's eight, doubling down on ten against an ace and surrendering half his bet (an option the Galaxy allowed its customers) with an eighteen against the dealer's nine upcard. Meanwhile, his stack grew.

Then, as rapidly as the count had soared, it plummeted to the negative side of zero. And within three hands, the player had reduced his bet to the original twenty dollars.

"I think we've got him. Let's just check the computer to be sure."

All pertinent information about known players was stored in the casino's mainframe and could be accessed from any terminal with the right password. In addition to the player's name, Social Security number, home address, and business address, a complete historical record of all his or her visits—wins and losses right back to day one—was available. The computer kept statistics on the player's average bet and number of hours of play per visit. For premium players, personal information such as birthdays, anniversaries, spouse's name, even the player's favorite liquor, could be programmed in to the card. Washington punched his keyboard and a monochrome computer screen below the video monitor flashed a readout.

"We don't have any Harry Jackson," Steve read as Washington scrolled through the names on the screen. "But that's not surprising. Let's check the blacklist."

A rogues' gallery of known cheaters, including card counters, was also programmed into the Galaxy's database. This information, provided by the various casinos' own security forces and by local police departments throughout the state, was shared freely among major Nevada casinos. It included MOs, mug shots, arrest records, and any other facts that might assist the casinos in protecting their bankrolls.

"Okay, Steve," said Washington, warming to his task. "I'll look in the card counter's section. Then I'll narrow down the list by bet size and the guy's physical appearance. If he's ever been nailed, we'll find out."

For several minutes the operator tapped on his keyboard. Faces and descriptions flashed by on the screen.

"Bingo!" exclaimed Thurman.

Forrester leaned in closer. "Jurgen Voss," he read aloud. "Caught once in Reno—by house security at Harry's—for card counting."

"That's got to be him. Look at the picture." A coarse but recognizable photo scan stared back at them from the monitor. "This was taken, what, ten years ago? Same big head, same skinny neck. Take away a little hair . . ."

"Jesus, only one pinch in ten years? The guy must be good."

"Yeah, but we're better."

"You're absolutely right, ol' buddy. I guess I owe you one." Forrester picked up his coffee cup and rose to leave. "Why the hell did I ever write that memo? Now I've got to get in there and play the heavy. Let's go, Buster."

9 "Excuse me—Mr. Voss, isn't it? I'm Steve Forrester of the Galaxy and I wonder if I could have a word with you," he said pleasantly.

Jurgen Voss froze for an instant. Then he frowned in disbelief. How did they know who he was? He had felt the bad vibrations from the lady pit boss and ignored them. A mistake, his first in ten years. But he was confident he could talk his way out of this.

"You have the wrong person. My name is *Jackson*. Harry Jackson. I am here on a convention."

"Which convention?"

Jurgen was silent for a moment, trying to decide between lie and indignation. He chose the latter. "That is my business."

Steve noted the man's pronounced foreign accent. He certainly didn't *sound* like a Harry Jackson. "Sir, we know who you are, and we know what your business really is. I'll have to ask you to step away from the table."

"What for?"

"We can't allow you to play blackjack here anymore," said Forrester mildly. "Now, please step away."

Emboldened by Steve's courteous, diffident manner, the card counter swung round on his stool and scowled at the interloper. "Who the devil *are* you, anyway? Why must I leave this table?"

"I'm in charge of security here at the casino, and if you'll just look over there, I'll show you a very good reason." On cue, Buster Malloy moved up and flanked Jurgen.

"That is not a reason. That is a big stick."

"I'm afraid it's all the reason we need. Now please stand."

Steve had hoped to avoid a noisy confrontation, but those hopes were fading as a curious crowd began to gather.

Lucy Baker, the young floor supervisor who had spotted the card counter and had informed the eye, looked on quietly as the handsome casino executive and the sinister security guard with the eye patch confronted the little man with the big head.

"What kind of cheap people are you?" the counter protested. "Can you not afford to let the players win once in a while?"

"Sir, we can do this the easy way, or the hard way," said Forrester. "It's your choice."

"I have rights," he blustered.

"Wrong. You have *no* rights in here—you're a card counter and you've just taken us for over two grand."

Voss's voice rose an octave. "I will get a lawyer! I will sue—"

Forrester cut him off brusquely. "Sergeant Malloy," he said, "I believe you have something to read to this *gentleman*."

Malloy planted himself in front of Jurgen Voss and extracted a plastic-coated card from the breast pocket of his uniform. In a sullen, unenthusiastic monotone he read from the card: "You are considered to be a professional card counter. You are not allowed to gamble at a blackjack table in this casino. If you attempt to do so, you will be considered a disorderly person and be evicted from this casino. If you subsequently return to the casino, you will be subject to arrest—"

"Arrest me? You cannot arrest me! I have broken no law! Are you the Gestapo?"

"Sir, we're trying to be civilized about this," said Steve. "But if you persist in arguing—"

At this point, foolishly, the little man's tremendous ego overcame the caution he knew he should be exercising. He shouted: "I will argue if I wish! You stupid people do not know with whom you are dealing! I have more intelligence than all of you together!"

"Then you admit you've been counting?" Forrester asked quietly.

"I have been using my brains . . . something you know nothing about—"

Steve's eyes hardened. "Okay, that's it," he said. "Sergeant Malloy, take Mr. Voss to the station. Ask Lieutenant Marshall to contact me when you get there. You can sign the complaint form."

Engrossed in the confrontation, Steve Forrester never noticed Lucy Baker, the young table supervisor, standing in the pit.

She, however, was fascinated by this handsome casino executive and could not help wondering if he was married.

10

Dan Shiller was ready to call it a night.

The card cheat had been hand mucking at a five-dollar table in Diamond Lil's, one of the smaller downtown joints on Casino Center. Maybe just one more hand; he had an ace concealed in his palm, and he hated to waste it. All he needed was for a ten or a face card to be dealt to him in order to produce a "blackjack" and be paid sixty dollars for his forty-dollar bet.

Just like clockwork, the dealer gave him a queen and a six facedown. He picked up the cards in his right hand, smoothly substituting the ace for the six, and tossed the natural twenty-one faceup on the table.

"Blackjack," the dealer announced.

"Hold it right there," growled a deep voice directly behind Shiller. "Don't pay that bet."

In a heartbeat, the hand mucker's right wrist was clamped to the table in an iron grip. Dan twisted his head around in alarm and saw that his captor was a beefy six-foot security guard backed by two others and a tough-looking man in a dark suit. Tightening his grip, the guard forced Shiller's wrist over, revealing the hidden card.

"Okay, mister, come with us," said the man in the dark suit menacingly. "Leave your chips on the table." Grasping the cheater firmly under each elbow, the other two guards dragged him off his stool. It fell to the floor with a crash.

A cold shiver ran down Dan Shiller's spine. He remembered how they'd broken his colleague's fingers in Tahoe. His mind raced. Maybe there was a chance, a slim chance, to get out of this in one piece. He was sandwiched between two guards, each of whom had a firm grip on his upper arm, while a third guard stood behind. Gathering his wits, he forced a wan smile and addressed the man in the suit: "Guess you've got me, gentlemen. I'll go quietly."

He feigned resignation and pretended to be escorted along willingly. As he had hoped, the guards relaxed their hold on him slightly. Suddenly he ducked, twisted his body, and wrenched free of their grasp.

With the guards in hot pursuit, fruitlessly shouting at him to stop, the exposed cheater barged through the packed casino, bowling over a hapless slot-change girl and knocking the plastic cup from an elderly woman's hand. Quarters rained down on the floor in a silver shower. If he could only make it to the street, maybe he could get lost in the crowd. He was almost at the door, but they were gaining. With a supreme final effort, he shouldered his way through a group of dumbfounded Japanese tourists, his momentum popping him out of the doors like a cork exploding from a champagne bottle. He flew across the sidewalk in a half stumble and careened helter-skelter into the roadway.

At which point his luck ran out.

Over a decade earlier, the Southeast Area Command of the Las Vegas Metropolitan Police Department had set up an experimental bicycle squad to improve patrol efficiency and speed up response time among the crowded sidewalks and congested traffic of the Strip. The experiment proved such a success that within a year the Northeast Area Command had established its own bicycle squad to patrol the downtown casino core. When Fremont Street was converted to a pedestrian mall, the practicality of this approach became even more evident. Helmeted cops on ten-speed bikes now constituted the frontline of law and order downtown.

Officer Al Dodd had signed up to be a Las Vegas bicycle cop not only because he enjoyed exercise but also because he liked people.

So far, the job had lived up to his expectations. He'd met numerous fascinating people—apart from cooling off the odd drunk or breaking up the occasional fight, most of his time was spent schmoozing with tourists, providing them with information and directions.

Dodd took great care to avoid running into pedestrians on his bike. Hordes of them, fascinated by the overhead neon spectacular, bumbled their way through the Fremont Street Experience without ever looking where they were going.

Apart from an occasional brush, he had never actually collided with a pedestrian.

Until today.

In a tangle of flying arms and legs and spokes and pedals, Dan Shiller, escaping grifter, ran squarely into Officer Al Dodd on his bicycle.

Stunned and disoriented, Shiller attempted to scramble to his feet, but it was too late.

"Officer! Hold that guy!" one of the Diamond Lil's guards shouted.

Recovering first, Officer Dodd grabbed Dan Shiller under the armpits and stood up, carefully pulling the man to his feet.

"Are you hurt, sir?" the policeman inquired solicitously, looking Dan over for apparent damage but nonetheless retaining a firm grip on his jacket.

"No—no harm done," Shiller panted. "I'll just leave now, Officer—"

"One moment," said the man in the suit from Diamond Lil's. "We caught this grifter hand mucking in the casino. He was attempting to escape custody when he ran into you."

"I see," said the cop. "Do you wish to press charges?"

"Damn right," replied the suit, who privately would have preferred to administer his own brand of justice in the casino's back room. It was lucky for the bastard that he ran into this cop. But at least he wouldn't get away. "If you'll take him in—"

"You have witnesses?"

"Yeah. Myself, these three guards, and the dealer. We were just about to call you guys," he lied, "when he ran."

"Okay," said Officer Dodd, not believing the casino security man for a second. "I'll call for a patrol car."

"It's all a mistake," Dan pleaded. "I didn't—"

"Sir, you're under arrest for fraud," said the policeman as he applied handcuffs to Shiller's wrists. Dodd glanced meaningfully at Dan's would-be captors and lowered his voice: "Just between us, buddy, you're lucky I came along when I did."

"Believe me, I know," replied the grifter quietly, dismayed to have been apprehended, yet grateful to have avoided a fate that could have been infinitely more painful.

"You have the right to remain silent. . . ."

11

Anger, frustration, and relief churned within Buster Malloy's soul as he reluctantly escorted Jurgen Voss out the back entrance of the casino to where the Galaxy's security cars were parked.

He was still furious about the baccarat incident; that fucking zip should be the one going to jail, not this poor little wanker. He was frustrated about having been obliged to suck up to that cocky bastard Forrester. Yet he was more than a little relieved that he still had the job; the prospect of being fired and looking for another one at his age, with his lack of education, was not a pleasant one.

He felt quite sympathetic toward his prisoner. In Malloy's opinion, anyone who had the brains to beat his shithead employers out of a few bucks deserved a fucking *medal,* not a trip to jail.

"Wanna ride up front with me?" Buster asked the card counter, unlocking the passenger door of a white Caprice sedan with blue roof flashers and GALAXY SECURITY lettered on the sides. Obviously, the little fellow posed no threat to the big security guard; otherwise, he would have cuffed him and tossed him in the backseat behind the Plexiglas divider.

Surprised, Voss nodded.

"Don't try nothin' funny," Malloy warned sternly as he walked around to the driver's side. Settling himself behind the wheel, he added, "Not that you look like the type that would."

Sensing an ally in the security guard, Jurgen ventured, "Will I be put in jail?"

Malloy started the car and slipped it into gear. "Well, kinda. But not exactly. They'll keep you in a holdin' cell until you go to court. But it ain't really *jail.*" Here Malloy spoke from experience, having himself been convicted of common assault twice in Southie. The second conviction had gotten him a thirty-day sentence in the South Boston Municipal Detention Facility. He had also earned several sojourns in the brig in Saigon for brawling. "The holdin' cell is kinda like a waitin' room, except you're locked in. Jail is where you go after they find you guilty."

"You are saying that they will *not* put me in jail?"

"Most likely not," replied Buster as they drove out of the Galaxy parking lot onto the Strip. "You'll be out in a few hours. The Galaxy don't really give a shit what happens to you. It ain't like them sawdust joints downtown where they'd as soon break a fella's arms as look at 'im when they'd catch 'im cheatin'. Not that *I* think you were. Cheatin', that is. I figure a guy's got the fuckin' brains to beat their games, more power to 'im." They were forced to crawl past Treasure Island as motorists slowed down to catch a glimpse of the hourly battle between the Royal Navy and the buccaneers—Steve Wynn's carefully orchestrated drama of sound and fury. Just once, Malloy would like to see the goddamn pirates *lose*. "They'll just charge you with DC."

"DC?"

"Disorderly conduct. They'll keep you for a few hours in the lockup, prob'ly fingerprint you an' take a mug shot. Then the judge'll let you go."

"This is all? I will not be given the opportunity to defend myself?" Suddenly Voss felt cheated. He had already begun to visualize his courtroom debut, a superintelligent David against a powerful but dull-witted Goliath, impressing judge and jury with his genius-level IQ, his clear logic, his flawless reasoning.

"You won't need to. I ain't never seen 'em throw a card counter in jail yet. My boss jus' wanted to put the fear o' Christ in you." He pronounced it *Chroyst*.

"I see. I have obviously made an error in judgment when I have argued with Herr Forrester."

"Maybe. But in a way, I don't blame you. Like, why should you buy that crap from them? You jus' told it the way it is. You wasn't cheatin'. You're smart an' they're a buncha jerkoffs."

The card counter took off his thick glasses and wiped them with a dirty handkerchief. "You are right, of course, Officer—"

"My name's Buster Malloy."

"—*und* yet I wonder. If I am so smart, why are *they* the ones with the money?"

"Because they kiss their precious fuckin' slanty-eyed customers' arses an' treat their employees like shit."

Jurgen could not quite grasp the logic of this statement, but he quickly understood that this was an angry, bitter man. "Then why do you work there?" he asked, genuinely curious. How *sonderbar* this Malloy was!

"When you ain't got but one eye an' a grade-eight education, you can't be too choosy. For guys like me, jobs don't grow on trees."

"I am sorry to hear this."

"Ah, shite, it's a livin'," said Malloy with a grimace as he hung a left onto Tropicana Avenue. "If I could do what you do, *I'd* be in there countin' the cards right alongsid'a you. In fact, I'd take their fuckin' money any way I could."

"You mean, steal it?"

Buster laughed bitterly. "Goddamn right. But there's a fat chance o' *that* ever happenin'. They're tighter'n choirboys' arseholes with their cash. They don't trust nobody. *Especially* their employees."

"This I have observed."

They drove for a few more moments in silence. On any other day, Jurgen would have enjoyed the drive along the Strip. The massive marquees blazed relentlessly, advertising Liza at Bally's, Englebert at the Roman Palladium, Siegfried and Roy at the Mirage, Dolly at the Desert Inn. The big stars needed only first names, the card counter thought abstractedly.

"Well, here we are." Malloy swung the car into the parking lot beside the Southwest Area Command Station on Spring Mountain Road. "Sorry about this, boyo. I'm jus' doin' me job."

"I understand."

They entered and Buster Malloy greeted the desk sergeant. "Got another'un for you, Fred. Oh yeah, an' Mister High an' Mighty Steve Fuckin' Forrester wants Lieutenant Marshall to call 'im before you do the paperwork."

As Malloy had predicted, Jurgen Voss was charged not with cheating, nor fraud, nor any other exotic offense, but with that mundane catch-all of the American justice system, disorderly conduct. The LVMPD desk sergeant, an affable middle-aged man with a graying walrus mustache, confided to Jurgen that charges of card counting were difficult to prove and seldom resulted in convictions. "The lieutenant spoke to Mr. Forrester," said the sergeant after Voss had cooled his heels for several minutes. "And they agreed on the DC charge. You'll go in front of a judge this afternoon."

"Will I need a lawyer?"

"Well, sir, that's up to you. We can get you one if you want. Have you got any priors?"

"Priors?"

"Ever been arrested before?"

"No." His capture at Harry's in Reno a decade earlier had been effected by private security guards, not cops.

"Then I wouldn't bother with a lawyer. You'd have to wait at least another day while they found you a public defender. And the judge'll probably let you go anyway. Minor offense, no priors. It's only a misdemeanor. If he's in a bad mood, you might catch a fifty-dollar fine. But I doubt it."

The complaint form was typed up in triplicate by the sergeant on an old IBM Selectric. Buster Malloy signed it on behalf of the Galaxy without so much as a glance at its contents.

"Good luck, mister," said Malloy, turning to leave. "Don't let the wankers grind you down."

"*Danke schön,* Herr Malloy," said Jurgen.

"An' don't do no more card countin' at the Galaxy," Malloy called back over his shoulder as he barged out the front door.

Voss was relieved of his wallet, belt, and shoelaces and taken to a small room where he was photographed and fingerprinted. Ashamed of his mutilated fingertips, Voss avoided eye contact with the police fingerprint technician, who involuntarily shuddered in disgust at the sight of Voss's scabbed and bloody appendages. Following this procedure, a sweaty, overweight desk officer escorted him politely but firmly to the holding cell. The mesh-walled area measured about sixteen feet square and was furnished with wooden benches bolted to the concrete floor. A strong disinfectant odor failed to mask the pervasive underscent of stale perspiration, urine, and vomit. Fluorescent ceiling fixtures cast an unforgiving white glare upon the cell's three tenants.

The officer unlocked the door, ushered Jurgen through, and closed it behind him with a clang that made the little man jump. Voss folded his thin arms protectively across his chest and glanced furtively around at the occupants of the cell as his escort vanished down the corridor and left him with—who knows what? Murderers, rapists, muggers? The unfrocked card counter had not felt so alone and vulnerable since the Reno incident, when the casino security men had roughed him up. He remembered with distaste the blows to his stomach: only two punches, but his abdomen had ached for days. But those were private security men; surely he was safe in this fortress of the law! Taking some comfort from this thought, yet keeping his back to the wall, Voss sidled over to a spot on the benches as far as possible from the other prisoners.

He noted a well-dressed, prosperously bronzed man, looking for all the world like the president of General Motors, seated casually in the opposite corner, legs crossed elegantly. An expensive-looking camel-hair jacket lay folded neatly on the bench next to him. At first glance, the man seemed out of place in this cell . . . yet Voss sensed an aura of larceny about him. In Jurgen's line of work, you learned that appearances could be misleading. After all, wasn't casino camouflage one of his own specialties? The card counter wondered what this man had done to deserve arrest.

Ten feet away from the smartly dressed man a Hispanic youth was curled up in a fetal position on one of the benches, moaning softly in Spanish. He had bundled a dirty windbreaker into a makeshift pillow. From the bruise on his cheek and the slightly bloody gauze pad on the boy's temple, Jurgen surmised that he had been involved in a fight, or perhaps he had been injured resisting arrest.

The third occupant of the enclosure caused Jurgen to shiver involuntarily. He was a mountain of a man, obviously a biker, all hard fat, at least equivalent in weight to a full-size refrigerator and considerably taller. He leaned insouciantly against the steel-mesh wall and chewed on a toothpick. Clad in faded jeans, steel-toed boots, and black leather vest, he sported a diamond stud in his left earlobe. Colorful tattoos festooned his bare arms. A fringe of greasy black hair encircled a large bald spot atop his head. As if to compensate for the lack of growth above, a Fu Manchu mustache and a stringy beard adorned the lower half of his face. The man's florid, pockmarked cheeks resembled pepperoni pizza; a bulbous, purple-veined nose testified to a lifetime of excessive drinking. Cheap plastic wraparound sunglasses hid the biker's eyes, yet Voss could feel the penetrating stare bore into him. It caused his scrotum to shrivel with apprehension.

Unsure of the etiquette of the occasion—did one acknowledge one's fellow captives, or did one ignore them?—Jurgen opted for the latter, averting his eyes and sitting down timidly on one of the hard wooden benches. He sighed, dejected. Why had he acted so foolishly, flaunting his intelligence, *daring* that Steve Forrester to arrest him? He could have walked away and been home by now instead of in this holding cell. Even the satisfaction of denouncing his persecutors in a court of law was to be denied him. And to make matters worse, the police would now have his photograph and a record of his activities on file—information that Voss was fairly certain would be circulated to all the casinos on his "paper route." It probably meant that he was finished as a card counter in Las Vegas—probably all of Nevada, for that matter. He would be forced to move to another state, to give up his apartment, all because—

"Where the fuck d'you think yer sittin'?" said a deep voice.

Startled, Jurgen looked up to see the biker looming over him like a monstrous avenging angel. An irrational fear gripped the card counter. Or was it irrational? Could this be Harry's all over again? Was he about to suffer another beating—or worse? Should he call for help? After all, this was a police station, not the back room of some grindout joint in Reno—

"I asked you a question, dickhead."

Voss cowered as the biker moved closer. He flinched at the powerful odor of marijuana, motor oil, and sweat that now engulfed him. "I . . . I am sorry," the card counter gulped. "I do not understand what . . . what you want."

"Move yer ass, boy. This here's my spot."

"Yes, of course." Jurgen hastily rose to his feet and scuttled over to the next bench.

"Not there, either, asshole."

"But where . . . ?"

"You sit on the floor."

Voss looked pleadingly at his tormentor. "I do not know you. Why are you doing this to me?"

"Because you remind me of a piece of shit stuck on a toilet bowl." The biker removed the toothpick from his mouth and hawked on the concrete floor, narrowly missing Jurgen's feet. "Because you talk funny. Because you ain't no American." The biker removed his sunglasses, revealing a pair of bloodshot eyes with grossly dilated pupils. "What are you, a Jew boy?"

The card counter quavered indignantly. "I am not Jewish."

"So you must be one of them fuckin' non-Aryan mongrels, huh?" With an arm as big around as Voss's waist, the biker pushed the little man lightly on his scrawny chest, causing him to stumble backward and nearly fall. "You a homo, too?"

Jurgen glanced around in desperation. Where were the police? What if he cried out for help and they did not hear him? Would that incite this bully to more violence? How ironic that the superior intelligence which had landed him here in the first place counted for absolutely nothing in dealing with such mindless brute force. In this arena he was totally helpless.

The man grabbed a fistful of Jurgen's shirt and with ridiculous ease lifted the little man so that only his toes touched the ground. "You know what we do to mongrel homos where I come from?"

"Please—"

"Hey, you," said the well-dressed man in the corner, quietly.

Without letting go of his victim, the biker turned his head. "You talkin' to me, man?"

"Who else?"

"This ain't none o' yer business."

"Knock it off, for Chrissake. Leave him alone." The man fixed a steady gaze on the biker. He did not rise from his bench.

"What the hell do you care about the little prick?"

"I don't. But you're annoying *me*. So put him down."

"Or what?" said the biker contemptuously.

"Or I'll call the desk officer and I'll testify that you threatened and assaulted this guy. And I'm sure he'll back me up. Right, pal?"

A trembling Voss, still in the grasp of the biker, nodded his head vigorously.

"Not only that," the man added, "but we'll tell them that you tried to rape the Spanish kid."

Jurgen's assailant hesitated. He knew he could beat the shit out of both men with one arm tied behind his back—but then where would he run? And despite a drug-induced fog, he recognized the validity of the man's threat. He was in enough trouble already, what with the possession and the resisting-arrest charges. He didn't need assault and rape added to his tab with the cops.

The biker released his grip on Voss's shirtfront and backed away. "Ah, fuck it anyway," he mumbled as he returned to his spot by the wall. "The little fag ain't worth the trouble."

"Good. Maybe now we'll get a little peace around here," said Dan Shiller.

A pale and shaken Jurgen Voss collapsed onto a bench near his rescuer. His heart was pounding like a jackhammer, and he observed that his hands were trembling—yet he felt the relief wash over him like a warm wave.

"Thank you for . . . what you have done . . . to help me," Jurgen stammered.

"It wasn't to help you," replied Shiller icily. "That blowhard just happened to be getting on my nerves."

"Nevertheless, I am grateful." Jurgen's pulse rate was returning to normal. "It is good to know there are still decent people in the world."

"Nobody's called me that for some time." Dan smiled sardonically. "Decent. A decent person! If I was really such a decent person, I wouldn't be cooling my heels in the LVMPD Hotel now, would I?"

"I do not know. May I ask—of course, it is not my business—but why *are* you here? You do not look like you belong in a place like this."

"Neither do you."

"Perhaps you would rather not talk. I have no right to ask—"

"No, that's okay. I don't mind trading war stories. But you go first."

Voss snorted. "The only crime I have done is using my intelligence to win a little money at cards. I have not cheated and have not broken rules. And still like a thief the casino treats me!" The little man's voice rose in frustration. "They build their *gefeckte* palaces with the money of people who play their games like idiots, yet they will not allow to play even the one person in a *tausend* who knows how to play correctly! And the law says that they can arrest such people." Even the lingering fright from his confrontation with the biker had paled in comparison to the anger he felt toward the Galaxy— mingled with disgust at himself for having allowed the whole debacle to happen in the first place. "And yet . . . and yet, I should have said nothing. What a dummkopf I was! I should when I had the chance have left quietly instead of losing my temper. I knew of their policies. And now this—"

"You're a card counter, right?"

"*Ja, ja,* of course. I did not explain that clearly. And yourself?"

"I'm a casino cash-removal specialist."

The card counter looked puzzled for just a fraction of a second, then chuckled as he realized his new acquaintance had made a joke. "I have never heard it said exactly like this. How do you remove the cash?"

"Lots of ways. Lately I've been working this roulette scam."

"Past-posting?"

"You got it."

"This must be difficult. Also risky."

"Not really. Not if you're well prepared. It's much safer than chip hustling at dice, but then again it's usually not as profitable—"

"You are also a rail thief?" Voss asked, a note of admiration in his voice.

"Yes, to put it indelicately. It's the best-paying thing I do. I picked up five yellow checks at the Palladium a couple of weeks ago."

"Five thousand dollars! That is more than I make in a month at black-jack!"

Suddenly the biker coughed. In his fascination with Dan's story, Jurgen had completely forgotten about his confrontation with the bearded monster. In the opposite corner of the holding cell the big man was slouched on a bench, mumbling to himself. He coughed again and spat on the floor. The kid appeared to be asleep.

Voss returned to his conversation with the grifter. "Are you also a card counter?"

"No, I don't have the brains for that. But I admire people like yourself who do. I do play the game, though. You could call me a reasonably competent mechanic. Except this time I got caught at it."

"Hand mucking?"

"Yeah. I was holding out cards at Diamond Lil's. Usually I can spot heat a mile away—you know, the way they whisper, the way they avoid looking at you, the way your balls tingle—"

Jurgen smiled ruefully. "I know exactly what you mean. I myself actually felt some heat, but I ignored it. Again, I was a dummkopf. Even after they spotted me, *ja,* I could have walked away. But I chose to remain and argue."

"Worst thing you could have done." The man rose to his feet, stretched, and yawned. "By the way, my name's Dan Shiller. What's yours?"

"Jurgen Voss. I am very happy to meet you."

"Likewise." The two men shook hands, a ritual Voss hated because it forced him to expose his fingertips. Shiller noticed the disfigured digits but managed to avoid shuddering. "Where did they nail you, Jurgen?" he asked.

"At the Galaxy."

"Steve Forrester?"

"*Ja,* Forrester." Voss sounded surprised. "You know this man?"

"We've never been formally introduced. But I've heard all about him. He's an ex-cop. Just last month at the Galaxy he nailed Mel Garfinkle, one of the best in the business. Mel was in cahoots with a dealer—dumping off black chips. Forrester spotted the scam right away. He's tough and smart. There are plenty of guys in our business who found *that* out the hard way. Since he took over security at the Galaxy, I don't go near the place."

"I am afraid I now will not be able to go near *any* place in Nevada," Jurgen reflected gloomily. "After this incident my name and also my photograph will be in every casino database from here to Reno."

"Mine, too."

"And next time I may not be so lucky . . . if you know what I mean."

Shiller laughed humorlessly. "I know exactly what you mean, my friend." He held his thumb and forefinger a fraction of an inch apart. "I came *this close* to getting the shit beat out of me at Diamond Lil's. If that cop hadn't come along on his bicycle when he did . . . they'd probably be feeding me through a tube right now."

Both men sat silently for a few moments, Jurgen reflecting on his plight, Dan deep in thought. The biker had ceased muttering and was engrossed in picking small objects out of his beard. The Hispanic kid snored softly.

Shiller broke the silence. "You know, we're both in deep shit."

"I know," said Voss.

"I don't mean with the law. You'll probably walk, and the worst I'll get is a few days in the local slam."

"You mean with the casinos."

"Like you said, they've got our pictures. They'll be watching for us. From now on, it's going to be damn tough for us to make a living."

The card counter nodded glumly. "That is certain."

"Besides which, I'm not getting any younger. I'm tired of grifting. I need to get out of this racket."

"Perhaps you should."

"Trouble is, I can't afford to quit."

"Really? Even with the *tausends* of dollars you make by hustling checks?"

"Never saved any of it. I seem to piss it away as fast as it comes in. Sometimes faster."

"I am in much the same . . . predicament. True, I have managed to put aside a little money. But nowhere near enough to live on for . . . always." He grimaced. "I suppose I must now move far away . . . to somewhere else in America."

"Maybe not." The grifter paused, thoughtfully sizing up his companion. "There may be a way—"

At that moment, the sweaty desk officer reappeared outside the holding cell, carrying a tray loaded with cellophane-wrapped sandwiches and coffee in Styrofoam cups. "Chow time," the cop called out. "Compliments of the management." He slid the tray through a horizontal slot in the door. The biker got to the tray first and grabbed the lion's share of the food. Jurgen and Dan shared the rest. The kid never woke up.

After picking at a soggy egg-salad sandwich and taking a couple of sips of lukewarm coffee, Voss said, "I am curious. What were you going to say?"

Shiller swallowed the last of his coffee. "Suppose I told you I had a plan for a major score. Big enough to retire on. I mean *really* retire. None of this Social Security and golden-age-discount-coupon shit. What would you say to that, my friend?"

Jurgen thought for a moment. "Well, I am a realist. Please do not take offense, but I would have to say you are dreaming," he replied. "On the other hand, it is always pleasant to dream. What else is there to do in a place like this?"

"Man, this is no dream. It's an idea I've been developing for some time now. But it's way too big to handle alone." Shiller lowered his voice. "I'd need a team. Somebody like yourself, somebody with brains. And at least one other person."

"Is it some kind of scam? A swindle?"

"No, it's way bigger than that. I'm talking millions of dollars here. *Tens* of millions."

Voss blinked. "Tens of millions! Incredible! But please go on."

"Okay. Follow the bouncing ball. First of all, who are the fattest pigeons in this town?"

"That is easy. The casinos."

"You're goddamn right! Now, who are the most vulnerable marks?"

"Most probably the same answer."

"Right again! The casinos! Think about it. At any given time they've got five to ten million dollars in cash in their counting rooms. Sometimes more. Any schmuck can walk into any casino at any time. There's no security to speak of—"

"*Aber,* Dan . . . if there is no security, then why are we here?"

"I don't mean *that* kind of security. Sure, they've got people trained to protect their cash from guys like us. But they don't have real security like there is in airports and courthouses and military bases. Even after Oklahoma City and Nine-Eleven, this town is pretty slack in that department. No metal detectors, no baggage searches, no ID checks. You could walk in with a fucking *arsenal* in your suitcase and they'd never know."

"You are not planning to *hold up* a casino?"

Shiller laughed. "No way, pal. That would be far too risky. And it isn't my style. I'm just reminding you how much cash they've got floating around . . . and how easy it is to get inside their candy store."

Voss shrugged. "All right. So. It is not a scam and it is not a holdup. *Bitte*—precisely tell me what is your plan."

"Not unless you're in."

"I must agree first to join before you explain?"

"Yep."

"I would have to think about it. How much is the . . . payoff?"

"Could be as high as fifty million. Split three ways."

"Fifty million dollars? Only in America! What would I do?"

"Help me with the planning. I've got a broad outline worked out, but I need to focus on the details. I'm not good at logistics—but I suspect you might be."

"I have an IQ of two hundred and five," replied Jurgen with barely concealed pride. "In addition, I possess a photographic memory. I am familiar with computers. My hobby is electronics. Does that qualify me?"

"My God, does it ever. You are *exactly* the guy I've been looking for."

"*Ja,* perhaps. And you have mentioned a third person. Who would that be?"

"We'd need an inside man. Somebody who knows the workings of the casinos."

"Do you have in mind someone?"

"There are a couple of guys I could ask. But I'm open to suggestions."

Voss remembered the ride to the police station with the embittered security guard, Malloy. "Perhaps I can recommend somebody. That is, if I decide to . . . join you."

"Take your time, Jurgen. I'm not going anywhere for a while."

"I will admit it sounds . . . *interessant.*"

Shiller lapsed into silence. After a moment he turned to the younger man, his expression serious. "Before you come in, there's something else you should know."

"Ja?"

"My plan will involve . . . violence."

"Violence? You mean someone will be hurt? Who?"

"I don't know. And frankly, I don't care. It'll be totally random. Luck of the draw. The upside is, they'll never find out who was responsible. The downside is . . ."

"Ja?"

"People will die."

12

Buster Malloy skidded his ancient pickup truck to a halt outside the trailer, raising a cloud of dust and barely missing the neighbor's dog. He slammed through the cheap aluminum screen door, almost knocking it off its hinges. Instantly awake, Helga Johanssen saw that there was anger in Buster's eyes. Violence. And she was scared.

"What happened, Buster?" she asked nervously.

"I got shit on again," he said bitterly. "An' guess who done it to me."

"I-I don't know."

"Some fuckin' zipperhead in the baccarat pit. 'E's yellin' at the caller, see, so I go into the pit an' ask 'im real polite to calm down, an' the goddamn slope t'rows 'is drink in me face!"

"Jesus, Buster, you didn't . . . get yourself fired?"

"Almost. I'm tellin' you, I was ready to beat the shite outta the little bastard. But Al stopped me."

"So . . . everything's okay?"

"No, you dumb bitch, everything *ain't* okay. I 'ad to kiss some major ass to keep me job." Malloy took off his shirt and lit up a Camel. "An' then, jus' to make me day perfect, I 'ad to take this card counter to jail."

The blond woman looked at him questioningly, afraid to ask why *that* had upset him.

He slumped onto the couch and answered her unspoken question. "Poor little fucker was jus' tryin' to make a livin', smart guy like 'im, it ain't right. They grind everybody into the fuckin' ground like fuckin' bugs."

"Sorry, Buster. Sounds like you had a rough day. Let me make you something to eat—"

"Fuck that. Jus' get me a beer."

Malloy was utterly pissed off. Not just at the Galaxy and the little yellow scumbag who had thrown the drink at him but at the whole goddamn *system*—the system that kept a man down, the one he'd been at odds with for his entire life, the one that still treated a man like dirt at age fifty-four, when he should be getting a little respect at last. But no—that would be asking too much. Who gave a shit that you'd fought for your country for five years in 'Nam? Who cared that you'd lost your eye keeping their fat asses safe from fucking communism?

In the end it all came down to money. If you had it, you were king of the hill. If you didn't, you were pond scum.

Helga's voice, tremulous, interrupted his dark thoughts.

"There's no more beer in the fridge, Buster."

"Then gimme that bottle of Irish."

She opened the cupboard door and extracted the whiskey bottle. "Do you want a glass?"

"No fuckin' glass. I said, *gimme that bottle*."

He half rose, threateningly. Disconcerted, she fumbled with the slippery bottle; it fell to the floor and smashed in a starburst of brown liquid and broken glass.

"Now look what you've done, you clumsy bitch," he roared, leaping to his feet in a blind fury. Impulsively, he clenched his fist and punched her hard on the side of the head. She collapsed to the floor with a moan.

"Get up," he hissed. "Get your butt over to the package store an' buy me another bottle."

She struggled to a sitting position. "O-okay, Buster. I'll go. But I don't have any money—"

He kicked her hard at the base of her spine. "Well, peddle your fuckin' arse on the way over."

With a cry of pain, she struggled to her feet but fell back against the chair. "Oh, Buster," she said through gritted teeth, "I'm hurt—"

He leaned over and slapped her hard across the mouth. "Not as hurt as you're gonna be if you don't move it out—right now."

"I-I can't. . . ."

Malloy seized her by the hair and dragged her bodily to her feet. "You lazy good-for-nothin' whore," he hissed. "Now I'm gonna show you who's boss around 'ere." He punched her again, hard in the jaw; her eyes rolled up and her body went limp. Only Buster Malloy's grasp kept her in a semi-upright position. Blood trickled from the corner of her mouth.

During the beating of Helga, Buster had become aroused. He shook her, gently at first, then more violently. There was no response. "Come on, you slut," he growled. "Let's get it on. Now you got me in the fuckin' mood."

It took several minutes for the big man to realize that she was dead. By the time this fact had registered, Buster Malloy was so horny that he was obliged to masturbate in the bathroom.

It was not the only murder he had committed in his lifetime.

The first had happened thirty-eight years ago.

Sean Malloy *was a South Boston cop, a first-generation Irish immigrant. The big red-haired son of Erin was as mean as they came, a drinker, a wife beater, the latest link in a genetic chain of violence whose origin was shrouded in the mists of Hibernian history. Malloy was a* walkin' *man in District Six, twirling his billy club like a baton of office five days a week from seven-thirty to four along the sidewalks of East and West Broadway and Dorchester Avenue.*

Malloy rarely bothered to make an official arrest; for all but the most serious of crimes he generally administered his own brand of instant street justice, using his baton and his hamlike fists in the graffiti-smeared alleyways of Southie. It was a crude but effective deterrent to would-be transgressors, few of whom repeated their misdeeds on Sean Malloy's beat.

Just as Malloy found no cause to allow the letter of the law to interfere with his application of the criminal code, he saw no reason to permit the job to constrain his drinking. Officer Sean Malloy's morning routine seldom varied: a quick nip of Powers at the Silent Man to start the day, another at the Black Rose midmorning, and two or three glasses of Guinness at the Triple X for lunch.

"Hiya, Sean, how's it goin'?" the pub keepers would inquire in a friendly and respectful manner as he slid his black-uniformed bulk onto a barstool.

"Ah, shite" was the invariable response. "It's t'irsty fookin' work."

Afternoons followed the same pattern. An elbow bender at Finnegan's, two or three more at the Legion, and a shift capper in the union hall before signing out for the day at the D Street station. Years of practice had taught him to project the illusion of sobriety at log-out time—you just walked straight and avoided breathing on anyone.

After exchanging his uniform for street clothes, Sean Malloy would embark upon the night's serious drinking at Feeney O'Rourke's Pub, his favorite, the only place he actually paid for his booze. By eight o'clock he was pretty well lubricated; by ten-thirty he was mean drunk, and God help the man who crossed him.

O'Rourke's Pub was conveniently located within five minutes of Malloy's flat, at the very corner where Dorchester Avenue divided Southie into east and west. Dorchester was a kind of reverse Berlin Wall, separating the established families in their comfortable Victorian town houses on East Broadway from their less-fortunate neighbors in grungy flats and walk-ups to the west. If the Irish were the dregs of Europe, then the new arrivals west of Dorchester were the dregs of South Boston. It habitually required a generation's struggle to climb the hill to the more prosperous part of town.

The Malloys occupied a cheap but respectable five-room flat at West Fourth and E Street. Sean Malloy did not aspire to the heights of East Broadway. What more comfort did a man need? Compared with the slums of Dublin that had spawned him, the meanest quarter of Southie was a utopia.

All but one of Sean Malloy's kids had fled the nest, scattered to the four corners of America, driven off by their father's addiction to alcohol and his proclivity for violence. Only the youngest, a late addition to the brood, unplanned by his mother and unwanted by his father, remained under the Malloy roof.

Early on the morning *of Buster Malloy's twelfth birthday, he was roughly shaken awake by his father, Sean.*

Rubbing the sleep from his eyes, the boy beheld a look on his father's face that he had never seen before: panic, helplessness, a fearfulness that for some reason frightened Buster more than any of Sean's violent rages ever could have.

"Wha . . . what is it, Da?" he cried, now wide-awake.

"It's your ma, boy. Come quick. She's sick."

"Ma? Sick? What've you done to 'er?" He leapt from the bed and raced into his parents' bedroom.

Maureen Malloy lay pale and sweaty, wrapped in a tangle of damp sheets. There was a fresh bruise on her cheek. Seeing her son enter the room, she struggled to raise her body to a sitting position but failed in the attempt, collapsing feebly back into the stained pillow.

Buster knelt by his mother's bedside and clasped her worn left hand between both of his. Her fingers felt cold and clammy. Terrified, the boy croaked: "Ma, what's the matter?"

"Oh, son," she whispered. "It feels like there's a great stone on me chest—"

"We'll get help, Ma. You're gonna be all right—"

"Give 'er this, boy," said Sean, shakily pouring a hefty measure of Paddy's Poteen into an unwashed glass. "Maybe she jus' needs—"

Enraged, Buster knocked the drink out of his father's hands. "What are ya tryin' to do, you ol' souse—finish 'er off?" He shouldered past his father, tears of rage and frustration welling in his eyes, and raced next door to Mrs. O'Shaughnessy's.

Two hours later in St. Brigid's Charity Hospital, his mother died. They said it was a massive coronary, she worked too hard, but Buster Malloy knew better. Sean Malloy was responsible—the years of beatings and verbal abuse had taken their toll, wearing her rag-thin, breaking her heart. He renewed his determination to get square someday with the stinkin' drunken bastard who had killed his ma.

After the funeral, his father began to hit the bottle in earnest. When he left the Boston Police Department a few months later, they called it voluntary early retirement. But there were few secrets on West Fourth Street.

"The ol' pisshead was lucky to get reduced pension," Mrs. O'Shaughnessy confided to the milkman.

Sixteen-year-old Buster Malloy stalked out of Sister Immaculata Mary's office with clenched fists. He was thoroughly pissed off. What fuckin' business of hers was it that he'd beaten up Tommy Sullivan—off the school grounds? The little toe rag had been asking for a thrashing for weeks, and Buster had enjoyed applying it more than he cared to admit.

Not that he really minded being expelled from Gate of Paradise School; he'd been thinking of quitting anyway. But he resented having the choice forced on him.

He walked the five blocks to the dingy sixth-floor walk-up on Burrill he now shared with his father. They'd had to give up the flat on West Fourth to save money.

"What the hell you doin' home at thish hour, boyo?" It was only eleven in the morning, but the old sod was already feeling no pain. He sat at the *kitchen table, reeking of Paddy's Poteen. An unread copy of the* South Boston Tribune *served as a coaster for his whiskey bottle.*

"I got kicked outta school," the youth replied sullenly.

"You what?" the elder Malloy sputtered.

"I got kicked out. Expelled. They don't want me back."

"Why you little arsehole—I alwaysh said you was good for nothin'. It'sh time you learned a lesson. I'm gonna break yer fookin' head right now." His father lurched unsteadily from the kitchen chair. He was a big, heavy man, outweighing his son by a good five stone. But most of it had run to fat. Buster Malloy coldly calculated his chances.

"Keep away from me, you drunken old wanker," he hissed angrily.

"You t'reatenin' me, boyo?"

"Fuckin' right. Touch me an' I'll lay you out like a carp."

The older man raised his beefy fist and aimed a blow at his son's head. The boy ducked smoothly and landed a hard punch into his father's blubbery belly. The ex-cop collapsed to the floor, gasping for breath. Surprised and thrilled at the ease with which he had felled the big man, Buster pressed his advantage, kicking his father in the kidneys as he lay doubled over in agony.

He kicked him again, harder this time. "That's for bein' a useless old tosspot. . . ."

Again, his nuts aching with the excitement of it. "That's for all the bullshite I've ever taken from ye. . . ."

Yet again, with all the force he could muster. "An' that's for drivin' me ma to an early grave. . . ."

His father moaned and tried unsuccessfully to struggle to his feet. "God 'elp me, boy, I'll kill you dead. . . ."

Buster Malloy laughed merrily. There was a pure sexual pleasure in the power he now wielded over this pathetic drunk. It wasn't just his father he was punishing anymore; he was hitting back at everything and everyone he hated—the kid who had squealed, the God Almighty holier-than-thou nuns, the whole rotten system.

"Kill me, then, will ya? How ya gonna do that, you old sack o' shit? How ya gonna do that when it's me that's got the power?" Triumphantly, he picked up a heavy wooden chair, raised it high, and slammed it down full force on his father's head.

Suddenly the kitchen was silent.

Blood trickled in a thin line from his father's ear. There was a pro-nounced dent in his skull.

And Buster had a definite hard-on.

This felt good, way better even than torturing and killing neighborhood pets. It was amazing how focused, how together, he felt. His mind was in-credibly clear; colors seemed brighter, objects appeared sharper. The act of inflicting pain had always turned Buster on. Killing was just a natural extension of this act: a higher high, an even more thrilling stimulant. That the victim was his own father bothered Buster Malloy not one whit—in fact, it intensified the sensation.

As a practical matter, he extracted the wallet from his father's hip pocket and counted the bills. The old cheapskate only had nine bucks on him. Well, he sure as hell wouldn't be needing it anymore.

It only remained to cover up what he'd done. Young Malloy thought for a moment, then smiled to himself. Grasping the dead weight of his father's body under the armpits, he dragged it across the worn linoleum, down the hall to the rear fire escape.

The back of their building overlooked a dirty, garbage-filled alley. Peering over the railing, Buster noted with satisfaction that there was no one around. With a mighty heave, he hoisted Sean Malloy's mortal remains onto the rusty railing as if he were hanging out an old mattress to air. The corpse's feet trailed pigeon-toed upon the deck of the balcony; its arms swung limply in space beyond the railing. Malloy picked up the body by the ankles and, with a final effort, worked it outward until gravity took hold and it slid over the railing, temporarily disappearing from his view. He ran to the edge in time to observe it land headfirst with a satisfying splat next to a bundle of old newspapers, sending a large brown rat scurrying for safety.

He stopped to consider his next move. This had to look convincing. He returned to the kitchen and carefully wiped the blood from the floor and off the chair. Then he brought the chair out onto the fire escape, placing it in the corner where his father often sat on hot days. He returned in a moment with the half-empty whiskey bottle, holding it with his shirttail in order not to leave any fingerprints, and set it down beside the chair.

It was that easy. He'd tell the cops that the old fart had gotten drunk and fallen off the fire escape.

He went back inside, humming "Mack the Knife," and dialed the operator.

Thirty-eight years later, the sensation was just as real, just as vivid. Buster Malloy hadn't meant to snuff his girlfriend, but what was done was done. He buried her that same night.

Finally, Helga Johanssen's piece of the American Dream was reduced to a few square feet of rough desert floor in Piute Valley.

13 Buster Malloy's confrontation with Mr. Ling, the Hong Kong high roller, was duly noted in his personnel record. By way of punishment, Malloy's captain assigned him a month's elevator duty. This was a job he hated. Standing at the base of the Saturn rocket checking would-be riders for room keys was not his idea of meaningful work. You couldn't even sneak out for a lousy smoke and too bad if you needed to piss because you were stuck there until your break. The one-eyed security guard and recent murderer still had an hour and a half to go at the elevator when he felt a tap on his shoulder.

He turned to see a vaguely familiar face. It took a few seconds for Malloy to recognize the little card counter he'd hauled off to jail less than two weeks ago. "Jesus Christ, what are you doin' here?" he said.

"I wanted to discuss with you a matter of . . . business," Jurgen Voss replied, glancing about nervously. Out of habit, he stuffed his hands in his pockets.

"If they spot you in here again, you'll get the fuckin' business all right. An' it won't be no disorderly conduct this time. They'll throw everythin' but the kitchen sink at you. I t'ought you was *smart*."

"I have taken a chance. There was no other way to reach you."

"Why the hell would you wanna reach *me*?"

"A . . . colleague and I have made a plan that you might possibly find *interessant*. We would like to talk with you about this plan. To explain will take some time. Perhaps after your work we could meet somewhere—"

"Hold it," Buster interrupted. "What are you, runnin' some kind of scam?"

"Not a scam. You will, however, earn a great deal of money. So much, you could never spend it all. You would be able to leave this job you hate so." He pronounced it *zo*. "In fact, you would never need to work again." Jurgen paused for effect, knowing that he had just pushed all the right buttons. "*Aber,* if you are not interested . . ."

"Wait a minute."

"*Ja?*"

"Maybe there'd be no harm in talkin'. What was your name again?"

"Jurgen Voss."

Malloy looked at his watch, the Seiko Helga had given him for his forty-sixth birthday. He sure as hell wouldn't be getting any more presents from her, not from her new home under four feet of sand. "Okay, I get off at eight. I'll meet you outside, on the Strip, under the Galaxy sign. Meantime, you better get your skinny arse outta here, boyo."

For his hand-mucking endeavors, Dan Shiller was awarded a ten-day all-expenses-paid vacation to Clark County Jail. On the evening that he was released, Shiller drove the BMW to Billy Bob's Saloon at Sam's Town for a meeting with Jurgen Voss and the potential recruit, a security guard Voss had met at the Galaxy. The meeting had been tentatively arranged while Shiller and Voss were sharing a cell and was confirmed by phone with Voss the minute Shiller got out. Sam's Town was a safe location; Shiller and Voss had discovered through a process of elimination that neither man had ever practiced his profession there. It was well away from Vegas, out on the Boulder Highway, where they weren't likely to be recognized or disturbed.

Voss, who did not own a car, was driven to the meeting by his recruit, Buster Malloy, in Malloy's old pickup truck.

Entering the saloon, the hulking Irishman lumbered along behind his diminutive companion like an overweight Oliver Hardy following an underfed Stan Laurel. They found Shiller in a quiet corner booth.

"Dan Shiller, I present Buster Malloy," said Voss, involuntarily clicking his heels.

Shiller rose to his feet and extended a hand in greeting.

"Pleased to meetcha," said Malloy, inadvertently crushing Shiller's manicured hand in his own huge, freckled hamhock.

Shiller winced. "How are you?" he managed with a grimace of pain. He extricated his hand as quickly as possible and flexed the fingers, surreptitiously checking for damage. Relieved to find none, he said briskly, "Let's sit down. Can I buy you gentlemen a drink?"

"Irish with a beer back," said Buster.

"A schnapps, *danke*," said Jurgen.

Dan signaled the waiter and ordered. "Okay, Jurgen. How much have you told . . . our friend here?" he asked, rubbing his hands together to re-store circulation.

"Only that we have a plan, that there is much money to make . . . and that in the plan is necessary violence. Buster has no problem with the vio-lence."

"Somehow I didn't think he would," Shiller answered wryly. In his profession it was important to evaluate people quickly. Based on what Jur-gen had told him and judging by what he had observed in the past few min-utes, the character of security guard Buster Malloy appeared to be pretty much an open book. "Okay, Buster," he said, "I've already explained the . . . project to Jurgen here. Before I tell you any more, I need to know—are you in?"

There was a pause as the drinks arrived. Once the waiter had left, Shiller looked inquiringly at his new acquaintance.

Malloy said, "I'll listen."

"No. You don't listen and then decide. If you're not with us one hun-dred percent *up front,* it was nice knowing you. Finish your drink and we'll look for someone else."

"How much did you say the gig was worth?"

"Millions. *Tens* of millions."

"And there's to be . . . killin'?"

"There will be a few deaths." Shiller stressed the word *few*. "It's unavoidable."

Malloy licked his lips. "That don't bother me."

Jurgen Voss wondered how anyone could be so cavalier about murder. He had privately agonized for days over the necessity of actually *killing* anyone. Violence was contrary to the card counter's nature; the prospect of complicity in a murder-for-profit scheme had caused him to spend many hours in restless soul-searching. The factors that tempted Jurgen to partici-pate in Dan's scheme were a real fear of pursuing his card-counting profes-sion since his arrest at the Galaxy—and the concomitant necessity of moving away from an area that he liked. In the end it was the little man's monstrous ego that tipped the scales; he convinced himself that any plan with which *he* was associated could only succeed.

"So," said Dan Shiller. "What's it going to be, Malloy? In or out?"

"Shite," replied the Irishman thoughtfully as he swilled the last of his beer and lit a Camel. "All things considered, I guess you boys can count ol' Buster in."

Unlike Voss, Malloy harbored no reservations about the homicidal aspect of the plan. During the ensuing discussion he immediately and with thinly disguised relish volunteered his services for those particular aspects of the operation. Shiller resolved to keep a close eye on the big Irishman whose psychotic tendencies, he observed, lurked dangerously close to the surface.

Willing himself to ignore the latent violence that he sensed in Malloy, Dan Shiller looked around and leaned closer to the others. He lowered his voice conspiratorially, and began: "Okay, the target is the Las Vegas Casino Association. It's kind of a secretive group of big shots who run all the major casinos. Their president is the head honcho at the Galaxy—Emmett Druperman. These guys have more cash on hand at any given time than the goddamn Bank of America." He paused and lit a thin, hand-rolled cigar. "Here's the plan. It's in four parts. I call the parts *phases*. Now in order to achieve our objective, we may only need to implement phases one and two, but I believe it's far more likely we'll have to go at least as far as phase three. Might even need phase four—Druperman's a tough nut to crack." He smiled wryly. "If it goes beyond phase four, gentlemen, he's won and we've lost."

Shiller continued for over an hour, outlining each of the four phases in detail and assigning preliminary tasks to himself and his two associates. He was interrupted only by the occasional question from Voss. Malloy merely listened.

When Shiller was finished, the three men agreed not to be seen together again in public. It was decided that the next meeting would be held at Voss's in two months, allowing time for each of the conspirators to complete his preliminary assignments.

LAS VEGAS,
JUNE

PART III

14 **Because of its location** less than two blocks from busy Interstate 15, Jurgen Voss's apartment building in North Las Vegas was continuously washed by the hum of highway traffic—a steady drone that was often augmented by the thunder of freight trains on the nearby Union Pacific tracks.

On the agreed day Dan Shiller and Buster Malloy arrived almost simultaneously, each parking his vehicle on the shaded side of Gorman Road. As Shiller set the Beamer's alarm and locked the doors, he dubiously surveyed the run-down neighborhood and wondered whether his hubcaps would survive this visit to Voss. By contrast, Malloy merely removed the key from the ignition of the crumbling Ford pickup and casually banged the door shut, releasing a cloud of rust particles. He did not bother to lock the vehicle or even roll up the windows. The two men greeted each other, filed silently through the front door, and pushed the bell marked J. VOSS on the bank of battered brass mailboxes.

A scratchy voice answered, *"Ja?"*

"It's us," said Shiller curtly into the dusty speaker.

Within a second, the inner glass door buzzed and the lock was released. Buster and Dan pushed through the door, both involuntarily wincing as a medley of Dustbane, cooked cabbage, and pee assailed their nostrils. They marched single file up the chipped terrazzo stairs to the second floor.

"Gentlemen, I have been expecting you," Jurgen announced, releasing the dead bolt and ushering his visitors inside. "Please excuse the mess. I am living alone; my housekeeping is not good."

"Don't bother me none," Malloy muttered.

"We're not here to admire the decor," Shiller said as he gazed around with barely concealed distaste. "But if we're gonna set up shop here, you might as well show us around," he added. "I wanna see this awesome computer stuff you keep raving about."

The grimy two-bedroom apartment was furnished with the barest essentials for the little man's ascetic lifestyle. Jurgen slept in the smaller bedroom, but it was in the larger one that he spent most of his leisure time and virtually all of his disposable income. This was Jurgen Voss's computer room—his nexus between reality and fantasy, a plexus of technological treasures that he alone commanded.

"Holy shit!" Shiller gasped in disbelief at the sheer complexity of it all. His overwhelming first impression of the room was that of a millennium-class communications center haphazardly deployed among the dusty relics of a twentieth-century computer graveyard. Malloy merely gawked.

Inside the room it was impossible to tell night from day. Opaque plastic blinds were pulled down past the sills, and thick curtains overlapped in the center, completely obscuring the room's two large west-facing windows. Years of afternoon sun on the windows had baked layers of dust into the heavy cloth drapes and the yellowed plastic blinds. Were he ever to open the curtains and raise the blinds, Jurgen would doubtlessly be faced with a virtual avalanche of dead houseflies. An ancient through-the-wall air conditioner, necessary to protect the equipment from the heat of the desert day, failed miserably to actually *freshen* any air, which felt stale and heavy. It was difficult for Jurgen Voss's visitors to suppress sneezes.

Voss proudly swept his hand around the room.

"Have you ever seen such a place, gentlemen?" he began proudly.

"Not me," said Shiller.

"Me, neither," said Malloy.

"I have gathered here much unique equipment," Voss continued, indicating a large, crowded desktop on the wall opposite the door. Its most prominent occupant was a twenty-one-inch monitor whose flared metal case pointed slightly down, suggesting a jet-black hooded cobra. A single track light suspended over the monitor illuminated the top of the machine and the keyboard, leaving the screen itself in shadow. Two smaller monitors flanked the large one, their screens coated with the dust that permeated the room.

Below the work surface was a bank of tower and mini-tower computers, all humming and emitting occasional sharp clicks as their hard disks were accessed. He pointed to the largest of the beige boxes. "As you see, gentlemen, the server is an IBM Itanium. It contains the most powerful chip possible, which I can upgrade to the next two generations of CPUs. The latest version of Windows is on it. Also Linux. To my ISP I am running a wi-fi connection; therefore, I have the *schnellest*—fastest—possible access to the Internet."

"Here on the shelf you see a magnetic card reader and writer—"

"I suppose you're gonna tell us you take American Express, too," Shiller interjected sardonically.

"*Nein*. It is just another useful tool. Like this plastic lamination machine—"

"Now *there's* a handy gizmo," Shiller remarked. "I suppose you use it to create fake IDs, huh?"

"*Jawohl*. Also other things."

Shiller surveyed the bizarre vista, his gaze falling on what appeared to be video-editing equipment. "What's this, Jurgen?"

"I will explain. To the video tape recorder and DVD player you see on the shelf is connected a video-editing card. With specialized software, I can perform completely digital editing of video and also make an output to VHS or any other format you wish. . . ."

At this point, unable to grasp much beyond the occasional familiar word, both Buster and Dan began to lose the thread of Jurgen's lengthy technosoliloquy. As the little man droned on, his associates focused their attention elsewhere.

Behind the door they noted a pile of boxes, stuffed with sheets of bubble wrap, blocks of Styrofoam, and unmailed warranty reply postcards, preventing the door from opening any more than ninety degrees.

The entire right wall was occupied by a shelving unit composed of plastic milk crates stacked on their sides. The topmost shelf was piled with more equipment boxes. The next one down contained a jumble of books, magazines, floppies, and compact discs. The lower two shelves contained a collection of computer peripherals, including a color flatbed scanner, a color inkjet printer, and a DVD burner. Cobwebs of various sizes adorned the corners of the crates.

Against the remaining wall sat a large 1200-dpi laser printer, capable of outputting high-resolution color sheets up to eleven by seventeen inches. Next to it on the floor were three additional plastic crates. One was full of parts: a collection of screws, metal plates removed from expansion card slots, floppy disk drives, electric fans, odd keys from old keyboards, and other unidentifiable components. One was overflowing with disks: CDs,

DVDs, 5¼-inch floppies, and 3½-inch disks of several densities, some missing their metal shutters. The last crate contained tools—two incomplete precision screwdriver sets, variously sized pliers, wrenches, a hammer, and a collection of anti-static wrist straps.

Obsolete hard disks, old PCs, and a broken-down dot-matrix printer occupied most of the remaining floor space.

As Jurgen continued his lecture, Buster Malloy gave up on any attempt to make sense of it and slowly developed a glaze over his one good eye. Dan Shiller was more astute. With a considerable effort, and only because some of this verbal diarrhea might be significant, Shiller forced himself to refocus on what the little pencil-necked Kraut was spouting.

". . . power failures cannot hurt my system," Jurgen continued, indicating four squat, humming boxes, one in each corner of the room. "These are uninterruptable-power-supply boxes. There is in the batteries enough power stored to keep all of this equipment working for several hours. If the power ever should fail, even if I would be out, a controlled sequence of shutdowns would occur and I would lose no data."

"How come you have three monitors?" Shiller asked.

"A good question!" replied his host in the manner of an indulgent college instructor. "The large one in the center is my main workstation. The smaller one on the left is connected to the machine that stores my information."

"Impressive, I guess. How about the one on the right?"

Voss blinked. "Basically a spare. It monitors my security system."

"Security system?" Shiller asked.

"It is not important," Jurgen replied. He edged toward the door, indicating that the tour was over. "Perhaps we could continue our meeting in the other room. . . ."

In fact, Voss's hardware and software were configured with security as their highest priority. A screen-saver program would black out the display and lock all inputs after only minutes had passed without use, and reaccess would not be granted until the correct time- and date-dependent password was entered. The computer cases themselves were constructed with solid locks and antitampering devices; opening the cases without unlocking the two obvious and the two hidden locks would completely and irrevocably destroy all data . . . and because of certain deterrents contrived by Jurgen, quite likely cause severe physical injury to any intruder.

Deep inside his system, Jurgen Voss had concealed dark, shameful secrets that must never be revealed, no matter what the cost.

Voss's small living room was furnished with only a thinly upholstered two-seater couch and a single worn armchair. Most of the available wall space in that room was given over to reading material of all description: bookshelves lined with hardcover volumes, cardboard boxes filled with paperbacks, magazines stacked in corners. The subject matter of all this literature was invariably technical: textbooks on electronics and physics, volumes about advanced programming, software manuals, computer catalogs, and industry trade magazines.

As Buster Malloy settled heavily into the armchair, it creaked in protest at the unfamiliar weight. "Have you actually *read* all that shit?" inquired Malloy, scanning the book-lined walls with the unabashed awe of the chronically unread. Computers were beyond his comprehension, but at least he could understand the principles of the printed word.

"Never mind that," Shiller snapped. "Look, we've got a lot to cover. Let's get on with it."

Malloy fixed the con man with a malevolent glare from his single good eye. "Chill out, Shiller. Who died an' made you the boss?"

"This is a business meeting, Buster. We're not here to admire Jurgen's library."

"What am I, some kinda dummy that ain't allowed to talk?"

"When you've got something relevant to say, I'll listen. Until then, please keep quiet."

The big man half rose menacingly from his chair. "You're askin' for it, boyo—"

"Sit down, Malloy," said the grifter. "Or I guarantee you'll be sorry."

Fearful that a physical confrontation between the two men might scuttle the project before it ever got off the ground, and even more fearful that he might get hurt during the course of it, Voss interjected: "Gentlemen, please. Let us not make a fight among ourselves."

Shiller took a breath, relaxed, and realized that the little card counter was right—a further sharp answer would serve no purpose. He renewed his earlier resolve to remain alert and watchful around Buster Malloy. The fact that the big man was prone to violence and enjoyed inflicting pain were character traits that would be extremely useful in carrying out the operation, yet were traits that Shiller sensed might be difficult to control. He decided to cool it, at least for now. "Hey, you're absolutely right, Jurgen," he said lightly. "Sorry, Buster. Now where were we?"

"I can start if you wish," said Voss nervously, chewing on the ragged remains of a fingernail.

"Good." Dan glanced quickly at his associate's raw fingertips, winced, then averted his gaze, focusing for aesthetic relief upon his own beautifully manicured and polished nails. Unable to resist the natural comparison, he glanced at Buster Malloy's huge hands, noting the cracked, black-framed fingernails. Shiller returned his attention to the plan. "Have you worked out the technical details?" he asked Voss.

"*Ja.* It required a good deal of research, but fortunately I was able to find all the materials and techniques we need. Through mainly the Internet."

"Can you be more specific? How about phase one?"

"The material for phase one was the most difficult to find. However, I have succeeded in identifying the ideal compound for our purposes." Voss paused for effect, a smug expression on his owlish face.

"Well, spit it out, for Christ's sake," growled Malloy, still miffed.

"*Jawohl,* I would definitely spit out this substance!" said Jurgen, hugely pleased that Buster had unwittingly handed him the perfect straight line. It was not often that the little man received an opportunity to display both his knowledge *and* his wit, so he decided to make the most of it. "Gentlemen, I have selected cantharidin." He smiled conspiratorially, revealing a mouthful of crooked, off-white teeth. "You may know it with a different name—especially if sex interests you!"

Malloy looked puzzled. "Do you know what the fuck 'e's talkin' about?" he asked Dan Shiller.

Shiller shrugged.

"Spanish fly!" Voss shouted triumphantly. "It has been for years known as Spanish fly! In minute quantities it is said to possess—how do you say it? *aphrodisiac* powers—"

"So what?" said the grifter, irritation in his voice.

"So, in larger doses it becomes a level-six toxin. That is as potent as possible. It is a white powder, virtually tasteless."

"Will it do the job?" asked Shiller.

"Of course! Or I would not suggest it! Once the . . . subject has taken the poison, death is inevitable." Voss related this fact quite casually, as if he were describing the benefits of a headache pill or the side effects of a cough medicine. Having made the decision to participate in Shiller's scheme, the little German genius had managed over the intervening weeks to insulate himself from the reality of his involvement in an actual murder. In his mind he had gradually transformed the whole operation into an intellectual challenge, abstract problems in chemistry, electronics, and computer science requiring elegant solutions that only he could provide. "For this substance there is no known antidote."

"Okay, Jurgen. It sounds like the right stuff. Where do we get it from?" said Dan.

"I have in L.A. located a pharmaceutical supply house that will not ask too many questions. But they will ask for identification. So I have already prepared several sets of papers. All I must do now is to print them out and laminate them."

"No problem. Mr. Malloy here can pick 'em up when you're ready." The grifter shifted uncomfortably on the thin cushions of Voss's couch. "Okay, Buster, it's your turn," he said conversationally, careful not to sound confrontational. "How do we deliver the envelope to Druperman?"

"I go right past the mailroom at least once a day. Easy to drop shit off in Druperman's box. There usually ain't nobody in there."

"Excellent. Just make sure you don't leave any fingerprints on it. Now what about phase two?"

"Piece a' cake. I've got a master key that'll open any suite in the hotel with the right code. I can buy the materials in any fuckin' hardware store. An' I already got the tools."

"Phase three?"

"No problem. I bought the backpack and the toy cars."

"Very good, Buster. And phase four?"

"Stealin' the vehicle was easy. Nickin' the uniform was the tough part. But I done it."

Shiller nodded approval and rubbed his hands together. "Jurgen, you got all the chemicals and shit?"

"Everything is in the garage you rented. Here is what we need to do." Jurgen spoke earnestly for several minutes, taking pains to emphasize his own brilliance. Shiller wondered briefly why he had saddled himself with a full-blown egomaniac and a borderline psycho as partners but consoled himself with the notion that these very flaws were the foundation of their usefulness to him.

When Voss finished, Malloy said gruffly, "Okay, Shiller, we done our part. Now what about you?"

The con man nodded. "Fair enough. Let's talk about the presentation of our demands first."

"You have at our last meeting said that to capture their attention and convince them of the seriousness of our intent, the presentation must be of dramatic nature," observed Voss.

"And it will, Jurgen, believe me, it will," promised Shiller. "I've given the matter a great deal of thought. And you sure as hell have the technology in that room to make it happen. I believe videotapes are the answer."

"Videotapes?"

"Right. Tapes of . . . relevant incidents. Stuff they can *see* and *relate to*. I want those fuckers to sit up and take notice. I want them to *feel* the pain." He described to the other two men in some detail the proposed content of the videos. Voss offered a couple of suggestions, to which Shiller agreed. As usual, Malloy merely listened.

"What about the money?" asked Jurgen. "How do we carry all the cash? I have made calculations that the mass of so many hundred-dollar bills would be too large to fit into—"

"Whoa," interrupted Shiller. "There is a way. We don't need to handle cash. I've met with some people from . . . overseas. They can help us with this thing. Naturally, it's going to cost us. But there'll still be plenty left." He paused to make sure he had their full attention. "Now here's how it works. . . ."

While Voss and Malloy listened to Shiller explain the intricacies of international money transfers, both men had the feeling that their con-man partner was not telling them the entire story.

LAS VEGAS, OCTOBER

PART IV

15 **In Las Vegas and Atlantic City** the competition to attract heavy gamblers is fierce. The profit to any casino from the action of just one unlucky high roller can easily outweigh the combined profit from hundreds of nickel-and-dime players.

All the major casinos will comp big players to the eyeballs—with first-class airfare, luxury suites, unlimited booze, and whatever else it takes to keep them happy while they blow small fortunes at the tables.

With every casino offering essentially the same inducements, the problem of how to compete effectively with one another for these premium players loomed large.

One solution involved offering bigger and better attractions. But only of a certain type. Whereas theme parks and circuses, rock singers and Broadway-style revues, magic shows and comedy shops were all useful in drawing the middle-class and family trade to the tables, the casinos had long since learned that these were not the enticements that drew North American high rollers. That constituency, composed primarily of wealthy middle-aged businessmen, responded mainly to two kinds of attraction.

The first was championship boxing, which over the past three decades had established itself more or less permanently in the converted show-rooms of Las Vegas and Atlantic City.

The second was big-name entertainers. Tom Jones, Tony Bennett, Engelbert Humperdinck—you could probably count these guaranteed casino-fillers on the fingers of one hand. They had endured for decades, retaining the unwavering loyalty of their fans, many of whom associated them with pleasant memories of earlier, simpler times.

One of the brightest of these stars—if not *the* brightest—was Tony Francisco. The Galaxy had Francisco under exclusive contract in the Las

Vegas market for three separate weeks every year, a multimillion-dollar investment on the casino's part that had paid off handsomely as a drawing card for big players—a fact that Francisco and his agent, Solly Greenspan, were keenly aware of. As a result, the pair had decided to try to sweeten the pot for Francisco's services, slyly waiting until after the Galaxy had invested heavily in an ad campaign to promote the entertainer's next scheduled appearance before springing their demands on Galaxy CEO Emmett Druperman.

Following Greenspan's message to Druperman, an urgent videoconference call between the two men had been arranged. During the call, the agent had issued a thinly veiled threat to cancel the gig unless the Galaxy upped the ante from $2.5 million to $5 million for Francisco's week of service.

When Druperman pointed out that the entertainer was bound by contract to appear at the lower rate, Greenspan smiled apologetically and reminded the CEO that the contract *did* provide for cancellation in case of illness and hinted broadly that Tony was not feeling too well.

"He seems to be coming down with a sore throat, Emmett. If it gets any worse, there's no way he can perform. . . ."

Druperman's brow knotted in anger. "Great timing, Solly. Right after I've spent a fucking *fortune* promoting this gig."

"These things happen."

"Whose idea was this, anyway? Yours or that goddamn old dago's?"

"Tony's always taken an interest in the business side of things."

"And I suppose the extra two and a half will take care of this convenient sore throat?"

"Like a trip to Lourdes, Emmett."

Druperman snorted in disgust. "So that's the way it is now, huh, Solly? I remember when a man's word meant something. When you made deals on a handshake." He took off his bifocals and rubbed the bridge of his nose. "Now even a signed contract isn't worth shit." Druperman watched the five-inch videophone screen intently as Greenspan shrugged helplessly. The gesture was amplified by the jerkiness of partial-motion transmission.

"Don't shoot the messenger, Emmett."

"I'll get back to you." Druperman hung up.

Having delegated the extortion business to Steve Forrester, Emmett Druperman returned his attention to the Tony Francisco situation.

The Galaxy stood to increase its drop by 10 or 15 million dollars during Francisco's week, so he could well afford the extra money the entertainer was demanding. But it was a matter of precedent: once it became known that Emmett Druperman had caved in under pressure—and Druperman had no doubt that it *would* become known—his bargaining position would be weakened. Not only in his negotiations with the entertainment industry but, far more important, in his present and future dealings with the unions.

He was convinced that once you showed weakness, you became easy prey for every alligator in the swamp. He needed to find a way to solve the Francisco problem without losing money—or face.

Emmett Druperman lit his third and final cigar of the day, exhaled a cloud of aromatic blue smoke, and closed his eyes. Everybody had weaknesses. What were Tony Francisco's? How could he exploit them? After a few moments, a smile flickered across his lined face.

He opened his eyes and pressed a button.

"Edith," he said, "get me Solly Greenspan on the videophone."

"Solly? How are you? How's Tony?"

Greenspan's image faded in on the videophone screen. He looked somewhat taken aback by Druperman's apparent cordiality. "Fine, Emmett," he said warily. "How about yourself?"

"All right, considering."

"Considering?"

The warmth evaporated from Druperman's voice. "Considering the crap you and your dago asshole boss are trying to pull," he snapped. "Now, listen carefully and don't interrupt. Here's what I'm prepared to offer—it's a take-it-or-leave-it proposition, and it's more than you greedy bastards deserve.

"First, I'm prepared to write off the three million dollars Francisco owes this casino." The performer, who had a weakness for gambling, had incurred substantial losses at the blackjack and craps tables and had tried to avoid paying off his losses by claiming he was only "shilling" for the house. The Galaxy had vehemently disagreed, pointing out that Francisco always collected on the rare occasions when he won. The debt remained on the books, although it was money that Druperman privately never expected to collect. However, Francisco did not know this. Druperman continued: "And let me remind you, Mr. Agent, that in your boss's tax bracket and with his overhead which includes ten percent to you and Christ knows how much to those other leeches that suck his blood, he'd probably have to earn *three times* that amount to pay this debt off."

"Now wait just a—"

"No, *you* wait," Druperman barked at the phone. "Just shut up and listen.

"Number two. After we wipe the slate clean, the Galaxy will give Francisco a two-million-dollar credit line, noncumulative, any time he's performing here. And this time we won't be too gung-ho about collecting when he loses." Which Emmett Druperman was reasonably certain would happen. It would probably not cost the casino anything because Francisco was a notoriously inept gambler. And even if he got lucky and occasionally won a million or two, it was still considerably less than the extra money he was demanding.

"Number three. The paycheck for the week remains at two and a half million as per our agreement. And if you try any more stunts like this, you and your goombah boss will be spending so much time in the courthouse, they'll name the fucking building after you."

"You can't just—"

"Believe me, we can and we will. We've got more lawyers than you've got pimples on your ass, Solly."

There was silence from the videophone. That plus Solly Greenspan's hangdog countenance told Emmett Druperman he had won. You just had to know which buttons to push, and you had to have the guts to push them.

"I'll speak to Tony. But I don't know if he'll—"

"Sure he will, Solly. See you soon."

Druperman hung up, pleased with himself. There was no doubt that he deserved the self-bestowed title of toughest son of a bitch in Vegas.

16

Technically, Tony Francisco was a singer. But to his legions of adoring fans, he was far more. A bobby-sox idol of the late forties, movie actor of the fifties and sixties, television star of the seventies and eighties, he was a part of their lives. Even now, at the age of sixty-nine, his albums still sold in the millions and his concert tours were always sellouts.

He was certainly no paragon of virtue. But despite—or perhaps because of—his failed marriages, barroom brawls, and bullying ways (as colorfully detailed in the tabloids and in several unauthorized biographies), the fans loved him. Tony Francisco was the stuff that legends are made of.

Having reluctantly agreed to Emmett Druperman's counteroffer, he was at the Galaxy for his contracted week's appearance.

As usual, the number of premium players attracted by his presence, trumpeted to the world on the hotel's mammoth Stripside electronic billboards, more than justified his $2.5 million paycheck.

And as usual, Francisco was being an unmitigated prick.

Surrounded by sycophants, he was seated at a reserved blackjack table. A curious crowd had gathered around the table, kept at a respectable distance from the aging superstar by a red-velvet rope barrier and four heavyset Galaxy security guards.

The dealer, a young Philippine woman, was close to tears.

Lucy Baker, the floor supervisor, normally enjoyed her job. But tonight was an exception. Facing an impossible situation, she was pale and tense.

"One more time. I want those cards dealt *single deck*. And I want mine *faceup*," Francisco said ominously. "Or I'll make sure you two broads get your walking papers."

Struggling to maintain her composure, Lucy replied, "You know our rules, Tony—"

"*Mister* Francisco to you, lady."

"Sorry. Mr. Francisco. We can deal to you faceup from the *shoe* or facedown from a *double* deck, but I can't authorize single-deck, faceup play." Lucy was stuck between a rock and a hard place. They had all been told to treat Francisco with kid gloves, but at the same time, she knew that casino policy on blackjack dealing was inviolate. "Maybe if I called the shift supervisor—"

"Fuck the shift supervisor. *You* make the decision. And it better be the right one."

Steve Forrester's phone buzzed softly.

"It's Thurman Washington on three," came Suzy's voice over the intercom.

He punched the flashing button and picked up the phone.

"What's happening, bro?" he asked his eye-in-the-sky officer.

"Looks like trouble on BJ seventeen. Francisco's up to his old tricks. Giving the crew a hard time."

"Christ, not again."

"He wants to change the blackjack rules."

This isn't the first time that arrogant son of a bitch has created problems, Forrester thought. There was the incident in which he drunkenly drove his Ferrari up the front steps of the hotel, slightly injuring a doorman in the process. There were the unpaid gambling debts. Not to mention the broken mirrors and wrecked furniture that were often strewn in his wake. Yet the Galaxy always forgave and forgot, because, as Steve realized, we still need this egomaniac more than he needs us. And he knows it.

The only question was, who picks up the pieces this time? He could pass the buck to Emmett Druperman. Or he could handle it himself.

Forrester decided to bell the cat.

"Okay, Thurm, I'll take care of our friend."

He replaced the receiver, grabbed his jacket, and grinned at his executive assistant on the way out. "Better get our résumés ready, Suzy. We may not have jobs when I get back."

The confrontation had degenerated into a Mexican standoff as Forrester ducked under the rope and approached Tony Francisco. As always, Steve marveled at the star's relatively youthful appearance; he looked a decade younger than his almost seventy years. Thin, elegant, with a full head of silver hair, Francisco was living proof that good genes occasionally compensated for even the most dissolute lifestyle. Extending his hand, Steve greeted the venerable entertainer.

"How are you, Tony? Anything I can do for you?"

Francisco ignored the outstretched hand. "Yeah. Tell these bimbos to deal me single deck, faceup."

While Steve disliked hypocrisy, he realized that he was obliged to defuse the situation without ruffling the feathers of the Galaxy's prime attraction. Thinking quickly, he whispered confidentially to Francisco, "Suppose we set up a personal game just for you in the Jupiter Room"—a small private casino off the main gaming area, reserved for VIPs—"and we'll deal the game any way you want." This way, Steve reasoned, the Galaxy wouldn't be setting any public precedents in its blackjack-dealing policies. Francisco could make all the fuss he wanted behind closed doors . . . and Steve would make sure that the assigned dealers and supervisors were thick-skinned veterans of the green felt jungle who wouldn't be rattled by this egotistical bully.

"Sounds like a plan to me, mister. Let's go, troops."

Forrester picked up the pit phone and quickly made the arrangements.

"Why don't you take the rest of your shift off, Maria," he said to the dealer. "You've had a tough time, and you deserve a break."

Still shaken, she smiled gratefully at Steve and headed for the dealer's lounge.

Forrester turned to the young floor supervisor. LUCY BAKER, her name badge read. "Thank you, Lucy, for keeping your cool. I appreciate the way you handled the situation."

"Thank you for coming along when you did, Mr. Forrester."

"I'm surprised you know my name." With more than four thousand employees spread over three shifts at the Galaxy, it was impossible to know every one of them. "Have we met before?"

"Kind of. You nailed a counter in my pit about six months ago. I guess you were too busy to notice me. . . ."

"Oh, right. The little fellow with the foreign accent and the large head—the one who wouldn't shut up and leave quietly. It was you who called it in. And I never even said thank you!"

As Lucy's color slowly returned, along with her composure, Steve couldn't help but remark what a startlingly attractive woman she was. How had he missed noticing her before? With short dark hair framing a classically beautiful face, she had the bluest eyes he had ever seen. Great body—athletic but not overdeveloped. Forrester surreptitiously admired Lucy's shapely ankles and well-proportioned calves, nicely accentuated by the medium heels she wore. *She looks after herself—and she's got guts, too,* he thought. *I'd like to get to know this lady better.*

"It's good to see you again, Mr. Forrester." They shook hands. *And she isn't wearing a ring.* "Honestly, I don't know how much longer I could have held out. He's such a . . . *thug.*"

"Please, call me Steve." He sensed that the attraction might be mutual. "If you're free for dinner tonight, maybe we could talk more about it."

She hesitated.

"Of course, if you're involved with somebody else . . ."

"No, it's not that. It's just . . ."

"Just . . . ?"

"Well, it's just that we both *work* here." *Could I be exposing myself to an awkward situation because of his position?* "You know what they say about mixing business and pleasure."

"Who said anything about *pleasure?*" Steve replied, trying but not altogether succeeding to maintain a poker face. "We're talking about a *business dinner* here. I think it's vital that we discuss this incident fully and . . . *set policy* for future occurrences of this nature." He winked. "Now if we just happen to have a little fun while we're at it, where's the harm?"

Ever since her failed affair on a cruise ship, Lucy had been supercautious in her relationships, choosing to go out with nice, interesting, *nonthreatening* men—men she could control, men she could keep at arm's length. This would be different, she knew. She felt herself attracted to Forrester's power, his competence, his sense of humor. *What if I grow to like him too much? And what if—*

Steve seemed to read her mind. "Look, I don't mean to pressure you," he said, more seriously now. "I understand your . . . misgivings. Maybe we should take a rain check on the dinner."

Well, kid, the ball's in your court now. Are you going to run scared for the rest of your life? Lucy gathered her resolve. "How about," she offered tentatively, "meeting for coffee after work? No strings attached."

"No strings."

"Good evening, Lucy, Mr. Forrester," said Gladys Adams, hostess of the Cosmic Café. She prided herself on remembering people's names, especially important ones such as casino executives. "Smoking, if I recall correctly?"

"Not for me, Gladys. I quit."

Steve looked inquiringly at Lucy, who nodded approvingly. The Galaxy's twenty-four-hour coffee shop—actually a full-service restaurant—was only half full. Armed with a stack of menus, Gladys shepherded the couple toward the booths ringing the floor. "Any preferences?" she asked.

"Maybe something near the orchestra," said Forrester with a grin, trying to lighten the moment and put Lucy at ease.

"Best I can do is put you near the kitchen door," replied their hostess, playing along dutifully with the old joke. As Steve had hoped, Lucy smiled.

"Your waitress will be right over," said Gladys as they slid into a leatherette-upholstered booth. "Have a good evening, folks."

"Thanks, Gladys."

She left them alone.

"Just a coffee, Lucy?" Forrester asked.

"That's fine."

There was a moment's awkward silence, then they both spoke together.

"Do you—"

"I think—"

They laughed.

"You first," she said.

"I was going to ask if you came here often," he said. "But then I realized what a dumb question it was. I must sound like a fifteen-year-old on his first date."

"No, you don't, Steve." She smiled prettily. "To answer your question,

I hardly ever go to any of the restaurants here. Usually I brown-bag it. To save money."

"Makes sense. Now, what were you going to say?"

"Nothing important. Only that I think our Mr. Tony Francisco needs to learn some manners and—"

At that moment, the waitress arrived. Steve ordered coffee.

One coffee turned into two, then three.

Forrester could sense Lucy's relaxing in his company. The conversation began to flow more easily—mostly small talk, trade gossip, nothing too serious. But there was definitely chemistry happening. They both felt it.

"What do you like to do in your spare time?" Steve asked.

"Nothing special. I collect art. Mostly Impressionists. I can't afford originals, of course, so I concentrate on prints. The only originals I have are a few landscapes by local artists I got at home."

"Where's home?"

"Back East."

"So how'd you ever wind up here?"

"My family was in the hotel business. Dad and Mom ran a country inn in Newport, Vermont, just across the border from Quebec. As a matter of fact, they still do. Anyway, to make a long story short—or is it too late for that?—I started in the family business right after college. Which led to a job in a bigger hotel in Burlington. Which led to working on a cruise ship, in the casino." Lucy decided not to mention the heartbreak she'd suffered on board. "Which led to this."

Forrester smiled. "And I, for one, am very glad that it did."

She looked at her watch. "Steve, do you realize we've been here for over an hour?"

He smiled. "And we *have* talked business. As agreed."

"True."

"Now that you know I'm a man of my word, how about that dinner? The invitation still stands."

Lucy had known this moment was coming. She didn't realize exactly *when* in the past hour she'd made up her mind. But all her instincts told her that this was a man she could trust. She decided to follow them. "I'd like that, Steve."

"Tomorrow night?"

"Tomorrow night."

17 **Stepping out** of the Chaisson Motor Cars showroom into the bright Vegas sunshine with a cashier's check for eight thousand dollars in his pocket, Barney Leopold took a deep breath of the fresh desert air and hummed a joyful snatch of "We're in the Money."

With the two grand cash he'd got from the pawnbroker, that made ten thousand altogether. And that was all he needed to get it all back, every last cent of it and then some, because the losing streak was over. He knew it as surely as he knew the sun would set tonight and rise again tomorrow.

Leopold decided to walk to the Strip because he had better things to spend his money on than cabs.

For over five years, Barney Leopold had managed to conceal the truth from his family, his business partner, and himself.

On the surface, he was living the American Dream.

Barely into his fifties, the El Modena resident was of above-average height with thinning sandy hair, faded blue eyes, and a permanent California tan. Publicly, he was a successful homebuilder, a happily married man with a Stepford wife named Shirley who loved him quite unconditionally and three picture-book teenagers who trusted and respected him. He was active in his Orange County community, a member of the vestry at St. Augustine's Episcopal Church, and a member of the PTA.

Privately, he was living an emotional turmoil.

On the good days his spirit soared to the heights of ecstasy; on the bad days he plumbed the depths of hell.

His partner in A&L Construction, George Anderson, had been the first to suspect.

"Barney, how come I keep getting calls from our subs about unpaid bills?" Subcontractors were the lifeblood of A&L—the carpenters, roofers, plumbers, electricians, painters, plasterers, and other tradesmen who provided the skilled labor to build the medium-priced tract housing in which their company specialized. *"I thought you'd taken care of them weeks ago."*

Leopold had always handled the sales and finances, while Anderson looked after the logistics of building. *"Don't worry about it, George. Everything's under control."*

"That's bullshit. Two of them are threatening us with liens."

"Liens?"

"Court action. Seizures. Do I have to spell it out?"

"Okay. Maybe I've had a few personal expenses to take care of."

"Personal expenses? *With company money? Goddamn it, Barney, what kind of expenses?"*

Leopold took a deep breath. *"I owed big bucks to some guys. And frankly, they wouldn't wait."*

In the beginning, *it had been the horses. Small bets—fifty, a hundred. He thrived on the action and had actually come out ahead for a while. The gambling made him feel* alive.

But inevitably, the losses started mounting. At first, they had been easy to cover, because A&L was a successful enterprise and Leopold took a substantial salary for his efforts. To recoup, he began betting larger amounts—five hundred, a thousand at a time. Sometimes he'd win, but more often he lost. Both his wife and his partner knew that he liked to gamble, but neither had any idea of the magnitude of his losses.

Vince Morini, the bartender at the Lido with whom he booked most of his action, was sympathetic. "Barney, you've dropped over eight grand this month alone. Maybe you ought to quit for a while." Leopold was a good customer who always paid his debts, and the bartender hated to see him get hurt. "At least cut back a little."

But Barney Leopold would have none of this well-intentioned advice. The gambling was in his blood now. He liked the uncertainty, *the joy of winning, the threat of losing. Besides, he intended to get it all back. There were plenty of ways to get even. Bigger bets, some fresh action. "Maybe I'll lay off the ponies for a while, Vince. What's the line on the Lakers-Knicks game?"*

"Lakers by eight. But, Barney—"

"That's like a gift. I'll take the Knicks. For five."

"Five hundred?"

"Five thousand."

The bartender almost dropped the glass he was wiping. *"Holy Mother of God, Barney, are you out of your mind?"*

"I can't lose. I feel hot."

The bartender recovered his composure. He started to say something, then shrugged in resignation. *"Let me call Sal,"* he said. Morini couldn't lay off more than a grand on his own ticket; he needed authorization from the man for whom he fronted.

"Okay. But hurry."

As the bartender dialed the private number of the local book, he looked at Leopold strangely. The man had a problem. He'd seen this before. But what the hell, it wasn't *his* problem; he'd done his best to slow the guy down. He turned his back to the gambler, spoke quietly on the phone for a moment, and hung up. *"Sal wants to talk to you, Barney. He'll be over in ten minutes."*

Sal Tantorello would have topped any Hollywood casting agent's dream sheet for the part of the mobbed-up bookmaker.

Sleazy, greasy, slick-haired, he'd have fit the role to perfection. Leopold's skin crawled as he gingerly shook the hairy bejeweled hand, noting with disdain the pointed shoes, the black shirt buttoned to the top, the ice-cream-colored Armani suit with a discernible orange stain on the right lapel. People who wear white suits shouldn't eat pasta, *Barney thought.*

"Mr. Leopold—Barney," he said smarmily. *"Nice to meet you after all this time! I hear you're looking for some heavy action."*

"Right. I want the Knicks for five."

"Let's sit down and talk. Can I buy you a drink?"

"Sure. Vince knows."

The book nodded to his agent and shepherded Leopold to a corner booth. Morini delivered the drinks and returned to his post behind the bar.

Tantorello extracted a cigarette from a silver case, lit up, and blew a stream of smoke at the ceiling. *"I'll need the cash up front, Barney,"* he said.

"I haven't got that kind of money on me now. It's too late to get it today. And the game's tonight."

"I don't know. Five thousand's a lot of dough."

"Come on, Sal. You want the action, or not?" Leopold was starting to feel the anxiety again. He needed *the action. Somewhere in the back of his mind, a little voice was saying,* Don't beg this slimeball. You've got an out now. He won't give you the credit. *But Barney disregarded it and persisted. "I've always paid on time. You know that."*

"Where will you get the money if you lose?"

"I won't lose. Anyway, I've got over fifty thousand sitting in the bank." That was a lie; he had less than twenty.

The bookmaker sized up his mark. He looked prosperous enough. "Okay, Barney, I'll take a chance on you. But this is a cash business. I ain't no finance company. I pay on the nose when I lose, and I collect on the button when I win."

"Don't worry," replied Leopold.

As Barney Leopold's *cash reserves dwindled, his bets increased in frequency and magnitude.*

The checking account was soon depleted, but there were plenty of other sources of cash. He maxed out his gold cards, all three of them, to the tune of more than $75,000. He took out a large personal loan at the local S and L. Without telling Shirley, he remortgaged the house, clearing another hundred grand. When he won, he was happy, but it was never enough to satisfy him. When he lost, which occurred with somewhat more regularity, he felt depressed, sometimes even suicidal, but strangely cleansed.

Sal Tantorello knew a good thing when he saw it. He now gave Leopold all the credit he asked for—on the unwritten understanding that the losing bets would be paid promptly, or, Barney suspected, matters could become very unpleasant.

The day finally came when there wasn't enough ready cash to cover the last bet. He had taken Georgia Tech over Brown with a six-point spread, for Christ's sake, *and Tech had blown it.*

Leopold was suddenly in debt for $25,000 that he didn't have. It was a strange feeling.

"Sal, give me a few weeks on this one," he asked the book. "I've been a good customer."

"No can do, my friend. I told you up front, I pay you when you win, you pay me when you lose."

"Can you give me any time at all?"

"A week, max. And I'm doing you a big favor."

"That's really going to be a problem." Sales at A&L had been slow. They were closing on a couple of houses, but not for a month.

Tantorello paused theatrically, lit a cigarette, and pretended to consider Leopold's dilemma. In fact, he'd costarred in this particular movie many times before and had been expecting a rerun for some time now. *"Okay, maybe I can help. I've got a friend who might possibly lend you the money. But don't play games with him."*

"Hey, thanks. How do I reach your friend?"

"Here's his name and number." The book scribbled it on a Post-it note.

Carmine Vincelli resembled more closely a chartered accountant than a juice man. Yet he wore an air of menace like a cloak of office. It was not his size or his stature that threatened—he was a compact, slope-shouldered man of indeterminate age with a sallow, cratered complexion, wearing a conservative gray suit and quite an ordinary tie. The menace was in the eyes: hooded slits with dead black pupils that seemed to look right through you. This was not a man you fucked with.

Vincelli did not offer to shake hands but came straight to the point. *"Sal tells me you're stuck for twenty-five large."*

"I just need it for a couple of weeks." So this is a shylock, *Leopold thought.* Funny how their names always end in vowels.

"What kind of collateral do you have?"

"My house. My car. And my business, I guess."

"Your business? Tell me about it."

"We're in residential construction. I'm a fifty percent partner."

"Numbers. Give me numbers." Vincelli produced a small black notebook and a gold Waterman ballpoint pen.

Barney reeled off the figures from memory. *"Gross sales last year, three and a half million. Net profit before taxes, four hundred thousand."*

"I'll need the name of your company and the address. Plus where you live." Leopold shuddered inwardly as the shylock wrote the information down in his black book. *"And the name of your partner."*

"Don't get him involved in this."

"I won't unless I have to. How much salary do you draw?"

"You really need to know that?"

"I got to know who I'm dealing with. I need to reassure my associates that you can handle this."

"Ten thousand a month."

"Pretax?"

"Yeah. Listen, Carmine, I'm good for it."

"Okay, Mr. Leopold, I believe you. Now let me tell you something just so we understand each other perfectly. The vig is two points a week. On twenty-five thousand dollars, that comes to five hundred dollars cash, *payable every Friday. No delays, no excuses."* He calmly replaced the pen in his inside pocket. *"Do I make myself clear?"*

"Sure. Where do I sign?"

The loan shark laughed humorlessly. *"You don't."*

Which was how Barney Leopold became a regular customer of Carmine Vincelli and the men whose names ended in vowels, under conditions that inevitably led to further indebtedness. Between the credit cards, the mortgage payments, the bank loan, and the shylocks, Barney Leopold's interest payments were becoming an insurmountable burden. He didn't dare think about the capital amounts he owed. To cover his mounting debts and to feed his ever-growing appetite for action, he sold his stocks and bonds, liquidated the kids' college accounts, and eventually dipped into company funds. Because, sooner or later, he knew he'd win it all back. It just hadn't happened yet.

Meanwhile, he had to face his partner.

"Is it the gambling?" his partner, George Anderson, had asked. "Is that where the money's gone?"

In exchange for Leopold's share of the business, Anderson agreed not to press charges, nor to seek the return of the money. "It's the best deal you'll ever get, Barney, when you consider the alternatives. The shares aren't worth anything near what you . . . took. Believe me, I'm only doing this out of concern for your family."

"And you won't tell anyone?"

"As far as anybody else is concerned, it's a buyout, pure and simple."

"One day I'll pay it all back and we can be partners again."

"Maybe, maybe not. Right now, you'd better do some painful thinking."

"What do you mean, George?"

"I guess what I mean is, when you come to terms with why you're do-ing this to yourself, we'll talk."

Leopold stared blankly at his ex-partner.

He didn't dare tell his wife the real reason he wasn't going into the of-fice anymore. Fortunately for Barney, Shirley had never taken an interest in the business and scarcely knew his ex-partner. He told her he'd sold out and ascribed his leaving to a "disagreement" with Anderson; she accepted the explanation at face value.

It was more difficult to explain the growing shortage of household money. Shirley had always handled the day-to-day family finances and was beginning to feel the pinch.

After a couple of weeks, she had asked innocently, "When do you get the settlement for your part of the business?"

"Soon, I hope," he lied, "but it's tied up in escrow until the final papers are signed."

It isn't a *complete* lie, *he thought to himself.* I *am* going to get the money. I'll win it back the same way I lost it. But this time, I'll be smart— no more sports action. I'll get hot at the craps table. Somehow, it'll all work out, *he fantasized. He wasn't completely broke. There was no cash or credit left, but he still had the car. And the Rolex watch, if push came to shove. As long as he could find action—any kind of action, it didn't matter—he'd be more alive than ever. He'd be master of his destiny, a risk taker, pushing the envelope, daring Fate to destroy him.*

And so it was that Barney Leopold found himself in Las Vegas on a sunny autumn day with a receipt for his Audi, a pawn ticket for his Rolex, and ten thousand dollars burning a hole in his pocket. He knew his luck would change.

What Barney Leopold didn't know was that it would get worse.

Much worse.

18 **It was a magnificent October morning** in southern Nevada. A cloudless, intensely blue sky stretched from mountain to mountain as Steve Forrester pushed through the swinging saloon doors of Zeke's Bar on Spring Mountain near the Southwest Area Command. The previous day Forrester had sent the envelope containing the threatening letter, the video, and the Dunes chip via Galaxy Security to LVMPD Lieutenant Frank Marshall and later phoned him, suggesting that they meet away from the station.

Marshall had not been enthusiastic about the idea. "What's the problem, Steve? Afraid of a leak?"

"I'd have to log in. And there could be reporters hanging around the house."

"Don't trust your old partner to keep a lid on it, huh?"

"It's not that. It's just that I promised Droopy I'd keep this thing low-profile."

"All right. You're the boss." There was the unmistakable ring of sarcasm in the cop's voice.

"Come on, Frank, lighten up."

"What do you mean?"

"You know what I mean. It's been almost three years and you're still pissed."

Marshall snorted. "Why should I be pissed? Just because you're there and I'm here?"

"Frank, it wasn't a contest. I wish to hell you wouldn't try to lay this guilt trip on me every time we talk."

"So much for promises, huh?"

"Goddamn it, Frank, I followed through and you know it. I'm not an employment agency—"

"Yeah, right." Marshall sighed audibly. "Look, just meet me at Zeke's in half an hour. If it fits in with your busy executive schedule, that is."

Exasperated, Forrester brusquely agreed to the rendezvous and hung up the phone.

Three years earlier, both men had applied for the post of VP Security at the Galaxy, a move that would effectively triple the chosen candidate's then-current salary as an LVMPD detective. Neither man had known that the other was applying for the position until after the selection had been made. When Forrester announced that he had landed the job, he was surprised at his partner's unenthusiastic reaction. It was only then that he learned of Marshall's own application. As time wore on, despite his promotion to lieutenant, Frank Marshall proved to be increasingly resentful of his ex-partner's success, blaming Steve for the relative slowness of his own career advancement.

There was no question that Marshall was a good detective, and Forrester had attempted to mollify Marshall by offering to keep an eye open for similar opportunities within Summit Enterprises. But Steve was torn between a genuine desire to help Frank advance his career and his knowledge that the latter had a drinking problem, a problem that made it difficult for Forrester to truthfully endorse him for any kind of sensitive position at Summit. And selfishly, Forrester realized that his old partner was far more valuable to him on the force than off it—the Galaxy was often obliged to enlist the aid of the LVMPD, and as Vice President of Security, he needed a reliable, talented contact on the force. Drinking problem or not, Frank Marshall was the best cop Forrester knew.

So Forrester compromised.

He recommended positions at Summit that he hoped Marshall would turn down for a variety of reasons—undesirable locations, unappealing terms of employment, uncompetitive salaries. And as Marshall obliged by remaining on the job, Forrester's "career offers" gradually dried up.

A marked coolness now hung between the two men. Their relationship had declined to the level of professional contact and an annual corporate Christmas card from Forrester to his ex-partner.

"Over here, Steve," said Marshall as Forrester entered the dimly lit bar, the former team's favorite after-hours watering hole. The policeman had commandeered a booth at the back of the room. He half rose to meet his ex-partner but did not offer to shake hands. Frank Marshall was a tall, gray-complexioned man, wearing a drab business suit and a perpetual frown. Forrester, who had not seen him for several months, noticed that Marshall's thinning mouse-brown hair was now arranged in an artful comb-over. He also observed that Marshall had already consumed most of his drink.

"Ready for a refill, Frank?"

"Why not? Just put it on your expense account."

Forrester decided to ignore the barb and get down to business. He signaled the bartender for two drinks. "Any luck with the package I sent over?"

"Nada. There weren't any usable prints on the stationery or the cassette or that Dunes chip—except for your boss and the mail boy. As far as tracing the stuff, forget it. The stationery is dime-store shit, and the tape cassette is a common brand they sell by the millions." He extracted a pack of Marlboros from his shirt pocket. "Want one?"

"No, thanks. I'm trying to butt out."

Marshall smiled faintly as he lit up and exhaled a luxurious cloud of smoke in his ex-partner's direction. "Sure you don't want one, old buddy?"

"I didn't say that, old *pal.* I'm just trying to stay off them is all."

"Let me know if you change your mind."

"Yeah, right. Thanks for your support."

"No problem, Steve. Thanks for yours."

"I give up, Frank." Forrester sighed. "So you got nothing at all?"

"Like I said. Do *you guys* have any idea who might be behind all this?" the lawman asked.

"Not a clue," Forrester replied flatly, trying to ignore the tempting aroma of the cigarette smoke. "Nobody saw the package delivered. It just *materialized* in Droopy's box. Could be a disgruntled ex-employee. Maybe a sore loser at the tables. Or just some wacko that we'll never hear from again." He sipped his Jack Daniel's. "I was hoping the lab might have found something."

"There was nothing to find."

"How about the tape?"

"It's from a movie called *Seven.* Released a few years ago." Marshall pulled a small black notebook from his inside pocket and consulted it. "The actors are Morgan Freeman and Brad Pitt. It's obviously a second-generation copy. The movie they copied it from is widely available in video-rental stores. We even checked for residual frames. Sometimes if a tape's been used before, there can be a few seconds at the beginning from previously recorded material. But this one was virgin."

"And the chip? I mean, they blew up the Dunes, what, fifteen years ago?"

"Not hard to find. There are all kinds of chips from defunct casinos in circulation. They sell 'em by the thousands in gambling-supply houses and souvenir stores."

"I know. I'm just wondering what the hell it means."

"Could be the perp's trademark." Marshall smirked. "So we don't get *him* confused with all those *other* shakedown artists sending you threatening letters," he added sarcastically.

"Like the signature isn't enough? What was it—Thanatos?"

Marshall consulted his notebook again. "We looked that up, too. Thanatos was the Greek god of death."

"So we've got the god of death. A chip from a casino that was blown up. A letter and a video that threaten us with a poisoning. . . ."

"No fingerprints and no suspects. All of which adds up to squat. There's nothing else we can do unless we hear from these skells again."

"Even if we do, Druperman says he's not paying."

"Paying what? Nobody's even *asked* you guys for any specific amount of money yet. All you've got is a vague threat by some nut with a flair for melodrama."

"That's true. I sincerely hope this thing just goes away," Forrester said. "You know better than anybody that we've gotten threatening letters before at the Galaxy—and nothing ever came of them. But . . ."

"But what?"

"But there's something *convincing* about this one. I've just got this weird *feeling* about it. Something about the letter and the tape and that stupid chip just seems too damn serious, too carefully worked out, to be a hoax. Why would anybody go to all this trouble for a sick joke?"

"I don't know." The police lieutenant shifted impatiently, butted his Marlboro, and swallowed the last of his drink. "Look, if you insist, I could call the Feebs in—"

Forrester shook his head. "Thanks anyway. Droopy doesn't want you to start an official investigation yet. You know what a hardheaded bastard he is. But maybe if you could make some discreet inquiries . . ."

Marshall sighed. "Yes, sir. When the Galaxy talks, we listen. Okay. Get me a list of whoever's been fired from the Galaxy since it opened—and for that matter, anyone else you can think of with a grudge against the place. At least I can have the names run through NCIC."

"Good."

"Call me if they contact you again."

"You bet. And thanks, Frank. Maybe one day we can be friends again." Forrester rose and extended a hand, which Marshall took reluctantly. "Or not."

The police lieutenant smiled thinly and signaled the bartender for a refill.

19

Barney Leopold was invincible, unstoppable, immortal.

He was Manolete braving the *corrida,* Saint George slaying the dragon, Chuck Yeager pushing the envelope.

The gambler had held the dice for an eternity. They were *alive* in his hands. When he whispered to them, they complied. When he shouted at them, they obeyed. And the crowd was riveted. A great roar would ascend to the very peak of the Galaxy's atrium each time he made a winning pass, followed by a breathless silence while he massaged the gleaming red cubes in preparation for the next.

Without actually counting his chips—that was bad luck—the gambler was vaguely aware that he'd parlayed the ten grand, his last money on earth, into a small fortune. But right now the money didn't matter. It was the *action,* the thrill, the adrenaline rush. It was the courting of disaster on every roll. It was the thrill of anticipation as the dice tumbled through the air, seemingly in slow motion, ready to do his bidding time after time.

Barney wasn't just hot, he was *sizzling*.

The boxman had been obliged to replenish the table's chip supply twice, and still the Californian hadn't cooled down. Leopold was a do bettor, playing the pass line and placing the numbers, pressing up his bets.

Each time a new point was established, he backed up his pass-line bet with another bet—the free double odds—which effectively tripled the amount of his original bet.

He also *placed* large bets on the other five numbers.

All he needed was for the place numbers to happen, and ultimately the point to repeat, before a seven was rolled.

And they happened. And repeated. And happened. And repeated. Barney's fingers were magic.

"Six, six, the point is six," chanted the stickman.

Leopold stacked a pile of chips behind the pass line for his free odds bet. "Gimme twenty-six hundred on the numbers," he commanded, tossing the dealer a handful of black and white chips. The dealer quickly placed five hundred each on the four, five, nine, and ten and six hundred on the eight.

Leopold rolled two deuces.

"Hard four. Pay the man nine hundred," said the stickman.

"Press it up—with another hundred," Leopold shouted over the excited clamor of the other players. The numbers kept coming.

"Easy four."

"Five alive."

"Ten easy."

"Three craps." This made no difference to Barney; he had dodged that particular bullet on the come-out roll.

"Nine."

"Hard eight. No field."

He rolled number after number, but never a seven except on his come-out rolls.

Finally, "Six easy, pay the line."

Leopold had held the dice for over an hour. He was running out of space for his chips. He had filled the rack in front of him several times and his pockets were bulging.

Somewhere in the back of his mind, cutting through the euphoria like a TV commercial, a persistent little voice was trying to make itself heard.

You've done it, said the voice. *You've got it all back even though God knows you don't deserve it. You can pay off the sharks and the mortgage and the loans and get the car and the watch back, and Shirley doesn't ever have to know how close you came to the edge. Maybe you can even buy your way back into the business.*

For once in his life, Barney Leopold listened.

You've been given another chance. Don't blow it this time.

With the Boston Red Sox cap and mirrored wraparound sunglasses, Buster Malloy felt reasonably confident in his anonymity.

As usual at dinnertime, there was a long line at the Cosmic Café. Malloy was obliged to wait almost half an hour to be seated.

"A single, sir?" inquired Gladys Adams, the hostess, when he finally reached the head of the queue. "Perhaps you'd care to sit at the counter?"

"Give me a table," said Malloy brusquely.

"Smoking or nonsmoking?"

"I don't care."

"Yes, sir. Right this way, please." Gladys glanced at her customer curiously. There was something *familiar* about him, she thought as she wove through the tables with the big man in tow. *Where have I seen him before?* But without Buster's uniform and his telltale eye patch, she failed to make the connection.

"How about this one in the corner?" Malloy demanded, indicating a table that was shielded from general view by a large potted palm.

"No problem, sir. Enjoy your meal."

Malloy knew he'd have to wait several minutes to be served. He had carefully planned this little visit to coincide with the café's busiest time. Making certain that he was unobserved, he pulled a pair of cotton work gloves from his windbreaker pocket. After surreptitiously slipping them on, he removed a padded brown envelope from inside his windbreaker and stuck it, using the double-sided tape he had applied earlier, to the underside of the table. Finally, he produced a small, clear plastic bag from his shirt pocket and unscrewed the chrome cap from the glass sugar dispenser.

By the time the waitress arrived to take his order, he had vanished.

"**Sir,** that's five hundred and seventeen thousand, four hundred we owe you," said the casino cashier. "Would you like a bank draft?"

Barney Leopold thought for a moment and smiled. "No, I'd prefer cash." A check was so impersonal. Besides, he was aching to feel those crisp Ben Franklins between his fingers. The cash would substantiate his triumph; somehow it would *justify* his journey to the edge of the abyss.

"That will take some time, sir. I can give you a receipt for the chips now and have the money ready in a couple of hours."

"Okay. I'll grab a bite to eat while you do that," said Barney. The cashier wrote out a receipt, which Leopold carefully folded and put in his shirt pocket. "See you later."

The newly reformed gambler marched purposefully toward the coffee shop, eyes front past the scene of his recent victory, supremely confident in his newfound self-control.

The dinner crowd had left and there was no longer a line at the Cosmic Café. So far, Barney Leopold's luck was holding.

He just didn't realize how little of it he had left.

There were eight restaurants in the Galaxy complex, offering diners a choice of menus and ambience ranging from fast food at the Asteroid Snack Bar to the finest French cuisine in the four-star Zodiac Room. One of the perks senior Galaxy executives enjoyed was complimentary meals for themselves and their business guests in any of these restaurants—a privilege that Steve Forrester seldom abused. This time he intended to make an exception. There was no business talk on the menu tonight.

The maître d' of the Zodiac Room greeted the Galaxy's vice president of security warmly as he arrived for dinner. "Weel you be seated now, Monsieur Forrestair? Ze table is ready."

"Thanks, François, but I'll wait in the bar for my guest. Lucy Baker. When she arrives, please show her over."

"Très bien, monsieur."

The restaurant was configured in a circular shape and featured a domed roof painted in Renaissance style with each of the twelve signs of the zodiac. Twinkling lights set into the paintings represented the stars that formed the constellations.

Fiber-optic sprays lit each table with a sprinkling of rainbow colors. The tables were arranged in tiered concentric circles around a small central podium upon which a string quartet was lightly underscoring the patrons' conversations with a pleasant selection of dinner music.

Every detail was artfully conceived to enhance the overall effect— which was nothing short of spectacular, Steve Forrester reflected with some proprietary pride as he surveyed the tableau from his barstool. There was no doubt that he worked for a classy joint.

The musicians paused momentarily to a scattering of polite applause, then picked up their instruments again. Forrester signaled the bartender for a double Jack Daniel's, reflected briefly, and changed it to a single. There never was going to be a perfect time to ease up on the drinking, he mused as he sipped the drink, enjoying the warm glow it always imparted. But what the hell, tonight was as good as—

"Hello, Steve. I hope I'm not late."

Forrester swiveled round on his stool and almost dropped the glass. She looked absolutely delicious in a deep blue velvet sheath that accented her slim figure and perfectly matched the color of her eyes. Her dark hair was haloed with reflections from the zodiac stars. She wore very little makeup— just a touch of complementary eye shadow, but it was enough.

He smiled and took Lucy Baker's arm.

Seated in the Cosmic Café, Barney Leopold was still under the influence of the euphoria he'd experienced at the craps table. He'd never felt so alive! Too bad his gambling days were over. He extracted the receipt from his pocket and unfolded it. In his heart he'd known all along that his luck would change; now he had the proof right here in his hands. Five hundred and seventeen thousand, four hundred dollars. No more sharks, no more stealing, no more lies—he was through with gambling. Permanently.

But then again, once he was back on his feet, who knew what might happen? In this life there were no absolutes; nothing was for sure, nothing was forever. And Lady Luck finally seemed to be swinging in his direction. . . .

The busboy appeared at his table.

"Your waitress will be right over, sir," he said. "Would you like a coffee while you're waiting?"

"Sure."

The kid inverted the cup and filled it. Leopold tucked the receipt under the keno rack, careful not to spill coffee on it. He poured a heaping teaspoon of sugar from the chrome-and-glass dispenser into his cup, stirred it, and gratefully swallowed a mouthful of the steaming brew.

At which point, the last of his luck ran out.

"Well, this time we really *did* get a seat near the orchestra," Lucy Baker said as she and Steve Forrester were seated by the maître d' at a table on the innermost concentric ring surrounding the music podium in the Zodiac Room. "Would you believe I've never been in here before?"

"You're kidding. My God, after all those comps you've written for other people, it's about time you got to enjoy it yourself."

"Strictly for research purposes, huh? Okay, you're the boss."

Forrester laughed. "Only sometimes. But not this evening, not with you. I promised myself there'd be no business talk tonight."

"That sounds nice. But do you think first, you know, before we don't talk business, do you think maybe you could answer one little question—"

"Yes?"

"I heard there was some kind of terrorist threat against the Galaxy. And since you're the Vice President of Security, I thought you'd be the one to—"

Steve stiffened. "Where did you hear that?"

"Oh, around. You know."

"No, I don't know. Lucy, this could be important. Please tell me where you got this information."

Disconcerted by her escort's sudden seriousness, Lucy quickly realized she had better come clean. "Well, sometimes I eat my lunch with Edith Frick. You know, Mr. Druperman's secretary. I'm sorry, I guess I shouldn't have mentioned it. . . ."

"No, that's all right. I'm glad you did." Forrester made a mental note to confront the old douche bag, who must have been listening in on Droopy's intercom, first thing in the morning. "In fact, it'll enable me to plug a leak."

"God, I feel like Linda Tripp."

"Believe me, you did the right thing."

"That's not what Monica Lewinsky said."

Forrester smiled. "This is different."

"So, tell me more. I promise not to breathe a word."

"What exactly did Edith say?"

"Something about poisoning everybody in Las Vegas. Apparently she didn't get the whole story—"

"Guess we'll have to increase the volume on her intercom. Or her hearing aid."

"That's not nice."

"Neither is eavesdropping. Druperman doesn't want the story spread around, for obvious reasons. But I'll tell you if you really want to know. It's kind of ugly, though."

"I can handle ugly. It's curious that always gets me."

"All right. We received an envelope addressed to Druperman in his capacity as president of the Las Vegas Casino Association—you've probably never heard of the LVCA, but that's the way they like it. Anyway, inside the envelope, there's this letter and a videotape. It's a movie clip that features a poisoning. Presumably to show us as graphically as possible that we're vulnerable."

As Steve talked, Lucy's expression went from lighthearted to concerned.

"God, you mean somebody's actually going to get *poisoned*?"

"We don't know. This could all be some sick joke."

"What are they asking for?"

"That's the funny part. They didn't make any demands. In the letter, they just told us they were going to demonstrate their power and said they'd get back to us. I guess this poisoning, if it ever happens, is going to be some kind of warning shot across our bow."

"That is kind of scary. What are you going to do?"

"Officially, nothing. Off the record, I've talked to the police, but there's not much they can do without more to go on. Whoever sent the envelope didn't leave any fingerprints or other clues. Besides, Emmett's afraid that if this gets out, it could seriously hurt our business."

"I appreciate your telling me."

"I feel that I can . . . trust you."

"Funny you should say that," she said thoughtfully. "I don't know why, but I sort of feel that way about you, too."

It was a moment, the first real one they'd shared, and Forrester wondered if this might be the start of something he hadn't experienced for years, if ever. Could she be feeling the same way? All the signs seemed to be right, yet still he sensed a reserve. . . .

The waiter arrived with menus. After some discussion, they decided to share an hors d'oeuvre of escargots Galeries Lafayette—broiled snails with garlic butter and parsley. As an entrée Steve selected the boeuf Bastille; Lucy chose the feuillette d'homard Louis XIV. They agreed on a 2001 Clos de Vougeot Burgundy. It was a superb meal, yet Forrester hardly tasted it. All his attention was focused on his dinner companion, this wonderful young woman who had unwittingly taken over his thoughts—and stirred his libido. He silently thanked Tony Francisco, the bullying megastar whose misbehavior had brought them together. Lucy Baker was so different from anyone he'd ever met. She was worldly, as you'd expect from a casino floorperson, yet without the hard shell most of her coworkers had grown. Her sense of humor was delightful. She was genuinely interested in him, his job, his life.

They laughed about the Tony Francisco incident. They compared their tastes in music and books, finding a great deal in common. They shared experiences and explored each other's background.

"Tell me about Vermont," Forrester said, topping up her glass with the rich Burgundy Grand Cru.

"Not much to tell. My grandparents were French-Canadian. Our real family name is kind of hard to pronounce, especially for you westerners, so I changed it to Baker."

"What *is* your real family name, then?"

"It's Boulanger." She pronounced it *boo-lonh-zhay*. "It means Baker in French."

He raised an eyebrow and gave her his best suspicious-policeman look. "So, ma'am—you've been operating under an alias?"

"Yes, officer. And that's not the half of it. My real first name isn't even Lucy."

"Whoa—who am I dating here anyhow, a CIA agent? What *is* your real first name? I suppose you're going to say you'll have to kill me if you tell me. . . ."

"No, silly." She made a face. "It's Lucette. And I hate it. In fact, not counting Personnel, you're the first person at the Galaxy I've ever told."

"I'm flattered. I think. But—why do you hate it?"

"I just don't like the way it sounds in English. *Loose set.* Loose set of what? Teeth? Other parts . . . of my anatomy?" Forrester thought he noticed a slight blush, although the subdued lighting in the Zodiac Room made it hard to be sure.

"I kind of like it, actually. Lucette Boulanger, right?"

"That's what it says on my driver's license, Steve. And by the way, your pronunciation of it . . ." She fake-frowned, held out a hand palm down and waggled it.

He chuckled apologetically. "That bad, huh? Okay, I'll stick to Lucy Baker."

"Merci, monsieur."

"So, Miss Lucy Baker, you apparently speak French."

"Oh sure. I learned to speak it before I learned English. Half my friends were French, and we got a lot of French Canadian guests at the hotel. You needed to be able to serve them in their own language."

"Impressive. Personally, I never got past *la plume de ma tante*. What the heck was it doing on my uncle's bureau, anyway?"

"I don't know—maybe it's a *thing* that French aunts have. I'll ask one of mine next time I go home." Her laugh was easy, reminding Steve of rippling water. "Tell me about yourself, Steve. You sound like you're a westerner."

"I'm from here, born and bred. Third-generation, as a matter of fact."

Steve decided not to risk boring his date with an overly long genealogical dissertation. In fact, it had been quite a while since he'd given any thought at all to the Forrester family history. . . .

Had it been *almost three-quarters of a century since his grandfather had coaxed an aging Model T across the desert to the embryonic gambling town of Las Vegas with its saloons and brothels and faro games? Was it really that long since Henry Forrester, desperate for a job, had risked his life for three years as a high scaler on the Boulder Canyon Dam Project? In the 1930s thousands of unemployed men came to this desolate canyon and for a few dollars a day worked in unspeakable conditions and almost unbearable heat to harness the raging Colorado River. Big Red, the workers called it. Too thick to drink and too thin to plow. One hundred and twelve men died on the job, but Forrester survived. He married a schoolteacher and became a construction worker in Las Vegas.*

Henry's only son, John—Steve Forrester's father—was less than a year short of retirement from the Las Vegas Police Department when his wife of almost thirty years answered the bell to find a grim-faced chief of detectives and police chaplain on her doorstep. Right away, Steve's mother knew the worst—because they don't send brass and chaplains around for minor injuries. As gently as possible the chief told her that John Forrester and his partner had stumbled upon a bank robbery in progress and that John had been fatally shot by one of the bandits. If it was any consolation, the chief continued, the man who killed your husband was himself gunned down, and both his accomplices taken into custody.

A grieving nineteen-year-old Steve, then a freshman engineering student at UNLV, decided to honor his father in the only way he knew how—by changing his major to criminal justice. If his father could sacrifice his life to protect this town, the young man reasoned idealistically, then at least he could carry on the tradition. The Forresters had a stake in the future of Las Vegas, Steve thought, because two generations of them had helped build it and protect it.

Twenty years later Steve Forrester still believed in his city, but with the hundreds of thousands of modern-day carpetbaggers flooding into what has become the fastest-growing city in the United States and the depersonalization of the gaming industry by the faceless megacorporations, his civic pride was becoming a little tattered around the edges. Las Vegas just wasn't the town he'd grown up in. Too many people, too much pressure. He already had one failed marriage to prove it.

But Vegas was still home.

Snapping himself out of his reverie, Forrester continued with the condensed version of his bio for Lucy Baker's benefit: "Anyway, after college I got into law enforcement. I was a cop for eleven years until I lucked into this job."

"I'm sure luck had nothing to do with it."

He smiled and met her gaze frankly. It was another moment, and they both felt it wash over them like a warm tide.

"Did you ever . . . marry?" she asked.

"Just once," he replied with an apologetic shrug. "It didn't even last three years. No kids, thank God. She was a cocktail waitress at the Nugget. I'm still paying for my foolishness." This could be serious, he thought, repressing a growing desire to take this woman in his arms then and there, and to hell with what the diners and the staff of the Zodiac Room might think. He forced himself back to reality. "How about you?"

"Uh-uh. I was engaged once. It happened on the cruise ship. I fell head over heels for this wonderful, charming man who turned out to be a real *bastard*. I was an assistant casino manager, and he was the manager. I'm kind of ashamed about what happened, to be perfectly honest."

"I'm sorry. What did happen?"

"Maybe one day I'll tell you about it. But not now. I don't want to spoil this evening."

"Nothing could spoil this evening," he said, smiling.

Only if I let it, thought Lucy. For the hundredth time, she wondered if she really was doing the right thing. Once bitten . . . but she pushed the thought away. "Tell me," she said, gazing intently at this attractive, likable man, "are we going to have a relationship?"

He met her gaze openly and frankly. "I think so. I hope so."

The quartet was halfway through Pachelbel's Canon as their waiter approached. "May I bring you coffee or dessert, ma'am, Mr. Forrester?"

Forrester looked questioningly at Lucy. Laying her hand gently on his, she heard herself say, "Why don't we go to my place for coffee?"

Steve Forrester needed no further persuasion. "Have François send the check to my office in the morning, please," he said quietly to the waiter, leaving a generous cash tip on the table.

Behind the potted plant in a remote corner of the Cosmic Café, Barney Leopold clutched his chest, turned waxy pale, and spewed a geyser of bright red blood, spattering the table with a pattern of scarlet gore. His body jerked, twitched, and stiffened, knocking over the keno rack. The coffee cup swung loosely down on his rigid index finger, neatly depositing its contents into his lap. His eyes rolled up in their sockets and he crumpled to the floor, crimson-chinned, a brown coffee stain spreading across his white Dockers.

The piece of paper tucked under the keno rack fluttered unnoticed off the table and into the foliage of the potted plant.

"Somebody help. . . . This man has collapsed!" cried one of the patrons.

People at nearby tables looked over in horror, then quickly turned away. Others appeared to be frozen to their chairs. Still others picked up their checks and beat a hasty retreat. One heavyset woman whispered to her companion, "Let's get out of here, Lydia. We don't want to get *involved*."

Drawn by the commotion, Gladys Adams, the hostess, materialized. She knelt by the fallen man and gingerly felt the carotid artery in his neck. No pulse.

A waitress arrived and came close to supplementing the casualty list by nearly passing out at the sight of the blood- and coffee-stained victim.

"Is he . . . alive?" the waitress asked the hostess in a trembling voice.

"He's stiff as a board. There's no pulse," said Gladys. "Call Security and tell them to get the paramedics over here *fast*." Relieved to be liberated from the carnage, the waitress raced for a phone.

She need not have hurried.

Mr. Barney Leopold, recently reformed compulsive gambler from El Modena, California, would be dead long before help arrived.

20 Forrester drove Lucy home, top down under the starlit desert sky. A velvet-smooth Tony Bennett ballad played on the CD; the warm breeze mingled delightfully with the scent of her perfume. In his peripheral vision he noted that her skirt had somehow ridden up to mid-thigh. *She keeps glancing at me, too—encouraging signs,* he thought.

"I'm so glad you're playing Bennett and not Francisco. Not tonight, anyway," she said.

"Are you warm enough?" he asked solicitously. "I could put the top up—"

"No, this is perfect, Steve. It's fun watching the stars go by."

Forrester reached over and took her hand. She made no objection; his pulse quickened slightly.

For the next few minutes only the gentle rush of the breeze over the windshield broke the silence as they made their way along the broad reaches of Eastern Avenue toward the Green Valley area of Henderson. Forrester drove slowly, regulating his speed to catch the lights, savoring the moment, anticipating whatever the rest of the evening might bring. To the east, the malls and office buildings were dark and deserted. To the west, the twin landing lights of a jumbo jet signaled the arrival of yet another planeload of tourists at McCarran Airport, another wave of excited gamblers ready to help feed the town's voracious appetite for cash. Far behind the big Mercedes sports car, the neon brilliance of the Strip faded to a faint glow.

"This is it," she said as they approached a gated apartment complex. Lucy lived in Arbor Court, a modest but neat grouping of two-story white stucco buildings in West Henderson, just outside the Las Vegas city limits.

Her second-floor apartment on Violet Lane was reached by an outside staircase that led onto a private balcony with French doors. Forrester admired the carefully tended window box decorating her sill.

Lucy's taste in furnishings had not been tainted by the glitz of Las Vegas, Steve was pleased to note. The decor was definitely Vermont. Her furniture was New England cozy, flowered chintz and pine antiques. Good quality, nothing cheap. Adorning the walls of the modest but immaculate living room were a number of Impressionist prints and a few original oils— covered bridges, farm scenes, snow-covered mountains. A cluster of framed family photos sat on a side table: Mom, Dad, Lucy, and a dark-haired youth who could only have been a younger brother. Forrester even detected a faint scent of pine.

He loosened his tie and settled back comfortably on an invitingly over-stuffed Ethan Allen couch.

"Would you like anything in your coffee?" Lucy asked as she busied herself in the neat, cheerful kitchenette. "I've got Courvoisier. . . ."

"You know, this is something I don't say very often, but I think I've had enough booze for one night. You're a good influence on me."

"Honestly, I don't mean to be," she said, walking over with two steam-ing cups of coffee on a silver Paul Revere tray. She sat beside him—keeping a decorous cushion's width between them—and placed the tray on the an-tique pine musket box that served as her coffee table. "I kind of like you the way you are. It's been a wonderful evening."

"It has. And there's something I've been dying to do since you walked into the restaurant."

"What's that?" she asked nervously, knowing exactly what it was.

He gathered his nerve. "Kiss you?"

He looked at her questioningly. She blushed, tempted, still uncertain of her feelings. Yet coming up here had been *her* idea. What could she have been thinking?

"Oh, Steve, I—"

He slid closer and touched her cheek tenderly. "Stop me anytime—"

Brrring! A warble emanated from Forrester's inside jacket pocket. They both jumped. The spell was broken.

"What's that?" she said.

"It's my cell phone," said Forrester. "Goddamn it."

"You'd better answer it," said Lucy. Disappointment fought with relief at this last-minute reprieve from a confrontation with her feelings. Somehow, at that moment, disappointment was ahead by a considerable margin.

He pressed the SEND button. "Forrester."

"Sir, it's Jim Roper at the Galaxy. I'm really sorry to bother you so late, but I think you should get over here right away."

Steve grimaced. "Right *now,* Roper? What's so important, it couldn't wait until morning?"

"We've just had a death in the Cosmic Café. Ordinarily I wouldn't bother you—"

Forrester recalled the threatening letter and the videotape. "Oh Christ. I hope this isn't what I think it is," he muttered to himself. On the one hand, fatalities were not uncommon in any large hotel, Forrester knew. You hated when they happened, but with a transient population of thousands—many of them elderly—seizures, heart attacks, and strokes were a fact of life. Or death. On the other hand, Jim Roper was a pretty levelheaded guy and it wasn't like him to bother his boss with a routine natural death.

"It looks like a seizure of some kind," the guard said. "This guy threw up blood, collapsed, and croaked. Kind of messy, but these things happen. I wouldn't have called you except that we noticed something odd—there was a package taped under the table where he was sitting. Addressed to Mr. Druperman. We haven't touched it."

"Describe the package."

"It's a brown envelope, one of those padded types, about nine by twelve inches and maybe an inch thick. There's a printed white address label stuck on it."

"Shit." So it had happened, just as the letter had promised. The warning shot. "Okay, Roper, you did the right thing by calling me. Don't let anyone touch the body. Just secure the scene, and I'll be right there." He disconnected and folded up the phone. *Why did the bastards have to pick tonight of all nights to do their dirty work?*

"Looks like we've got a problem, Lucy," he said. "They may have poisoned somebody in the coffee shop."

"Oh God, Steve. That movie came true. You'd better go." She hoped the brisk practicality in her voice would conceal the disappointment.

"I'm sorry."

"Don't be sorry. Just go."

"Rain check?"

"Sure. Call me."

Steve Forrester was thoroughly pissed off, and it showed in his driving. The leisurely drive to Lucy's earlier in the evening had taken about half an hour; it took him less than eight minutes to make the return trip, redlining the big SL 500 convertible most of the way and ignoring traffic lights. En route, he used the cell phone to leave a terse message for Lieutenant Frank Marshall at Las Vegas Metro. Then he called Emmett Druperman at home. Fuck it. If *he* could be disturbed, so could Droopy. The CEO reluctantly agreed to meet his VP Security on the Bridge in an hour.

Steve arrived at the Cosmic Café in the middle of a heated argument between Galaxy security guard Jim Roper and two paramedics who wanted to transport Barney Leopold's body to their waiting ambulance.

"I told them what you told me, sir," Roper said. "But they won't listen."

"Sorry, fellas," Forrester said to the white-coated attendants. "I'm going to have to ask you to wait for the police before you move him. Shouldn't be long."

"We can't tie up the ambulance all night," said one of the paramedics. "There's only two crews on call tonight for the entire Strip—"

"I see. Well, you'd better leave him here. We'll make other arrangements to move the body."

"We still have to bill you for the call—"

"Fine. No problem. Thank you for coming." Forrester managed to control his temper. He noticed that Roper had a familiar bulge in his uniform shirt pocket. Screw it. "Roper?" he said through gritted teeth.

"Sir?"

"Give me a cigarette, please."

By the time Frank Marshall arrived, accompanied by two uniforms, Steve Forrester was smoking his third bummed cigarette.

The patrons had been asked to leave, and the Cosmic Café was temporarily closed. Yellow tape draped across the entrance bore bright witness to human tragedy.

Steve showed Frank to the area where the body still lay frozen in death like a bloody wax effigy. Evidence of the man's violent demise was sprayed across the marble tabletop, crimson gore clinging to the salt and pepper shakers, the sugar dispenser, the keno brochure rack. He pointed out the package still taped to the underside of the tabletop.

"I guess these guys weren't kidding after all," the LVMPD lieutenant remarked.

"Guess not, Frank. I told you I had a feeling."

"You also told me you quit smoking. So what's that in your hand? Caving under a little pressure?"

Forrester grimaced and shrugged.

"All right, Steve. Give me a rundown."

"Apparently the busboy served him a coffee. Then he hurled blood and collapsed. One of my guards found the package taped under the table and called me. Nobody's touched anything, Frank. I figured I'd let your boys remove the package . . . and the body."

"Good. I called the coroner. The Bomb Squad and Crime Scene should be here any minute. But, then, you probably remember the routine." The cop fingered his comb-over thoughtfully. "Any witnesses?"

"I don't think so. Maybe Gladys Adams can tell us something. She's the hostess."

"Let's get her over here."

Forrester beckoned to the woman to join them. "Are you okay, Gladys?" he asked gently. She nodded hesitantly. "This is Lieutenant Marshall of the LVMPD. He has some questions for you."

"Why don't you sit down and tell us what you saw," said Marshall.

"I-I didn't really see anything," she told the police lieutenant. "The customers said he just collapsed. It couldn't have been anything he ate. The waitress hadn't even taken his order yet."

"All he had was the coffee?"

"Yes, sir."

"Served by the busboy?"

"Yes."

"Which one?"

"Manuel. His shift is over and he's gone home."

"We may need to talk to him."

"He's in again tomorrow."

"All right, now, Gladys, just a couple more questions and you can go. First of all, do you know who this man is?"

"No. I remember showing him to the table, but I don't recall having seen him before."

"Okay, Gladys. Now I want you to think carefully," said the cop. "Who was sitting at this table before the man arrived?"

"Golly, I can't remember. Dinner is such a busy time for us. . . ."

"This might be important."

Gladys closed her eyes. "I'm trying to recall. It's kind of hard to concentrate after all this excitement." She furrowed her brow. "I'm sorry, Lieutenant. . . ."

"I understand. Look, keep trying. If it comes back to you, please get in touch with Mr. Forrester or me." He gave her one of his cards, and she left the area, shaking her head sadly.

"We'll have to bag all this stuff and take it to the lab for analysis," Marshall said. "I've got a hunch there just might be some very nasty stuff in that sugar dispenser."

"What about the envelope, Frank?" Steve said.

"The Bomb Squad should be here any minute. Before we open it, we'll make sure it doesn't contain any kind of explosive device—although I doubt it. It looks exactly like the previous package you got."

"I'd lay odds there's another video inside."

"You'd probably win that bet."

"Druperman's on his way over. Maybe we could look at the tape in his office once your people have checked out the envelope."

"Why not? It *is* addressed to him. And we wouldn't want to delay the personal mail of the Chief Executive Officer of the Galaxy Hotel and Casino, now, would we?" Marshall slipped on a pair of clear plastic gloves and awkwardly reached inside the dead man's jacket. "Meanwhile, let's find out who this poor bastard was."

Buster Malloy quietly rose from the video poker machine near the entrance to the Cosmic Café, where he had sat unnoticed during the confusion of the past hour. He smugly congratulated himself on having obtained precisely the desired result. There was a tingling in his groin—not the rush he had experienced when he'd offed Helga, but pleasant enough.

He looked forward to phase two with heightened anticipation.

21 **While he and Marshall waited** for Druperman in the CEO's outer office, Forrester telephoned Lester Kinnear at his home and issued a series of crisp instructions. Kinnear was the hotel's food services manager.

Just as Forrester hung up, Druperman walked in.

"Emmett Druperman, Frank Marshall of the LVMPD," said Steve as he and the policeman rose. Druperman and Marshall shook hands briefly.

"Let's go inside," said Emmett without ceremony, barging through the heavy double doors onto the Bridge.

"Sorry about all this," Marshall began as they settled in around the massive conference table that dominated one end of the CEO's office. "But it looks like you and your association have a real problem. These people are obviously serious. There appears to have been an intentional poisoning in your coffee shop."

"Goddamn it," said Druperman. "Are you sure it was intentional?"

"We can't be a hundred percent positive until the coroner gets back to us. But I'd bet my miserable pension it was. Meanwhile, you guys better not take any chances."

"I spoke to Kinnear," said Forrester. "He's having all our restaurant managers dispose of any food that's been removed from its original packaging. That includes everything edible in the kitchens: meat, vegetables, baked goods, fruits, seasonings, flour, shortening. We're replacing glass sugar dispensers and salt and pepper shakers on the tables with individual sealed paper packets. I also told him to contact his opposite numbers at the other hotels and alert them. Probably a case of closing the barn door after the horse has escaped, but I thought it was . . . *prudent*."

"Prudent, eh? Won't the managers ask questions?" said Emmett.

"Kinnear's telling *them* what I told *him:* that there was a case of food poisoning in the Cosmic Café," Forrester replied. "I just didn't happen to mention that it was probably intentional."

"Good. The fewer people know what's going on, the better." Druperman picked up a plastic-sleeved letter that was lying atop his spacious mahogany desk. "What's this?"

"We took the liberty of opening your, ah, latest mail," said Frank. "They're asking for a huge sum of money. . . . See for yourself."

Stone-faced, the CEO sat down and read aloud: "'ATTENTION LAS VEGAS CASINO ASSOCIATION! WITH THIS POISONING ACTION WE HAVE PROVED OUR POWER. PREPARE TO PAY TEN MILLION DOL-LARS!' Ten million dollars! Fucking thieves!" Druperman's eyes narrowed to feral slits. He tossed the letter aside and addressed Frank Marshall. "I already made myself clear on this subject to Steve, and I'll tell you the same thing," he rasped. "I will not pay one cent to any fucking shakedown artist or extortionist or whatever the hell you want to call them. I don't give a rat's ass what they threaten us with. You just put a few of my goddamn tax dollars to work and nail these bastards before they do some real damage."

"That may not be so easy," said Marshall quietly, glancing at Forrester, who nodded agreement. "These people are not stupid. Look, why don't we at least play the video they sent?"

"Do what you want," said Druperman, folding his arms across his chest. "Just don't expect any money from this hotel or the association or . . ." His voice trailed off to a dark muttering as Steve inserted the cassette in his boss's VCR and pushed PLAY.

Once again, it was a movie clip.

"Who do these assholes think we are," Forrester sighed. "Ebert and Roeper?"

The scene opened in a gloomy subway tunnel. Staccato mood music lent a sense of impending danger to the atmosphere. One man appeared to have his foot caught in the train tracks. Another man carrying a length of what looked like metallic pipe rushed up behind the trapped man and raised the pipe threateningly. The trapped man yelled, "Frank!" A third man, tall, blond, whom Forrester knew he had seen before in the movies or on TV, raised a pistol and shot the man brandishing the pipe. As the man fell, his foot on one rail, the metal pipe he was holding touched the third rail and a cascade of sparks exploded from his body. Quick cut to a close-up of the trapped man. Cut again to yet another character running away down the tunnel. Back to the electrocuted man, smoke issuing from his collapsed body and residual sparks winking out around him like dying embers. The clip ended, the screen went blue.

"So now what are they going to do?" Druperman snapped. "Electrocute somebody?"

"Looks that way, Mr. Druperman. Anyway, you didn't finish the letter," said Marshall. "Let me read you the rest. It says, 'TERRIBLE RESULTS WILL HAPPEN IF YOU REFUSE TO PAY THIS MONEY. DO NOT FOOL YOURSELVES! ON THE VIDEO HEREWITH IS OUR NEXT OPERATION. THE POLICE CAN NOT STOP US. TO AVOID THIS ACTION, PLACE ON OR BEFORE FRIDAY A CLASSIFIED AD IN SECTION 260 OF *LAS VEGAS REVIEW-JOURNAL*! CONFIRM AGREEMENT TO PAY THEREIN! SIGN IT, LVCA! WE WILL CALL YOU WITH INSTRUCTIONS ON FORRESTER'S CELLULAR TELEPHONE. THANATOS.'" Frank laid the letter down and picked up a small plastic bag containing two red chips. "Oh, and by the way, this time they enclosed *two* five-dollar chips. These Dunes chips must be their calling card. And a cute way of letting us know how much the pay-off is. Ten dollars in chips equals ten *million* dollars in blood money. I wonder who writes their material."

"Anybody recognize the movie?" Forrester asked.

"What difference does it make?" said Druperman. "Now that they've delivered their message—"

"Don't be too sure about that, Mr. Druperman," Frank said. "You'd be amazed how much information our guys will be able to infer from that video. Not just physical evidence; we've got people who can get right into these guys' heads."

"Today's Wednesday, gentlemen," Forrester said. "Do we run the ad?"

"Why not?" replied Marshall. "Maybe it'll buy us more time to track down the perps."

"Run it, don't run it, makes no difference to me," said the CEO grimly. "I'll speak to the other members of the Las Vegas Casino Association and bring them up to speed. Just as a courtesy, you understand? Because I know how these boys think. In fact, I can tell you right now exactly what they're going to say."

"What's that, sir?" the policeman asked.

"My associates will say that for ten million bucks they can zap all the *ferkochte* tourists they want."

At the Cosmic Café, the last of the Crime Scene Investigation team had departed, leaving the Galaxy's night cleaning crew to wipe down the table and swab the bloodstains from the floor.

"What kind of shit they servin' in here, bro'?" one of the cleaners asked his associate.

"I dunno," replied the man. "But it sure as fuck done disagreed with this dude." He picked up a folded piece of paper that was lodged in the foliage of the potted plant and casually tossed Barney Leopold's receipt for five hundred and seventeen thousand, four hundred dollars into a bright orange trash bag.

22 The thunder of a Union Pacific freight train shook Jurgen Voss's apartment until the dishes rattled and books threatened to topple. Buster Malloy covered his ears with his hands. Dan Shiller looked up from the classified section of the *Las Vegas Review-Journal* he had spread out on the kitchen table and shouted, "Jesus Christ, Jurgen, how do you stand the noise?"

"I have grown used to it. It no longer bothers me. In fact, there is from the noise a definite advantage."

"Really?"

"*Ja*. Because of it, here the rent is lower than in buildings farther from the tracks."

"Yeah, right, Jurgen." Shiller rolled his eyes in exasperation over the petty financial concerns of his accomplice. "Well, you won't have to worry about rent money much longer. Look what I found in the paper."

The trickster's two confederates leaned in closely as Shiller pointed a manicured finger at the personals column. Malloy began reading loudly over the diminishing rumble of the freight train, " 'Married white male seeks—' "

"Not that one, stup— I mean, Malloy," said Shiller, catching himself just in time. "The next one down. Here, I'll read it. 'We agree to your terms. Contact ED soonest. LVCA.' "

"All *right*!" Malloy grinned triumphantly, slapping Voss on the back and causing the little man with the big head to stumble and cough. "They backed down just like the fuckin' chickenshits they are!" He reflected for a moment, and a brief flash of disappointment clouded his florid features. "Guess that means we won't need to go through with phase two, huh? I was, you know, kinda . . . lookin' for'ard to it."

"Don't worry, Buster," Dan answered, speaking slowly as if to a child. "They are not going to pay. Not yet. All they're doing right now is jerking us around—playing for time while the cops try and identify us. That little operation in the coffee shop was only a warm-up. It isn't going to scare them enough to cough up ten million dollars, let alone twenty-five or fifty—"

"I know you have believed this all along, Dan," said Voss. "You said that Druperman would not pay the first time. You expect nothing from LVCA this time and even next time. *Aber* my letter and the video of the electrocution has made clear the consequences of not paying! How can you be sure they will not pay? How can they be so stupid not to pay when we have *proved* our power to hurt them? I am still hoping for not so much killing—"

"You're dreaming, my friend. Believe me, all we've done so far is catch their attention. Now we've got to light a big fire under their fat asses to persuade them to pay." Shiller lit a cigarillo as if to illustrate his point. "But you know, I'm ninety-nine percent sure even phase two isn't going to do the trick. So we'll just keep raising the ante until—"

"You cannot be so certain. They *have* agreed to our terms."

"Words, that's all. Look, smart guy, you may know all about computers and electronics, but I know people. And I know these guys, these casino executives. They're tough, hard-nosed sons of bitches. Especially Druperman. They didn't get to where they are by giving in to every schlub who tried to shake them down. But they *are* vulnerable. And we *will* win eventually. Okay?"

"*Ja,* okay, but should we not at least provide them with the instructions for depositing the money now? One never knows—"

"Of course we will, for Chrissake. But I guarantee they won't be depositing anything yet, no matter what they say. But, what the fuck, they'll have the deposit instructions for next time. In fact, let's do it right now. Let's call them. Jurgen, have you set up the phone relays?"

"*Natürlich.* You will please note that when I make a promise, I do it. I said I would make an untraceable telephone relay, and that precisely is what I have done. Even the telephone company could not have done this!" The little man was fairly bursting with pride. "I shall route the signal through several blind addresses on the Internet. You will be required to converse through the built-in microphone on one of my PCs. *Und* you will note that the signal is fully duplexed. Also I have used software that will make your voice—what is the word?—*indistinguishable.*"

By this time the sound of the freight train had faded away; only the steady hum of Interstate traffic relieved the silence that followed Voss's monologue. Malloy looked blankly at Jurgen, then at Shiller.

"What the bejaysus did 'e just say?" the big Irishman asked.

23 Frank Marshall always felt a little uncomfortable when duty forced him to visit the Clark County Coroner's Office. It wasn't so much the cadaverous tenants housed in the refrigerated drawers that disturbed him—he'd seen plenty of stiffs in his police career, usually at the worst possible time, right after they'd suffered their final indignities and before the undertakers had cleaned them up. What made the police officer uneasy was the sobering reminder of his own mortality: the fact that here was an enterprise dedicated to the absolute certainty of death, staffed by people who relied upon a constant supply of fresh corpses—whose ranks every human being, including the policeman himself, was someday guaranteed to join. Marshall avoided the place whenever possible.

But Frank Marshall was above all a professional. Despite his feelings toward his ex-partner, he was beginning to take a personal interest in this case. Which was why he found himself on a sunny Friday morning in the inner sanctum of Chief Medical Examiner Dr. Chester A. Pike.

"How's business, Doc?"

"Standing room only, Frank." The balding, heavyset ME shepherded his visitor to a battered leather chair and ensconced himself behind a scarred gunmetal gray desk. "We don't see you in here often. This is a rare pleasure."

"Not as rare as I'd like, to be perfectly candid. Nothing personal, Chester, but you know this place gives me the creeps."

The ME shrugged and grinned sympathetically. "I know that, Frank. As usual, we'll do our best to give you the revolving-door treatment."

"Thanks. What did you find out about our friend?"

"Interesting case. Definitely poison." Pike donned a pair of reading glasses and opened a file folder. "Barnaby Galt Leopold. Age fifty-one.

Three eighty-five South Alameda Drive, El Modena, California. Did you call the next of kin?"

"Uh-huh. Wife's flying in. In fact, she should be here anytime now."

"Well, she's in for a shock, Frank. You won't believe what killed this guy."

"You said poison."

"I know. But wait till you hear what *kind* of poison. I haven't come across it in twenty-five years of ordering tox screens. Are you ready for this?"

"Come on, Chester, don't keep me in suspense."

The doctor could not keep a straight face. "Spanish fly!" he chuckled. "Otherwise known as cantharidin. That's what killed your guy. There was enough of it in that sugar dispenser to snuff an army. He was a goner as soon as he ingested the stuff."

"You're kidding. I thought Spanish fly was an aphrodisiac."

"Me, too. So I did a little research. And guess what? The aphrodisiac thing is bullshit. An urban legend, like alligators in the sewer. I don't know how these stories get started, but this one's obviously been around for a while. Oddly enough, the only record I could find of Spanish fly poisoning anybody was a case that happened in London in the fifties. This British chemist, Arthur Ford, was convicted of manslaughter in the death of two of his female employees. Apparently he had heard about the aphrodisiac qualities of Spanish fly while he was in the British army. Then he discovered that cantharidin—technically, *cantharis vericatoria*—was the generic name for Spanish fly and that the stuff was actually available in his own shop. To make a long story short, Ford disguised it in candy, gave a piece to each of the women, and took one himself. I guess he was trying to get all three of them horny. Anyway, his plan backfired. The substance is an incredibly potent toxin. He survived somehow, but the two women died almost instantly."

"That's quite a story. Whoever dreamed up our little extortion must have done some heavy research themselves. Where would they have gotten the stuff?"

"Hospitals. Pharmaceutical companies. Medical supply houses. Drugstores—but you'd need a prescription."

"I scc. Is it traceable?"

"Difficult, if not impossible. I can generate a list of manufacturers and distributors, but I doubt if it will help. Meanwhile, here's a copy of my report."

"Thanks, Doc."

Back at the Southwest Area Command, Lieutenant Frank Marshall studied the coroner's formal report. In it the pathologist had chronicled a terrible litany of destruction: necrosis of the esophageal and gastric mucous membranes, intense congestion of blood in the genital and urinary organs, damaged cells in the renal tubules.

In plain language, Barney Leopold's internal organs had literally been burned away by the searing, blistering effects of the powerful poison.

24 Steve Forrester and Emmett Druperman sat in comfortable chairs at the oversize conference table in the Bridge. They rose to greet their scheduled visitors, LVMPD Lieutenant Frank Marshall and another, slightly older man.

Marshall said: "Mr. Druperman, I'd like to introduce Sergeant Morris Jaworski. He heads up our Forensics Division. Which includes profiling, electronics, and Crime Scene Investigation." Jaworski was a short, rotund man whose graying hair badly needed cutting. He wore scuffed mallwalkers, baggy gray trousers, and a tweed sports jacket bearing traces of fingerprint ink on the cuffs.

The scruffy sergeant shook hands with the casino executives. "Glad to meet you, Mr. Druperman. And it's good to see you again, Steve. How many years has it been?"

"Three years since I left the department, Moe."

"They still talk about you at the house. You and Frank were a hell of a team."

"The operative word is 'were,' " Marshall remarked acidly.

"Am I missing something here, fellas?" Jaworski asked innocently.

"Nothing important, Moe," said Forrester, glancing daggers at his ex-partner. "Maybe we should get down to business."

"Steve's right." Druperman looked at his watch and addressed the two law enforcement officers: "Gentlemen, I don't have a lot of time. Thank you both for your interest in our little problem. As we all know, these assholes have murdered one of our guests. All *I* want to know is, what is the police department going to do about it?"

"May I answer this one, Frank?" Sergeant Jaworski asked courteously. Marshall nodded, and Jaworski continued: "Sir, now that we've had a couple of days to analyze the data, I believe that we may be closing in on a solution to your 'little problem.'

"Our primary objective, of course, is to identify the extortionists, this 'Thanatos' group. The first and most obvious source of information about them is the letters they have sent. Despite their cleverness in avoiding fingerprints or other identifying marks on the paper, my people have still managed to infer a great deal. We know the type of computer that generated the letters and the type of printer that output them. Not greatly significant in and of itself, but in combination with other evidence, it's information that may secure a conviction later on. Of course, that doesn't help us right now. We need to find these people and stop them before anyone else gets hurt.

"What's far more interesting, and this could really lead somewhere, is the actual wording of the letters." Jaworski pulled photocopies of the extortion letters from his battered briefcase and spread them flat on the conference table. "Have you noticed how stiff and awkward the wording is? I'll give you a couple of examples." He picked up one of the copies. "Our writer talks about the 'stake,' presumably referring to money, when he means the 'stakes.' Instead of saying, 'What will happen is shown here on the videotape,' he writes, 'What will happen is on the videotape herewith shown.' The words are all there, but it's not the way you or I would phrase it. And this: rather than writing, 'There is no defense against us,' he twists it around to read, 'Against us there is no defense.' Nothing grammatically wrong, but it doesn't exactly roll off the tongue, does it? So what does this tell us about the writer? In our opinion, he is highly intelligent—but English is obviously not his first language. Here's another tipoff: on both envelopes, the label say, 'President of LVCA.' Standard American business English would be 'President *comma* LVCA.' He writes 'can not' as two words instead of one—something no computer spell-checker would ever catch. Anyway, the rather convoluted syntax, the insertion of adverb clauses in front of the verb, the placement of exclamation marks after imperative sentences—all this leads us to believe that this writer's native language is German." Jaworski consulted his notes. "Our linguistics people have also noted certain unusual adverbs that confirm this theory. 'Herewith' and 'therein' are rarely used in English, except perhaps in legal documents, yet their direct translations, *'hiermit'* and *'darein,'* are everyday words in German.

"Now for the signature. As we all know by now, Thanatos was the Greek god of death. This allusion reveals that our writer is well versed in the classics, but that's not all it tells us. Taken in combination with the tenor of the letters, our profiler believes that the writer is a small male with a massive superiority complex. He likens himself to a god. He uses expressions such as 'we have the knowledge and the power' and 'against us there is no defense.' Egomaniacs are usually male and often smaller than average in stature—just think of Napoleon!

"There is also some rather inconclusive evidence that the subject's sexual urges are . . . abnormal. We can infer with some certainty that he is not married. At least, not in the accepted sense."

Morris Jaworski paused momentarily to survey his audience. Forrester was fascinated by the policeman's discourse. Druperman appeared impressed. Only Marshall, who had heard it all before, looked bored. Jaworski continued, "Another thing the letters tell us: our subject is at least computer-literate, and most probably quite knowledgeable. For example, according to the second note, he has evidently secured Steve's cell-phone number—even though Frank has pointed out that it isn't listed. He could have got the number from one of your staff, except that I understand only a few of your more senior people know it. Is that correct, Steve?"

"Some key people have it for contacting me in emergencies. I doubt if any of them would have divulged it."

"So, most likely, he hacked his way into the Sprint database. Probable conclusion? He's a computer freak.

"And the writer is very likely living in this area. He knows about Steve. He knows of Mr. Druperman's position as president of the LVCA. And just logically, gentlemen, it would be extremely difficult for anyone to pull the strings in an extortion scheme like this from any distance.

"All right. With your permission, I'll summarize. We're looking for a physically small, very intelligent, and highly egocentric man, probably with a German accent. He is a computer expert and he's from this area. Of course, there are still many people who fit this profile, but the information does narrow our search parameters significantly."

"Do you think this man is acting alone?" Steve asked. "The letters keep saying 'we' and 'us.'"

"Good point, Steve. The simple answer is, it's highly unlikely he's running this scheme by himself. If he were, with his ego, he'd definitely be expressing himself in the first-person singular. And quite frankly, it's just too big an operation for one man to handle. Somebody had to prepare the videotapes, somebody had to obtain the cantharidin and slip it into the sugar . . . somebody had to plan this whole thing. No, it's almost certainly not the work of just one individual. We believe Thanatos—I guess that's what we'll call them—is a gang.

"One of the gang members had to have been very familiar with the operations of this hotel in order to have successfully slipped the first package into Mr. Druperman's mailbox without being spotted. This suggests the possibility of his being a Galaxy employee. We've already run the list that Steve gave us through the NCIC computer in Washington, but so far there just isn't anybody on your staff who fits the profile—*and* who has access to the mailroom. It's another reason to believe we're dealing with more than one subject here.

"Anyway, gentlemen, that's what the letters tell us. Now—and this may surprise you—the other potential source of information about Thanatos is the movie clips they included. We can tell that they weren't recorded off the air or from cable TV. Which means they must have been copied from videotapes." The police scientist leaned back in his chair. "Frank is coordinating this aspect of the investigation."

"It's going to take a lot of shoe leather, but we're putting three teams on it, starting today," said Marshall. "The first clip was from the movie *Seven* with Morgan Freeman and Brad Pitt. The second one turns out to be from *Extreme Measures.* Starring Gene Hackman and Hugh Grant, among others. But again, it doesn't really matter what the movies are about or who's in them. The point is, we know the titles, so we can canvass video-rental stores in the metro area to find out who's taken out these two specific movies over the past month or so. As Moe said, Thanatos had to have rented or purchased originals to make the copies from. Neither one of the movies is a new release, so that should make for a shorter list.

"Once we've got this information, we'll cross-match it with Steve's list of possibles among Galaxy employees. Finally we'll check the results of that search with the NCIC database again and see what shakes loose this time."

Morris Jaworski picked up the discourse again. "Meanwhile, we've asked local law enforcement departments from San Francisco to Phoenix to check pharmaceutical suppliers and see if we can nail down who purchased the cantharidin. Unfortunately, it's a needle-in-a-haystack situation, and there's not much chance of a quick breakthrough there.

"The last thing I wanted to mention is the cell phone. We assume from the letter that Thanatos has obtained Mr. Forrester's number. Well, working with the phone companies, our technicians can easily discover the phone number that the subject is dialing from—unless he routes his calls through some kind of electronic relay. If he calls you over regular landlines, Centel can tell us precisely where he's phoning from. If he's using a cellular unit, it's trickier but still doable. Every cell phone has a built-in electronic MIN—a mobile identification number—so the Sprint people can provide us with the name and address of the person to whom the unit is registered. Unless they're using a purchased phone card, in which case we're out of luck."

Druperman rose from his chair and began to pace. "Gentlemen, this is all highly fascinating. But let's get back to reality. What do we do right now?"

"Step one, I suggest we put a reverse trace on Mr. Forrester's cell phone," said Jaworski. "I'll have our technicians contact the Sprint computer switch. They can monitor the line and get us the originating number that Thanatos is calling from. Step two, in case they call from a wireline, we'll have Centel activate a central office trace and use *their* surveillance software to bridge us in."

"You do that," Emmett said impatiently. "But you haven't answered my question. I'm asking, what do we do about the money? What do we say when they call? Why did we even humor these killers by running that ad and agreeing to their cockamamy terms?"

"Mostly to buy ourselves some time," Frank Marshall reminded the CEO. "The longer we have to work the case, the more likely we are to catch the perps."

"Good," said Druperman, "because I spoke to some key guys in the association and they backed my position a hundred percent. We're not paying, and that's it. So you people are gonna have to work around the money thing."

Marshall nodded his head. "I hear you loud and clear, Mr. Druperman, and I agree with your decision. We always discourage payments to kidnappers and extortionists. We don't tell *them* that, of course. We need to keep their hopes alive while we work.

"And that's where you come in, sir. Please don't let them know you don't intend to pay. I suggest that when they call, you try to negotiate their price down. Offer five million instead of ten. If that doesn't work, play for time. See if you can get us a week, two weeks, or even more. I can practically guarantee that if you swing that for us, we'll nip this little operation in the bud before anybody else gets hurt."

Druperman winced as one of his hemorrhoids flared up, a reaction Marshall misread as skepticism.

"Don't get me wrong here, Mr. Druperman—I don't mean to sound patronizing. I'm sure you don't need negotiating lessons from the police department."

"It's not that," said the CEO. "You guys are the experts, and I'll take your advice. Now if there's nothing else . . .?"

"I assume we have the Galaxy's permission to tap Mr. Forrester's cell phone. . . ."

Steve nodded, and the two police officers left the Bridge.

Still in some discomfort, Druperman walked bandy-legged over to his desk, indicating that the meeting was over. "Okay, Steve," he said. "If they're gonna call me on your phone, I'll need the goddamn thing handy."

"I'll leave it with you, Emmett," said Forrester, taking it out of his pocket and handing it to his boss. "Oh, and one more thing." He leaned over Druperman's massive mahogany desktop and rotated the speakerphone so the microphone side was facing him.

"What are you—?"

Forrester raised a finger to his lips, then spoke loudly into the speakerphone: "Did you get all that, Edith?"

There was no response, but after a moment a distinct click could be heard.

Druperman looked puzzled. "What was that all about?" he asked.

"Nothing important, Emmett. Just tying up a few loose ends."

For a moment, the suggestion of a twinkle relieved the extreme droopiness of the CEO's features. Then another wave of hemorrhoidal pain washed it away.

A crimson-faced Edith Frick refused to meet Steve Forrester's eyes as he stood over her desk in Emmett Druperman's outer office.

Forrester addressed her pleasantly. "Hello, Edith."

"H-hello, Mr. Forrester."

"I wonder if you could help me with something, Edith. You wouldn't by any chance know how rumors about that poisoning got started—even before it happened, now, would you?"

"I-I'm sure I don't know. . . ."

"I'm sure you don't, either, Edith." Forrester said sympathetically, maintaining a poker face with some difficulty. "But just in case anybody's intercom *accidentally* happens to get turned on during any more of Mr. Druperman's private meetings, I'm having certain electronic equipment installed in his office. It'll tell us who's listening so we can have criminal charges brought against them for . . . *wiretapping* and *invasion of privacy.*"

"I-I don't think that will be n-necessary, Mr. Forrester," Edith Frick responded in a shaky voice. Eyes downcast, she pretended to be busy with the papers on her desk.

"Well, golly, Edith, that *is* a comfort." By this time, Steve was fairly bursting inside and was forced to beat a hasty retreat before he exploded into laughter.

The call came sooner than anyone expected.

Alone in his office, less than an hour after the others had left, Emmett Druperman picked up Forrester's cell phone and flipped it open. "Hello."

"Druperman?" It was an echoey voice, strangely high-pitched.

"Yes. Who's speaking?"

A distinct pause. "This is Thanatos. Did you enjoy my sneak previews?"

"You murdering bastard!" Emmett did not need to fake the anger; he merely augmented and intensified what he already felt. It added credibility to his negotiating position. Keeping opponents off guard had always been the cornerstone of his bargaining technique. Whether he was stonewalling unions, haggling with entertainers, or buying time from extortionists, he firmly believed that the best defense was a good offense. There'd be no groveling to these scum. "You killed that man in the coffee shop!"

There was another noticeable pause before the mechanical voice answered. "Fucking right, Mister Cee-Ee-Oh. Want to find out who's next?"

"Get to the point, sicko."

Pause. "I'll ignore that remark, Druperman. Like the letter said, you will transfer ten million dollars to the following account—"

"Now listen, you greedy son of a bitch." Two miles away, in a windowless room at the Sprint switching center, the LVMPD technician winced and adjusted her headphones. "There's no fucking way the association's gonna authorize that size of . . . payment. *However*—I might be able to convince them to kick in something, you know, just to avoid any future incidents and get you off our back. Would you be willing to settle for a smaller amount? How about five million?"

Pause. "Absolutely not. The ten million is nonnegotiable. Wire the money to the following numbered account."

"Wait a minute."

Pause. "Don't interrupt again, Emmett, or I'll hang up and you'll be sorry. Be a good boy and wire the money to the Banco Internacional de Panamá in Panama City, account number two-three-six-sev—"

"Whoa—go slower; I'm trying to write this down."

Pause. "Don't bother. I'm sure the cops are taping the conversation. Hey, fellas, how are you? How's the trace going?" The caller laughed, an odd squawky sound, and repeated the account number. There was another noise in the background: some kind of interference, the police technician thought. She'd be able to check it later on the tapes. "You have until Monday at five P.M. If we haven't received confirmation from the bank by then—"

"Wait a minute. Today's Friday. You're only giving us three days, and there's a weekend in there, for Chrissake. We'll need at least . . . two weeks to get the money together."

Pause. "Bullshit. Just pass the hat 'round to your pals in the casino association. They keep more than that in their fucking petty-cash drawers."

"Give us a week, anyway." The background noise on the line became louder.

Pause. "Monday. Ten million. That's final." Pause. "This will be our last voice communication with you."

There was a click, and the strange voice was replaced by a hollow silence.

"**Christ,** Jurgen, I could hardly hear myself think over the racket from that goddamn train," said Dan Shiller to his associate, who was busy unplugging the microphone from the back of the PC. "I wonder if they heard it at the other end."

"Most probably they could not hear it. Anyway, it does not matter. There is absolutely no way to trace the call." Voss tapped out a command on the keyboard, then pushed two keys simultaneously and the screen went blank. "Your conversation was routed through four independent Internet servers on four continents. And a special voice filter has disguised completely your identity. Even with the most sophisticated equipment available, they will never be able to generate a usable voiceprint."

"So now we wait, huh?" said Buster Malloy.

"Not for long, Buster," said Shiller emotionlessly. "I guarantee you'll be back in action in three days."

Okay, Christie," said police scientist Morris Jaworski to his young audio technician. "What do you make of it?"

"I don't know, Sergeant," she replied, removing her headphones. "They used some kind of filtering device or digital signal processor. No way a voiceprint analysis is going to help us here. I can check out that background noise, though. Maybe it'll tell us something."

"What about the trace, David?" Jaworski asked another technician.

"Well, the call didn't come from any cell phone—and it didn't originate from any wireline, either."

"So where the hell did it come from? Outer space?"

"Close, Sarge. The call originated in cyberspace."

"You mean the Internet?"

"Yep."

"Can it be traced back to the source?"

"I doubt it. You know that pause just before the guy spoke every time? I'm pretty sure that was lag."

"Lag?"

"You know, the time it takes a signal to travel to the satellite and back. Probably bounced up and down three or four times, if they routed the call through a number of Internet servers. It's like when they're talking to somebody across the world on TV—that's only one relay, but even then you get a noticeable pause. The speed of light ain't all *that* fast, Sarge."

25 LVMPD Detective Carl "Big Swede" Hansen casually surveyed the new-release shelves at the VegasVideo store in the seedy strip mall. At the counter his partner, Len Traver, listened with growing impatience as the teenage clerk explained once again why he couldn't provide the information the two cops wanted.

"Like I said, mister, if you give me a name or a membership number, I can enter it in the computer and tell you right away if that person's ever rented those movies," said the clerk, a long-haired beanpole with a severe case of adolescent acne. "Or I can print out separate lists of who's rented each movie. But you'd have to correlate the lists yourself."

"How long would these lists be?"

"Hey, man, a popular movie like *Seven,* we'd have maybe fifty copies on the shelf to start with. And each copy would be rented out, you know, like about a hundred times."

"Jesus Christ, that's five thousand names," Detective Traver said glumly. Then he brightened, remembering the suggestion Frank Marshall had given them before they left. "How about just the past month? Can you narrow the list down to customers who have taken out the movie over the past month only?"

"I don't think so. Lemme check." The kid pecked on his computer keyboard while the policeman drummed his fingers impatiently on the counter. "Nah. There's no field to isolate rentals by date. Maybe you better talk to head office."

"Hey, Swede, come here a minute," Traver called to his partner. "We got problems."

Hansen ambled over with a movie in his hand. "Look what I found, Len. I didn't know it was in the stores yet. Ingrid's been dyin' to see this—"

"Never mind that," his partner returned testily. "This guy says the best they can do is give us everybody who's ever rented the movies—on separate lists. You know, thousands and thousands of names. He says they can't isolate them by date. And this is only one store. You know how many freakin' video outlets there are in Vegas?"

It was almost midnight at the Las Vegas Metropolitan Police Department on Spring Mountain Road.

By the time Morris Jaworski had listened to the Druperman tape for the thirtieth time, every word was burned into his brain. Ensconced in the audio room with a group of technicians and specialists, the police scientist was at once pleased and frustrated—pleased because their profiler had confirmed that the caller was definitely *not* the writer of the letters, thus validating their earlier assumption that Thanatos was made up of at least two people; frustrated because all attempts to trace the call had so far met with failure.

Jaworski tossed his Styrofoam cup into the trash basket, atop the remnants of the pizza that the department had provided by way of compensation for the enforced overtime. "Let's recap what we know," he said, not bothering to conceal his tiredness from the others. It had been a long day. "Christie, why don't you start?"

The young audio technician referred to her notes. "There isn't much on the graphs we can use to identify the speaker. Their filtering device was quite efficient. As David said, the pauses before each reply represent the time their signal took to reach us through a number of relays.

"However, we do know one thing for certain: the caller is definitely a native U.S. English speaker. His use of American colloquialisms and obscenities proves that beyond a doubt.

"Also, there's that extraneous noise on the tape, just at the end. It could be RF interference—or it could be something else. I'll scope it out more thoroughly tomorrow, but right now I'm bushed, Sergeant." She closed her notebook and looked up at Jaworski.

"I understand, Christie, and thanks; we won't be here much longer. Warren, how about the profile on our caller?"

"We faxed a transcript of the conversation earlier this evening to Lyman Schiff, the dialect specialist at UNLV. Since there was no recognizable speech to actually listen to, Dr. Schiff said a printout would do. He just got back to me. I'm sure none of us wants to hear the rationale for his conclusions at this late hour?" Warren looked up at Jaworski, who shook his head. "Good. I'll cut to the chase. The subject is a male in his forties or fifties, reasonably well educated, probably from the Midwest originally. He appears to be a good judge of character and may well be some kind of professional scam artist. The surprising thing about the doctor's report is that he doesn't believe the man is a killer." The specialist paused. "But Lyman says this is only a preliminary report and he'll analyze the transcript more closely tomorrow. Considering the lateness of the hour and the short notice, this is all he can give us for now."

Jaworski did not appear impressed. "Except for the part about the subject's not being a killer, I don't think there's much in Schiff's report we couldn't have figured out for ourselves. But . . . it's a start." He yawned and stretched. "Okay, David, your turn. Let's hear the bad news from the trace team one more time."

A bespectacled technician wiped his glasses and shuffled to his feet. "Bad news is right," he reported. "All we know is that the call was routed to the Sprint switch off the Internet. We've traced it back to AOL, but that's as far as we can get. Beyond that, it could have come from anywhere in the world—from Australia or from the next room; we just don't know. And, of course, you can't get a phone dump from these Internet service providers, because they don't keep records."

"That's too bad, David. But . . . now that we know how they did it, would we have more success tracing the next call—if there is one?"

"I doubt it, Sarge. These dudes are sharp. They go to incredible lengths to cover their tracks."

A momentary silence enveloped the room. Sergeant Morris Jaworski looked around at the others, stood up, and reached for his jacket. "All right, everybody, I guess that's it for tonight. Let's go home and get some sleep. It's going to be a busy weekend."

26 **Jack and Sheila Wilson** had not let the gym bag out of their sight since they boarded America West Flight 1787, nonstop from SeaTac Airport to Las Vegas.

Right now it was nestled under Jack's feet, next to the small overnight bag they were sharing. The moment of truth was approaching; win or lose, they'd be leaving Las Vegas in the morning. He touched his waist for the hundredth time. The money belt with the reserve fund was still there, under his shirt. They had agreed to preserve a tenth of the total amount he'd "expropriated." God-forbid money, Jack called it.

Wilson squeezed his wife's hand. "Nervous?" he asked.

"Petrified," she replied, returning the pressure. "But excited. Look, Jack, I know what I said earlier. It's just that we've been so *honest* all our lives. I never thought we'd ever get involved in . . . anything like this. And in a way, I never believed it was actually going to happen. But we're in it now. And I guess whatever happens, you know, we're in it together."

He leaned over and kissed her cheek just as the seat-belt lights flashed on. The two-hour flight had passed in what seemed like minutes.

"In preparation for our landing at Las Vegas's McCarran Airport," the flight attendant droned mechanically over the speakers, "we ask you to please make sure that your seat belts are securely fastened and that your tray tables and seat backs are returned to their upright and locked positions. All carry-on baggage should be stowed under the seat in front of you or in the overhead bins. And thank you for choosing America West."

They landed just as dusk was settling over the airport. The heat still shimmered on the desert floor, and the mountains that ringed Las Vegas took on a blue, then a purple hue as the evening light became increasingly diffuse. With no checked baggage to collect, the Wilsons were able to walk directly out of the airport and hail the first cab in line. The illuminated triangular billboard on the vehicle's roof advertised Tony Francisco at the Galaxy and exhorted readers to LIVE THE LEGEND. They settled back in the Whittlesea cab for the short ride to the Strip. Scrubby vacant lots riddled with billboards gave way to seedy motels, mini-malls, and apartment blocks. Then suddenly they were in another world. Confronted with the brilliance of the Strip, nature's showy display faded behind the lights of the Tropicana, the Roman Palladium, the Flamingo, the Galaxy, and all the other brightly lit domains of decadence.

"Where are you folks from?" the driver asked.

Sheila answered, "We're from Red—"

"Tacoma," interrupted Wilson, nudging his wife gently. With a good-natured grin, he cupped his hand around her ear and whispered, "If we're going to be 'Fred and Dorothy Langdon from Tacoma,' we might as well start now."

She smiled self-consciously and whispered back, "Sorry—*Fred*, I forgot."

Within a few minutes their driver turned left off Las Vegas Boulevard and pulled up under the giant cantilevered space wheel of the Galaxy Hotel and Casino.

Jack tipped the Latino cabdriver ten dollars and the Klingon doorman another five. "After all," he murmured to his wife, "those Langdons can afford it."

Jack Wilson was a native Washingtonian, born and raised within the salt smell of Puget Sound. At the age of forty-five, he was a cut below average in height, a pleasant, prematurely balding man who smiled easily and generally enjoyed life. Somewhat atypically, he was still happily married to his high-school sweetheart, Sheila. They had a son and a daughter, both now in their late teens. The kids had turned out well—there had never been a problem with drugs or alcohol or any of the other temptations to which today's young people were exposed. For which Wilson gave full credit to Sheila's firm hand.

Sheila was petite, dark-haired, and vivacious—and *totally straight,* as the kids were fond of pointing out with comic exasperation. She had planted the seeds of honesty and integrity deep into their consciousness at an early age and tolerated no deviation from the high standards of conduct that she set for her family and for herself.

Which is why Jack Wilson had expected far more resistance from her when he proposed the Plan.

"My name is Fred Langdon," said Jack Wilson. "I believe you have a room for us."

"Yes, Mr. Langdon," replied the female Galaxy desk clerk, tapping on her computer. She wore a uniform resembling that of a Romulan—or was it a Vulcan? Wilson would not have been overly surprised had Mr. Spock himself beamed down then and there to offer help with their bag. "Have you stayed with us before?"

"Ah, no—actually, we haven't." That much was true; they usually stayed at the Roman Palladium. No one knew them here, which was one reason the Wilsons, alias the Langdons, had selected the Galaxy for their desperate gamble. The other reason, equally crucial to their plan, was the Galaxy's no-limit betting policy.

"I have you down for one night in a nonsmoking room with a king-size bed. Will that be satisfactory?"

"Perfect."

"And how will you be paying, sir—cash or credit card?"

"Cash. I'll pay now."

"Thank you, sir." She tapped on her keyboard. "With tax, it comes to one eighty-nine. However, I will need your credit card on file for incidentals."

Wilson had foreseen this detail and confidently handed her a very real-looking but totally counterfeit gold American Express card. Along with a fake driver's license and Social Security card, it had been the last of his purchases for the Plan.

Jack remembered his delight when he picked up the documents and the credit card. The old counterfeiter was a genius; his work had been perfect. *And the proof of the pudding is in the eating,* Wilson thought as the Galaxy's Vulcan desk clerk handed the bogus Amex card back without a trace of suspicion. He had no intention of using the card for purchases; its sole purpose was to facilitate checking in and later to confirm his cover identity.

"Do you need any help with your luggage, folks?" the clerk asked.

Jack tightened his grip on the gym bag. "No, we can take it from here."

"Enjoy your stay with us, Mr. and Mrs. Langdon."

In the hotel room, Sheila tried to hide her nervousness. She made a great production of unpacking and arranging the contents of their single overnight bag. Her clothes went in one drawer, his in another. Nightgown and pajamas were laid out neatly on the bed; toothbrushes, toothpaste, cosmetics, and shaving kit were aligned symmetrically on the bathroom vanity.

She busied herself opening the curtains. She turned the TV on and off and adjusted the table lamps. She fussed and fidgeted, all the while maintaining a bright, nervous stream of chatter: "Look at the view, Jack. You can see the whole Strip. I just love this wallpaper, don't you? I'll hang our coats up in the closet. Honestly, they give you so much space in these rooms. Do you think anybody actually uses all these drawers? Have you got the extra room key in your pocket? Can we—"

Finally, Wilson could take no more. Putting his left arm around his wife's shoulders, he held the tip of his right index finger to her lips. "Hey, relax, girl. Take a deep breath. *It's going to be all right.*"

"Oh God, Jack, we're really going to do it, aren't we? I'm *scared.*"

"There's nothing to be scared of. What's the worst that can happen? Even if we lose, we've still got the reserve." They had set aside part of the money in the event that their big gamble lost. It was only a fraction, about 10 percent of the amount he intended to bet, but it was enough to give them a bare-bones fresh start.

"You could be arrested for . . . embezzlement."

"You're having doubts again, Sheila. Look, I've covered my tracks pretty thoroughly. And even if they do catch me, they probably won't press charges. Can you imagine how incompetent that would make Defcon look in the eyes of the Matsutachi people?"

"I still can't help feeling guilty about what we've done."

"I sure as hell don't. And you shouldn't, either. Technically, I may have committed a crime. But morally . . . let's face it, they reneged on their promise to me. We're only collecting on that promise."

The whole sordid affair had angered and embittered Jack Wilson.

He saw it in black and white, his first inkling of the shocking news that was to destroy his career, spread over three full columns in the Sunday financial section of the Seattle Post-Intelligencer. It had knocked the wind out of Jack Wilson like a blow to the solar plexus.

MATSUTACHI BUYS CONTROL OF DEFCON

TOKYO, January 6—Electronics giant Matsutachi Electric Company of Japan has purchased a controlling interest in Defcon Industries Incorporated, America's sixth-largest defense contractor.

Kenzo Onishi, chief executive officer of Matsutachi, made the announcement today at a Tokyo press conference. Defcon chairman and principal class A shareholder William B. Swinden confirmed the buyout in a simultaneous press release from his company's headquarters in Everett, Washington. Swinden said the sale will bring "a vital new competitive edge" to Defcon, adding that the transaction had been approved by U.S. regulatory agencies in return for "significant bilateral trade concessions" by Japan.

Financial details of the multibillion-dollar transaction were not released, but industry analysts believe . . .

That was his company they were writing about! The company he had joined twenty years ago and helped build with his blood and sweat! How could he not have known? How could those bastards not have told him? It wasn't like Swinden to keep him in the dark. Or was it? He thought back to those mysterious recent occasions when his inadvertent interruptions of Swinden's earnest conversations with Defcon president Fred Harris and executive vice president Harvey Feldman had been met with brief, embarrassed silences. He hadn't attached much importance to the incidents at the time. Then there were those unexplained trips Swinden had made to Japan. It had been happening right under his nose. He should have seen it coming. What an idiot he'd been!

Jack read the article a second time, and a third. At the end of the article, a footnote directed him to the newspaper's editorial pages.

Here the Post-Intelligencer *pulled no punches. In a stinging condemnation of the foreign buyout, the newspaper mirrored his own rising anger:*

THE SELLING OF AMERICA

The consumer electronics business was the thin edge of the wedge. Then came the invasion of our automobile industry. Yesterday's announcement by Matsutachi Electric Company of its purchase of Defcon Industries Incorporated, a leading U.S. defense contractor, represents an alarming assault on one of the last bastions of American entrepreneurship by Japanese multinationals.

By relinquishing de facto control of even a small segment of this sensitive industry to foreign interests, no matter how well intentioned, we are effectively mortgaging our collective birthrights. Furthermore, in sanctioning this encroachment, the federal government is risking an increased imbalance in the balance of economic power. . . .

At eight o'clock that Monday morning, Wilson had intercepted Swinden in the executive parking garage beneath the Defcon One building.

"Got a minute, Bill?"

"Sure, Jack. You're in early."

"Obviously not early enough. I guess I missed the meeting where you advised your key people about this . . . Japanese takeover."

The CEO ignored the sarcasm. "Let's walk up together."

"Right. Well, are you going to explain why I wasn't told about this Matsutachi thing? Or do I just wait for another press conference and read about it in the paper?"

"Sorry, Jack, honestly. It was a tough call." They reached Swinden's office, and he unlocked the massive oak door. "In the final analysis, we decided we couldn't risk a leak. You know what that would have done to share prices."

"You couldn't risk a leak? Goddamn it, Bill!" Wilson followed Swinden inside, controlling his temper with difficulty. "If you couldn't trust my discretion after all these years—"

"Really, it was nothing personal, Jack. The only people besides myself who knew about the buyout were the lawyers and, ah, the Commerce Department

people. Plus Fred and Harvey, of course." Between them, Swinden, Harris, and Feldman controlled over 50 percent of Defcon's preferred stock.

Jack's eyes narrowed. *"What about the CFO position?"* Based on Swinden's verbal assurances, he had assumed that the recently vacated post of chief financial officer was to be his. With a salary of five hundred thousand and stock options worth over a million.

The chairman hesitated. *"Ah, I'm afraid there's been a slight . . . reorientation in that area—pardon the pun."* Wilson was definitely not amused. *"You know how the Japanese prefer to import their own people for these top jobs, especially in sensitive areas like finance—"*

"This is my life we're talking about here, Bill! This is twenty years of helping you build this company from a hole in the wall to number six in the business! I thought I had your word—"

"We were, ah, in an awkward position—"

"Just tell me this, Bill. Am I out?"

"Of course not. As far as I'm concerned, you're still a key player on the team." The CEO forced a thin, insincere smile. He turned away for a moment to raise the blinds on the huge picture window that overlooked the plant, and added something which Wilson didn't quite catch.

"What did you say, Bill?"

"Hmmm?"

"I didn't quite hear that."

"Oh, I just said, 'At least as long as I'm around.' "

Jack Wilson leaned over his boss's desk and stared directly at him. *"At least as long as you're around? I see. And precisely how long will that be?"*

Bill Swinden avoided eye contact, and Jack knew. Right then and there, he knew that it was over. *"I've signed an eighteen-month contract with Matsutachi,"* said Swinden lightly. *"To smooth out the transition. After that, who knows?"*

Well, I guess I do now, *thought Wilson.* You deceptive bastard, you've negotiated yourself a sweet little deal with your new masters—and totally abandoned the people who helped you on the way up. Your word isn't worth shit. You'll serve a year and a half of well-paid servitude, then you'll get that megabuck golden handshake. You've taken care of number one quite handsomely. But where does that leave me? I'll be forty-seven years old with two kids in college, nothing in the bank, and more than likely no job.

The Plan had occurred to Jack Wilson during their last trip to Vegas. He and Sheila had flown in for the weekend, right after the bad news about Defcon. They needed to get away and forget their worries about his future, at least for a couple of days. Wilson was playing at a twenty-five-dollar-minimum craps table in the Roman Palladium and had engaged the floorman in idle conversation during a lull in the activity.

"That was some hot streak huh?" The previous player had held the dice for close to twenty minutes before he finally "sevened out." Like the majority of crapshooters, the man had been playing the pass line, betting that the first number he rolled would repeat before a seven came up.

"Yeah, he was hot, Mr. W. And he walked away a winner. Most of 'em don't."

"I know. They get greedy and they give it all back."

"And then some. How do you think we pay for all these lights?"

Wilson chuckled. "Losers are what keep you guys in business."

"True. But we let just enough folks win to keep 'em coming back. Yesterday we gave away two hundred large to a guy from Philly."

"Jesus, you mean he won two hundred thousand dollars? How much was he betting?"

"Well, the limit here is five thousand on any line bet."

"That's gotta be about the highest on the Strip, huh?"

"Just about. Mind you, there are some casinos that'll let you bet any amount you want."

Something clicked in Wilson's mind. Any amount you want.

"No kidding. Ah, which casinos are we talking about here?"

"Well . . . there's Binion's Horseshoe Club downtown. And the Galaxy right here on the Strip." Wilson had never visited either establishment. "I hear the Galaxy faded half a million dollars on one pass for some Arab king last year." The floorman paused. "Don't tell me you've got that kind of money burning a hole in your pocket, Mr. W!"

Wilson thought for a moment.

"Not yet," he replied. "Not quite yet."

Convincing Sheila was the hardest part of the Plan.

"Honey, are you asleep?"

She snuggled closer to him. "That depends. What did you have in mind?"

"Not that." He smiled. "Not right now, anyway. I wanted to talk to you about the work thing. What if I told you I had a way for us to come out of this mess with all the money we'd ever need for the rest of our lives?"

"I'd listen!"

"So listen. But you've got to promise to hear me out, okay? No matter how crazy it sounds, just hear me out." She nodded, frowning slightly, and he paused to organize his thoughts. "How can I explain this? Okay. You re-call that movie we watched on TV the other night? Going in Style? *About the three old guys who rob the bank. George Burns was in it. And Art Carney. And who was the other one . . . ?*

"Lee Strasberg."

"Right. Lee Strasberg. He dies after the robbery. The other two take some of the money and fly to Vegas and win a fortune at craps."

"I remember you laughed and said you wished it were that easy." She sat bolt upright in bed and looked wonderingly at her husband. "Jack, you're not planning to rob a bank?"

"Not exactly. But what if I . . . in effect . . . borrowed *some money from the company? Then I doubled it at craps, kept the winnings, and* returned *the original amount? They'd never know."*

"But wouldn't that be . . . embezzlement?"

"Not really. Not if I paid it back."

"That's fine, but what if you lose?"

"The way I figure it, even if we do lose, we've still got about a ninety-five percent chance of getting away with it." As a certified public account-ant, Jack was on familiar statistical ground now as he explained the odds. "First, we've got close to a fifty percent chance of winning immediately, in which case I return the money I 'borrowed' and all our problems are solved.

"Second, if we don't win, I calculate the chances of the auditors spot-ting the discrepancy and linking it to me are about the same: fifty percent. Fifty percent of fifty percent leaves about a twenty-five percent downside risk. Which is the same as seventy-five percent in our favor.

"And we wouldn't bet all *the money. We'd hold back a reserve to tide us over in case we did lose.*

"Third, if *we lose and* if *I get caught, what are the chances they'll prosecute? One in five? Big corporations avoid publicity about these*

matters like the plague. It makes them look incompetent. Twenty-five per-cent divided by five works out to maybe a five percent element of risk."

Sheila was dubious. "How do you intend to double the money? Most of the time you play craps, you lose."

"I know. But that's because I make a lot of bets. And every time I make a bet, the house edge gets bigger. This time, I intend to make one bet, and only one bet, at the most favorable odds they offer."

"I don't understand."

"Okay, honey, let me explain. Suppose the house advantage is one per-cent. And suppose every bet I make carries an even-money payoff, like the pass line with no odds. If I start with, say, a hundred dollars and bet it a dollar at a time, reinvesting the winning bets, on average I'd win ninety-nine dollars and lose a hundred and one. By reinvesting, I'd actually be putting two hundred dollars into play . . . and wind up losing two dollars, which is one percent of the money I'd bet. If I kept playing, I'd lose on av-erage one percent on every sequence of bets, and eventually I'd lose it all. Or just not be left with enough to cover the table minimum." He paused. "Now, supposing I took that same hundred dollars and bet it all just once. The odds against me would be only one percent. In other words, forty-nine and a half percent of the time, I'd win; fifty and a half percent of the time, I'd lose. That's what I meant when I said we'd have close to a fifty percent chance of winning."

"It's still a bit confusing. You know I've got no head for numbers." *Sheila tried to absorb her husband's logic. "What you're saying is that the more you play, the less chance you have of winning."*

"Right. And the less you play, the better your chances."

"How would you get the money out of the company?"

"I'd submit dummy invoices and pay them to ourselves."

"You could do that?"

"Easily. Don't forget, I've been with Defcon for twenty years and I know the accounting system inside out . . . mainly because I designed it."

"How much would you . . . take?"

He told her, and she gasped. "You can't be serious."

"I am. Dead serious."

"I don't know, Jack. All our lives we've been honest—"

"And look where it's got us."

"We don't know for sure you'll lose the job. Maybe—"

"There are no maybes. Swinden as good as told me in his office."

"Oh, Jack, it's scary. This just isn't like you."

"I know. But I've done a lot of thinking lately."

"What about the kids? All their lives I've tried to teach them honesty. How do we tell them?"

"How do we tell them we can't afford to pay for their college tuition anymore? How do we tell them their parents are broke? They don't need to know what we've done."

"There must be another way."

"Sure. We can scrimp and get by somehow. Maybe I could get part-time work doing people's books. You'd probably have to get a job to help out. There wouldn't be any more company car. We'd have to give up the house—there's still ten years left on the mortgage. Not to mention the taxes and insurance. And forget about the charge accounts at Neiman's and Sears. We'd be Kmart shoppers."

Sheila felt herself weakening, falling into her husband's mind-set. *"Maybe you could get another job in the industry—"*

"We've already talked about that. At my age I've got about as much chance of landing an equivalent position as a snowball in hell. Come on, babe, what have we got to lose? There's only one chance in twenty that we'll (a) lose, (b) get caught, and (c) get prosecuted. It's still a gamble, but the odds are way better than just waiting for the ax to fall at Defcon."

She was silent, her brow knotted in indecision. *"Let me think about it."*

Neither of the Wilsons got much sleep that night.

The next morning over coffee, Sheila said: *"I'm getting goose pimples just thinking about it. But those corporate cannibals really owe you. Let's just* do *it."*

For Sheila Wilson, it was her husband's remark about shopping at Kmart that finally tipped the scales in favor of the Plan.

In the hotel room, Sheila appeared thoughtful. "Jack, since we've gone to all this trouble, why don't we just . . ."

"Just what, babe?"

She hesitated, unsure of the morality of what she was about to propose. Then she plunged ahead. "I mean, now that we're criminals anyway, why don't we just *keep* the money? Why gamble it?"

"We've talked about that."

"I know, but—"

"Look, Sheila, I don't *want* us to be criminals. I don't want us to be forever looking over our shoulder. I want us at least to have a fair shot at replacing the money. That way I can thumb my nose at Matsutachi and Defcon and Swinden and his cronies with a clear conscience."

"I suppose you're right."

"I know I am. Besides, I'm kinda looking forward to our big gamble. Can you imagine the rush when we win!"

"*If* we win."

"George Burns and Art Carney did it. And they started out with a lot less cash than us."

She perked up. "And they didn't have *me* coaching them."

"That's the spirit." He hugged her.

"You know, I'm amazed that we could fit all that cash into one gym bag. Maybe we should buy another one to take our winnings home in."

"If—or should I say, *when*—the Plan succeeds, we'll buy a whole new set of Gucci luggage. And we won't even ask the price." Jack Wilson held his wife a little tighter. "Hey, babe, I've got an idea," he said. "Let's go downstairs and hit the crap tables."

Just as the Wilsons stepped off the elevator at the casino level, the Galaxy's star attraction, the giant Saturn rocket, embarked on its hourly spectacular. A floor-shaking rumble emanated from powerful hidden speakers as a disembodied voice deeper than that of James Earl Jones counted down the seconds. ". . . T minus three seconds . . . two . . . one . . . we have ignition!" Brilliant red, orange, and yellow fire spewed from the mighty exhaust manifolds in holographic splendor as the rocket actually appeared to lift off, rising higher and higher in the great atrium. Realistic plumes of liquid oxygen blended with swirling clouds of simulated exhaust at the base of the rocket while the thunderous sound effects peaked to a mighty crescendo.

The fiery exhaust died away, the sound faded, and the smoke cleared. The deep voice continued: "The Galaxy welcomes you to the future—the future of mankind, the future of entertainment. We hope you enjoy your visit, and we invite you to explore with us the wonders of the universe at our Final Frontier theme area, open daily from eight A.M. to midnight. And may Lady Luck smile on you in the Galaxy's fabulous casino. . . ."

She'd better smile on us, Jack thought, shrugging off a feeling of unreality as he and Sheila walked hand in hand toward the dice tables.

They stopped at a five-hundred-dollar-minimum game. There were only two other players at the table, high rollers with respectable rows of black, white, and yellow chips in their racks. Both were betting with the dice.

"I think this is our table," Wilson whispered to his wife.

"I'm so nervous," she replied. He squeezed her hand.

Jack gathered his resolve and caught the eye of one of the floormen. "I'd like to make a large bet," he said, indicating the gym bag.

"No problem, sir," the floorman replied. "We have no maximum limit here. How much did you have in mind?"

Wilson took a deep breath. "A million and a half," he said casually.

At precisely five P.M. Jurgen Voss initialized a preprogrammed sequence of commands that generated a direct voice connection between his computer and a telephone on the twelfth floor of an office tower in downtown Panama City.

Dan Shiller listened as the phone rang twice and a voice answered.

He spoke briefly, then motioned to Jurgen to sever the connection.

"I did not understand all this banker said," Voss commented.

"He said exactly what I expected him to say," Shiller replied. "The money isn't there."

27 **The floorman** at the craps table was momentarily speechless, but he recovered quickly. "Did you say a *million and a half,* sir? One bet?"

"That's right," said Jack Wilson. "On the don't pass line. Straight up. No odds." Wilson had studied the mathematics of casino gambling, and he knew that this was the single best bet of any table game. The mechanics were simple: you placed your bet in the don't pass area of the layout. If the first roll of the dice—the *come-out roll*—was a two or a three, you immediately won an amount equal to your original bet. If a seven or an eleven came up, you lost it all. Twelve was a push, or a stand-off, and another come-out roll had to be made. If any other number was rolled—a four, five, six, eight, nine, or ten—that number became *the point* and you had to hope that a seven was rolled before the point repeated. If it did, you won even money. If it didn't, you lost.

The house edge on a straight-up don't pass bet was only 1.4 percent. Jack knew full well that he could decrease that percentage even further by backing his bet with free odds, but that would mean he'd have to hold at least a million dollars in reserve. He'd miss out on doubling his entire stake instantly if a two or a three appeared on the come-out roll. And even if he won, the odds portion of his bet would not be paid off at even money but rather at the *true odds,* which could be as low as one to two—fifty cents won for every dollar bet—depending on the point. Essentially, he'd be making two bets instead of one. For Jack Wilson, alias Fred Langdon, this had to be a one-shot deal.

The floorman said: "Sir, this is too big for me to authorize alone. Would you mind waiting for a moment while I call my supervisor?"

Wilson nodded assent. As the man walked to the pit phone and spoke briefly, Jack whispered to Sheila, "I told you they'd check us out. Don't forget who we are!"

"Right now I'm a nervous wreck," she whispered back, trying to smile bravely.

The floorman returned with two casino executives in dark suits. "Sir, I'd like you to meet my shift supervisor, Ed Kelly. And my pit supervisor, Rick Bloom. My name is Bob Sinclair." Wilson had already noted the man's name on the brass badge he wore. "And you're Mr. . . . ?"

"Langdon. Fred Langdon. From Tacoma. This is my wife, Dorothy."

"Are you a regular player here at the Galaxy, sir?" asked Kelly. "I don't remember seeing you before."

"No, as a matter of fact, this is my first visit to your casino."

"And you're playing for cash?"

"A million and a half. I have it right here in the bag."

Kelly appeared cautiously impressed. "Mr. Langdon, as you know, there's technically no limit to the size of your bet. However, we do have to be careful with amounts of this magnitude. In addition, the state requires that we record the details of any cash transaction over ten thousand dollars. Regulation six-A, you know. So I *will* need to see some identification—"

"Really? Okay, that's no problem." Wilson pulled out his wallet and produced his custom-made driver's license and Social Security card. Kelly examined them and passed them along to his subordinates, Bloom and Sinclair.

"Do you have any other ID, sir? I'm sorry for the inconvenience, but we have to be certain who we're dealing with. Credit cards, perhaps?"

"Sure. I only carry one card. American Express. Gold." Jack handed over the counterfeit card.

"Thank you, Mr. Langdon." After a few moments Kelly returned the documents and the card to Langdon/Wilson, who had observed Sinclair copying the fictitious information in a notebook. By the time they checked it, if they ever did, the "Langdons" would be long gone. "Just one other question, sir, and I'm a little embarrassed to put it to you. I hope you'll understand that I'm not questioning your integrity or . . . prying into your private business. But with an unusually large wager like yours, we've got to ask. *Where did you get the money?*"

Wilson's heart skipped a beat, but he remaincd outwardly calm. He managed a conspiratorial chuckle. "Actually, I *won* it," he replied. "Washington State Lottery."

"I see," said Kelly. "Not that I doubt your word, Mr. Langdon, but do you happen to have any *proof* of this win. . . ?"

Jack had rehearsed this scene over and over in his mind. It was time to add credulity to his story with a touch of impatience. "Listen, Mr. . . . Kelly, is it?—if this is too big for you guys to handle, there are plenty of other places who'd be glad to book my action. I didn't come here to be hassled and, believe me, if you have a problem—"

"No problem, sir," Kelly replied quickly. "Please bear with me for just one more moment. This is standard procedure when we're meeting big bettors like yourself for the first time."

My ass, thought Wilson, *you've probably never booked action this big in your life.* With the air of a man who has just about had his fill of bureaucracy, he sighed and said aloud: "All right, just a second. Dorothy, do you still have that Xerox in your purse?"

"Yes, I think so, dear. Let me look." Jack was proud of her self-control. Her voice was steady, and she looked calm and composed. He knew how difficult this was for her. She rummaged for a moment and "found" the paper. "Here it is," she said, handing it to Kelly. "Sorry, it's kind of dog-eared. . . ."

Once he'd embarked upon the Plan, Jack Wilson had taken steps to avoid any potential problems with the placement of his bet. He remembered reading how Caesars Palace in Atlantic City had been forced by the New Jersey Casino Control Commission to close for an entire day as punishment for "willfully" helping a compulsive gambler from Toronto lose millions of dollars he had embezzled from the bank he worked for. In addition, fines ranging from $3,000 to $10,000 had been imposed personally on six of Caesars's employees. Casino executives across the country had taken note. You couldn't just walk in and lay down huge sums of money if they didn't know who you were or where you got it. Besides, Nevada state regulations required casinos to record the name, address, and Social Security number of any person who made cash transactions, including bets, exceeding $10,000.

To get around this requirement, he'd need to establish an alternative identity, one that would stand up to close scrutiny. This could be accomplished with the use of fake ID, which (somewhat to his surprise) Jack discovered was relatively easy to obtain.

He'd also be required to explain the source of his cash, to avoid questions about embezzlement or money laundering. So Wilson hit upon the idea of pretending to be a lottery winner. For proof, he decided that a fake newspaper article would suffice. So he created a story about the fictitious Fred Langdon and his big win. Using QuarkXPress, a computer typesetting program, he set the story in type on his Macintosh, carefully matching the size, style, and layout of an existing article on the front page of the Tacoma News Tribune. *He then output a hard copy on his laser printer and glued it directly over the original article. He also reset the dateline to read four years earlier and made a laser print of that line of type, covering the original dateline with his version. Wilson made a preliminary Xerox copy of the pasted-up section of the page. He then used Wite-Out to eliminate cut-and-paste marks and completed his cover-story prop by making a clean second-generation photocopy.*

At the craps table, shift supervisor Ed Kelly unfolded the paper that "Dorothy Langdon" had pulled out of her purse. It looked perfectly natural to him: a slightly shopworn photocopy of a *Tacoma News Tribune* front page dated four years earlier. Kelly quickly scanned the story:

41-YEAR-OLD TACOMA MAN
WINS $12 MILLION IN LOTTO

News Tribune Staff—An independent certified public accountant from Lakewood Center will be busy managing his own funds now that he has won $12 million, the grand prize in the biweekly Washington State Lottery.

Frederick C. Langdon became the 32nd jackpot winner from the Tacoma area, confirmed lottery spokesman Paul Richardson, with winning numbers he generated randomly on his home computer. The win was the second-largest in the history of the Lotto and will be paid in twenty annual installments of $600,000.

Langdon and his wife, Dorothy, plan to use part of their winnings to pay off debts and finance their children's education.

"Other than that, we don't intend to change our lifestyle. I'll keep on working, although maybe not quite so hard, because I enjoy my job," Langdon told *News Tribune* staff.

Langdon, who says he has always been fascinated by games of chance, purchased five tickets at the Safeway store at 10595 Gravelly Drive S.W. but didn't check the winning numbers in Sunday's newspaper. When he bought more tickets for Wednesday's draw, he had a Safeway clerk check his earlier numbers. The machine issued a "claim jumper" ticket.

"The clerk jumped up in the air and yelled, 'You won the jackpot!' " Langdon said. "The only response I could think of was, 'You've got to be joking!' "

Langdon wasted no time claiming his winnings once he learned of his good fortune, arriving at the lottery's Olympia office within the hour.

"I like casino gambling and poker, but I never thought I'd win anything like this," Langdon stated.

And what about the future?

"We still intend to buy lottery tickets," he said. "You never know—lightning can strike twice."

Kelly stopped reading. Jack's heart was pounding, and his mouth was dry.

The shift boss handed the photocopy back to Wilson. "Mister," he said, "you've got yourself a bet."

Pit supervisor Rick Bloom surveyed the neatly wrapped piles of cash stacked in the Wilsons' gym bag. "Mr. L., we're going to have to exchange this money for player's checks. There isn't room on the table to stack all these bills."

"I understand," said Jack.

"We'll have it converted in the cage. Shouldn't take more than an hour. Would you care to be present while it's counted?"

"No, that's okay. I trust you." Wilson knew that the bigger casinos were scrupulously honest and extremely accurate in their transactions. On many occasions he'd observed players leave large quantities of chips on the table while they took a break from the action, relying on the casino staff to watch over them. On one occasion, late for his plane, Jack had forgotten to pick up a couple of hundred dollars in chips at one of the Palladium's craps tables. The chips had been returned intact to him on his next visit.

"Perhaps you'd like to wait for your checks in the VIP lounge?" Bloom suggested respectfully.

Wilson glanced at his wife, who shook her head. "Thanks, but we'll stay here and watch the game," he said. "You know, get a feel for the dice."

28 Accompanied by **LVMPD** Lieutenant Frank Marshall and Sergeant Morris Jaworski, Steve Forrester stepped up onto a raised speaker's platform in one of the Galaxy's meeting rooms.

"Good afternoon, ladies and gentlemen. May I have your attention, please?" Forrester called out to the seventy-odd men and women who made up the evening security shift. Some were in uniform, others plainclothes. "Can everybody hear me? Good. I'll make this short.

"You've all probably heard rumors about threats against the Galaxy. Well, I'm here to tell you that there is some basis to those rumors. That's why we've asked the Las Vegas Metropolitan Police Department to investigate. I must point out that these threats are directed against all members of . . . a certain association—not just the Galaxy, but every Strip casino and most of the downtown ones. We don't know where, if anywhere, these people are going to strike, but in case the Galaxy is targeted, we want you to be prepared. Now because these gentlemen"—Steve gestured toward Marshall and Jaworski—"are conducting an ongoing investigation, there are certain details I can't give you at this time. The main thing is, we need you to be extra-alert for suspicious activity. You see or hear anything at all out of the ordinary, please report it to your supervisor immediately.

"One activity I want you to specifically watch for is any unauthorized attempt to modify or interfere with the hotel's electrical system. Please pay particular attention to access panels, breaker boxes, cable trays, and the like. If you see any wires or extension cords where they shouldn't be, again, inform your supervisor right away.

"Now Lieutenant Frank Marshall would like to say a few words." Forrester stepped back as his ex-partner cleared his throat.

"Thank you, *Mister* Forrester. Ladies and gentlemen, I just wanted to add that there will be undercover police officers posted throughout the hotel, the casino, and the amusement complex. They will identify themselves to you upon request. We would appreciate your cooperation and assistance if they should ask for it." A buzz of conversation emanated from the assembly. Steve Forrester raised his arms for silence.

"Just a few more things," Marshall said as the noise died down. "There will be unmarked cars patrolling the grounds until this . . . situation is resolved. I just wanted to warn you all that the people who have issued these threats should be considered armed and dangerous. Unfortunately, we can't provide you with any physical descriptions. Please don't get yourselves into any situations where you feel threatened—just call for help on your radios and a Metro officer will be there in seconds."

One uniformed guard muttered to his associate, "What do they expect for twelve bucks an hour? Human sacrifices?"

Steve Forrester raised his voice as the room again broke into a cacophony: "Okay, that's it. Thank you, everybody. And good luck."

While the security people filed out of the room, Steve Forrester motioned to the two law enforcement officers to join him for a quick conference. "Thanks, guys," he said as they drew up folding chairs and arranged them in a semicircle. "I appreciate your taking the time to speak to the troops. I know how busy you are. But I do need to ask you both for one more quick favor. Droopy is wondering what's going to happen now that the deadline's passed. As you know, he didn't wire the money, and he's getting a little antsy. If you could brief me on your progress, I could pass the word along to him."

Frank Marshall answered first. "When Druperman speaks, we listen," he said cynically. "Okay, here's the story. Getting a handle on these videos is not as easy as I thought. None of the stores can correlate more than one title with specific renters. Our guys have been walking into the station with armloads of printouts, but all they tell us is who rented *each* movie, not who rented both. And they can't organize the rentals by date. I'm sure our suspect's name is somewhere on these lists, but unless we get real lucky, it's going to take days to manually cross-check them. Do you have any idea how many times these two movies went out?"

"You're saying that you basically have two lists—one for each movie?"

"You got it, pal. I'd estimate that if we combined all the printouts from all the stores, we'd have at least a hundred thousand names per movie. No wonder those Hollywood studios make so much money."

"What if . . . ?" Forrester's voice trailed off, and he closed his eyes to concentrate. After a moment he said to Marshall: "What if you went back and asked the stores to put the names *on diskette* rather than on paper? And then we got Moe's data people to write a small subroutine and correlate the lists? I don't know much about programming, but I'm pretty sure that's doable. . . ."

Marshall unconsciously fingered his comb-over while considering Steve's suggestion. "I hate to admit it," he said slowly. "But that might just work. What do you think, Moe?"

"It's worth a try. We've got a couple of computer whiz kids in the lab. If your boys can get the data files, I'll put them right on it."

The resentment in Marshall's voice was difficult to disguise. "Hey, Moe, remember what I was telling you? Now you can see why Steve got picked for the job here at the Galaxy!"

"I'm beginning to see a lot of things," Jaworski replied thoughtfully, shifting his gaze between the ex-partners.

"Well, let's not get too excited in case it doesn't pan out," Forrester said quietly. "And let's keep this thing on a professional level, okay, Frank?"

"Yes, sir. We'll just do our jobs."

Steve decided to ignore the sarcasm. "How's it going at your end, Moe?"

"Interesting developments on our analysis of the Druperman tape, Steve. We've got this bright young audio technician, Christie Newman, and she thinks she's identified that background noise we hear near the end of the tape. Are you ready for this? She believes it's the sound of a train! There was a definite Doppler shift in the frequency, just like you get when a train passes a fixed location—plus a couple of sharp spikes in the signature, which she's ninety-nine percent sure were caused by a train whistle. So now we're checking with Union Pacific, trying to ascertain what rolling stock was where at the exact time that Thanatos called.

"Also, I asked my captain to contact the CIA in Washington to see if we could get a line on this Banco Internacional de Panamá. Apparently, it's out of their jurisdiction, but they'll find out what they can unofficially."

"All right, fellas, thanks for the input," said Forrester. "At least I'll have something tangible to tell Druperman. Everybody here at the Galaxy really appreciates the effort you guys are putting in to this case. I know I'm not your favorite customer, Frank."

29 **The Orion Showroom** was packed. An hour into his set, Tony Francisco was perched comfortably on a solitary stool, center stage, illuminated by a single blue spotlight. He had shed his sequined dinner jacket; his shirt collar was open and his tie hung loosely.

As usual, Francisco held the crowd in the palm of his hand. He had started slowly with some of the familiar favorites from his early years, the ones they always asked for. Between songs, he bantered with the audience, establishing a rapport, creating the easy mood of sparkling sophistication that was his trademark.

He built gradually to the climax of his performance. Timing was everything, and Francisco was a master of the art. His delivery was relaxed, his phrasing smooth and melodious. Behind the performer, partially hidden by a diaphanous curtain, a thirty-piece string orchestra played sweetly and harmoniously, complementing his song stylings as only the very best musicians in the business could.

Every eye was riveted on the entertainment legend as he launched into a medley of his biggest hits. Enthusiastic applause greeted each new title as people recognized the ballad from their favorite album, that unforgettable movie theme, the music they danced to at the senior prom. Almost every piece was "our song" to some moist-eyed couple holding hands under the table.

Francisco's entourage—his current girlfriend, an ex-Vegas showgirl named Gloria Latorella; his manager, Solly Greenspan; his personal assistant, and two bodyguards—were seated around a deluxe banquette in the front tier of the showroom.

"He may be a mean-tempered son of a bitch, but he hasn't lost the magic. Even after all these years," Greenspan whispered to the personal assistant,

Mario Mastrodicasa, who in many respects shared his colleague's private opinion of their mutual meal ticket.

One of the bodyguards, a swarthy ex-boxer, stifled a yawn. "Don't you guys ever get tired of watching the show?" he asked.

"It's kind of a drag when Tony has an off night," Solly admitted. "But when he's hot, which is most of the time . . . I got to say that I could listen to him forever." He glanced at his gold Rolex, a gift from Francisco after a particularly successful tour. "Anyway, the show's over in fifteen minutes."

Not coincidentally, fifteen minutes was all the time Buster Malloy needed to complete his current project.

Malloy knocked on the door of Tony Francisco's penthouse suite, expecting— and receiving—no response from within. After all, it was showtime and Francisco was currently downstairs entertaining the high rollers. Had anyone answered the door, Buster had rehearsed a totally plausible reason for his visit. "Galaxy Security," he would have said. "We've had a report that there's an intruder on this floor. They asked me to check the suite while Mr. Francisco was out." But the ploy wasn't necessary.

With a furtive glance down the corridor, Malloy opened the massive oak door, using his master key card and the universal access code which he had memorized.

He slipped inside, closing the door quietly behind him.

The suite was magnificent. Arranged on two floors, its focal point was a massive copper-hooded fireplace flickering with the glow of slow-burning Vermont maple logs, set in the middle of a sunken living room. Expensive, comfortable-looking armchairs and sofas were artfully scattered around the big room. A two-story picture window overlooking the bright lights of the Strip dominated an entire wall.

Upon a raised platform in front of the window a stately concert grand piano occupied center stage; on its polished ebony top were arranged the traveling trophies and memorabilia of a career that had spanned over half a century. A *Masterpiece Theatre*-style camera zoom across the piano top would have revealed a dazzling array of gold records and awards and statuettes, along with a panoply of expensively framed photographs: Tony Francisco shaking hands with presidents, Tony Francisco schmoozing with celebrities, youthful Tony Franciscos with pomaded hair, middle-aged

Tony Franciscos with miscellaneous offspring from various marriages, older Tony Franciscos in yachts and private jets and luxury sports cars. Malloy cast a derisive glance at the ostentatious display and resisted a strong impulse to sweep it all to the floor.

To the right of the suite, he noticed a full-size kitchen hung with gleaming copper pots. Next to it was a formal dining area featuring a richly burnished rosewood table with floral centerpiece and crystal chandelier. To the left stood a matching rosewood-and-brass bar with velvet-upholstered stools, softly lit by concealed overhead lighting. Above him, a brass-railed balcony formed a semicircular mezzanine that could be reached from the living room by a wide, curving staircase. Five bedrooms led off the mezzanine, four with a single door and one with a set of double doors. This was obviously Francisco's private room, and Buster Malloy headed directly for it.

Lifestyles of the filthy rich, he muttered to himself, glancing disdainfully around at the huge circular bed, brocade draperies, and lavish mirrors. He waded through ankle-deep broadloom, passed through the dressing area, and strode purposefully into the huge bathroom en suite of Italian marble, white shag carpet, and glistening brass.

Malloy opened the shower door, removed various items from his pockets, and set to work.

The crowd cheered and applauded as Tony Francisco's performance reached its climax and ended with a haunting rendition of his theme song, "My Town."

Mario Mastrodicasa had dutifully rushed backstage and was waiting in the wings with a glass of ice water and a towel. He was a small, slender, dark-complexioned man in his mid-forties who wore his hair in a tightly pulled back ponytail. "What a set, Tony. You knocked 'em dead."

"Yeah, right. That's what I do." The megastar slumped into a nearby chair. The stage presence had vanished; suddenly he was just an aging mortal, tired and irritable.

The applause continued. Mario peeked through a slit in the curtain. "They're standing up and begging for an encore."

Francisco wiped his face with the towel and took a sip of water. "Fuck 'em," he snapped. "They've had enough. All I want now is a stiff drink and a hot shower."

Steve Forrester walked reluctantly across the casino floor in the direction of the deserted executive offices. There was work piling up on his desk; decisions had to be made, business had to go on, extortion or no extortion.

His attention was attracted by a huge crowd surrounding one of the five-hundred-dollar-minimum craps tables. He walked over and caught the eye of the shift supervisor, Ed Kelly.

"What's going on, Ed?" he asked.

"You're not going to believe this, Steve, but we've caught ourselves a whale." *Whale* was casino insiders' irreverent jargon for a massive bettor. "This guy is going to bet a million five on the don't side. One bet, win or lose, he said. No odds."

Forrester whistled softly. "Is he one of our regulars?"

"No, he's a walk-in. We've never seen him before. He's a cash player, but he checks out. As far as we can tell, there's no theft or money laundering involved. The guy won his poke in a *lottery,* for Chrissake."

"Where is he?"

"That's him over there, watching the game. With his lady. Rick's doing a check change now in the cage."

"Why the crowd?"

"I don't know. Somehow the word got out." Kelly spotted Rick Bloom, the floor supervisor, weaving his way back to the table through the throng of onlookers. He was flanked by two security guards, one of whom was bearing racks of chips in a Plexiglas case. "Excuse me, Steve. I've got to look after our whale."

"Good luck. I'll stick around and do a little whale watching myself, if you don't mind."

Like a Holy Week procession in Little Italy, Tony Francisco's retinue slowly wound its way across the crowded casino floor toward the bank of elevators in the Saturn rocket, where they were holding a private car for the great man's ascension to the penthouse. As always when he was obliged to run this gauntlet, the entertainer and his entourage were spearheaded by a phalanx of oversize Galaxy security guards.

An unusually dense throng around one of the craps tables caught Francisco's attention. "What's all the excitement?" he asked one of the guards.

"Some high roller's gonna bet a million and a half on the don'ts, Mr. Francisco," the guard replied. "One roll. That's him over there with his lady."

"A million and a half? No shit? This I gotta see," Tony said. "Let's go, troops." With the guards running interference and his sycophants in tow, the singer threaded his way through the crowd toward the center of the action.

Other Galaxy security guards had cleared the table of players and were keeping the spectators at a respectable distance.

Ed Kelly, the shift supervisor, spotted Francisco and his lady friend immediately and greeted them. "Mr. F! Miss Latorella! How are you?" he asked, smiling nervously—with good reason. Francisco's tantrums at the gaming tables were legendary. Even more disturbing were the stories about his shabby treatment of dealers and supervisory personnel. Of course, the entire staff had by now heard about Francisco's latest contretemps in Lucy Baker's blackjack pit. Crossing his fingers and uttering a silent prayer to Saint Jude, Kelly said, "If you'd care to watch, sir—"

"Let me get this straight," Tony interrupted brusquely. "This guy is betting a million and a half? On one roll?"

"I believe so, Mr. F. They're just arriving now with his checks, so it won't be long—"

"I wanna get in on this."

Saint Jude give me strength, the supervisor thought, *here we go.* "Well, it *is* a private game, Mr. F., and I believe the gentleman and his wife *would* prefer to play alone—"

"I don't give a shit what the gentleman and his wife would prefer!" Francisco said loudly. "My money's as good as theirs! Now you just get me a marker—"

"Problems here, Tony?" a familiar voice asked. Alerted by the arrival of the star, Steve Forrester had emerged from the crowd and joined the group. For Steve the feeling of déjà vu was almost tactile.

"You again!" Francisco snapped. "You're the smart-ass who sent me off to play blackjack in that fucking Jupiter Room. You know I lost my goddamn shirt in there?"

"I'm real sorry to hear that, Tony," Forrester lied.

"Yeah, *right.* Well, I wanna get into *this* game, and your pit boss here is giving me a hard time."

"Sorry, Mr. F. How about . . . right after this roll?" Kelly said pleadingly.

"Not right *after* this roll," Francisco hissed. *"This roll."*

"Oh, Tony," said Gloria, the star's ex-showgirl companion. "Can't you even wait for one lousy—"

"Shut up. I wanna play now!"

"Why don't we just ask the other gentleman," Steve suggested, "if he'd mind?"

Kelly grasped at the straw eagerly. "Good idea, Steve. I'll go check." He walked over to Jack and Sheila Wilson, alias Fred and Dorothy Langdon, at the other end of the table. "Excuse me, Mr. L., but do you mind if Mr. Francisco joins the game?"

Wilson shrugged noncommittally and looked at his wife, who was staring transfixed at the performer and his entourage. "Golly," she asked the floor supervisor breathlessly, "is that really him? Tony Francisco?"

"None other," replied Kelly, who was beginning to feel optimistic again about his chances of surviving this shift. "He just heard about your bet and he wants to get in on the action."

Sheila Wilson glanced at her husband, who shrugged and nodded. "Oh my God," she blurted, "w-we'd be *honored* if Mr. Francisco would join us. At least *I* would." She looked hopefully at her husband. "Dear . . . ?"

"I guess it *would* be something to remember," said Jack Wilson unenthusiastically.

Saint Jude had come through! Kelly whispered a silent prayer of gratitude. "Thank *you,* folks," he said with undisguised relief. The shift supervisor returned to Tony Francisco and Steve Forrester to report the good news.

"All *right,*" said the entertainer with a self-satisfied smirk; in the end he always got what he wanted. "Gimme a marker for the same amount as *him.*" Francisco waved at the Wilson/Langdons and flashed them his famous grin. Thrilled, Sheila Wilson waved back.

"One million, five hundred thousand, Mr. F.?" asked Kelly.

"What's the matter? You don't hear so well? Or are you saying I'm not good for it?"

"No, sir! No problem!" Ed Kelly nodded to the boxman. "Give Mr. Francisco a million and a half in browns." He turned to Francisco and asked, "How are you playing them, sir?"

"What d'you mean, how am I playing them?"

"Are you betting the money all at one time?"

"Fucking right."

"With the dice or against them?"

"That depends. What are those people doing?"

"I believe Mr. Langdon is betting the don't pass line. Straight up, no odds."

"Then I'll take the pass line."

Ed Kelly's heart skipped a beat, and he stifled the urge to rub his hands together in glee. Suddenly the casino couldn't lose! This was his day after all! Francisco had faded Langdon, and the two bets now canceled each other out! The shift supervisor raised his eyes heavenward and vowed to accompany his wife to Mass next Sunday like he'd been promising since Easter.

At the other end of the table, Jack Wilson laid his trays of brown chips on the don't pass line. Chocolate chips, they called them. Five thousand dollars each. Three trays, five rows per tray, twenty chips per row. One point five million dollars.

The boxman addressed Wilson. "Would you care to shoot, sir?"

Players who bet against the dice often preferred to pass, but Jack had no such compunctions. "Sure," he replied, then added impulsively, "but I'd like my wife to throw the dice."

The boxman nodded to the stickman, who slid several dice over to the Wilsons. Dozens of pairs of eyes stared at the transparent red cubes with the bright white pips set flush into their six facets, perfect cubes, machined to a tolerance of one ten-thousandth of an inch—wonderful, magical cubes that were about to seal the fate of two breathlessly hopeful people from Redmond, Washington, and provide a moment's diversion for a multimillionaire megastar from Jersey City, New Jersey.

"Good luck, everybody," said the stickman, ironically importuning the impossible; *somebody* had to lose, and this time it wasn't going to be the house. "Coming out!" he called.

All eyes were on Sheila, and she panicked momentarily. "But Ja— I mean *Fred,*" she whispered, wide-eyed, "I've never *done* this before."

"It's easy, babe," he whispered back. "All you've got to do is pick out two dice. Then you throw them down the table hard enough to bounce off the other end."

"Okay, I guess—if you really want me to, I'll do it. What number should I try for?"

"A two or a three, *we* win and Tony loses. Seven or eleven, *he* wins and we lose. Anything else . . . I'll explain later."

The crowd fell silent as Sheila selected two dice.

Down the table, Tony Francisco stood stock-still in anticipation. Gloria Latorella nervously chewed a glittery fingernail. Even Steve Forrester was mesmerized. The tension was electric.

Sheila Wilson caressed the dice for a moment and stole a glance at her husband. He smiled back as if to say, *This is it, I know we can do it.*

She drew her arm back and released the two dice. In suspended time, they floated gracefully through the air. Hitting the end of the table perfectly, they bounced off the foam-rubber grid and slowly, so slowly it seemed, rolled to a stop.

The stickman peered closely at the glistening red cubes. He hesitated, glancing over at the boxman. "Winner seven," he called. "Pay the line."

Tony Francisco clenched a fist and raised it in the air like a victorious boxer. Scattered applause was followed by an excited undertone of conversation among the spectators.

Jack Wilson paled. In a heartbeat, the million and a half was gone! Miserably, he fingered the money belt under his shirt, the reserve fund, looking for reassurance. All of a sudden, a hundred and fifty thousand didn't seem like so much money anymore. Sheila Wilson burst into tears.

"Oh Jack," she sobbed, the alias forgotten. "I'm sorry. I did it wrong. It's gone, isn't it? And it's all my—"

"Wait a minute," cried the boxman, *"Don't touch those dice!"*

Buster Malloy slipped quietly out of Tony Francisco's suite, carefully locking the door behind him.

He was confident that there were no visible clues to his handiwork.

30

"Don't touch those dice!" the boxman repeated.

Wilson glanced at his wife. Was there a ray of hope?

The triumphant grin faded from Tony Francisco's face.

From his position at the Wilsons' end of the table, Steve Forrester peered closely at the dice. Something was definitely wrong.

The boxman held a hurried consultation with Kelly, Bloom, and Sinclair.

"Gentlemen," the boxman announced, "one of the dice is *cocked*. No roll."

Sheila Wilson whispered feverishly to her husband: "What does he mean? Didn't I shoot a *seven*?"

Jack was jubilant. "No. Look at the dice. One of them is *leaning* against Tony's chip rack. Your roll doesn't count. *We're still alive!*"

One of the dice, the one that showed a four, was lying perfectly flat on the green felt. But the other one—the one the stickman had read from his vantage point as a three—had rolled to a stop against one of Francisco's chip racks and was positioned at a perfect forty-five-degree angle. Viewed directly from above, both the three-spot and the five-spot facets were equally visible.

"Sorry, ma'am," said the stickman. "You'll have to shoot again."

"Oh, please," Sheila replied excitedly, "don't be sorry. You've given us another chance!"

The entertainer muttered an obscenity and squeezed his girlfriend's arm painfully. For one glorious moment, he thought he'd won. To him, losing a million and a half wouldn't have been the end of the world; besides, he had no intention of paying if that happened. But still, he'd much rather *win,* if only to stick it to that cheap bastard Emmett Druperman.

"Same dice, sir?" asked the stickman.

"Why not?" replied Jack Wilson, a.k.a. Fred Langdon. "Dice have no memory. I hope."

The stickman passed the dice to the Wilsons. "Coming out!" he called.

Once again, a hush fell over the crowd. Once again, Sheila picked up the dice. But this time there was no hesitation. The dice flew through the air, bounced, and landed perfectly flat on the layout.

Snake eyes!

"Two craps," the stickman called with certainty. "Line away. Pay the don'ts."

The spectators cheered.

The Wilsons hugged each other in relief.

For them, it was over.

For the members of Tony Francisco's entourage, the next few days were probably going to be hell.

Buster Malloy couldn't wait for his shift to end.

There had been this pleasant tingle in his groin ever since he'd finished his work in the bathroom of the penthouse suite. But he knew the deeper satisfaction, the real thrill, would come only when he witnessed the results of his evening's handiwork.

In the end, it wasn't the money. For Malloy, the game was the thing. Especially when the game involved killing.

31 Tony Francisco kicked off his patent leather shoes and sank into the depths of one of the deeply padded couches in his palatial suite.

The entourage followed him in at a respectful distance.

"Hey, baby." He snapped his fingers at Gloria. "Get me a drink."

"Sure, Tony." She walked to the rosewood bar and poured the superstar a double shot of his favorite, Chivas Regal.

"Great show, Tony," said Solly Greenspan, fixing himself a Cutty Sark. "But . . . a million and a half?"

Francisco downed his drink and grunted, "Big deal. Anyhow, I've got no intention of paying. Mind you, if I'd won, I would've collected." The entertainer put his feet up on the rosewood coffee table and added snidely: "I figured I'd give it a shot, seeing as how my manager couldn't get any extra money out of Druperman."

"Sorry about that. He's a tough bastard."

"Maybe I need a tougher manager."

Solly sighed. "I work damn hard for you, Tony, and you know it."

"Bullshit. I do all the real work around here. And I'm getting tired. Maybe it's time I pulled the plug. Retired. Then you mooches would have to look for a real job."

"Come on, Tony," said Mario Mastrodicasa, his ponytailed valet. "You don't mean that. You've got a lot of good years left—"

"Don't tell me what I've got, you little faggot."

"Jesus, Tony," said Greenspan. "Leave him alone. If you want to piss away millions on the fucking crap table, that's your business. But don't take it out on us when you lose—"

"Hey, just what I need right now. Psychological guidance from *Doctor*

Solomon Greenspan, show-business Jew and adviser to the stars. *Vaffan-culo.*"

"You know, most of the time you're a great guy and I'm proud to know you," Greenspan sighed in exasperation. This was a depressingly familiar conversation, repeated more and more often lately. "But sometimes you act like the meanest son of a bitch—"

"If I want to act like a mean son of a bitch, I'll act like one. I've earned the right. I was the *definitive* son of a bitch when you guys were still shitting your diapers." Francisco paused and glowered at his disciples, daring anyone else to enter the fray. No one did. "Come on, Gloria, let's go to bed."

He dragged himself off the couch and mounted the stairs, pulling himself up by the handrail with some effort. At the top of the staircase, he turned and addressed his chastened entourage: "And don't any of you *disgraziati* wake me before noon, or I'll have your balls for breakfast. Except for you, Mario; you'd probably enjoy it."

Gloria opened one side of the double doors, and they entered the bedroom. She closed the door and reached up to put her arms around his neck. "Not now," he grumbled irritably, shrugging her off. "All I want right now is a shower and some sleep."

She pouted but remained silent. He could be brutal if he was crossed, especially when he'd had a couple of drinks. Unconsciously, she touched her face, remembering the shiner he'd laid on her a couple of weeks ago out of sheer meanness.

Francisco stripped to his shorts, carelessly tossing his clothes on the floor. "Give these to the little *finocchio* for cleaning and pressing," he commanded, reaching for a terry-cloth robe.

"Okay, Tony," she replied, obediently gathering up the great man's sweat-soaked garments as he padded tiredly into the bathroom, locking the door behind him.

Gloria Latorella picked up Francisco's discarded clothes from the floor and placed them on a hanger. Despite his overbearing ways, she couldn't help feeling a powerful attachment to the aging superstar. It wasn't just the glamour and the gifts and the jet-setting lifestyle, although they were nice. She had always been able to tolerate the bullying and the arrogance, because she knew that, deep down, he loved her and, more important, that he *needed* her.

Opening the door to the suite, she called downstairs, "Mario! Tony wants you to look after these."

Mastrodicasa was slumped dejectedly in an armchair. He was hurt. No matter how many times Francisco had slighted him, he had remained loyal. But it was getting harder and harder to take the abuse, the innuendoes about his sexual orientation. "Leave them up there. I'll do it in the morning."

Gloria draped Francisco's clothes over the brass railing and returned to the bedroom. She was tired, too, and had not really minded terribly when Tony spurned her advances.

She unzipped her Simon Chang evening gown and slipped out of her bra and panties. Selecting a lacy black negligee from the bureau, she pulled it on and crawled gratefully between the cool satin sheets.

There was no way she'd go to sleep before Tony returned from his shower. *You never know,* she thought, smiling to herself, *maybe the shower will mellow him and then . . .*

The memories came back. *Memories of the good days, the magic. Then, the sparks had flown between them. She was Cinderella at the ball, and Tony was her prince.* The Prince and the Showgirl, that was us, *she thought dreamily.*

Has it really been five years? Five years since the last curtain call at Bally's? It was Don Avon's Jubilation Revue, featuring twenty—count 'em, twenty, ladies and gentlemen—dazzling, sexy, topless dancers, including yours truly, Gloria Latorella.

She had good tits; excellent dancing got you past the first audition, but superb boobs were what landed you the job. Her nipples were always firm and pouty before showtime—she'd never been obliged to resort to preshow ice-cube massages like some of the girls.

Gloria fondly remembered the backstage pandemonium, the wisecracks, the fun times before shows.

"Robes off! Two minutes!" the line captain would yell out as the last touches were applied to makeup, scanty costumes were adjusted, feathers smoothed.

"Jesus Christ, my G-string just snapped!"

"What is this—the smiling snatch show?"

"Last chance for ice!"

"Oh look, it's the snow queen!"

"Where's my freaking eyelashes?"

"Under your nose—oh, sorry, darling, that's your mustache."

She smiled, recalling Teddy, the show's choreographer, a tireless per-fectionist. He would clap-clap for attention as they lined up in the wings. "Remember, girls," he'd sibilate. "Extension! Thrust! Tuck in those bums!"

The giggling, the whispered remarks: "I bet he's tucked his dick into a few bums."

"Don't be mean to Teddy. He's a sweetheart."

The excitement and the sheer energy of the show: Hit the lights. One, two, three, kick! Pulsing music. Four, five, six, piqué! Dazzling smiles. Seven, eight, nine, thrust! The sweat glistened on the sleek, firm-breasted young bodies as they lost themselves to the rhythm, the climax, the ap-plause. You never tired of the applause.

And then that special day, after the show: a gorgeous bouquet of white roses overflowing her section of the dressing table. Gloria's first thought was, This is a mistake—these can't be for me. There must be six dozen! *In-credulously, she extracted the envelope from among the blooms.*

"Yes, darling, they're for you all right," Teddy announced smugly from behind her. "Isn't this just too *exciting?"*

"Who . . . who are they from?" Gloria turned to the choreographer. "I'm afraid to look at the card."

"You'll never guess. Not in a million years."

"Jesus, Teddy, don't keep me in suspense!"

"What if I told you that Tony Francisco was in the audience. . . ."

"Don't play games with me. This is a joke, right?"

"No joke, lover. He wants to meet you. His manager just brought the flowers in five minutes ago. Solly Greenspan. I've known him for simply years."

With trembling hands, the showgirl opened the envelope. The gilt-edged card read: "I'd love to get to know you. Dinner tonight?—Tony."

"Oh, wow. Holy Mother, I must be dreaming. Why me?"

"Search me, kiddo. Maybe he likes your bazoos. Anyway, Solly asked me to call him if you're available—and interested."

"Am I interested? Teddy, I'm getting wet just thinking about it!"

The choreographer grinned self-deprecatingly. "Too bad, darling. I'd have gone in your place. Oh, well. I'll give Solly the word. He'll pick you up at your apartment in an hour."

That night Gloria's feet never touched the ground.

As promised, Francisco's manager picked her up in a blocklong limo

*and whisked her off to the Roman Palladium, where the star was perform-
ing at the time. Greenspan escorted her in a private elevator to the singer's
suite. Gloria's nervousness increased as the floor markers flashed by.*

"Oh, Mr. Greenspan—"

"Call me Solly."

"I'm shaking like a leaf, Solly. Does it show?"

*He laughed. "Don't sweat it, honey. Tony's just a guy; he puts his
pants on one leg at a time just like the rest of us."*

"Do I look all right?"

"You look great."

*After some agonizing, she had settled for the dark green peau-de-soie
dress with the modest scoop neckline that exposed just enough cleavage to
be interesting (she hoped) but not cheap. She put on fine mesh stockings to
show off her legs, and matching medium-heel shoes. She'd worn her hair
down, just a simple clasp in the back, no jewelry except for a single strand
of pearls. Light makeup completed the look she thought would be right:
a touch of blush and just a little eye shadow.*

*Greenspan continued: "Believe me, Tony's dying to meet you. Just be-
tween us, he's probably as nervous as you are."*

*The elevator doors opened on a magnificent multilevel suite unlike
anything Gloria had ever seen outside the movies. Crystal chandeliers
abounded, velvety broadloom cushioned her feet, hidden speakers dif-
fused soft classical music. She wondered if he ever played his own
albums. . . .*

"Gloria Latorella, may I present Tony Francisco?"

*There he was, large as life. Just like in the movies and on TV. Only he
was real. Gloria managed a nervous "hello."*

*He clasped her hand gently between both of his. Gloria thought she
was going to faint. Until he spoke—in that wonderful familiar voice.*

*"You were amazing in the show. Gloria, I couldn't take my eyes off you.
And I'm really happy you could come."*

Suddenly, she felt at ease.

"Thank you, Mr. Francisco—Tony—I'm so glad you asked me."

*Diplomatically, the star invited his manager to stay for a drink. Gloria
smiled gratefully at Tony. She knew he was breaking the ice by asking Solly
to remain for a while.*

*After her initial shyness had worn off—she was amazed how charming
Francisco was, how easy to talk to—Greenspan looked at his watch,*

pleaded a previous engagement, and wished the two of them a good evening.

"I hope you don't mind, Gloria," Tony said after his manager had left, "but I've . . . taken the liberty of ordering dinner for us. Up here. If you're ready, I can call for it now."

Gloria was not certain she could eat, but she said simply, "Sure, Tony, that sounds great."

Within five minutes, three waiters arrived, and in the blink of an eye had artfully created a table d'hôte worthy of Maxim's. Silver place settings sparkled in the candlelight on a snow-white linen tablecloth as one of the waiters dimmed the overhead lights. The table was set up in the suite's cantilevered two-story bay window, providing the diners with a splendid bird's-eye view of the Strip's neon kaleidoscope. Gloria gasped at the culinary splendor—chilled Dom Pérignon, sherbet, coq au vin, baked Alaska, and a selection of good liqueurs.

"Tony, I'm amazed. Do you always eat like this?"

"Not really." He laughed. "To tell you the truth, I had a Big Mac and fries for lunch today. This is all to impress you."

"Well, it worked."

"I wasn't sure what a dancer like yourself would like. I hope I ordered right. . . ."

"Well, we have to watch our weight. We eat boring stuff like brown rice and tofu and vegetables—no sweets or soft drinks. Usually. But every once in a while we get the urge to pig out. And I guess tonight's my night."

After dinner they danced, slow and easy. The conversation diminished to occasional whispers. Neither the singer nor the showgirl felt the need for talk; both knew they had found someone special in each other.

That night they made gentle love for the first time.

Inside the bathroom, Tony Francisco kicked off his shorts and opened the shower door, reaching in to pull out the single-lever scald-guard control and start the welcome flow of hot water.

He stepped into the marbled enclosure and closed the glass shower door behind him. For a moment, he luxuriated in the needlelike spray, allowing it to soak him from head to toe. He reached for the washcloth and soap and began to lather up.

"Shit," he mumbled as the soap squirted out of his wet hand

and landed on the floor of the shower. He bent down to retrieve it.

To keep his footing as he stood back up, Francisco instinctively grasped the grab bar.

Instantaneously, 115 volts of electricity coursed through him.

With his feet in half an inch of water and his hand on the wet metal grab bar, his body was transformed into a perfect conductor for the powerful current.

He shook spasmodically, his fingers locked in a death grip on the bar as the electricity unmercifully continued its lethal passage. His muscles locked, his teeth clenched involuntarily, and his eyes rolled unseeingly up in their sockets as the terrible shock paralyzed his heart. Within moments, Tony's circulatory system was transformed into a virtual electric kettle. His blood began to boil and a red mist emanated from his orifices, mingling with the spray from the shower.

Mercifully, there was no pain.

Lying in bed, Gloria Latorella brushed away idle remembrances of things past. That was then and this is now. *Nothing lasts forever,* she thought, *and I'm lucky to still be with Tony*. If you're smart, the showgirls used to say, you'll latch onto a man or a job for later on. So now this was later on, and for better or worse, saint or son of a bitch, she had her man. She picked up the remote control and idly flipped on the television set. They were just wrapping up the news.

". . . light southwest winds and a high tomorrow of eighty-five," the weatherman finished.

"Thanks, Randy," the attractive young anchorwoman said. "And that's it for tonight. Join us tomorrow evening at eleven for News Thirteen Inside Las Vegas. And stay tuned for our late movie, the classic favorite *Manhattan Memories*."

It was one of Tony's movies—the most famous one, the one that had revived his faltering career in the late fifties. Gloria wished she had known him as he was then. *This will definitely cheer him up,* she thought. During the commercials and the station promos, she helped herself to a chocolate mint from the bedside table and propped up the pillows behind her head. He ought to be out of the shower anytime now.

But by the time the credits finished rolling, Francisco had still not emerged. He normally took only a few minutes in the shower, especially when he was tired. She could hear the water running.

She waited until the first commercial, then got out of bed and rapped tentatively on the bathroom door. "Tony?" she called. "Are you all right?" No answer. She tried the handle, but it was locked.

Gloria was worried. This wasn't *like* him. She knocked more insistently. "Tony! Answer me!" Behind the hissing of the water there was an ominous silence.

She hesitated, but not for long. After all, at his age, anything was possible. A heart attack. A stroke. She ran to the vanity and grabbed a bobby pin. Inserting it in the emergency release hole of the brass lockset, she fumbled nervously until an audible click told her the door was unlocked.

Hesitantly, she stepped inside. The room was completely fogged with hot, damp steam. "Tony?" Still no answer. Her heart was pounding wildly as she ran to the shower. Something was terribly *wrong*.

She flung the shower door open. Francisco was crumpled in the corner, mouth agape in a ghastly rictus, eyes rolled back in his head, right hand still frozen to the grab bar. Wisps of crimson ran from his nose and ears, watered down to a sickly pink by the warm spray cascading from the showerhead.

"Oh, Tony," she cried as she bent to touch his twisted body. "What hap—"

The intense electric shock threw her back onto the hard marble floor. She lay there for a moment, hurting all over, stunned and gasping for breath. When she finally found the strength to stumble to her feet, she limped out of the bathroom and staggered to the bedroom door.

Tears were streaming down her face, and she was trembling from head to foot as she called weakly downstairs, "Mario . . . Solly . . . come quickly. Tony is . . ." She collapsed.

Francisco's assistant and his manager raced up the stairs, followed by one of the bodyguards. The other one reached for a phone, preparing to call for help. Maybe the performer's earlier remarks about pulling the plug had been prophetic. Mario knelt down by the stricken woman and gently raised her head. "Gloria, what's happened?" he asked.

She was ashen, fighting unconsciousness. "It's Tony," she managed weakly. "In the shower . . . don't touch him . . . there's electricity in there . . ."

She closed her eyes and passed out in Mastrodicasa's arms.

Steve Forrester surveyed the piles of paper on his desk.

Suzy had finished the first draft of the report for Druperman, and a quick scan of the neatly printed pages revealed that she had done her usual thorough job. But his in-basket was backing up. Letters to be answered, decisions to be made, telephone messages to be returned. At least the messages could wait until tomorrow; it was unlikely that any of his callers would be available at this hour. Reluctantly, he started on the paperwork. Somehow it all seemed so trivial, considering the events of the past few days and the threat that hung over the association like a modern-day sword of Damocles.

Just as he reached for a pen, the phone on his desk rang.

"Mr. Forrester? Herman Glockmeyer here, sir." One of the security guards on the swing shift, Forrester remembered. The man was obviously upset. "Thank God you're still here. There's been a terrible . . . accident. Mr. Francisco's suite. Can you come up right away?"

A cold fear gripped Steve's heart. Somehow, he knew. Without asking the guard for any details, he knew immediately and with instinctive certainty that this was Thanatos's work. "I'll be there immediately," he replied tersely, banging down the phone and racing out of his office in the direction of the elevators. The Saturn spectacular was in full blast, but Forrester ignored it.

"Would a cashier's check for the three million be acceptable, Mr. Langdon?" Ed Kelly inquired solicitously.

The Langdon/Wilsons were seated with the shift boss over coffee in the Galaxy's VIP lounge. They both felt elated but drained. Between the heart-stopping near loss with Sheila's misroll of the dice and the thrill of victory on the very next roll, it had been an emotional roller-coaster ride.

"I don't think so, Mr. Kelly," Wilson replied. "We want our original cash back, and we'd like you to match it."

"You do realize, sir, that there are no tax implications to worry about?" Kelly suggested hopefully. "It's a verifiable win at a table game. If you'd won the money at the slot machines or at keno, we'd have to withhold a certain amount for the IRS. But with a win at dice—"

"I'm aware of that, Mr. Kelly." More precisely, Jack was aware of the fact that he'd be unable to deposit a check made out to the fictitious Fred

Langdon. "I also know that it will take a while for your people to get the money together. But we don't mind waiting."

"We want to do a little shopping anyway," Sheila added helpfully.

"Very well, folks. We'll have your cash ready in the morning. And thank you for playing at the Galaxy. I hope to see you again soon."

Fat chance, thought Wilson as he and his wife walked out of the VIP lounge hand in hand. "What was all that about shopping?" he asked.

"Oh, Jack," she giggled, "you forgot. Gucci luggage, remember? To carry our winnings home in!"

32

Steve Forrester was met at the door to Tony Francisco's suite by security guard Herman Glockmeyer.

The entertainer's people were gathered numbly around the fireplace, the flickering light from the log fire accentuating the mixture of shock and disbelief on their faces. Gloria Latorella lay supine on the couch to which Mario had carried her, covered by a blanket.

The guard filled Forrester in as best he could. "Sir, it appears that Mr. Francisco was electrocuted in the shower," he began. "The lady touched him and received a tremendous shock herself. There's an ambulance on its way, and we're looking for the electrician right now. Meanwhile, I've posted a man at the bedroom door to keep everybody out. I don't believe there's anything that can be . . . done for Mr. Francisco."

Forrester's heart sank. "He's dead?"

"Yes, sir. No question." Glockmeyer's portable two-way radio crackled. He listened for a moment and reported to Forrester: "They've located the electrician, sir. He'll be here in five minutes." The guard replaced the radio on his belt and looked thoughtful. "Mr. Forrester," he said hesitantly, "excuse me for asking, but is this what you meant in that meeting when you said we were to watch out for . . . electrical stuff?"

The electrician said to Forrester, "Before we can do anything, I'll have to shut off power to the whole suite. I guess the folks downstairs will be okay—they'll be able to see by the light of the fire. We can work upstairs with a flashlight." He unlocked a small metal door in the kitchen area, flipped the master breaker, and relocked the door. All the lights went out.

Steve followed the electrician's flashlight beam up the stairs. The security guard stood aside to let them into the darkened bedroom. Forrester dreaded the scene he knew awaited them in the bathroom.

No one had dared shut off the faucet, and clouds of steam from the Galaxy's inexhaustible supply of hot water had suffused the room from ceiling to floor with a dense, warm fog. The flashlight shot a powerful yellow beam through the ghostly haze. Both men gasped involuntarily as they beheld the naked body of the Galaxy's star attraction crumpled grotesquely in the corner of the shower enclosure, his right hand still locked in a death grip on the grab bar. Donning a pair of heavy rubber gloves, the electrician reached in and turned off the water.

"I don't understand it," he said grimly. "This should *not* have happened. All the receptacles in the bathroom are GFI-protected. And the light fixtures are double insulated." He played his flashlight around the shower enclosure, its beam highlighting the dead man's face.

Steve was first to notice it. "What's that?" he asked, indicating the brass grab bar mounted to the shower wall. The flashlight had briefly illuminated the corner of some gray material partially hidden behind the bar.

"Better not touch it, sir. Let me handle it." The electrician gingerly peeled off the material. "It's a piece of . . . *duct tape*. Somebody's used it to stick the end of . . . this *wire* to the bar."

"My God," Forrester whispered, his premonition confirmed. "Those warped sons of bitches *did* do this."

The electrician pulled on the wire. It was a single copper conductor. The first inch was bare, the rest of it white-plastic-insulated. "It looks like half of an extension cord, slit down the middle, with one end stripped." He started to gather the wire, holding it carefully in his gloved hands as he followed it back to its source. "Look at this, Mr. Forrester. They buried the wire in caulking."

The wire had been artfully concealed in a bead of still-soft caulking running down the corner of the marbled enclosure and across the angle between the floor and the wall. A small hole had been drilled to allow the wire to pass through the brass molding that framed the glass wall of the shower. At this point the other wire from the extension cord, separated from its neighbor and shortened to the right length for its deadly purpose, had been taped to the molding. Beyond the shower stall the cord was intact, its twin leads unseparated. The two men continued to trace the cord to its origin. It ran under the white shag carpeting, beneath the bathroom door, around the baseboard of the bedroom. The electrician gathered more and more wire as the coil grew larger in his gloved hands.

Finally, they reached the end. It was plugged into a live wall outlet behind a Louis XIV *écritoir*.

"I thought so," said the electrician as he unplugged it. "It's just a cheap extension cord. But it was enough to kill the gentleman. His body completed a circuit between the two wires—like current running through a toaster."

But Forrester was not looking at the cord. His attention was riveted to the brown envelope lying on the carpet under the receptacle. In the halo of the electrician's flashlight, he spotted the now-familiar rectangular address label: EMMETT DRUPERMAN, PRESIDENT OF LVCA, CONFIDENTIAL.

Steve picked up the package and slipped it inside his jacket. Then he spoke quietly to the electrician. "I'm going to ask you to keep the details of this incident confidential for now. We'll be calling the police immediately, but any premature disclosure could jeopardize the investigation."

"I understand." The electrician paused for a moment and scratched his head. "What I *don't* understand is why the hell the breaker didn't trip."

By the time the two men returned downstairs, the EMTs had whisked Gloria away.

"Was it . . . an accident, Mr. Forrester?" Glockmeyer the security guard inquired.

"I can't tell you that right now, Herman." He gathered his thoughts and approached the hushed group gathered in the living room. Solly Greenspan clutched a Cutty Sark, his third in half an hour. Silent tears rolled down Mario's cheeks. The two bodyguards were pale and subdued. "Gentlemen, Mr. Francisco has suffered a fatal . . . *accident*. Please accept my sincere sympathies on your loss."

"How . . . how could you . . . let this *happen,* Steve?" Solly's words were thick and slurred. "How the hell could anybody get . . . electrocuted . . . in a fucking *shower,* for God's sake?"

"We'll leave the investigation to the authorities, Mr. Greenspan. Meanwhile, I'll have to ask you all to remain here until they arrive."

"Where the fuck else . . . are we gonna go?" Solly mumbled.

The electrician had just restored power to the suite. He peered closely at the breaker panel and reached inside. Then he walked over to Forrester and drew him aside. "Look at this, sir," he said quietly, revealing a strip of crumpled silver paper in his palm. "Whoever set this up knew what they were doing. There's foil stuffed behind the breaker switch. No wonder it didn't trip."

Steve nodded grimly, walked to the nearest phone, and dialed the Southwest Area Command. "This is Forrester at the Galaxy. Is Frank Marshall still there?"

"No, sir," replied the dispatcher. "He left an hour ago."

"We've got an emergency here. Please get in touch with him at once— I don't care if you have to get him out of bed—and ask him to come to the penthouse suite at the Galaxy. Meanwhile, please send a couple of officers up to secure the area."

"Yes, sir. What is the nature of the emergency?"

"There has been a . . . death. I can't go into details on the phone."

"Understood. We'll have some men there within two minutes."

"And please get hold of Sergeant Jaworski if you can."

He hung up and called Emmett Druperman's private home number. After five rings, a sleepy voice answered. It was the Drupermans' maid. "Druperman residence."

"This is Steve Forrester. Let me speak to Mr. Druperman, please."

"But, señor, he is *sleeping*—"

"Then wake him. This is . . . *muy importante*."

"One moment, señor."

After a several minutes, the CEO picked up the phone. The irritation in his voice was plain. "Steve, do you know what time—"

Forrester interrupted brusquely: "Listen to me carefully, Emmett." He turned his back to the entourage, cupped his hand over the receiver, and lowered his voice. "Tony Francisco is *dead*. And it looks like Thanatos is responsible." There was a deathly silence on the line. "You'd better get over here now and help me with damage control. Francisco's suite."

Casually smoking a Camel outside the rear service entrance of the Galaxy, Buster Malloy watched with dismay as the ambulance departed.

The paramedics had loaded a stretcher bearing what appeared to be a woman—unconscious but apparently still very much alive—into the waiting vehicle.

Not the result he'd hoped for, but he decided to hang around, just in case. In less than an hour his patience was rewarded.

This time, it was the Clark County coroner's black station wagon. This time, the big Irishman observed smugly, judging by the body bag, its cargo was very definitely deceased.

And Malloy was very definitely aroused.

Ignoring Dan Shiller's instructions to report back as soon as he knew anything, Buster decided to go and get laid.

33 **The Crime Scene people** had completed their grim task in Tony Francisco's suite. His body had been spirited away by the coroner to the Clark County morgue for its mandatory autopsy.

One of Francisco's daughters from a previous marriage was reached by telephone. After the screams faded and the tears subsided, she promised to take the next flight to Las Vegas to look after the arrangements.

Tony's entourage had been politely but thoroughly questioned by the police, with negative results. None of them had been in the suite during the show; none had seen or heard anything out of the ordinary.

"Why are the cops involved in this? And why the hell are you questioning *us*?" one of the bodyguards had asked Lieutenant Frank Marshall suspiciously. "It *was* an accident, wasn't it?"

Apart from the police, only Forrester, Druperman, and the electrician knew the real reason for the star's death. "Standard operating procedure, sir; just routine," Marshall had replied.

Solly Greenspan drained the bottle of Cutty Sark. The effects of the alcohol were beginning to transform his initial shock into outrage. "Routine?" Francisco's newly unemployed manager spluttered drunkenly. "You call this *routine*? Tony's dead and . . . and somebody's gotta *pay*. I'm calling our attorneys in the morning. They're gonna sue this hotel for . . . fucking *billions*."

"We're all terribly . . . upset, Solly," said Emmett Druperman. As CEO, he realized that the potential exposure of the Galaxy for Francisco's demise was enormous. If the real reason were covered up and the death recorded as an accident, their insurers could be liable for a massive settlement and the hotel's premiums would skyrocket. On the other hand, if the story of the extortion and the murder came out, the Galaxy's reputation would suffer irreparable damage. Either way, Druperman had plenty to explain at the next Summit Enterprises board meeting.

Nor would the Las Vegas Casino Association be pleased. Once the story got out, the incident would damage everyone's credibility, undermining the hard-won image of Las Vegas in the early twenty-first century as a safe, crime-free tourist destination—a destination that was only now beginning to recover from the cloud cast upon tourism in general by the tragic events of September 11, 2001. Of course, if Emmett were to be totally honest with himself, it was really the force of his own personality that had persuaded the other members to hardball the extortionists' demands. On the other hand, they had all assumed that the cops would act faster, and even if they didn't, what the hell, the next victim would just be some unimportant tourist, some visiting nobody whose death could easily be covered up. Who would have dreamed for a moment that the bastards would murder the biggest star in Vegas, if not the whole world? And under *his* fucking roof, to boot.

Druperman was beginning to dread the next chapter in the Thanatos saga, yet he needed to know what the extortionists had up their sleeve. Steve Forrester had quietly advised him that another package had been found; it only remained for the suite to be cleared of Francisco's people so they might talk freely.

Steve called Reservations and asked them to relocate Greenspan, Mastrodicasa, and the bodyguards. "I'm afraid you won't be able to stay here tonight, gentlemen," he said. "The bell captain will move your luggage to other rooms."

With grumbles and tears, the remnants of the entertainer's entourage filed silently out of the suite. It was the end of an era.

Finally, Emmett Druperman could vent his frustration. "What kind of fucking animals are we dealing with here?" he shouted angrily, staring fiercely in turn at Frank Marshall, Morris Jaworski, and Steve Forrester. "How could they disrespect . . . *defile* . . . this man we all loved so much?"

After a moment of skeptical silence and a glance at the others—was this Emmett's erstwhile "show business dago"?—Forrester fielded the rhetorical question. "They wanted to hit us where it hurt," he said, ascribing Droopy's saccharine eulogy to selective sentimentality. "And it appears that they've succeeded."

"All right, but tell me, why the fuck weren't these guys caught before it came down to this? You told me the cops were right on top of things—"

"Sir, we're this close to identifying the suspects," said Jaworski, making a U with his thumb and forefinger. "If we'd had just a little more time—"

"Don't blame me for that," Druperman cut in. "I tried to stall, but the schmuck just hung up on me. You heard the tape."

"Look, there's no use pointing fingers here," said Marshall. "Let's just look at the latest video and plan our next move. Agreed?"

Steve nodded and indicated a large cabinet with double doors. "There's a TV and a VCR in there, Frank." He walked over to the rosewood bar. "Anybody want a drink?"

"I'll read the letter while Frank's putting the tape in," Moe volunteered. He picked up the sheet and began: " 'ATTENTION LAS VEGAS CASINO ASSOCIATION! YOU HAVE SEEN OUR POWER. PERHAPS NOW YOU WILL TAKE US SERIOUSLY. AS PUNISHMENT FOR NOT SENDING THE MONEY, WE HAVE INCREASED THE PRICE YOU MUST PAY. YOU WILL NOW WIRE TO BANCO INTERNACIONAL DE PANAMÁ TWENTY-FIVE MILLION DOLLARS ($25,000,000.00). THE VIDEO HEREWITH SHOWS YOU OUR NEXT ACTION. YOU WILL PAY BEFORE WEDNESDAY 1700 HOURS. THANATOS.' That gives us less than two days." Jaworski paused and held up another object. "This time they've included a twenty-five dollar chip."

"Times a million," Marshall remarked.

"They're upping the ante again," said Steve. "These guys aren't going to stop until they get what they want. And it gets more expensive every time. Let's see the video, Frank."

The big screen came to life with grainy black-and-white footage that appeared to have been culled from some bygone news program. The subject matter of the news clip quickly became clear. There were fire trucks and plumes of smoke and flames shooting from windows. A solemn voiceover intoned:

"Just before seven o'clock yesterday morning a disastrous fire broke out at the MGM Grand, starting in the casino and spreading rapidly through the hotel complex. Latest reports indicate that close to a hundred guests and employees may have perished, most of them victims of the deadly smoke, many trapped inside locked stairways. At least two victims leapt from their hotel-room windows, desperately choosing a quick death over slow suffocation."

On the TV screen a dark shape below one of the windows, half hidden in the haze, suddenly came into focus. The camera zoomed in, revealing a woman literally hanging on for dear life from the ledge. She remained suspended for several agonizing seconds until either the choking smoke or her failing strength caused her to release one arm, then the other—and she cartwheeled earthward, obviously to her death, disappearing behind the dome of the casino.

"Equipment from as far away as Laughlin was called to the scene, but rescuers were unable to reach any of those trapped above the eighteenth floor."

A ladder truck, its skinny finger extended to the maximum, pointed to a balcony. A fireman and two rescued guests managed a shaky, painfully slow descent down the ladder.

"Some guests and hotel employees were able to reach the roof, from which helicopters ferried them to safety."

Thick black smoke mushroomed from the roof. Buffeted by the wind, its poisonous plumes chased a knot of people from side to side across the hot tar-and-gravel surface like a school of frightened fish. Finally, helicopters swooped in and picked up the rooftop survivors.

Then the video cut to a head-and-shoulders shot of a middle-aged man in fireman's gear, a reporter's microphone shoved into his soot-blackened face.

"According to the Clark County Fire Chief—"

Marshall pushed PAUSE and the picture froze. "These people are unbelievable," he said grimly to the others. "Now they're going to torch a hotel unless you guys cough up twenty-five million bucks."

"The question is, which hotel?" Forrester said thoughtfully. "And when? Surely they can't believe they've got a hope of successfully targeting the Galaxy for a third time. They must know that by now we'll have the place protected like Fort Knox."

"Once again, I believe you're right, Steve," said Marshall acidly. "What a loss to the department when you left."

By now even Druperman had sensed the tension between the two ex-partners. "Could we please stick to the matter at hand?" the CEO rasped.

"Of course," Marshall replied. "Like Steve so perceptively says, it's highly unlikely they'll strike here again. Which means we'll have to stretch our resources pretty thin to cover all the other hotels in the association. You know, Mr. Druperman . . ." He hesitated for a moment, unwilling to say what had to be said next. "I hate to ask you this, but we do need to . . . reaffirm your group's position. Do you still refuse to pay the money? You know our policy on extortion, but you're the guys taking the risk. Maybe you should consider—"

"I'll call an emergency meeting of the association right now and let you know what we decide," Druperman growled, fixing a droopy eye on his VP Security and the two policemen in turn. "But don't hold your breath. We're still counting on you people to stop these maniacs before they kill anybody else." He glanced at the frozen video image of Clark County's fire chief of a quarter century earlier. "You know, I remember that fire at the MGM like it was yesterday. It cost the hotel about a hundred and forty million in lawsuits. And that was in nineteen-eighty dollars. The same fire today, you're talking a couple billion, minimum."

The CEO stomped out of the penthouse suite, unceremoniously shouldering the uniformed cop on the door aside. Forrester's observation that the Galaxy was unlikely to be targeted for a third time had not escaped his attention.

"Anybody like a drink?" Forrester repeated from behind the bar. Marshall allowed as how *he* would; Jaworski, lost in thought, declined. Steve poured his ex-partner and himself each a generous measure of Jack Daniel's on the rocks. Then he lit a Vantage from his eleventh pack in three days. There was only so much pressure a person could take; for now, lifestyle improvements would have to take a number. Irrelevantly he added, "Well, I guess Francisco's gotten away with another marker."

"Meaning what?" asked Marshall.

"You didn't hear? He pissed away a million and a half at the craps table—on credit. One roll. Tonight, just before he got zapped. Somehow I doubt if we'll ever collect on that one."

"Hmm. I'd say that's the least of your problems."

"I'd say you were right. So let's talk about Thanatos. How's the video thing going, Moe?"

"Your idea worked," said the police scientist. "We got the diskettes from the stores and one of our programmers wrote a subroutine to correlate the lists. We've narrowed it down to about sixty names—people who have rented both *Seven* and *Extreme Measures* over the past month. Our perps' little flair for the dramatic may have cost them twenty-five mil—and their freedom."

"Let's hope so. What about the audiotape?"

"There was only one train in the Las Vegas area the night Thanatos called. At the time the whistle sounded, the front end of this Union Pacific freight train was somewhere between Washington Avenue and Craig Road. That's as close as the railroad people could locate it for us. So we're assuming the call came from an area within a couple of blocks of I-fifteen, where it runs parallel with the tracks between Washington and Craig.

"Now that the video-rental list is ready, we'll cross-reference it to those names you gave us, Steve, and also to the possibles we downloaded from the NCIC computer. Should be done by morning. Then teams of detectives will be given copies of the profile and start making house calls, concentrating on the area around the tracks."

"Any luck with the poison, Moe?"

"We're still working on a source, but so far, no results.

"Incidentally, the CIA finally contacted this Banco Internacional de Panamá on our behalf. It appears that they're one of the biggest money-laundering outfits in the area. Mostly South American drug money, but rumor has it they also do business with organized crime syndicates in this country. Anyway, these sleazeballs wouldn't tell our agents anything. There's no international law that requires them to reveal details of numbered accounts."

"Too bad. I guess it was worth a shot." Forrester stubbed out his cigarette and reached for his jacket. "Gentlemen, thank you. I've had it up to here with this business and I'm going home."

In reality, Steve Forrester harbored no desire to spend what was left of the evening at Conquistador Trail.

34

On his way to the underground garage, Forrester pulled out his cell phone and dialed directory assistance. Within a few seconds he was connected to the number he wanted.

"Lucy? It's Steve."

"Hi. This is unexpected."

"I was kind of hoping, if it isn't too late, to drop by your place and maybe pick up where we left off last time. Remember, you'd just made this pot of coffee . . .?"

There was a definite hesitation on the line. "I don't know, Steve," she said finally. "Are you sure you want to drive all the way out here at this hour?"

"I need to talk to somebody who isn't a cop or a coroner."

"God, what's happened now?"

"Well, I guess you could say it's good news and bad news."

"Give me both."

"Tony Francisco is dead."

Disturbed by the news, Lucy Baker replaced the receiver slowly.

Things were happening, events that were beginning to shake the very foundation of the cozy little world she'd created for herself. She felt insecure, dislocated. It wasn't only the awful crimes that were being committed under the same roof where she spent forty hours a week. It was more the terrifying prospect of a relationship with this exciting, charming, impetuous man who was filling her thoughts in a way she'd never have believed possible.

Kind of like being in a Hollywood movie, she thought, *with somebody else writing the script.* She tried to shake off this new feeling of unreality and failed, unable to come to terms with the surprises life kept handing her lately. Since coming to Las Vegas, her life, and her lifestyle, had been safe and predictable. It appeared that those days were over—and she just wasn't *ready*.

Lucy rose from the couch where she'd been reading and began to tidy up the already neat living room in preparation for Steve Forrester's arrival.

"**I want** to apologize for the other night," Forrester said. "And for not calling you sooner. But I've been up to my neck in this extortion thing, what with the poisoning—and now this."

Lucy sat upright in the armchair, her knees pressed closely together, while Steve perforce occupied the couch. "You don't have to apologize," she said. "I understand. It must have been awful for you."

"It was pretty awful for Tony Francisco, I can tell you that. No matter what we might have thought of him, he was still a human being, and no human being deserves to die the way he did."

"I'm almost afraid to ask. What happened?"

"They electrocuted him. The same people who poisoned that man in the coffee shop. They wired up his shower . . . and that was it. I guess the only blessing is he died instantly. At least, that's what the coroner said."

"My God. What do these people want?"

"Money. Lots of it. If the association doesn't pay, they're threatening to burn down a casino. But Droopy's hanging tough."

Lucy was silent for a moment, her eyes downcast, as she absorbed this news. When she looked up again at Steve, there was resentment in her voice. "Why does everything have to be so . . . complicated?" she asked plaintively.

Steve rose from the couch and knelt by her chair. "Are you talking about the extortion or . . .?"

"Or about us? I don't know. It's just everything, Steve. Things were so simple until . . ."

"Until I came along?" He tried to put his arms around her, but she stiffened. "What's the matter?" he asked, rebuffed in his attempt to comfort her. "I really thought we had something special the other night."

"I don't know, Steve. I'm still a little bit afraid."

"Of me?"

"Of the way my life is changing. Nothing's simple anymore. I need time to think things through."

Forrester sighed. "Okay, I guess. Maybe I should go." Lucy nodded sadly. He stood up and walked toward the door. With his hand on the knob, he turned and asked, "Is this really about your . . . experience on the cruise ship?"

When she didn't answer, he said good night and quietly closed the door behind him.

Aboard the Rio de Janeiro, *twenty-three-year-old Lucy Baker still could not believe her luck.*

The money was good, the work in the ship's casino pleasant and the fringe benefits marvelous. Kind of like being on perpetual vacation, she wrote her family. The days passed quickly under the tropical sun; the evenings were all her own. For Lucy, the best part of them was a relaxed stroll around the deck with the soft salt breeze caressing her face and ruffling her hair.

She loved the marvelous vista that extended to the horizon in all directions. Especially at night. The moon would paint a broad watery stripe through the sea, a radiant counterpoint to the faint phosphorescent glow that tinged the gentle swells. Overhead, in the velvet canopy of the Caribbean sky, the stars seemed close enough to touch. Somehow there were more of them, thousands more, than she ever remembered seeing at home in Vermont. Only the ship's wake disturbed the tranquillity of the water, creating a luminescent trail that sparkled for miles in an arrow-straight line behind the great vessel.

Because the casino staff—managers, assistant managers, dealers, cashiers, and office personnel—were frequently reassigned to different ships within the line, Lucy Baker met new faces on every cruise. She had been lucky; her own posting aboard the Rio *had lasted for over three months, during which time she'd visited almost every port on Holiday Lines' Caribbean itinerary.*

On that final, fateful western Caribbean cruise, Lucy met Nigel Fuller, a handsome, blond Brit in his early thirties, newly assigned to the post of casino manager. Fuller could not take his eyes off Lucy. He took advantage of his managerial position to assign her to his own shifts, where he "chatted her up" with extravagant courtesy at every opportunity. Lucy was flattered and thought to herself, Is he really interested in me? *She responded favorably to his advances.*

Encouraged, Fuller asked her for coffee on the Lido Deck. She accepted with some misgivings, but they were soon laid to rest by the suave Englishman's natural charm and easy conversation. He was from Stratford-on-Avon, he said, educated at Oxford, and this was his third cruise with Holiday. He had learned the casino business at the Playboy Club in London.

Lucy was fascinated by him and absolutely thrilled that this attractive, worldly man could be even remotely interested in an ordinary, unsophisticated person like her.

After working hours, their meetings became more regular. Whenever they weren't required to stay on board for port manning, they toured lush Caribbean islands and Mayan ruins together. At sea, they danced in the ship's nightclub or strolled the decks for hours, holding hands.

The first time he kissed her, she responded with a passion that surprised both of them. Halfway through the three-week cruise, he gently suggested that they might sleep together. Every fiber in her body ached to comply with his wishes, for by now she was hopelessly, head-over-heels in love with this man.

But Lucy was unable to overcome the deeply ingrained strictures of her Catholic upbringing. Unlike most of her unmarried friends, she was still a virgin, keeping a promise she'd made to her mother to save herself for marriage.

One warm starry night, snuggled together in a deck chair, he presented her with an engagement ring. It had been his mother's, he said. Lucy cried a little, laughed a little, and said yes. They spent that night, and the next, and the next, in his cabin.

The cruise passed in a whirlwind for Lucy. She telephoned home from the ship the morning after Fuller had presented her with the ring.

Her mother answered.

*"*Maman, *it's me. I've got super news. I'm engaged."*

"Oh, chérie, *that's wonderful! Tell me all about him. Did you meet him on the ship?"*

"Yes. His name's Nigel. Nigel Fuller. He's British. I know you'll like him."

"Have you set a date?"

"Honestly, Maman, *you're so practical! We only got engaged last night.*

But I know he wants to get married in Vermont. And he can't wait to meet you and Papa."

They talked for another half an hour, and Lucy promised to come home with her fiancé as soon as they could possibly get some time off together.

But it was not to be. When the Rio de Janeiro docked in Fort Lauderdale at the end of the cruise, Fuller quietly disappeared without a trace or so much as a note for Lucy.

She learned from Personnel that Nigel Fuller's contract had expired and that he had elected not to renew it.

The ring turned out to be a cheap cubic zirconia diamond imitation, which she threw overboard.

She cried for days.

Driving back to Conquistador Trail from Lucy Baker's apartment, a thoroughly fatigued Steve Forrester sighed and wished he'd never made the trip. The magic of two nights ago hadn't been there. Lucy was cool and reserved, and Steve was unwilling to chance a confrontation by pressing her. On the way home he stopped to pick up a carton of Vantage 100s.

So much for fickle women and good intentions, he thought glumly as he depressed the electric cigarette lighter in the burled walnut dashboard of the SL 500.

35

Steve Forrester awoke at seven-thirty with a dull throbbing in his temples courtesy of Jack Daniel's and the taste of burnt straw in his mouth thanks to R. J. Reynolds.

Blinking back the glorious desert sunrise that streamed through his bedroom window, he stumbled into the kitchen to make coffee. The goddamn Folgers jar was empty. He peered into the fridge—a half-full box of Arm & Hammer baking soda and a can of Coors Light. *Perfect,* he thought numbly, *I'll have the six-course American breakfast. One can of beer and five cigarettes.*

Back in the living room he flipped on the TV. The CNN announcer's voice was properly sober. "Sad news from Las Vegas last night," the announcer read from the teleprompter as a recent photograph of the extortionists' latest victim appeared over his left shoulder. "Legendary entertainer Tony Francisco is dead, apparently from an electrical accident that occurred in his suite at the Galaxy Hotel, where he was performing. No official report has yet been filed as to the exact cause of his death, but some sources have suggested suspicious circumstances. An autopsy is scheduled for later today, after which a press conference will be held at the Clark County Coroner's Office.

"Mr. Francisco's companion, Gloria Latorella, also sustained a severe electric shock when she went to the star's aid, but her injuries are not life-threatening and she is reported to be recovering at Sunrise Hospital." The announcer paused while his image dissolved to some grainy black-and-white footage from the singer's early years. All the major networks kept updated bios of well-known personalities on file for the inevitable obits. Over the familiar strains of "My Town," the announcer continued: "Francisco was a fixture in American show business for more than five decades. . . ."

Forrester pushed the OFF button. Still clad only in a pair of boxer shorts, he cracked open the front door and reached through for the paper lying on the doormat. A two-inch headline in the *Las Vegas Review-Journal* stared up at him accusingly. Over a four-column color photograph of the deceased star it read, FOUL PLAY SUSPECTED IN SINGER'S DEATH. He picked up the paper and squinted at the subhead: TONY FRANCISCO DIES IN "ACCIDENT" AT GALAXY. Steve wondered how they'd found out so quickly about the so-called foul play. The electrician must have blabbed—or maybe one of the cops did.

Not that it really mattered, because in the long run there was no way to cover up what had happened. Forrester shuddered when he imagined what the tabloids would do to the Galaxy when they got their claws into the story. *Droopy's going to pop his hemorrhoids,* he thought.

The Coors actually helped clear Forrester's head, and he began to feel semi-human as he stepped into the tiled shower stall. A quick flash of Tony Francisco's fatal shower scene caused him a second's hesitation, but he quickly purged that ghastly image. Steve had always exercised his most creative thinking in the shower; while he lathered up under the hot spray he considered the potential outcomes of Thanatos's latest threat.

Despite Druperman's bullheadedness, the Las Vegas Casino Association could decide to knuckle under and pay off the extortionists. It might not be the red-blooded American solution but, weighed against the risk of a major fire, hundreds of deaths, and billions in damages, maybe the wisest course.

Or the police might arrest the gang before they had a chance to carry out any more threats. End of problem.

In Forrester's opinion, the most likely scenario was neither of the above.

He believed that the LVCA under Druperman's leadership would continue to refuse to pay. The fact that the Galaxy was unlikely to be targeted a third time would certainly encourage Emmett to preach tenacity; he'd taken *his* lumps like a mensch and now it was *their* turn to tough it out.

And while Steve respected Frank Marshall's ability, he doubted that his ex-partner would be able to locate the extortionists before Wednesday night—even with the full resources of the Las Vegas Metropolitan Police Department behind him. These Thanatos bastards were just too goddamn *smart*. So far there simply hadn't been any chinks in their armor.

They probably would carry out their awful promise and then come back with even bigger threats and even steeper monetary demands. Because how do you stop them? In the real world, how do you find that needle in the haystack? How does even the biggest army of law enforcement officers cover every corridor, scope every stairwell, reconnoiter every room—in every hotel on the Strip and downtown? With seventeen of the twenty largest hotels in the world located in Las Vegas, the whole city was just so damned *vulnerable* that it amazed Forrester these extortions hadn't happened before. Perhaps this was the beginning of a trend; maybe the copycat criminals would move in to plow these fresh pastures, much as a spate of airline hijackings occurred after D. B. Cooper broke new ground with his notorious $200,000 parachute jump over the Pacific Northwest. Forrester shuddered, visualizing Las Vegas as an armed camp at the mercy of every psycho with a Bic lighter. He dared not equate Las Vegas's current dilemma with the awful events in Oklahoma City or New York. . . .

So, what could they really do about it? Should the casinos pay off this particular gang of extortionists and hope that this time it was merely an aberration, a minor stumbling block in Las Vegas's march toward its hoped-for future as the family entertainment capital of America? Or would the casinos, as Druperman believed, simply be opening the floodgates to more of the same, to a deluge of demands, a torrent of extortions that would make aircraft hijackings look like kindergarten lunch-money rip-offs?

36 LVMPD Detective Len Traver parked the battered beige Crown Victoria on Colton Avenue near the corner of Bruce Street. His partner, Carl "Big Swede" Hansen, pulled a computer printout from his inside jacket pocket and unfolded it. There were thirty-two names and addresses on the list; all but a handful had been crossed out with a red felt pen.

"Look at this, Len," said Hansen, spreading the paper out on the console so that Traver could see it. "We only got five left. Two on Colton and one each on Wagner, Delhi, and Gorman. That's all inside four blocks. Why don't we just park here and shag the rest?"

"Good idea, Swede. My arse is developin' bedsores from this car seat."

"We finish this list, we're outta here. Then I don't give a shit, ain't no more overtime for this Big Swede—it's strictly Miller time."

"In your dreams, man. You heard what the lieutenant said. Double shifts until somebody makes the collar."

"I dunno, Len. This is Tuesday. Ingrid and me always go to the movies on Tuesday night. She is gonna be one pissed-off lady."

"Would you rather have her or Frank Marshall pissed at you?" Traver laid a sympathetic hand on his partner's shoulder as they trudged off down Colton. "C'mon, Swede, could be we get lucky this time."

Jurgen Voss frowned in annoyance as the sudden, totally unexpected reverberation of the doorbell shattered the unfrocked card counter's concentration on his computer programming.

Who the devil could it be? He had not buzzed anybody upstairs. Maybe some door-to-door peddler had gained access by pushing bells until someone let him in. That was the irritating thing about this building: someone always did. Certainly, *he* was not expecting anybody. Except for Shiller's scheduled call to the bank in Panama City tomorrow, preparations for the next two phases of the Thanatos scheme were complete, so neither Shiller nor Malloy had any reason to come by today. And Jurgen had no friends—not in the accepted sense, no one who would ring his doorbell without warning.

He decided not to answer the bell. Let them go away, whoever they were.

He resumed tapping on his computer keyboard.

The doorbell shrilled again, longer and more insistently.

He stopped typing, his fingers poised uncertainly over the keyboard. Perhaps he should answer it. It could be important. Maybe the super had finally arrived to repair the toilet as he had been promising for weeks. With a sigh, Voss pressed two keys simultaneously and the monitor screen blanked out. He pushed back his chair on its rollers and rose from the workstation.

"All right! I am coming!" he yelled down the hall to his unknown visitors as the doorbell rang yet again. "Be patient!" A glance through the peephole revealed two middle-aged men wearing suits, standing stoically outside his door. Jehovah's Witnesses? Encyclopedia salesmen? Well, he knew how to get rid of those types.

"Yes?" he said, snapping back the dead bolt and opening the door a few inches—without releasing the chain latch.

One of the men, a chunky, sweating type with greasebags under his eyes, held up a badge on a leather flap. "Sorry to bother you, sir. I'm Detective Traver of the Las Vegas Metropolitan Police Department." He indicated his companion, a tall, heavyset man with thinning blond hair. "This is my partner, Detective Hansen."

A sudden fear gripped the little man, knotting his belly and causing him to blink rapidly. And yet, why should he be afraid? There was no way the police could have traced the murders back to him! He had been so careful to leave no loose ends! It must be a coincidence. He gulped and stammered, "Wh-what is it? I am very busy. Perhaps if you returned later—"

"Do you mind if we come in, sir? This won't take long."

"For what reason? I have done nothing—"

Traver smiled affably. "Just routine, sir. There's been some break-ins in the neighborhood recently, and we're wondering if you've seen anything suspicious."

"In this neighborhood, there are always break-ins, Detectives. I am afraid I cannot help you."

"Maybe we can help *you,* sir. If you just let us in, we could check your windows and doors and your alarm system—"

"I have no alarm system. Now *bitte,* let me return to my work." Jurgen still had not released the chain latch, and he started to ease the door shut.

Without warning, the blond detective slammed the heel of his hand against the door, pushing it back to the extent of the chain and nearly smashing it into Voss's nose. "You got a problem letting us in, mister?" the big man growled. "Something in there you don't want us to see?" Swede Hansen wasn't just playing bad cop; he was tired of all the leg-work, pissed off at the overtime, and all he wanted was to finish up with this asshole and hopefully go home. But there was something else, and a glance at his partner confirmed that Len sensed it, too. This guy was *right.* So far, he fit at least three of the points on the profile they'd been given. A small guy, German accent, living near the tracks—what else would they find inside?

The two detectives had no search warrant and, so far, no probable cause to enter the subject's apartment. But their combined thirty-five years on the job had taught them just how far you could bend the law to serve your pur-poses. If politeness didn't work, sometimes bluster would. As long as they didn't use actual physical force to gain entry, it was strictly their word against the suspect's that they weren't cheerfully invited in. And Hansen was determined to get in.

Hansen kept up the pressure on Voss's door—the scrawny computer expert could no more have closed it than he could have moved the wall—and added with a fierce scowl, "You don't let us in, mister, we'll think you've probably got drugs in your apartment and we'll be back with a search warrant. Or maybe there's stolen goods in there—and you're the guy we've been lookin' for!"

Jurgen Voss listened with growing apprehension. It was obvious that these *gefeckte* storm troopers were not going to leave. But then he thought a little further. They had not mentioned the extortion. Was the story about the neighborhood break-ins merely a ploy to disarm him—or was it genuine? Were they really here about the protection of his household goods—or did they suspect his involvement in Thanatos? Maybe it was better to find out. Even if he did let them in, they would find nothing. He had been scrupu-lously careful to leave no physical traces of Thanatos's covert activities. With a sigh of resignation, Jurgen said, "Okay, okay, Detective, if you in-sist. Stop pushing on my door and I will admit you."

"You are Mr. Voss?" Detective Len Traver asked. "That's German, isn't it?"

"How do you know my name?"

"Ah, we got it off your mailbox," said Traver smoothly as his partner scanned the dingy apartment. "Do you live here alone, sir?"

"Yes. Perhaps if we could arrive at the point—"

"Look, we're really sorry to bother you, but it's important we catch these . . . burglars. So, if you don't mind, we'll just look around for a few minutes and we'll be gone before you know it."

"What's in there?" Hansen inquired, indicating the feeble glow emanating from under the door at the end of the hall.

"That is merely . . . some computer equipment," Voss replied, nervously gnawing a ragged fingernail. "It cannot be your interest, *nichtwahr?*"

"I wouldn't be too sure about that, sir," said Detective Traver, thinking quickly. "It's just the kind of thing that gets stolen around here. Did you have the equipment engraved with your name and Social Security number? That's one of the services that the LVMPD offers to householders—you know, free engraving of valuables. Could save you a bundle on insurance premiums. Can we check it out?"

Jurgen shrugged helplessly. There was obviously no stopping these men. "If you must."

"Thank you." Traver could smell blood now. "Ah, perhaps you'd care to wait here, Mr. Voss, while Detective Hansen and me, ah, just look around in there for a minute. We won't touch anything, sir, I promise."

Without waiting for their reluctant host's formal assent, both men proceeded to the computer room, filed in, and casually eased the door closed behind them.

"What a fuckin' mess," said Hansen, repressing a sneeze. "Did you ever see so much dust and cobwebs?"

"Never mind that, Swede!" Traver whispered excitedly to his partner as soon as they were alone. "This is the guy! Every single point on the profile, this asshole fits it to a T! He's into computers. Plus I'll lay odds he's got the exact kind of equipment we're supposed to look for."

"Jesus, Len, you think so? What was it again?"

The sweaty detective extracted a typed sheet from his pocket. "Here it is: a Hewlett-Packard 8100 printer and an IBM Itanium computer."

Hansen crouched and peered under Voss's work surface. He brushed aside a colony of spiderwebs and dusted the nameplate on a small tower

PC with his finger. "Well, you're right about the Itanium. It's under the table."

"And the printer's over here on this shelf."

"Right on! Have we got enough to take this guy in?"

Traver grinned gleefully. "Are you kidding? What else do we need, you big dumb Swede? This little fart's got everything but 'perp' tattooed on his forehead!"

"All *right*! Let's bring him in.

"Happy ending, partner!" Len Traver chortled as he clapped his colleague on the back. "Now you can take your old lady to the movies after all!"

"Mr. Voss, would you mind comin' with us to headquarters?" Detective Carl Hansen asked with disarming courtesy. There was no need for the bad-cop routine anymore. They'd gotten in. They'd seen what they needed to see. He could almost have kissed the little dude for making it so easy. Let somebody else ask the tough questions; his day was almost over.

Jurgen's eyes bulged behind his Coke-bottle lenses. "Why are you arresting me?" he asked in a trembling voice. "I am no burglar."

"We're not arresting you, sir. We just need to talk to you."

"Where are you taking me?"

"The Southwest Area Command on Spring Mountain."

"This is not about break-ins in the neighborhood, is it, Detectives? This was a trick to come in my home. Am I right?"

"No, sir. You asked us in. It was all nice and legal," said Hansen, neatly evading the question.

"What is this really about?"

"They'll explain that to you later." The edge had begun to creep back into Carl Hansen's voice.

Voss swallowed and took a deep breath. "*Und* what if . . . what if I will not come with you?"

Len Traver stepped protectively in front of Jurgen, ostensibly shielding the little man from his partner. He spoke in a low and earnest voice to their suspect. "Number one, *sir,* we'd consider it to be uncooperative behavior on your part. Number two, we'd put a cop on your door while we drove all the way across town to get a warrant for your arrest and then drove all the way back here and cuffed you. Number three, that would *really* annoy my partner, Detective Hansen here, because it would mean extra work for him. And when he gets mad, I can't control him."

Right on cue, the big blond detective growled and took a step toward Voss.

"Wait a minute, Swede." said Len Traver, apparently restraining his partner only with the greatest difficulty. "I think Mr. Voss will cooperate. Right, sir?"

The little man looked around desperately. Once again, it appeared he had no option. "Yes . . . all right. You win. I will accompany you. Just . . . let me get my jacket."

"No problem, sir," said Traver with a reassuring smile. "Take your time."

Jurgen shuffled miserably into the bedroom and picked his windbreaker up off the floor. Was this it? Was the game over? Had Thanatos lost?

Impulsively, he stopped off at the messy kitchenette that adjoined his living room and picked up a couple of small pink packages from a cracked sugar bowl.

"What's that, sir?" Traver asked politely.

"Only some artificial sweetener, Detective." Voss showed the paper packets to his captor. "Sweet'n Low. For my coffee. I always bring with me some when I will be away from home . . . for a while."

"Good idea, mister," Hansen said impatiently, glancing at his watch. He and Ingrid could still make the seven o'clock if they hurried. "Now, let's go."

37 "**Mr. Voss,** this is Lieutenant Frank Marshall. I'm Sergeant Morris Jaworski. Please sit down. Can we get you anything? Coffee? Soda?"

"*Nein* . . . no, thank you." Jurgen glanced around at his new surroundings. Fluorescent ceiling fixtures cast a cold white light on the windowless interview room and its sparse furnishings: a scarred refectory table and a number of mismatched wooden chairs. There was a wall-mounted camcorder, a cork bulletin board with wanted posters and official notices thumbtacked to it, and a large mirror, obviously for one-way viewing from outside the room.

Uncomfortable and out of his element as he was, the would-be extortionist felt increasingly *un*intimidated. During the ride to the police station his confidence had grown. Except for the rather transparent scare tactics of the big blond detective, which in retrospect Voss realized were no more than a well-practiced routine to coerce reluctant subjects into cooperation, both men had treated him fairly courteously—far more courteously than he supposed an actual *suspect* would have been treated. They had made it clear that he was categorically *not* under arrest; he was being brought in only for questioning. Voss knew that he, Shiller, and Malloy had left no traces; under his technical direction, the planning and execution of the Thanatos scheme had been flawless. Additionally, he comforted himself with the fact that his computers at home were impregnable. He had erected so many barriers and firewalls—not to mention the deadly deterrents he had concealed— that the data was totally irretrievable to anyone without the codes and passwords that he alone possessed.

Somewhat more relaxed, Jurgen assessed his position. They obviously had *something;* otherwise, he would not be here. Yet there could not possibly be any hard evidence against him. Perhaps all this stemmed from his earlier arrest at the Galaxy; maybe the authorities were simply questioning anyone with any connection, no matter how remote, to the giant casino. As long as he admitted nothing, he had nothing to fear. He was actually beginning to look forward to matching wits with these Neanderthals.

"Well, gentlemen," said the unfrocked card counter with a thin smile. "How may I help the police?"

"Sir, we're looking into an extortion scheme against . . . certain hotels here in Las Vegas," said Marshall. "We believe you may have information that could help us."

So it *was* about Thanatos! Voss felt a surge of adrenaline. He struggled to remain composed. "Extortion? I know of no extortion."

"What do you do for a living?"

"This and that."

"Are you a professional card counter?"

He was right! But was this all they had? In any event, there was no point denying his former occupation; it was now a matter of police record. "*Ja*. However, I have not—"

"Do you like movies, Jurgen?" the other policeman cut in suddenly.

"I do not understand. . . ."

"From the video store," said Marshall. "Do you ever rent movies from the video store?" *Of course!* Jurgen thought. These plodders had actually checked the names of every person who had rented *Seven* and *Extreme Measures*! How many thousands of names would be on *that* list! Voss almost laughed aloud as realized exactly how these louts had arrived at their decision to question him—and how little real evidence they had. It was all circumstantial. The card-counting episode at the Galaxy, the movie rentals—that was it! Let them keep him here as long as they wished. Let them ask their foolish questions. He would admit to nothing.

"**What did you say** his name was, Frank?" Steve Forrester asked, lighting up a Vantage 100 with his free hand. He slid a ruled notepad closer to the phone and reached for a pen. "Jurgen Voss? No, don't bother spelling it. . . . I remember the crazy little bastard. A card counter. Sure . . . that's right . . . we sent him over to you guys for booking, what, six months ago?" Steve took a deep drag on his cigarette while Frank Marshall spoke. "What? Lunch with you and Moe? And you want me to bring Druperman? Sure.

He'd appreciate being brought up to speed. Why not swing over here, and the Galaxy will buy the lunch . . . yes, Frank, the casino *can* afford it." Thoughtfully, he replaced the receiver, rose from his chair, and walked to the window.

There was something bothering him, something about the mention of the little card counter's name. He gazed at all the glistening new hotel-casinos on the south end of the Strip—the Paris, the Venetian, the Bellagio—without really seeing any of them. What was it about Voss? He stared down at the All-Star Café and idly watched two taxicabs experience a near collision on the busy Las Vegas Strip below his window.

Forrester turned away and stubbed out his cigarette. If he left it alone, concentrated on other things, he knew it would come to him. Sooner or later, it always did.

"We've got the subject in custody, had him there all night, and I can guarantee you he knows more than he's telling us," said Lieutenant Frank Marshall as he picked at his potato salad in the Cosmic Café. "Not only that, but I get the distinct feeling the little bastard is laughing at us."

"Yes, I remember how cocky he was the day we sent him over to you at the station," said Steve Forrester. "He just about dared us to arrest him."

Emmett Druperman looked surprised. "You mean you've run into this character before, Steve?"

"Yep. Jurgen Voss is actually a professional card counter. Picked him up about six months ago. He was given the choice of walking or arguing, and he decided to argue. So . . . we turned him over to Frank's people."

"To the police? What happened?" asked the CEO, chewing on a pastrami sandwich.

"The usual. First offense, judge gives him a walk," Forrester replied. "All we wanted was to scare him a little. Doesn't look like it worked—if we're right. About his being part of the Thanatos gang, I mean."

"What makes you think he's part of the gang?" Druperman inquired.

"You recall that profile we developed of the person who wrote those extortion letters?" said Morris Jaworski. "Well, sir, this Jurgen Voss scores a bull's-eye on every single point. He's egocentric . . . he's highly intelligent . . . he's physically small . . . his first language appears to be German . . . and he's into computers.

"Not only that, he lives near the Union Pacific tracks . . . and he's also rented *Seven* and *Extreme Measures* from VegasVideo within the past month.

"And the icing on the cake is, before they brought him in, Frank's detectives identified one of his computers and his laser printer as the exact types of machine that generated the letters.

"Now, while this evidence is tremendously compelling, it's also totally circumstantial. There isn't a single shred of hard proof that Voss played any part in the murders or the extortion. However, the evidence was strong enough to get us a search warrant for his apartment. I've had a team of forensic programmers in there since before midnight, tearing his computer system apart. If there are any traces of his involvement in this scheme, or better still, if there are any indications as to which casino is targeted for the fire, they'll find them."

"Well, they better work fast," Druperman growled. "The latest deadline is five o'clock today—and I convinced the LVCA to hang tough and not pay the ransom. I told 'em to rely on you guys. It was a tough sell. If you don't come through, they'll be hanging me out to dry."

"Not to mention hanging a few hundred tourists out to *fry*," Frank Marshall added.

Forrester nodded grimly and said quietly, "You know, Frank, there's something that's bugging me about this guy Jurgen Voss. Something you or Moe said a while ago. I just can't get a handle on it. But I've got a feeling it could be important."

"Don't worry about it, O perceptive one. Just let me know when the revelation strikes you."

A silence fell upon the casino executives and their lawmen guests as the waitress reappeared at their table. "Can I bring you anything else, gentlemen?" she asked.

"How's the coffee here?" Jaworski asked innocently.

"From what I've heard," Frank Marshall commented dryly, "it either gets you horny or it kills you."

David Takahashi, freelance forensic computer programmer for the LVMPD, mopped the dusty sweat from his forehead with a soiled handkerchief and cursed softly under his breath. Between the dust bunnies, the cobwebs, and the oppressive heat, this assignment had become an endurance test for him and his crew. In fact, he'd had to send one of the guys home, a fellow with moderate allergies who could not stop sneezing in Jurgen Voss's dust-filled computer room. Takahashi was surprised that the equipment still functioned under such adverse conditions.

This whole assignment was unusual. Under normal circumstances, they would have disconnected the equipment and brought it back to the lab for analysis. But Morris Jaworski was worried that the system might have been rigged to trigger massive data destruction if any unsequenced physical disconnection occurred. In addition, Jaworski had made it clear that time was of the essence—if there was any information to be found about the location of the threatened fire, it was crucial to uncover it before the extortionists' five-o'clock deadline. Hence, the on-site investigation.

"Got you, you dusty bastard!" one of his technicians suddenly shouted triumphantly. "Check this out, Dave. That cunning son of a bitch had more than Intel inside! He's got two hidden locks in the case, and they're accessible only through these ventilation slots. But I got them open—and it's lucky I did. There's a tiny bit of plastic explosive pressed onto this internal RAID array. If I'd tried to force the case open without releasing the hidden locks, it would've gone off and destroyed the data." The technician shuddered and grimaced. "Might have blown a couple of my fingers off, too."

"My God," said Takahashi. "You okay to keep going, man?"

"Sure, Dave, no problem." The technician paused thoughtfully. "But I just don't get this guy."

"Meaning?"

"Meaning, what is Voss hiding that's so hands-off, he's willing to destroy all his data—*and* his computer—rather than let anyone in?"

"Who knows? Course, the data's probably backed up somewhere. And the hardware's replaceable. But that's beside the point. We've got to get in there and find some answers—fast."

"It's not gonna be easy. Voss has encrypted the whole system."

"How?"

"Military-grade IDEA encryption."

"Damn."

"It'll be tough to break in without the password. Any ideas?"

Takahashi shook his head slowly. The password could be anything from a sequence of numbers to a phrase, probably date- and time-dependent. Would Voss keep it in his head, or would he have it written down somewhere? It was more likely he'd keep it in some kind of off-line storage device. . . .

Suddenly Takahashi brightened and snapped his fingers. Of course! Didn't Voss possess a magnetic card reader—and a writer? And hadn't the detectives found a wallet when they tossed his bedroom? With credit cards in it?

The programmer turned to his technician. "I think I know where to look for the password. I'll have to call the Evidence Room first. If my idea works out, we'll be inside this mother in forty-five minutes."

38

"Mr. Forrester?" the voice on the other end of the phone was tentative. "It's me, Gladys."

"Gladys?" replied Steve Forrester, not immediately placing the name.

"Gladys Adams. You know, the daytime hostess in the Cosmic Café?"

"Of course, Gladys. I should have recognized your voice. How are you feeling? That was a terrible thing that happened in the café last week."

"Well, that's why I'm calling, Mr. Forrester. Remember how you and that police lieutenant asked me to try and recall who had been sitting at the table before that poor gentleman . . . died? Well, I've been thinking and thinking about it and finally it came back to me. I sort of remember now what he looked like. I don't know if this will help. . . ."

"I'm sure it will. And I'll be glad to pass it along to Lieutenant Marshall. Go ahead."

"Yes, sir. The best I can remember, it was a big man, tall, kind of heavy. I asked him if he wanted smoking or nonsmoking and he went, 'I don't care.' He had these wraparound sunglasses on, so I couldn't see his eyes."

"Good, Gladys. Do you remember what his voice was like? Any accent?"

"No . . . sorry, Mr. Forrester. I can't remember his voice."

"All right. Anything else?"

"Well, there was one other thing. He was wearing this baseball cap, you know, and it mostly covered his head, but . . ."

"But . . . ?"

"But I could still see a bit of his hair. He had red hair, Mr. Forrester."

That was it! Suddenly, Forrester felt as if a door had opened in his mind. This was what had been bothering him ever since Frank Marshall told him about Jurgen Voss! "Thanks a million, Gladys," he almost shouted into the phone as he banged the receiver down.

"Suzy," he said to his executive assistant, grabbing his jacket in one hand and his briefcase in the other, "I need you to call Personnel right now. Tell them to pull Buster Malloy's file. I'll pick it up on my way out."

"Right away, boss," she replied. "And might one inquire as to where you're going?"

"I'm headed for the Southwest Area Command to meet with Morris Jaworski and Frank Marshall. Call me on the cell phone if you need to reach me."

"And how long will you be gone, Steve?"

"I dunno, Suzy." Forrester looked at his watch. Two-fifteen. Less than three hours until Thanatos's deadline—for a $25 million transfer that he knew the association had no intention of making. "Don't hang around."

An exhausted, dirty crew of forensic programmers clustered excitedly around one of Jurgen Voss's monitors.

"I'll be damned," said the technician at the keyboard. "Somehow this guy's hacked his way into the California DMV database and downloaded a driver's license template."

"Obviously for the purposes of creating a bogus ID," said David Takahashi. "What's that file with the Photoshop icon?"

"Hold on . . . let me open it." The technician double-clicked on the icon. Silence fell over the group as the application was opened automatically by the computer and the file decompressed. A head-and-shoulders scan of a ruddy-complexioned middle-aged man loaded quickly and filled the screen. "Want me to make a hard copy, Dave?" the tech asked.

"Later. Right now let's download these files to the lab. Time's running out."

Dan Shiller waited until the Saturn spectacular was in full blast before he dared approach Buster Malloy at his post near the elevator.

"Psst! Buster!" the con man whispered fiercely, trying to make himself heard over the megawatt THX roar of the holographic rocket's engines.

The one-eyed security guard turned casually toward the sound, then froze as he recognized his accomplice. "Shiller! What the fuck are you doin' here? I thought you said we shouldn't never be seen together," he growled out of the corner of his mouth.

"Shut up and listen carefully. They've got Jurgen—"

"What?" Malloy wasn't sure he'd hcard correctly over the rumble of the Saturn blastoff. "Did you say they got Jurgen?"

"That's right. I've just come from his apartment. It's crawling with cops."

Buster's ruddy face fell. "Jesus Christ. What're we gonna do now?"

"Nothing, man. I figured we'd carry on. You know, go through with it anyway. We don't need him anymore. He's rigged the electronics for phase three and wired up the boom box for phase four. He's made the video and written the last letter—"

"What about the bank in Panama? Ain't you been callin' 'em on Jurgen's computer?"

"No problem, my Irish friend. I can call them from hotel-lobby phones. The way I do it, it's just as untraceable."

Malloy brightened. "Does this mean I still get to set the fire tonight?"

"Goddamn right you do, Buster—if the association doesn't cough up the twenty-five million. And I don't think they will."

Malloy licked his lips. "All right! Call me at home after—"

Shiller glanced around. The holographic smoke had begun to clear and the noise of the spectacular was fading away. It was time to leave. He couldn't put off the bad news any longer. "Buster, look, you can't go home."

"Why not?"

"Voss may have squealed. They may be onto you. In fact, you'd better get out of the Galaxy right now."

"But my shift ain't over until—"

"Never mind your fucking shift," Dan hissed angrily. "Would you rather spend the next thirty years in jail?"

"All right, all right. I'll go. Where do I meet you?"

"Billy Bob's. Come around five-thirty. Meanwhile, you better get rid of your truck. They'll be watching for it."

"What about you? Ain't you afraid they'll come to *your* place?"

"Let me worry about that."

Dan Shiller occupied no fixed address. Over the past three decades, he had lived in hundreds of efficiency apartments, hotels, and motels, never in any one location for more than a few weeks, always registering under assumed names. The constant migration was one of the few annoyances of the grifting business, but a necessary precaution and one he had learned to live with.

Shiller and Malloy left the Galaxy, each by a different exit.

"**Welcome back** to the Southwest Area Command, Steve," said Sergeant Morris Jaworski. "That's quite a sweat you've worked up."

"I kinda rushed over here, Moe. I've got something important to tell you and Frank."

"Sure, come on in. And by the way, thanks again for lunch."

"Well, I'll be damned." Frank Marshall looked up in surprise as Jaworski ushered Forrester into the police lab. "So you decided to honor us with a visit."

"Hello, Frank."

"Did you read my mind? I was just about to call you. You should see what our forensic programmers have dug out of Voss's computer system. I need you to—"

"Hold on a sec, Frank," Forrester cut in. "Before we get into that, I've got a news flash for you guys. Remember at lunchtime I told you there was something bothering me? Something I couldn't quite put my finger on? Well, it came to me. Right after Gladys Adams called."

"Gladys Adams—the hostess in the coffee shop?"

"That's right. You asked her to try and remember the previous customer at Leopold's table. Well, she came through. She remembers a tall, heavy man with red hair and wraparound sunglasses. And that description triggered the answer I'd been missing." The two lawmen looked at Steve expectantly. He continued: "Moe, after your preliminary analysis of the case, you suggested the probability of a Galaxy employee's being involved in this Thanatos gang. Okay, who is the only Galaxy employee we know of to have had any more than casual contact with Jurgen Voss? Buster Malloy, that's who! He's the security guard I assigned to take Voss to the station and sign the complaint after Voss was busted for card counting.

"Now, let's compare Gladys's description of this guy to Malloy's. She said tall; Malloy's personnel file lists his height as six-two. Heavy—I'm sure he weighs at least two-fifty. Red-haired—that's our boy. And here's the clincher: she said he was wearing wraparound sunglasses. Malloy has only one eye. Normally he wears an eye patch, but the sunglasses would conceal the missing eye just as effectively.

"And I happen to know that Malloy is not altogether a happy camper at the Galaxy. There have been incidents—at least one that I know of. Malloy resents our high rollers, especially Asians. Nothing serious enough to fire the man for—yet. Anyway, I brought Buster's personnel file with me. His full name is Francis Marion Malloy."

An electric silence fell upon the room for a moment as Jaworski and Marshall absorbed Forrester's hypothesis.

Then the police sergeant spoke up. "And I suppose he would have had access to the mailroom to deliver that first envelope?"

"You bet he would, Moe. And to Francisco's suite. Security guards all have a master key card."

"Hell, Steve, this guy sounds right," the police scientist said with controlled excitement.

"Steve Forrester scores again," Marshall muttered.

Jaworski frowned at his colleague, then shrugged and addressed Steve. "Now here's what we were going to ask *you*," he said. "Our forensic programming people downloaded a photograph from Voss's computer that they think was used to make up a phony ID. I was going to ask you if you recognized it. Then while you were talking, I was thinking, shit, could it be this fellow Malloy? Could it actually be Malloy's photograph? That would tie this whole thing up pretty neat, and we'd have two prime suspects to lean on.

"But then you said Malloy was missing an eye. This guy's got two. Anyway . . . we'll show you the picture. Maybe you'll recognize the subject. . . ."

Jaworski turned to a nineteen-inch Sony Multiscan 200SX monitor and pressed a button. As the screen slowly brightened and the photograph came into focus, Forrester gasped. "That's him!" he said. "I don't know how they fixed his eye, but that's definitely Malloy."

Morris looked thoughtful. "That explains why Voss imported the scan into Adobe Photoshop. It's a retouching program. He gave Malloy a new eye electronically!"

Malloy's trailer was deserted.

Detective Len Traver rang the bell of the neighboring mobile home. A skinny, underfed mongrel lying prone beside the steps thumped its tail halfheartedly, raising a small cloud of dust. The stench of cigarette smoke and cheap rum emanating from inside almost knocked him off his feet as a heavyset woman opened the door. He forced himself to brave the effluvium and said politely, "Good afternoon, ma'am. Detective Traver, LVMPD. Have you seen Mr. Malloy from next door?"

"Malloy? I always knew that sum bitch was trouble," she answered unsteadily. "Haven't seen him since yesterday. An' that blond girlfriend of his . . . haven't seen her for weeks. What's he done?"

"Just a routine inquiry, ma'am. Who is this girlfriend you mentioned?"

"Big blond whore. Stric'ly trailer trash. Name's Helga . . . Helga Johnson or somethin' like that."

Traver made a note. "I see. Does this woman live here with him? Does Mr. Malloy have any other friends or associates you know of?"

"What am I, his freakin' social secretary? I don't know nothin' about Malloy except he lives next door . . . an' mister, believe me, I don' *wanna* know nothin' about him. Onliest thing I can tell you, his truck wasn't there last night. I know because the thing makes such a God-awful racket." She paused. "I hope that one-eyed sum bitch is gone for good. There's somethin' . . . *weird* about him. He *scares* me."

"I understand," said Traver sympathetically, handing her his card. "If Mr. Malloy should come back, don't even mention that we were here. Just call me. And thanks for your cooperation, ma'am."

Carl Hansen, Traver's partner, reported back. "I checked the people on the other side and across the street, Len. DMV says he drives a 'seventy-nine Ford pickup. The men looked around, but it's not here. Nobody's seen him or the vehicle since early last evening."

"Somethin' must've spooked him, Swede. Marshall says he didn't even finish his shift at the Galaxy yesterday."

For Buster Malloy the elevated empty lot across Carey Avenue afforded a perfect vantage point from which to view his trailer unobserved. Astride the motorcycle, parked behind some scrub brush, he adjusted the focus of the field glasses to suit his own monocular vision. Inside the crumbling concrete-block wall that surrounded the park, the cops were getting back into their cars.

Malloy had gone home, packed a bag, and abandoned the trailer right after Shiller had told him of the computer expert's arrest. So the little scumbag *had* squealed. Why else would the cops have shown up?

One way or the other, it would all be over soon. Meanwhile, he could live in the desert. The big vehicle was perfectly concealed in a gully, and there was plenty of room inside to stretch out.

39 **Watching the interrogation** of Jurgen Voss from behind the one-way mirror in the Southwest Area Command Station interview room, Steve Forrester could not shake a pervasive sense of *déjà vu*.

Eventually he figured it out. It was the same feeling he always experienced in the catwalks at the Galaxy—he was once again the reluctant voyeur, keyhole peeking through the eye in the sky and feeling guilty about it. In fairness to himself, both Frank Marshall and Morris Jaworski had asked him to stay for a while and audit the interview. "Just in case us hack cops miss anything," Lieutenant Frank Marshall had added. Ignoring the sarcasm, Forrester had immediately agreed to the request and now watched, fascinated, as the two veteran police officers plied their trade. It had been three years since the casino executive had been on the other side of the glass, and he had to admit that he sometimes missed the job. He lit another Vantage 100 and returned his attention to the morality play being acted out under the bright lights just a few feet from where he sat in darkness.

"Jurgen, it's time to quit playing games," he heard Frank Marshall say. "We've got enough evidence against you right now to get an indictment—"

"You have nothing," said the little German, folding his arms resolutely across his scrawny chest and tucking his hands in his armpits, a move that also served to conceal his mutilated fingertips from his questioners. "I am a card counter *und* I rented some videos—like many other people. What does this prove?"

"Tell us where the fire will take place, Jurgen," said Marshall wearily. "Now, before hundreds of people die."

"I do not know what you are talking about."

"Who are your associates? What are their names? If you give us the information now, maybe we can cut some kind of deal."

"I have no information for you."

"Jurgen, where's the fire?"

"I do not know."

"Where's the fire?"

Voss shook his head stubbornly, set his thin lips in a firm line, and contemplated the ceiling. He knew his tormentors had no real evidence against him. They were clutching at straws, and it was only a matter of time before they would be obliged to release him.

Marshall glanced at Moe Jaworski, then at his watch. Less than two hours to go. Time to play hardball. He rose from his chair, opened the door, and beckoned to the men waiting outside.

Two of Jaworski's forensic programming technicians entered the room. One of the technicians was bearing a computer monitor; the other carried the computer itself and a keyboard.

"Set it up here on the table, please, so Jurgen can see it," said Morris Jaworski. While the technicians connected cables, Frank Marshall drew Jaworski aside. "Have we got it all, Moe?" he asked quietly.

"Enough to give this skell a real shock," Jaworski whispered back.

While they were talking, the technicians had plugged in the equipment and booted up the system. "All set, Sarge," one of them reported.

"Thanks, fellas."

The two men left the room. Under the harsh fluorescent lights, only Jurgen Voss, Frank Marshall, and Morris Jaworski remained. Steve Forrester continued to observe through the one-way mirror.

"You know, Jurgen, we could really make things easy for you if you'd cooperate. If it was somebody else that did the killings, tell us now," Marshall said pleasantly to their suspect, laying a friendly hand on Voss's bony shoulder. "Give up the names of your pals and tell us where the fire is going to be, you might even walk away from this."

Jurgen Voss had been momentarily puzzled by the introduction of the computer into the interview room, but he relaxed as he realized that this must be another of their simpleminded police tricks. And now this Marshall was apparently to be cast as the good cop. Would these *idioten* never learn? "To the police I have nothing to say."

Frank Marshall shrugged and nodded to Jaworski.

The police scientist depressed a button on the wall-mounted video camera. He then enunciated for the record the date, time, location, and identities of the three persons present in the room. He continued, "Jurgen Voss, you are under arrest for the murders of Barnaby Galt Leopold and Antonio Giovanni Francisco, and for attempted extortion against Emmett Druperman and the Las Vegas Casino Association.

"This interview is being videotaped.

"You have the right to remain silent. If you give up that right, anything you say can and will be used against you in a court of law. You have a right to an attorney and to have your attorney present during questioning. If you cannot afford an attorney, one will be appointed for you. Do you understand your rights?"

"Of course. Do I look stupid?" Jurgen was mildly surprised by the sudden shift in the attitude of the police and by the formalization of his status as a suspect. But he remained composed.

"Do you wish to have an attorney present?"

"*Nein.* I will get one only when I sue you for false arrest."

Frank Marshall, no longer the good cop, leaned in closer to the suspect. "Is that so, mister? Well, you may change your mind when you hear what we found out about Thanatos."

"Thanatos? *Ich kenne nicht diese Thanatos. . . .*"

"Don't act dumb, shithead, you know exactly what I mean. For openers, our forensic programmers have discovered some very interesting stuff on your computer—"

Voss suddenly sat bolt upright on the hard wooden chair. "What? You had no right—"

"Oh, yes, we did," said Marshall grimly. "We obtained a search warrant last night authorizing us to examine all your computer files."

"Really? Well, I am certain this has done you no good. My files are secure. *Und* my hardware is tamperproof—"

"Are you referring to the plastic explosive my guys found inside the computer cases, you little bastard?" Jaworski interjected. "Just be grateful we disarmed it before it blew somebody's fingers off. Otherwise, you'd be facing charges of aggravated assault on top of everything else."

Jurgen paled. "I did not expect you to—"

"And furthermore," Jaworski cut in, "you're not nearly as smart as you think you are when it comes to protecting your data with tricky barriers. Our forensic programmers found your password on a magnetic card in your wallet. After that it took them less than two hours to mine your entire god-damn system."

Voss slumped back in his chair and mumbled an imprecation in German. He prayed that they had not discovered his terrible secret, the one only a few special friends knew about, the real reason he had erected so many security barriers around his computer system.

"What was that?" Morris snapped.

"Nothing. I only—"

"We're wasting time," Frank interrupted. "Let's cut to the chase and tell Jurgen exactly what we know. Then maybe he'll tell us what *he* knows about Thanatos's coming attractions. Including the fire."

"All right, Jurgen, listen carefully," said Jaworski, straddling a chair in front of Voss. "We know you rented the movies that were used in the extortion packages—and we found the equipment you used to make the copies. We matched the type of printer used for the extortion notes to your laser printer. Our audio specialists identified the background noise on the phone call your pal made to Emmett Druperman—it was from a train that just happened to be passing through your neighborhood at the exact time of the call. Oh yes—and that DSP software of yours that we found incorporates a voice filter that precisely re-creates the voice pattern on your partner's call to Druperman."

"All this proves nothing," the little man protested weakly. So far, they had not mentioned his shameful secret. Perhaps his luck was holding and they had not mined deeply enough. . . .

"Shut up. I'm not finished. We have evidence that one of your accomplices is Buster Malloy. . . ."

Behind the thick lenses, Jurgen's eyes widened momentarily at the mention of Malloy's name, but he managed to suppress any other reaction.

". . . and look what we found on one of your hard drives!" Jaworski pressed a key to turn on the computer screen, then double-clicked on an icon. The retouched scan of the big Irishman's face stared back at his accomplice, who had begun to perspire visibly. "Recognize him?"

"I . . ."

"You and Malloy must have become *very* good friends on your way to jail last spring. And I have to congratulate you; that was a wonderful California driver's license you made for your new friend. With the color laser printer and the laminator, you could make up the whole thing in that dusty little room of yours, couldn't you?"

Morris paused and stared coldly at the little man. The bravado had faded; the police scientist noted a slight twitch, an almost imperceptible trembling. "Okay, Jurgen," he continued sarcastically. "Help me out here. What was the name you used on the license?" Jaworski raised an eyebrow quizzically and waited. "Don't tell me you've forgotten? Think hard!" There was no response from the shaken Voss. "Harry Jackson, wasn't it? Frank, correct me if I'm wrong, but isn't that the same alias Jurgen gave Steve Forrester at the Galaxy?"

"That's right, Moe," said Marshall. "I thought Mr. Voss here was supposed to be some kind of Einstein. I sure as hell didn't think he'd be stupid enough to pick a name he'd already used.

"And you know what else, Jurgen?" the police lieutenant continued. "Somebody purchased some cantharidin—that's Spanish fly to us laymen— at an L.A. pharmaceutical supply house just a few days before the poisoning at the Galaxy. Using a California driver's license in the name of Harry Jackson as ID! And—guess what?—somebody who looked a lot like Buster Malloy was seen in the Cosmic Café just before Barney Leopold's last coffee break. Sitting at the same table. How's that for a bunch of coincidences, Jurgen?"

Voss's brain reeled, but he remained silent.

"Okay, Mr. Jurgen Voss," said Morris Jaworski. "We'll give you one more chance to save your miserable ass. All we need right now is for you to answer two questions, and I can guarantee you that you'll be very, very sorry if you don't. Who else is involved in Thanatos? And—*where's the fire?*"

Now uncaring who saw, Jurgen raised a ragged, bleeding thumbnail to his mouth and began to chew. He must be strong. He must admit to nothing. He was afraid that if he tried to speak, his voice would break. And there could be no weakness now. With a supreme effort, he swallowed hard and managed to stammer, "I-I am sorry. I still have . . . nothing to tell you."

"In that case," said Jaworski sternly, rising from his chair and picking up the mouse, "we will have to advise federal authorities about the filth we found on your computer."

Voss's heart almost stopped. Finally, the truth was out.

Jurgen Voss *had always felt superior to the other boys in the village of Löcknitz. The smallest and weakest of his peer group, he knew nonetheless that he, Jurgen, was more intelligent than any of them. From an early age the stick-frail boy with the large head had inured himself to the insults and the catcalls, refusing to dignify them with a reaction, scuttling home every day after school to escape the harassment and to bury himself in his father's engineering manuals and mathematical textbooks.*

Because, for as long as he could remember, Jurgen Voss had experienced an ongoing love affair with numbers. To him, they were not simply symbols on paper, they were living things. They spoke to him, they invited him to explore their delicious intricacies, they entranced him with their perfect logic. They were his friends, his protectors, his refuge from the storm. Life for the small boy in the East German village was tolerable.

Until the night of his seventh birthday.

After that, there was no escape from the night terrors.

He did not know which was more unbearable—the physical pain or the awful shame he felt that night. Upon leaving Jurgen's bed after repeatedly ramming the horrible great thing into him, his father had sworn him to secrecy and promised terrible retribution if the boy ever mentioned the incident to his mother or anyone else.

Two nights later the event was repeated. It became a recurring nightmare for the seven-year-old, happening with increasing frequency. There was no one the boy could turn to for help. He was afraid to tell his mother and doubted in any case that she would believe him. He could not turn to the priest; how do you tell a man of God that you have sinned so terribly? One day he haltingly tried to blurt out his awful secret to his ten-year-old brother; the older boy paled and turned away, refusing to speak of the matter. Jurgen thought he noticed tears welling up in his brother's eyes.

Jurgen's father was a civil engineer, an employee of the East German government. Life was difficult for the Voss family; they lived in the cold northern reaches of what was then East Germany, near the Baltic Sea. Food was scarce and luxuries nonexistent. Yet when the elder Voss announced that the family would flee to America, Jurgen's only reaction was to hope that perhaps in the new land the visits from his father would cease.

But his hopes were dashed. Immediately after settling in the modest Minneapolis house, the night terrors became more frequent—and more ferocious. For two more years they persisted, until Jurgen could tolerate no more. Gathering his courage, the fifteen-year-old tremblingly told his father that the nocturnal visits must stop, that he would quite simply kill himself if the older man continued his incestuous practices.

The threat worked. Jurgen's father finally stopped doing the shameful thing, and from that day forward rarely even spoke to the boy.

In high school Jurgen Voss fit the profile of the archetypal nerd. Moderately severe strabismus forced him to wear thick glasses; he was skinny and totally unathletic. An innate shyness compounded the problem. Jurgen became something of a loner, developing a persona among his unsympathetic fellow students as the dorky-looking whiz kid with the funny accent—which he never lost—and the bad haircut. His intellectual superiority did not promote any kind of serious social life, while the baggage he carried from a thousand nights of abuse had robbed him of any chance for a normal sex life.

Many of the boys in his class, their hormones raging, dedicated a large portion of their teenage energy to the active pursuit of girls. Others, too shy to date, nevertheless bragged incessantly to their friends about imagined conquests or fantasized privately about their female classmates.

But not Jurgen. He knew that he was somehow different. Certainly girls held no attraction for him—in fact, they frightened him. He felt empty and alone. He told himself he did not care; he had his numbers.

And yet there were the urges. Always the urges. Secret fantasies he could tell no one about, private yearnings so terrible that Voss tried desperately to deny them. For years, right through his teens and early twenties, he believed that he was alone with his unspeakable desires.

Then came Jurgen's awakening: his introduction to the wonderful world of computers and his subsequent discovery of the Internet. The message on the 'Net was plain: this is the one place where you do not have to be ashamed of your feelings, where you are not alone, where there are others like you who have banded together in secret to fulfill these forbidden fantasies.

But we must be careful; even in cyberspace there are those who would revile us for our desires.

We must never be found out by those who would shame and punish us.

Voss slumped in his chair, feeling now the full measure of his inquisitors' contempt.

Jaworski clicked on a file and began to scroll through color photographs of small boys in various lewd poses—some naked, some being brutally abused by adults, some being tortured by men dressed in leather and rubber garments. There seemed to be an endless supply of pictures, many accompanied by lurid, graphic text.

"We've counted over three hundred pictures like these, Jurgen. Did you know it's a federal offense to possess or transmit child pornography?" The police sergeant clicked another file open. " 'The Pedophile Plaza,' " he read from the screen. "Looks like Jurgen's got his own chat room, Frank. And guess who's been making dates on it to meet little boys—in Arizona and California?"

"Not Jurgen?"

"Yep. Wonder if he knows that traveling across state lines with the intent to have sex with a minor is also a federal crime."

"I'll bet he knows he could get ten years for it. And I'll bet he knows what happens to pedophiles in jail."

A now pale and trembling Voss had a sudden flashback to his narrow escape from the biker in the holding cell at Spring Mountain.

"That's gotta be why he was so protective about his computer files."

"Look at this, Moe. He's got the names and addresses of his little boyfriends and even how much he paid them. Plus the names of his buddies in the Pedophile Plaza."

"The feds would eat this guy alive, Frank."

Frank Marshall returned his attention to the exposed sex offender. "Okay. No more fucking around, you perverted little son of a bitch," he said quietly. "Tell us what we want to know and maybe—just maybe—we'll forget about turning this garbage over to the FBI."

Jurgen's head swam and his ears rang.

They had the evidence about Thanatos. Probably enough to convict him. He had gambled and lost. Suddenly the murders he had helped plan were no longer abstract problems in science; they were real and he would be made to pay for his part in them. The hopelessness of his position slowly penetrated the darkest recesses of Jurgen Voss's mind. Under the harsh fluorescent lights, the enormity of his crimes became clear to him. No longer could he delude himself that Thanatos had simply been an elegant intellectual exercise. He had participated in the killing of two innocent men—and these policemen knew it. At this moment he stood on the threshold of allowing hundreds more to be burned alive.

But what was even more unbearable, his awful secret had been exposed. Now the entire world would see him for what he was: a disgusting, despicable molester of little children, a predator of the sickest kind. The little man's shoulders heaved; he removed his thick glasses and buried his face in his hands.

250   JOHN GOODGER

Should he try to clear his conscience by saving others?
Or should he take the other way out?

"**That's right,** operator," said Dan Shiller into the mouthpiece of the Tropicana's lobby phone. "Charge the call to my room. William Smith in twenty-seven fourteen."

For a few moments, strange sounds filtered through the line. Beeps, buzzes, a hollow burbling. Finally, a distant voice answered, *"Buenos dias, Banco Internacional de Panamá."*

After a brief exchange, Shiller hung up the phone and smiled grimly.

Druperman was still hanging tough.

"**Glimme an Irish whiskey** with a beer back," said Buster Malloy to the bartender at Billy Bob's.

"B and B, easy ice," Dan Shiller added.

"Did you call the bank?"

"Uh-huh. And guess what. Not a nickel in the account."

"Too bad," said Buster with an unpleasant grin. "Looks like I'm gonna have to warm things up."

"Everything set?"

"Yeah. Took me five trips with the backpack, but it's all there."

The two uncaptured members of Thanatos lapsed into silence until the drinks arrived. Malloy snorted his whiskey in one gulp and turned to Shiller. "The cops raided my place this afternoon," he said flatly. "Just like you said. The little wanker must've squealed on me."

Shiller nodded. "I see. Well, look on the bright side, Buster. Now we're talking a two-way split."

"Yeah. I guess that's good," the big Irishman said unenthusiastically. An expression of concern clouded his ruddy visage. "Listen, Shiller, do you think maybe Jurgen blew the location of the fire?"

"I dunno. It's entirely possible. Get there early. If the place is crawling with tourists and not cops, he hasn't blown it. In that case, wait till eight-thirty to push the button. *But no later, you understand?*"

"Why no later?"

"Because eight-thirty is their peak time. And they close the rides at nine."

"Okay."

"If it's the other way around—I mean police all over, then he probably *has* squealed. Doesn't mean they'll have found all the devices, though. Set 'em off right away. At least you'll get some cops."

Buster's pulse quickened slightly in anticipation of the carnage, albeit limited. He smiled broadly.

Dan noted the reaction to his mention of killing. It made even the totally amoral grifter a little uneasy. There was no question now that the big man *enjoyed* killing. He'd already proved it twice. Shiller wondered how many other times Malloy had murdered. To cover his discomfiture and fill a potentially embarrassing void in the conversation, Dan blurted out the next thing that popped into his mind: "So, ah, Buster, did you stay in the boom box last night?"

"Where else? It ain't bad except for the stink of fertilizer. You?"

"I . . . move around a lot. They'll never find Dan Shiller. Jurgen knew jack shit about me. He couldn't have told 'em anything."

"You got the envelope with the video and the letter?"

"Voss's last contributions to the cause. Yeah, it's in the car. I'll courier it to Druperman tonight."

"And then . . . ?"

"Meet me here again Friday, same time."

Malloy swilled the last of his beer. "You know, Shiller," he said, sliding off the barstool, "I gotta say my piece now in case things . . . get fucked up. I didn't like you at first, an' I still think you're a real bastard. But you sure are a smart one. Not book-smart like that little prick Jurgen, but street-smart."

Dan Shiller grunted in surprise. "Coming from you, Buster, I'll take that as a compliment." Seeing that Malloy was in the mood for truth—and tired of pussyfooting around the subject—he added impulsively, "For a borderline psycho, you're not such a bad guy yourself."

Buster Malloy's expression froze. He stared hard at his accomplice. Then he turned on his heel and walked away.

At that moment, Dan Shiller wished he'd kept his big mouth shut.

40 **Steve Forrester felt** somewhat useless, unable to help in the interrogation of Jurgen Voss. He lit yet another Vantage 100 and returned his attention to the drama unfolding under the bright lights just a few feet from where he sat in darkness.

It seemed that Voss was finally ready to cooperate; springing the kiddie porn on him seemed to have turned the trick. Steve watched in fascination as Jurgen took off his glasses and buried his face in his hands, his thin shoulders racking with sobs. Marshall looked down at the exposed pedophile with unconcealed disgust while Jaworski turned off the computer screen and pulled a chair up beside him.

"Jurgen," said the sergeant neutrally, "it's time to tell us what we need to know."

The little man continued to sob.

"Jurgen! Time's running out. Give it up!"

With an effort, Voss raised his head. His eyes, sunken and beady without the thick lenses to magnify them, were red-rimmed. He pulled out a dirty handkerchief, wiped his face, and replaced his glasses. "I am sorry," he muttered. "Please excuse me. I will tell you what you want to know." Jurgen paused and swallowed. "But first . . . my throat is very dry. Could I have something to drink? Perhaps a coffee?"

"Sure, Jurgen," said Morris. "How do you take it?"

"Black, please."

"There's a machine outside. I'll be right back."

Neither Frank Marshall nor Voss spoke while they waited. The police lieutenant did not trust himself to conceal his contempt for this pervert; he was afraid of shattering the fragile prospect of confession that hung so delicately in the room. Jurgen sniffled quietly.

On his way back from the coffee machine, Morris Jaworski paused for a moment in the anteroom behind the mirror and whispered enthusiastically to Forrester, "Watch closely, Steve. Our little bird will be singing real soon."

"I hope so, Moe."

Jaworski reentered the interview room bearing a steaming Styrofoam cup, which he placed on the table in front of the suspect. Voss nodded his thanks, reached into his shirt pocket, and pulled out a couple of pink envelopes.

"What's that?" said Morris suspiciously.

"Artificial sweetener. For my coffee."

The cop nodded and relaxed. Jurgen ripped the top off both paper envelopes simultaneously and shook the white powder into his coffee. Wrapping his hands protectively around the cup, he looked directly at Jaworski, then at Marshall.

"*Gott* forgive me for all I have done," he said simply.

Outside the room, Steve Forrester watched idly as the little man emptied the white powder into the Styrofoam cup and lifted the hot brew to his lips. Suddenly, a flashbulb exploded in his head and he knew instinctively what was happening. Forrester leapt from his chair and burst into the interview room, causing Morris and Frank to turn their heads in surprise.

"Hold it!" Steve yelled. "Don't let him drink that coffee!"

The two lawmen hesitated for a split second, confused by Forrester's sudden noisy entrance. Steve's momentum carried him toward the suspect; he lunged desperately across the table in an attempt to knock the cup out of Voss's hands. But he was a fraction of a second too late; Jurgen squeezed his eyes shut and quickly gulped down the entire contents of the paper cup.

"Jesus Christ, Steve," said the LVMPD detective, puzzled and alarmed at his ex-partner's odd behavior. "What was that all about?"

Forrester stood up and brushed himself off. "I've got this sinking feeling, Frank," he panted, "that Jurgen's just poisoned himself."

Buster Malloy parked the motorcycle next to Vegas Vic's Bar and Grill, half a block south and across the Strip from his target. It only made sense to give himself a clear escape route after the place went up.

There was no record of Malloy's possessing the bike. He had stolen it the previous afternoon near where he had abandoned his truck: Willow Beach, Arizona, a small town just across the border. He was smart enough not to have ripped one off in Nevada—any vehicle stolen locally would be on the state and Metro police hot list, and right now was not the ideal time to be picked up for motorcycle theft. For extra insurance, he made sure that the license plate was covered with just enough dust to render the numbers illegible. It wasn't hard; a few moments' drive in the desert had done the trick.

With the visor pulled down on his helmet, Buster felt confident that he wouldn't be recognized by any of the cops buzzing around Vegas like bees round a hive. To complete his biker disguise, he wore a black leather jacket, jeans, and steel-toed boots.

Malloy's groin tingled with suppressed excitement as he noted that the parking lot surrounding his target across the street—even this early on a Wednesday evening—was already full to overflowing. Which meant the structure would be packed.

He checked his watch. Shiller had said if the place was crawling with tourists, that would mean Jurgen hadn't given up the location. And that Buster should wait until eight-thirty, but not later—the crowds would be densest then, and traffic on the Strip the most choked.

With a little over an hour to kill, Buster Malloy decided to slip into Vic's for a couple of drinks.

"**Goddamn it,** Jurgen," Frank Marshall roared, grasping the prisoner by his shirtfront and dragging him to his feet. "What the fuck have you done to yourself?"

"Try and make him talk—I'll get help," said Morris Jaworski as he disappeared through the door, unable to phone for help because of LVMPD policy banning telephones from interview rooms.

Voss jerked spasmodically in Marshall's grasp. "Help me with him, Steve," the policeman said. "Grab his legs and we'll lay him down on the table."

Forrester did as he was asked. They laid Jurgen as gently as they could on the wooden table; Frank rolled up his jacket and tucked it under the man's head.

"Jurgen! Can you hear me?" the police lieutenant shouted.

Voss nodded weakly and coughed violently. He tried to speak, but it was too late—blood had begun to well up in his mouth, and the words burbled out unintelligibly.

Marshall impatiently lifted the oversize head. "Jurgen! Try and tell us! Where's the fire?"

Suddenly Voss convulsed violently and projectile-vomited a stream of bright-red blood, splattering Forrester, Marshall, and the tabletop with scarlet gore. He thrashed wildly, then shrank back into a fetal position, breathing shallowly.

"Jurgen! *Where's the fire?*"

Voss's mouth opened and closed soundlessly like that of a landed fish. His eyelids fluttered and his pupils started to roll upward. With what appeared to be a final supreme effort, his hand shaking, the little man drew a shape with the gnawed tip of his right index finger in the rapidly congealing film of blood on the tabletop. Then, after a final spasm, his thin body stiffened and he lay still.

Frank Marshall noted the fixed pupils and collapsed chest. "I think he's dead," the policeman said, anger and frustration evident in his voice. "Well, pal, you beat me to the punch again."

Irritated, Forrester turned his attention from the recently deceased Voss to his ex-partner. "Beat you to the punch? Frank, why do these things always have to come down to a pissing contest?"

"Because I'm tired of getting pissed on."

"By me, I suppose."

"By you? Oh, no. Look at all those career opportunities you found for me at Summit—just like you promised. Jesus, Steve, I could be heading up the chicken-snatcher squad at that supermarket chain right now. Or maybe checking uniforms at some rent-a-cop outfit in Armpit City, New Jersey. How about—"

"Look, I did what I could for you, okay? Under the circumstances. Like I told you on the phone the other day, I'm not an employment—"

"What's that supposed to mean?"

"What?"

"Under the circumstances."

"You want it straight?"

"Why not? It'll be a first."

"Number one, you've got a drinking problem—"

"Bullshit. It's under control."

"No, it isn't, Frank. And I couldn't risk the repercussions if I recommended you for any kind of top-level position at Summit." He paused, half expecting his ex-partner to take a swing at him. When it didn't happen, Forrester continued: "Number two—"

"There's more?"

"Number two. You're the best cop I know. Why do you think I call on you every time we have a problem? Maybe I'm being selfish, but, goddamn it, Frank, I need you right where you are. Especially now, with this thing happening."

"So I'm a drunk, but I'm useful to you. Well, that's a comfort."

"You asked for an honest answer. None of it's personal. Never has been."

"Okay, Mister—"

Morris Jaworski burst through the door, forcing Forrester and Marshall back to the gruesome reality of the moment and the exigencies of a now seemingly hopeless situation. He was followed by the desk sergeant carrying an emergency medical kit. "How is he?" Jaworski said breathlessly. "My God, you guys have blood all over . . ."

"The little asshole's fucking gone and killed himself, Moe," Marshall snapped, still angry at himself for not divining Voss's intentions, and smarting from Steve's revelations.

"Are you sure?" Jaworski gingerly felt for a pulse on Voss's carotid artery. As he did so, the desk sergeant opened the kit, unscrewed an oxygen bottle and connected it to a respirator mask. Morris waved him off. "Never mind," he said. "Frank's right. Forget the oxygen. This guy's gone. We might as well wait for the ambulance."

"Guess we've lost any chance to find out what he knew," said Forrester.

The police lieutenant stared at the bloody tabletop. "Maybe not," he said. "Maybe he did leave a message for us. Look at this."

In the coagulating gore on the table, the dying man had drawn an odd pictograph, a shape reminiscent of an old-fashioned fountain pen nib:

"What do you make of it, Frank?" Forrester asked.

"Let me think about it for a minute." Marshall stared at the strange diagram. "A bomb? An arrowhead? Neither of which makes much sense to me. But then, I'm just an old lush—or maybe a good cop. Sometimes hard to tell which, eh, Moe?"

The Forensics chief frowned at his associate, shrugged, and said, "I'll get some Polaroids of it."

Perched on a barstool in Vic's Bar and Grill, Buster Malloy focused his good eye on the Seiko watch, all he had left to remind him of Helga. Impulsively, he raised the shot glass and silently toasted his deceased companion. Some days he missed her more than he cared to admit—but then, he thought philosophically, what was done was done. Besides, he rationalized with alcohol-induced sincerity, that Swedish bitch had always liked the desert. Maybe he'd done her a favor. Amused by this conclusion, the big man in the biker's outfit grinned slyly at the bartender and ordered another drink. There was plenty of time; all he had to do was take a leisurely stroll across the Strip and push a button.

The preparatory work was all done. Malloy had needed the better part of the previous day, Tuesday, to carry in and conceal all twenty of the thermite incendiary devices. Five trips with the backpack loaded, five times up and down those stupid elevators, but at least nobody had paid the slightest attention to him—despite the fact that the entire town was overrun with cops and security guards.

Buster chuckled as he recalled how he'd successfully placed every single one of the devices, right under their stupid noses. Five in the restaurant, taped under tables. Three in the gift shop, concealed beneath piles of T-shirts and magazines. Three more in the cocktail lounge, hidden in heavy fabric drapes. Three in one of the wedding chapels, under wooden pews. One in each of the five high-speed elevators: these were the most crucial of all the devices because their function was to burn out the control panels and disable the elevators, precluding easy escape by those trapped above, as well as ascent by rescuers. They had also been the most difficult to plant; Malloy had been obliged to wait for each elevator to empty before hiding the firestarters behind the emergency-access panels. After that task was complete, he had strategically placed one last device in the stairwell, thereby blocking the only other means of escape from the planned conflagration.

Earlier, he and Shiller had mixed the simple but deadly cocktails—equal parts of powdered aluminum and powdered iron oxide—and packed them in innocuous cardboard boxes. Voss had assembled the ignition devices: explosive squibs connected to battery-powered receivers that the diminutive electronics expert had stripped from radio-controlled toy cars. Jurgen had coded all the ignition devices to one frequency and had provided Malloy with a single transmitter designed to set off all the devices simultaneously at the push of one button. When ignited, Jurgen had explained, the aluminum would burn fiercely, extracting its combustion oxygen from the iron oxide. The resultant exothermic reaction would produce a temperature of almost four thousand degrees Fahrenheit for several minutes, in twenty different locations, virtually guaranteeing a raging, uncontrollable inferno within seconds of primary ignition.

In a way it was too bad the little wanker had gotten himself nabbed, Malloy thought. But like Shiller said, they didn't need him anymore. And there'd be that much more money for each of *them*. Judging by the crowds he had seen flocking unhindered into the target structure across the street, Buster reassured himself that Voss hadn't revealed the location of the upcoming fire.

He fingered the transmitter in the pocket of his leather jacket and downed the last of his beer chaser.

He glanced at his watch.

Plenty of time for another round, maybe two, before the fireworks.

I should have seen it coming, Frank," said Morris Jaworski glumly.

Marshall nodded wearily. "So should I, Moe. Especially after what they did to Barney Leopold. But then, who knew the little bastard was suicidal? With an ego like that, who'd have ever thought he'd *poison* himself?"

The two lawmen and Steve Forrester were huddled over coffee in the police cafeteria. Marshall kept glancing at the Polaroids of Jurgen Voss's terminal scrawl in the pool of tabletop gore.

"Well, we knew the evidence from his computer would shake him up," Jaworski offered. "It just worked a little better than we thought."

"Yeah, right. Let's face it, Moe, we both screwed up. Only Mr. Wizard here guessed what was happening, and by the time he could react, it was too late."

"I doubt if any of us could have stopped him," said Forrester. "And even if he didn't take the poison, he would have hanged himself in his cell or something."

"But in the meantime," Marshall replied tiredly, "we could have squeezed info about this goddamn fire out of him."

"The only hope we've got now is to nail Malloy," Jaworski said. "That APB should be in the field by now. Every cop and security guard from here to Reno will be looking for him."

"Right," sighed Marshall. "But, you know, somehow I can't get too optimistic about our chances. This guy's too street-smart. He knows we're looking for him. I'm sure he's ditched the truck by now—and probably changed his appearance." The cop paused and picked up one of the Polaroids of Voss's death scene. "I wonder if he could be hiding out at a friend's place. One of his neighbors in the trailer park mentioned this woman who used to stay with him—Helga Johnson, if I remember correctly. We ran the name, but there's no record of it."

"Maybe someone at the Galaxy knows him socially."

"Could be." Marshall slowly rotated the Polaroid print.

"I can ask his captain at the Galaxy," said Steve. "But I don't think he had many fr—"

"Hey, check this out!" Frank Marshall interjected, his mood becoming more positive as personal issues were forgotten in a sudden flash of enlightenment. "We were just looking at it the wrong way." He turned the Polaroid ninety degrees:

"Christ, Frank, you're right," said Steve, quickly grasping his ex-partner's meaning.

Jaworski peered more closely at the photograph. "I still don't—"

"Look closer," Frank urged. "Jurgen Voss has told us exactly what we wanted to know."

"Wait a minute—I think I see it," Moe said slowly. "It's got to be . . . yes! When you look at it this way, it's got to be a drawing of that new hotel-casino tower at the south end of the Strip . . . what do they call it. . .?"

"The Obelisk," said Marshall.

41

At twelve hundred and fifty-two feet, the Obelisk dominated the skyline of Las Vegas.

Literally and figuratively topping the roster of superlatives that obsessed this world capital of hyperbole, the Obelisk claimed to be the tallest freestanding structure west of the Mississippi. Originally the tower was to have been built even higher; however, the FAA scotched those plans, citing danger to air traffic at McCarran. Nevertheless, the owners proclaimed triumphantly, the tower's elevation still exceeded that of its nearest rival, the Stratosphere Tower.

A gracefully tapered square concrete tower terminated in a ten-story pyramid featuring an observation deck, Cleopatra's Needle Restaurant, a 250-seat cocktail lounge, the ubiquitous Las Vegas gift shop, and two wedding chapels. Like many of the new destination resorts along the Strip, the Obelisk offered its share of fairground-type amusements.

Corkscrewing down inside the tower, the Helix Roller Coaster offered thrill seekers "the ride of your life," combining centrifugal force and vertigo in a stomach-dropping spiral halfway to the base. At the end of this ride, those hardy souls who wanted more had the option of completing their descent in the free-fall Terminal Velocipede, actually four-passenger gondolas mounted on vertical steel rails that plunged their occupants to the tower's base at zero gs, slowing suddenly near the end and subjecting them to a deceleration force of over four gs.

As with most Vegas theme attractions, the fun seekers were disgorged through the adjoining casino, in the hope of their dropping a little more cash on the way out.

At the core of the structure, five high-speed double-deck elevators, each with a capacity of thirty passengers, whisked riders to the observation level in less than a minute. A single staircase, restricted to the public except in case of emergency, spiraled down around the elevator shafts.

Since the disastrous fires at the MGM Grand and the Las Vegas Hilton in the early eighties, all new public buildings in Las Vegas were required by code to be sprinklered—and the Obelisk was no exception. However, as Jurgen Voss had pedantically informed his associates, the extreme heat of the thermite incendiary devices would render the sprinkler system virtually useless, a condition exacerbated by low water pressure due to the pyramid's altitude. By disabling the elevators and blocking the staircase, there would be no escape from the blaze, no immediate means of rescue. The fatality list on a busy Friday evening could easily run into the hundreds.

During their planning sessions for the fire, the three conspirators had demonstrated very different attitudes to the potential carnage their handiwork would create.

Jurgen Voss had managed to block the terrible consequences from his mind by the simple expedient of classifying the project as an intellectual undertaking—no more than an exercise in electronics, chemistry, and physics. Only when it was too late did he concede the enormity of the crime.

Dan Shiller had demonstrated no emotion, no last-minute attack of conscience, no regret whatsoever. The suffering of other people was not a concern of his; in Shiller's dog-eat-dog universe, there was no room for sentiment.

Only Buster Malloy, a twisted, sinister smile on his pink boozer's face, had demonstrated a genuine enthusiasm for the project. He had made it abundantly clear to the others that he hoped the association would not pay, not just yet, thereby forcing him to joyfully torch the tower.

Despite bumper-to-bumper traffic on the Strip, the LVMPD Bomb Squad reached the base of the Obelisk within six minutes of Lieutenant Frank Marshall's urgent warning. Hampered by their size, the first fire trucks did not arrive for another five minutes.

In retrospect, it was determined that two factors had prevented a calamitous loss of life. The first was the emergency radio communication by Marshall to police officers patrolling nearby, directing them to organize an immediate evacuation of the tower.

The second was the decision by Buster Malloy to order one more Irish whiskey before he strolled across the street and pressed the button.

The additional time unwittingly provided by Malloy allowed police and security guards enough time to quickly send down several elevator-loads of older people, young children, and the handicapped and to hurry them away from the tower. Those who appeared capable were asked to take the stairs.

As a further precaution, an orderly evacuation of the hotel-casino complex adjoining the structure was conducted by a hastily assembled team of LVMPD police officers and Obelisk security guards.

Meanwhile, search teams of Bomb Squad members and LVFD fire-fighters arrived and began to methodically comb the tower, hunting for evidence of planned arson. Not knowing what to look for complicated their search. Were the arsonists themselves present, preparing to manually torch the structure? Or had they concealed incendiary devices? If so, were they booby-trapped, timed, or remote-controlled?

It was Mike Morgan, a rookie fireman, who provided the answers. He and Fireman Henry Oakes had been searching Cleopatra's Needle Restaurant, now empty of diners. Half-eaten food, spilled drinks, and crumpled napkins attested to the speed of the patrons' exodus.

The two firefighters had followed standard operating procedure in organizing the search. First, they stood quietly in various parts of the restaurant with their eyes closed, listening for a clockwork mechanism. When no such mechanism was detected, they embarked upon a visual search. Based on the furniture and contents of the room, they determined to what height their first sweep should extend. Hip height appeared to be logical; it would encompass all the tables, chairs, miscellaneous serving buffets and cabinets. Each man took half the room. A large part of this first sweep would necessarily involve crawling on hands and knees to look under furniture. And it was from this position that Mike Morgan made his discovery.

"Check this out, Henry," Morgan said to his associate. Concealed by the hanging tablecloth, a cardboard container about the size and shape of a cereal box was taped to the underside of a table.

"Jesus, Mike," Oakes exclaimed. "We better call the Bomb Squad." He clicked a button on his shoulder mike and reported their find.

When Buster Malloy finally unglued himself from the barstool at Vegas Vic's Bar and Grill, he was in a mellow mood. This feeling of exhilaration sprang partially from the pleasant afterbuzz of four Irish whiskies accompanied by beer chasers and partially from sexual excitement about the incredible thing he was going to do.

Unfortunately for Malloy, his mood was rudely shattered when he stepped out into the gathering dusk on Las Vegas Boulevard and observed the flashing lights of a fleet of emergency vehicles drawn up around the base of the Obelisk like twinkling fireflies.

"Shite!" he whispered with a sharp intake of breath. "The fuckin' little wanker *did* spill 'is guts!" Buster glanced at his watch: 8:41. Shiller had told him to blow the place no later than 8:30. Was it too late? No, there were still people streaming out of the casino! There must still be others inside! He raced across the Strip, dodging traffic and pulling the transmitter from the pocket of his leather jacket as he ran.

The big man in the cowboy hat was adamant. He had planted himself like an oak tree at the entrance to the roller-coaster ride, one beefy arm braced against the doorjamb, the other protectively encircling the shoulders of his chesty, ash-blond wife. "Mah name's Elford T. Blaine, an' we been linin' up *two hours* for this here ride," he explained patiently but firmly to Police Sergeant Drew Rogers. "An' mister, me and the missus ain't leavin' until we git our turn on that there Helix."

"Elford, for Chrissake, you're actin' like a real asshole," said the wife, ineffectively trying to squirm free of his grasp. "Forgit about the roller coaster. Jes' do like the man says."

"Sir, your wife is right. You have been asked to leave for your own safety," said Rogers, noticing a strong odor of alcohol on the man's breath. "As I told you, there has been a . . . threat against this building. If you don't go right now, I'll have to use force to evict you."

Blaine snorted derisively. "You and whut army, son? Ah'm from Texas, an' we don't like bein' pushed around by nobody—specially cops, y'hear?"

The policeman did not bother responding. Instead, he stepped back and spoke briefly into a shoulder mike. Within thirty seconds, the large Texan found himself being duck-marched toward the elevators by Drew Rogers and three burly firemen.

As they bundled the unwilling passenger and his wife into the elevator, Sergeant Rogers asked one of the firemen, a grizzled lieutenant, "Are they the last?"

"I think so," the lieutenant replied, reaching inside to push the G button and stepping back quickly as the car doors closed. "Nobody left up here but us smoke-eaters and the Bomb Squad. And yourself. Maybe you should think about leaving."

"I'm the last cop up here in the pyramid? How many incendiary devices have you guys found so far?"

"About a dozen that I know of. The wedding chapels, the restaurant, and the cocktail lounge are clean now. There were none in the washrooms or the observation deck. They're just checking the gift shop."

"And these devices were all radio-controlled?"

"Yeah. The Bomb Squad boys have neutralized the ones we've found so far. God knows how many more there are. They say we're lucky the bad guys haven't transmitted a detonation signal yet. A lot of people could have died."

"Right, Lieutenant. Well, I guess I'll take your advice. Time for me to leave."

"Take the stairs. It's safer."

Buster Malloy tried to remember his instructions. How close did he need to get for the transmitter to work? With difficulty, he recalled what Jurgen had said. At least get as close as the sidewalk in front of the building, the little wanker had advised. Trouble was, that was now impossible, with the cops busy shooing people away. There was no way they'd let him get inside the police lines. He stopped and considered his options. The parking lot! If he could get around back, he'd be plenty close enough. He ran down Clancy Street and vaulted the low fence that surrounded the Obelisk's parking lot. Weaving his way through the parked cars, Malloy emerged less than fifty feet from the west corner of the giant tower.

The would-be mass murderer uttered an imprecation and pushed the button.

When the thermite incendiary devices went off in the elevators, four of the five were empty. In the fifth, Mr. and Mrs. Elford T. Blaine of Texas died almost instantaneously as a white-hot fountain of blazing aluminum powder showered the inside of the enclosed area, robbing it of oxygen and raising its temperature briefly to almost four thousand degrees Fahrenheit.

Fireman Mike Morgan was incinerated beyond recognition by another device that happened to be concealed beneath some T-shirts in the gift shop, not three feet from where he was searching. His partner, Henry Oakes, on the other side of the room, suffered second-degree burns to his face and hands.

Police Sergeant Drew Rogers was trapped in the Obelisk's stairwell when the thermite incendiary device ignited ten feet below him. He was rushed by ambulance to Sunrise Hospital with third-degree burns.

Three Bomb Squad members suffered mild smoke inhalation.

Besides Morgan and Oakes, there were no casualties among the fire-fighters in the pod. Equipped with respirators, the rest of the crew was able to bring the blazes in the gift shop and the elevator shafts under control inside an hour and extinguish them completely within two hours.

Damage to the Obelisk was later estimated at $30 million.

Dan Shiller twisted the tuning knob on the car radio, momentarily unable to find a local newscast. He had seen the smoke pouring from the Obelisk like a gigantic smoldering highway flare and had heard sirens wailing in the distance. "Come on, come on," he muttered. Country music. A Sears commercial. Jesus saves. Then finally ". . . in a fire that started at exactly eight forty-four this evening. Apparently Las Vegas police had received a warning that an arson attempt would be made against the tower." Shiller turned up the volume as the newsreader continued: "Because of this early warning, officials were able to evacuate the building in time to prevent massive casualties. However, reports from the scene indicate there have been at least three deaths, including a Las Vegas firefighter and two out-of-state visitors. One police officer is in critical condition at Sunrise Hospital. Several others are reported to be suffering from mild smoke inhalation. Preliminary estimates put property damage in the tens of millions of dollars. We now return you to the scene of the fire, where KLVX reporter Kim Allen has further details—"

Shiller snapped off the radio in exasperation. If the fire had started only at 8:44, then Buster Malloy had fucked up. The goddamn psycho was supposed to get there early and detonate the incendiary devices *immediately* if the cops had beaten him to it—otherwise, he was supposed to do it at *eight-thirty*. Something had gone wrong; Jurgen must have talked somewhere along the line, and Malloy had managed to screw up the timing.

The grifter-turned–mass murderer consoled himself with the fact that there had been *some* fatalities during phase three. And quite obviously extensive property damage. Druperman and his cronies in the LVCA didn't know just how goddamn lucky they were. At least they'd see that Thanatos was capable of carrying out its threats. Next time, faced by the terrible consequences Shiller and the others had arranged for phase four, he knew they'd pay.

Dan wheeled the BMW into a mini-mall on Paradise Road. He parked by the Kwik Kourier storefront depot, donned a pair of sunglasses and a baseball cap, and walked inside.

"I want this envelope delivered first thing tomorrow morning," he told the clerk, a sallow, gum-chewing youth who appeared more interested in watching television coverage of the Obelisk fire than in his latest customer.

"Cash or charge?" said the kid unenthusiastically.

"Cash."

Holding the envelope by its edges to avoid leaving fingerprints, Shiller slid it across the counter. The clerk checked the waybill. "Galaxy Hotel? That's zone one. Cost you six forty-two, including tax."

"Just make sure it gets there early," said Shiller.

"This is News Thirteen Inside Las Vegas. Our top story this morning: a suspect in the Obelisk fire has apparently committed suicide in police custody. Jurgen Voss, a local resident, had been arrested in connection with an alleged extortion attempt against a number of Las Vegas casinos by an organized group.

"An arrest warrant on charges of murder, arson, and extortion has now been issued for a second suspect in the case, Francis Marion 'Buster' Malloy, a security guard at the Galaxy Hotel and Casino." The Galaxy's personnel file photograph of Malloy appeared on the television screen. "Anyone with knowledge of Malloy's whereabouts is asked to contact Las Vegas Police."

"Some sources have suggested that the same group was responsible for the recent tragic death of entertainer Tony Francisco at the Galaxy Hotel. Police spokesmen have refused comment on this allegation.

"Meanwhile, the police officer who suffered burns in the Obelisk fire died early this morning in Sunrise Hospital without regaining consciousness. This brings to four the total number of deaths in the conflagration.

"Damage estimates have been placed at thirty million—"

"Bastards!" Emmett Druperman shouted at the TV screen. Drooping vulturously over his massive mahogany desk on the Bridge, he angrily thumbed the remote, muting the local TV news report.

"It could have been worse, Emmett," Steve Forrester observed. "A hell of a lot worse."

"I suppose so," Druperman allowed testily. "It could have been another fucking MGM all over again." More benignly he added, "I understand it was you guys that figured out where the fire was gonna take place."

"It was Frank Marshall," said Forrester, lighting his sixth Vantage 100 of the morning. "He saved a lot of lives yesterday. The cops are getting close to an arrest."

"Humph. Where I come from, close only counts in horseshoes and hand grenades. I won't believe it's over until these motherfuckers are all behind bars. Or better still, dead."

"Well, one of them *is* dead—and we've identified another."

"You mean this security guard Malloy—the one that works here?"

"Used to work here. I'm definitely firing him."

Emmett chewed on an unlit cigar, ignoring the dark humor. "This was the guy that slipped the first envelope into my mailbox?"

"Probably. We're pretty sure he poisoned the guest in the Cosmic Café. And I'd guess it was also Malloy who wired up Francisco's shower. Definitely an inside job."

The speakerphone on Druperman's desk buzzed. He pressed a button and snapped, "What?"

Edith Frick announced, "There's a package here for you, Mr. D. The courier slip says RUSH."

The two men looked at each other.

"Are you thinking what I'm thinking?" said Forrester.

"Let's find out right now, Steve. Bring it in," he said to the phone.

A chastised Edith Frick opened the door just enough to slip through, tiptoed nervously to the desk, and deposited the brown envelope in front of the CEO. Just as quietly, she left.

"I like her. She's scared of me," Emmett remarked inconsequentially after the woman had silently closed the door behind her.

"'Edith the Eavesdropper.' I think maybe these days she's a little scared of me, too," said Forrester with a grin.

Picking up the envelope by a corner, Druperman commented, "Same label. Same printing: EMMETT DRUPERMAN, PRESIDENT OF LVCA, CONFIDENTIAL.

Same brown envelope. So, Mr. Vice President of Security—do we wait for the cops, or do we open this one ourselves?"

"They're not going to find any clues on it. And it *is* addressed to you."

"My thoughts exactly." Druperman picked up a letter opener and carefully slit the sealed end of the envelope. He shook out the contents onto the polished surface of his desk: the usual tape and letter, plus two twenty-five-dollar Dunes chips.

"Let me guess, Emmett," Steve commented cynically as the two green chips rolled across his boss's desktop. "They're asking fifty million this time."

"We'll read the goddamn letter and find out. Then we'll look at the tape."

"After which we'll call Frank Marshall. Again," said Forrester, walking around Druperman's desk to look over his shoulder.

Emmett read the letter aloud: " 'ATTENTION LAS VEGAS CASINO ASSOCIATION! HERE IS YOUR LAST CHANCE TO STOP AN OPERATION WHICH WILL MAKE ALL OTHER ACTIONS APPEAR SMALL. THE PRICE IS NOW FIFTY MILLION DOLLARS ($50,000,000.00)—' "

"Hey, whaddaya know; I was right," Forrester cut in.

" 'IF THIS MONEY IS NOT SENT TO BANCO INTERNACIONAL DE PANAMÁ BY FRIDAY 1700 HOURS, ONE OF LVCA HOTELS WILL HAVE THE SAME DEATH YOU SEE ON THE VIDEO HEREWITH. THANATOS.' "

"What's that?" Steve asked, pointing to the bottom of the laser-printed letter, to an inscription handwritten in ballpoint pen.

"Kinda hard to see." Druperman donned a pair of reading glasses and squinted more closely at the sheet. "It says, 'P.S. Please excuse our associate's lousy English. You got lucky last time, but it won't happen again.' "

"They're referring to Voss. He must have prepared this little package of goodies before he was arrested. One of the gang obviously added the P.S. after the fire last night. So there's got to be at least one more member of this Thanatos group. Voss is dead, and Malloy doesn't have the brains to mastermind a scheme like this. Someone else is still pulling the strings. It has to be the guy you talked to on my cell phone."

The CEO looked thoughtful. "You know something? Those bastards knew it all along."

"Knew what, Emmett?"

"That we weren't gonna pay."

Forrester nodded. "Sure. Thanatos had to have had all these operations ready from the get-go, and they certainly couldn't have executed them without considerable advance planning." Druperman scowled agreement. "These people obviously realized that you personally wouldn't be an easy mark, so they knew they had to keep raising the ante until the *other members* of the LVCA folded under the pressure."

"Well, my boys haven't folded yet. And I'll do my goddamnest to make sure these shakedown artists don't win—"

"Right on, Emmett!"

"—no matter how high they stack the fucking chips."

Steve picked up the videocassette and walked to Druperman's media wall. "Speaking of which, I guess we might as well find out what their next little surprise is," he said, inserting the tape into a VCR and pushing a button.

Within seconds, the giant television screen filled with a chillingly familiar image.

"My God," Forrester breathed. "It's Oklahoma City."

42 **A pall** of amber cigar smoke floated over the Starlight Hotel boardroom like an L.A. smog bank trapped beneath a temperature inversion. Around the marble-topped conference table eighteen pairs of eyes, belonging to the most powerful men in Las Vegas, bored mercilessly into the drooping countenance of Emmett Druperman.

"Look, Emmett, we may be in the casino business, but none of us are gamblers," said the chairman of the Olympic Entertainment Corporation to the current president of the Las Vegas Casino Association. "Why take a chance on these crazies blowing up one of our properties?"

"Marty's right," added the owner of one of the newest megaresorts on the Strip. "We control, what, thirty-two hotels between us? So we pay these bastards fifty million—that's only a million and a half apiece, give or take."

"Cheap insurance," the CEO of the Roman Palladium interjected. "We can't afford to jeopardize this city's reputation as a safe family destination. People come to our casinos because they feel secure. We're giving 'em Disneyland with slot machines. It's already taken us too long to recover from Nine-Eleven. Let's not risk it now."

Druperman rose from his chair at the head of the table and began to pace. "I believe you're wrong, gentlemen," he began slowly. "If we give in to terrorism—and believe me, that's what this is—we might as well all close up shop right now and go home." Jabbing the air with his cigar for emphasis, he continued more loudly: "Every psycho with a bomb or a gun or a package of matches is gonna try and stick it to us. Do you guys want to greet your guests at the door with metal detectors and bomb-sniffing dogs? 'Welcome to Vegas, ma'am, excuse me while we strip-search you?' What the hell's *that* gonna do for our image?

"Look at Israel—they never give in to terrorists. For a very good reason:

they know that the more you give, the more these bastards take. Look at Eye-rack. Sure, Saddam was tough, but we were tougher. Yeah, I know, we had to clobber 'em three times, but in the end him and his rag-head pals got the message loud and clear—don't fuck with the U.S.A.!

"Why do you think we bombed Afghanistan back to the Stone Age? Because it's the only language these guys understand!

"History, gentlemen." He paused theatrically.

"Look back forty, fifty, sixty years. Look at the Cuban missile crisis in 'sixty-three—Dean Rusk just stared those Russians down. Look at Hitler. If Churchill hadn't had the balls to say no to the little prick, we'd all be *Sprechen-Sie Deutsch*-ing right now." Emmett stopped pacing and leaned on the table, scanning the faces of his fellow casino executives one by one. He lowered his voice and spoke more intensely: "I say we hang tough and let the cops do their thing. One of these guys is already dead. They know the name of another one. Right now, there's more cops swarming around our properties than a goddamn policemen's convention.

"And I'm talking to you as a guy that's already taken two gut shots from these killers. Don't give 'em a plug nickel, that's my advice."

Druperman resumed his seat. A silence fell upon the boardroom. Some of the men shifted uncomfortably in their chairs. Finally, the head of the largest group of hotel-casinos in Nevada, a world-famous business prodigy who had made his first million by the age of twenty, stood up.

"Emmett," he began, "we all appreciate your position, and we respect your leadership abilities. On your advice, we've toughed it out so far. But frankly, enough is enough. You said the police had things under control. But they couldn't stop the murder of Tony Francisco. They couldn't save the four people who died in the Obelisk fire—although I admit it could have been a lot worse if that guy they arrested hadn't talked.

"The point is, this Thanatos group has basically carried out every threat they've made, right back to the poisoning incident at your place. In my opinion, and I believe most of us around this table agree, we can't afford to gamble with a threat of this magnitude." He lowered his voice to a near whisper. "My God, Oklahoma City all over again . . . can you imagine the consequences?" The rhetorical question hung unanswered in the smoky atmosphere.

"Now, I'm sure the authorities will catch these people sooner or later. I *realize* that one of them is dead, and they've identified another one. But who knows how many more of them are still out there? It only takes one guy to pull off a stunt like this—look at Timothy McVeigh. We have less than two days to comply with their latest demands, and that just may not be enough time for the cops to do their thing.

"So, what I'm saying, Emmett, with all due respect, is that we should pay up this time—and this time only. Right now, with this immediate danger hanging over our heads, we shouldn't be worrying about opening the door to more terrorist demands. This is the time to protect our assets. *And our asses.*"

All eyes turned back to Druperman. "All right," their president sighed. "You know my position. But I'll go along with the majority. Let's have a show of hands. All in favor of paying these shakedown artists their blood money . . ."

Slowly, one by one, hands were raised around the table. The vote appeared virtually unanimous.

"Those opposed . . ."

Emmett Druperman lifted his hand. His droopy eyes scoured the gathering for some sign of support, some crumb of compromise, but there was none.

"Okay, gentlemen," Druperman said, his demeanor mournful. "We pay. Send me cashier's checks by tomorrow morning."

Dan Shiller glanced quickly around the lobby of the Monte Carlo. Once assured that he was not being overheard, the grifter picked up a house phone.

"Yes, operator," he said. "I want to make a call to Panama City. Charge it to my room. Harold Brown, eighteen twenty-three." Shiller suppressed a yawn while the operator punched up the unsuspecting Mr. Brown's name and room number on her screen. When it checked out, she asked for the telephone number in Panama City. Again, Dan waited while the usual cacophony of clicks and chirps echoed across the satellite connection to Central America. Within two minutes a Spanish-speaking woman's voice confirmed a successful connection with the Banco Internacional de Panamá.

"*Buenos dias* to you too, baby," said Dan. "Put me through to Señor Vasquez."

More clicks, a double ring, then, "Ricardo, how are you? Dan Shiller here." Shiller rattled off the account number he'd memorized. "Yes, fine . . .

I know, it should be there tomorrow before five P.M. . . . just confirming my instructions. That's right . . . the Libyan Arab Foreign Bank . . . you have the account number."

Shiller listened to the banker with growing impatience. "No, Ricardo, I am not asking you to lie. When I call tomorrow, you will quickly and privately confirm the transfer to me. A simple okay will do. Then, when my . . . associate comes on the line, you just tell him the truth: that there's no money in the account. Let him draw his own conclusions. Got that? . . . Good. I'm paying you guys enough money for this. . . . All right. Is an hour enough time for the transfer? . . . Fine. Then I'll call you tomorrow around six."

Lieutenant Frank Marshall could not disguise the frustration he felt. "So the association did cave," he snapped. "I had a feeling they might."

"Hey, Frank—no need to shoot the messenger," Steve Forrester replied. "Besides, I can understand where they're coming from. It's a hell of a risk for these guys to take just to uphold Druperman's principles."

"Shit, it's just I hate to see those bastards win."

"Well, they haven't won yet. If I know you, you'll catch up with them sooner or later."

"Damn right. What really pisses me off is that we're so close." The policeman pulled a pack of Marlboros out of his desk drawer and lit up, pointedly not offering one to Forrester. Marshall added defiantly, "Anyway, it ain't over till it's over. We've got till five o'clock tomorrow, and the whole team's on double shift. Sooner or later Malloy has to surface. The lab's going over those unexploded incendiary devices with a fine-tooth comb. In the meantime, we're not taking any chances with this bomb threat. Just because the LVCA has paid the money, I'm not trusting these killers to keep their word. We're closing all the doors, just in case."

"What do you mean?"

"Think about it. In the Oklahoma City incident, they used a four-thousand-pound truck bomb. Which is the kind of explosive power it takes to rip open a building that size. So until we nail this Malloy, we're going to search every single truck that goes anywhere near any of the hotels. I'm talking semitrailers, delivery trucks, even vans. As a matter of fact, we're asking the hotels to lend us their security people to help out in the vehicle searches. And that includes your guards at the Galaxy."

The late-afternoon sun beat down mercilessly on the Boulder Highway. With a sigh of relief, Buster Malloy pulled off the shimmering ribbon of blacktop and parked the motorcycle in a shady spot on the Sam's Town parking lot. He was sweating profusely under the leather jacket, and his black-helmeted head felt as if it had been baked in an oven.

Tucking the helmet under his arm, the big man slipped on a pair of sunglasses to help hide his face. Then he stepped into the cool recesses of Billy Bob's in search of Dan Shiller.

Buster found his co-conspirator seated with his back to the wall in a dark corner of the barroom. "Hey, Shiller," the Irishman said breezily, pulling up a chair. "How are they hangin'?"

Dan looked up sharply and slammed his glass down hard on the table, spilling half his drink. "Goddamn it, Malloy, what the fuck happened on Wednesday night?"

Taken aback by Shiller's angry greeting, Malloy said defensively, "What's your problem, boyo? Sounds like you got a hair across your arse."

"Fucking right I do. You were supposed to torch the tower by eight-thirty *latest*."

"Big deal. It was *around* eight-thirty."

"So how come they had time to evacuate the building?"

"Well, you see, I got a little t'irsty. An' I just decided to wet me whistle before I fried 'em. I couldn't help it if the cops got there while I was . . . otherwise occupied."

"That's exactly what I thought happened. Jesus Christ, do you realize what kind of damage you could have caused if you hadn't been boozing it up when you were supposed to be watching the place?"

Malloy gave Shiller a twisted smile. "Hey, man, I snuffed a buncha people, didn't I? *An'* caused plenty o' damage. If that little wanker hadn't squealed—"

"Jurgen's dead, you stupid fuck."

"I know. An' be careful who you're callin' stupid," Buster said levelly, a blank expression on his face.

"I'm tired of pussyfooting around with you, Malloy. You're not only stupid, you're so psychotic about the killing that I'm beginning to think you don't really give a rat's ass about the payoff. So the quicker I see the last of you —"

For a large man, Buster moved with snakelike speed. In one fluid motion he reached inside his biker's boot, pulled out a switchblade, and snapped it open. Before Dan could react, Malloy had seized his companion's wrist in an iron grip and pinned it to the chair arm. With the other hand he pressed the sharp point of the knife into Shiller's belly, just below tabletop level.

"You know, Shiller," he hissed, "Nobody calls me stupid—or crazy—and gets away with it. I'd just as soon spill your guts right here—"

The grifter did not move a muscle. Calmly, he stared at his own reflection in his attacker's sunglasses and said quietly, "Back off, Malloy. You kill me, you won't see nickel one of the fifty million bucks. I'm the only one who can access it." The Irishman relaxed his grip on Shiller's wrist but kept the knife pointed at his belly. "Think about it, Malloy. They know who you are. Your ugly face is all over the TV. You've only got one chance—and that's to get out of the country. You can't do it without money. And for that, you need me."

Buster's expression did not change, but he slowly withdrew the knife and folded up the blade. "All right then, boyo," he said suspiciously, "what about the money? Is it there yet?"

"Probably. I haven't called them yet."

"Well, then, let's do it."

"Don't you want to order a drink first?"

"Fuck that. I'll celebrate when I hear we got the money. Come on, let's go. There's a pay phone over there."

"We'll need change for the phone. I don't have a credit card."

"I'll get a bucketful from the slot girl. You stay right here."

Malloy disappeared in the direction of the casino. Shiller slumped back into his chair, closed his eyes, and allowed the trembling to take hold of his body. He hadn't come this close to the edge since his brush with those apes at Diamond Lil's six months ago.

"Hello, Señor Vasquez, please." A pause. "It's Dan Shiller, Ricardo. What's happening? Did the money get there?" The faintest hint of a smile flickered across Shiller's face as he listened intently to the banker for a moment. Then his expression changed; he frowned and appeared surprised. "What? What's that? You're kidding!" The grifter pressed his hand over the mouthpiece and spoke to Buster Malloy: "Bad news, Buster. The money isn't there."

"What?" said Malloy. "But you said—"

"I know what I said. But apparently the association doesn't believe we'll go through with phase four."

Buster's pink face reddened. "Are you sure?" he asked slowly, suspicion creeping into his husky voice. "You wouldn't be connin' me now, would you, Danny boy? You wouldn't be thinkin' of keepin' all that lovely money for yourself, by any chance?"

Shiller shrugged. "Here," he said, handing his accomplice the receiver. "Ask him yourself. His name is—"

"I know what 'is fuckin' name is," Malloy retorted, snatching the phone and placing it to his ear. "Hello, Mr. Vasquez. What about the money then? . . . You're sure about that? . . . Yeah, I got it. Nothin' in the account."

Slowly, deliberately, Malloy replaced the handset on the pay phone. "All right. That's it, then, ain't it? They think they won. Well, those cocksuckers are gonna learn that you don't fuck with Buster Malloy. I'll blast 'em to hell in a handbasket. It'll be more awesome than Oklahoma City. *An'* Nine-Eleven. *Together.* They'll be diggin' out bodies till Christmas."

"You do that, Buster. Blast 'em for Jurgen and blast 'em for me."

Malloy smiled bitterly. "I knew in me heart they'd grind us into the dirt again, boyo. You can't beat the fuckin' system. You think you've won, but in the end you always get the shaft." Clapping a beefy arm around his partner's shoulders, he added sentimentally, "Sorry about just now, Dan. I still t'ink you're a sneaky, low-life, lyin' son of a bitch. But I'm gonna miss you. An' I'm sorry you ain't gettin' nothin' outta this neither." Shiller nodded sadly in the manner of a fellow traveler who has also reached valiantly for the stars, only to fall facedown in the mud. *For the best performance as a disappointed co-conspirator,* he thought smugly, *may I have the envelope please. . . .*

Buster squared his shoulders and continued: "But don't worry. I'm gonna give those bastards a fireworks show they ain't never gonna forget."

"I know you will, Malloy. And I suspect that you won't *really* mind wasting all those people, will you?"

Buster Malloy did not answer. With an expression that was half malice and half anticipation, he jammed the biker's helmet down over his ears, turned on his heel, and strode toward the parking lot.

43

Lucy Baker's doorbell hardly ever rang in the evening; certainly never after nine o'clock on a Friday night. If it wasn't bad news, she wondered what *else* anyone could possibly want with her at such an hour. She clutched the terry-cloth robe tightly to her throat, padded barefoot to the door, and squinted through the peephole.

Distorted by the fish-eye lens, a funhouse image of Steve Forrester bearing a bouquet of flowers and a brown paper bag grinned foolishly back at her.

"Steve!" she cried, unlatching the chain and opening the door. "I never expected . . . what are you doing here?"

"I was in the neighborhood and I thought I'd drop in." He paused, the grin beginning to fade. "Actually, I wasn't in the neighborhood at all. The truth is, I drove all the way out here because I just wanted to see you again. Especially now. Now that it's over, I mean."

"What's over?"

"Well, Droopy and his pals in the association have knuckled under to the extortionists. They paid up. So, all threats are presumably off, although Frank Marshall isn't convinced yet. In fact, he's still at DefCon One around the hotels. Maybe an overreaction, I dunno, but he's not backing off until they get Malloy. Anyhow, I kinda hoped you might want to help me celebrate." He presented the flowers, a bouquet of lilacs and tiger lilies, with a flourish and extracted a bottle of champagne and two glasses from the bag. Donning his best orphan-on-the-doorstep expression, he added, "But to prove how pure my heart is, even if you don't let me in, you get to keep the flowers and the bubbly."

She laughed, and Forrester's heart melted at the music of it. "All right, wiseguy," she said lightly. "I guess I can't very well turf you out now. Come on in. But you'd better behave yourself."

Like a breaching silver whale, the boom box exploded from the bottom of the gully in a great shower of sagebrush, sand, and stones. As it rose from its gritty blind and breasted the rim of the depression, a pair of brilliant headlights pierced the velvet desert sky at a steep upward angle, gradually returning to horizontal as the huge vehicle found level ground.

Behind the wheel, a grim-faced Buster Malloy accelerated recklessly over the rough terrain, scattering rocks and sagebrush along the way and creating an extended dust cloud that hung motionlessly behind him in the still night air.

Five miles to the dirt road that led back to U.S. 93.

After that, if he obeyed the speed limit, it was less than an hour and a half to the Strip.

Lucy squinched her eyes shut and covered her ears against the forthcoming pop as Steve expertly thumbed the cork out of the champagne bottle.

Standing in the middle of her living room, he in a dark business suit and she in a fluffy white terry-cloth robe, Forrester filled the two glasses and they clinked a toast.

"To peace in the valley," he said solemnly, looking down into her eyes.

"Peace in the valley," she echoed, looking up into his.

"All's well that ends well," he added.

"Is that it for the clichés?" she asked.

"I guess. Look, do you mind if I sit down? It's been a long day."

"Sure. Give me your jacket." She hung it on the coat-tree in the tiny vestibule and joined him on the overstuffed Ethan Allen couch. "And to think, my big plans for tonight were to take a shower and wash my hair."

"Sounds fascinating. If you need anybody to scrub your back . . ."

"Hey—you promised to behave."

"Just kidding." He refilled their glasses. "But seriously, I *am* sorry about the other night. Was it something I said?"

She put her glass down on the musket-box coffee table and bit her lip. "No, it was me. I was a real bitch. It's just that . . . well, frankly, I was a little bit scared. Scared of getting too close to someone again . . . and maybe . . . getting hurt. That's why I kind of . . . pushed you away."

"Let me guess. Does it have anything to do with that . . . cruise ship affair you mentioned when we had dinner in the Zodiac Room?"

Of course it does, she thought. *It has* everything *to do with that.*

"I don't know what happened then," he said. "Maybe I never will; that's up to you. But this is now, and I can tell you one thing. There's just no way I could ever . . . do anything to hurt you. Because, quite frankly, Lucy Baker, I can't help it . . . I've got feelings for you . . . like I never had before."

"Damn. That's what I was afraid of."

"You mean . . . you don't feel the same way? Not even a little bit?"

"That's just the trouble: I do." She lowered her eyes. "Believe it or not, I really do. And yet . . ."

This was the moment she'd been dreading—yet wanting so desperately. Was this the time to abandon her reservations at last, to release the emotions that had been repressed for so long? Funny how it suddenly felt so right. . . .

He drew her closer, and she responded, timidly at first. He kissed her lightly, then more and more deeply. She trembled a little, still nervous, still unsure of herself. Yet he could feel her body responding, feel her yielding to the passion. He exulted in the softness of her lips, the eagerness of her supple body, the sweet young scent of her.

She was wearing nothing but a terry bathrobe, belted loosely around the waist, and his arousal was enhanced by a clear view of her wonderful pink breasts as the robe slipped open a little. "You know," he whispered. "That offer still stands."

"What offer, Steve?" she breathed.

"Scrubbing your back."

She blushed and rose from the couch, gently pulling him to his feet.

He reached down and loosened her belt. Shyly, she shrugged off the robe; it slipped unnoticed to the floor. *This is right,* she said to herself, really believing it now. *This is the time, this is the man.*

Forrester shrugged off his shirt; she admired the flat stomach and well-defined pecs, lightly strewn with salt-and-pepper chest hair. She unbuckled his belt, and he stepped out of his pants.

Hand in hand, they walked into the bathroom and across the tiled floor to their watery tryst.

Under the warm spray, they started slowly, savoring the closeness. He soaped her all over, enjoying the smooth, slippery perfection of her firm skin. She washed his hair and gently massaged his shoulders. Kneeling at his feet, she delicately pleasured his throbbing member, sliding her fingers up and down until Steve could stand it no longer.

He put his arms around her slim waist and lifted her easily off the tiled floor of the shower, lowering her tenderly onto his stiffness. She twined her legs around him, and he covered her wet hair with soapy kisses as their glistening bodies danced and pulsated in a steamy embrace.

Eagerly, Lucy clutched Steve closer to her, pulling him, forcing him deeper inside her with every thrust. The intense sensation of the rhythmic pulsing and the warmth of the shower pushed Forrester over the edge quickly. As he released, he let out a wild cry and his legs buckled, almost landing the two of them on the tiled floor.

Luckily, Lucy's apartment had the dual advantages of thick walls and discreet neighbors.

44

Buster Malloy cursed the traffic. It was backed up as far as he could see. He hadn't moved more than half a mile in the past ten minutes.

As he topped a rise on U.S. 93, he saw red and blue flashers in the distance, blocking the snail parade of taillights. It was single-lane traffic; there was nothing he could do but stop and go with the rest of the trapped motorists.

Finally, at the state trooper's signal, he pulled the big vehicle to the left and around the scene of the accident. From his raised driving position, Malloy enjoyed a bird's-eye view of the carnage. He observed one blood-covered motorist, obviously dead, trapped inside a crushed subcompact. Another victim was being loaded into the back of an ambulance.

"Stupid arseholes," Malloy snarled venomously as he pressed down angrily on the accelerator pedal. "Your lousy drivin' cost me a whole fuckin' half hour. Dyin's too good for you."

Although the $50 million had been paid to Thanatos, Lieutenant Frank Marshall and the LVMPD were taking no chances. Las Vegas was an armed camp. Inside and out, downtown and Strip hotels were awash with policemen, some in uniform, some in plainclothes. Orders from Marshall had been specific: until further notice, no trucks were to be allowed anywhere near the Strip or downtown casino core without proof of a scheduled delivery or pickup. No trucks would be permitted to stop, except for traffic lights, within a block of any hotel. Every truck or van entering the grounds of a hotel, even with proper documentation, was to be thoroughly searched.

Marshall was determined to maintain the precautions at least until Buster Malloy was captured—or killed.

One of the uniformed LVMPD police officers posted at the Riviera's receiving gates looked at his watch while his partner stifled a yawn. Behind them a flotilla of large trucks, mostly semitrailers, was backed up to loading bays, disgorging cargoes in a never-ending race to stay ahead of the huge hotel's insatiable appetite for everything from toilet paper to frozen shrimp.

Both cops were intimately familiar with the contents of every vehicle, having personally scoured each of them from bumper to bumper. They had searched inside and underneath the cargo compartments, they had examined the cabs, they had even tossed the sleeping quarters of the big interstate rigs.

"I thought all this freakin' overtime would stop once they caught that perp with the computers," one of the metro cops complained. "Especially after the stupid hump offed himself."

"I also heard the hotels paid the ransom."

"Guess they ain't takin' chances," replied his partner with a shrug. "Anyways, only two more hours of this crap and we're outta here."

The first cop peered casually down Paradise Road and his face fell. "Oh shit," he groaned.

"What is it?"

"Hold your nose, man. It's another load of fish."

I'm exhausted, clean, and smitten by the love bug," Steve Forrester reported languidly from the couch. "Not necessarily in that order."

Lucy Baker radiated an inner glow as she bustled around the compact kitchenette. She felt warm and safe with this man; she knew her instincts had been right. "Coffee?" she asked.

"Sure. Mind if I smoke?"

Lucy wrinkled her nose prettily. "Do you have to? Now that the extortion is over, can't you go back to quitting—like before?"

"Just one, I promise. For old time's sake. Then I really will quit."

She arched a disbelieving eyebrow. "So kill yourself—see if I care."

Forrester stretched and lifted himself off the couch. He walked over to where his jacket was hanging in the vestibule, stopping en route to plant a kiss on Lucy's still-damp hair. Just as he reached into the side pocket for his pack of Vantage 100s, a soft ringing from the inside pocket startled him.

"Is that your cell phone?" Lucy asked.

"Sure sounds like it."

"Well, at least their timing is a little more convenient this time." She laughed, remembering their previous interrupted tryst in the apartment.

Hc flipped the phone open. "Steve Forrester."

An unfamiliar voice said, "This is Thanatos."

With less than five minutes to go before final boarding of his Alitalia flight to Rome, Dan Shiller paced back and forth in front of the bank of pay phones at LAX's Gate 23.

So far, it had all worked out perfectly. He had used his two accomplices for as long as necessary, and now he was rid of them. He had everything he needed to start a new life—a confirmed seat to Rome, then a ticket to the Tunisian island of Jerba. Because of the United Nations air embargo against Libya, that was the closest he could get to Tripoli. The 250-mile drive to the Libyan capital was inconvenient, but after that he was home free. All the money—minus the exorbitant banking fees those Panamanian crooks had charged him—would be waiting for him in the Libyan Arab Foreign Bank.

He could have had it sent to the Cayman Islands or Switzerland or any other Western tax haven, but Shiller was a cautious man. He knew that U.S. law enforcement had a long arm, with agents throughout the free world—agents, Dan supposed, who would not be above bending international law to seize his money and put him behind bars. Or worse.

So he had ruled out Europe and the Western Hemisphere, which left what—Asia? Africa? *Well, why not?* thought Dan. If he could find a country that was unfriendly to America, that could use a few bucks, that wouldn't run brown-nosing to the U.S. embassy the minute they found out who he was . . . if he could find a country like that—say, in Africa—he'd feel a hell of a lot more secure. Once the money was safely there, he could relax a little and figure out where to send it. Maybe he could split it up between three or four of these anti-American countries. That might be safer.

For the money.

And for him.

A totally amoral man, both by tradition and by choice, Shiller had long ago taught himself to care only for numero uno. Don't pity your victims, he had learned. Never worry about the consequences of your actions. He could easily shrug off the deaths of six innocent people and attribute them to the luck of the draw. He had gambled and won; they had lost. The world was full of losers; what did it matter how they died?

Yet for some reason, the idea of another Oklahoma City–type catastrophe bothered him. He could handle the snuffing of a mere half a dozen strangers, but gradually the monstrous concept of destroying thousands of lives had aroused some long-forgotten shred of decency, sounded some deeply buried chord in the grifter's vestigial conscience.

He really should do something. After all, it would cost him nothing. He *had* their money; once he'd left the country, they wouldn't be able to touch him.

Dan unfolded a scrap of paper with a phone number scrawled across it—a number Jurgen Voss had tracked down, a number that Shiller had used only once before and had never intended to use again. He dialed it and deposited the amount of change that the pay phone's readout demanded. Maybe there'd be no answer; maybe the line would be busy. In which case he could always tell himself that at least he'd tried.

One ring. Two rings. Then, "Steve Forrester."

"This is Thanatos," Shiller said, not bothering to disguise his voice.

There was a palpable intake of breath at the other end of the line. Finally Forrester responded, "Did you . . . receive the money?"

"Yes. But that's not why I'm calling."

"Then why?"

"To warn you. Buster Malloy is on his way to blast one of your hotels. He's driving a twelve-thousand-pound bomb into town right now."

"Why, for Chrissake? You say you got the money."

"Malloy docsn't know that."

Steve thought for a moment. "You screwed him out of his share, right?"

"Maybe. Look, I've gotta go."

"Who are you?"

"Ncvcr mind that."

"Which hotel is Malloy going to bomb?"

"I don't know. That's up to him. My guess, one of the majors on the Strip."

The operator's voice interrupted. "Please deposit two dollars for another three minutes."

"I don't have any more ch—"

"Quick," Forrester cut in, "what kind of truck is he driving?"

"Truck?" Shiller laughed. "He's not—"

"Sorry, sir. Time's up."

Click. Silence.

His conscience relieved, Dan Shiller ran to the gate and just made his flight to Rome.

To save time, Buster Malloy decided to take the long way around.

He would stay with 93 until it intersected with I-15, then swing onto 15 South and exit at Flamingo Road. That way, he'd avoid crosstown traffic and wind up less than two blocks from his target.

Friday-night traffic on the Strip was bound to be snarled, and Malloy was running out of patience.

Steve Forrester flipped the now-silent phone closed.

"That was them, wasn't it?" said Lucy Baker. "They're going to bomb a hotel, aren't they? Oh God, Steve, which one?"

"They didn't tell me. Look, Lucy, I've got to go."

"Wait. I'm coming with you."

"No—"

"Don't argue. You're not doing this alone. Besides, you may need help."

He sighed. "All right. You can phone the cops while I drive. But hurry."

"Give me thirty seconds."

For over three decades the undisputed title of classiest joint on the Strip had belonged to a pseudo-Roman pile of marble and brass, set discreetly back from the Strip behind acres of manicured lawns and topiary gardens. Pedestrian visitors were swept to its magnificent cantilevered porte-cochère on an elevated, covered people mover, while those arriving by car drove in along a gated, cypress-lined avenue, past forty-foot fountains and oversize statuary.

Inside, the splendor continued unabated. Acres of lush broadloom cushioned visitors' feet, while ornate chandeliers and gleaming brass appointments dazzled their eyes.

No expense was spared, no detail overlooked, to maintain an image of immaculately tended luxury. Ashtrays in public areas were always clean, the casino's logo carefully impressed into the white sand that filled them. An army of cleaners picked up trash almost before it touched the floor. Fingerprints on brass and glass were quickly polished away. In the finest tradition of the Roman baths, the restrooms sparkled.

For sheer opulence, none of the upstart megaresorts along the Strip could come close to matching the giant hotel-casino's aura of impeccable *grand luxe.* The biggest stars played there, the biggest gamblers stayed there.

In every respect, the Roman Palladium magnificently re-created the grandeur of that august bygone era.

Buster Malloy, however, was patently unimpressed as he waited for the green arrow that would permit him to turn left and proceed through the gates leading up to the Palladium's main entrance.

"**Hello,** Lieutenant Marshall? This is Lucy Baker. Steve Forrester's friend. Yes . . . that's right. Listen, I'm in the car with Steve right now. He just got a call from one of those extortionists. . . . No, we don't know his name. Apparently, this Buster Malloy is going to bomb a casino tonight. . . . What? Yes, I know the money was paid, but Malloy doesn't. Steve thinks the guy who called us ripped Malloy off. . . . No, he didn't know which casino. Probably a big one on the Strip, he thought. He said something about a twelve-thousand-pound bomb. Steve asked the man what kind of truck we should look for, and he laughed, kind of like it wasn't a truck. Then we got cut off. . . ."

Forrester pushed the big Mercedes-Benz SL 500 convertible hard left around a corner, squealing the tires and forcing Lucy to clutch the dashboard. Now heading north on Las Vegas Boulevard, he accelerated hard, unleashing the full power of the mighty 302-horsepower V-8.

In the open convertible, Lucy gave up trying to hold her hair in place. She listened for a moment and then spoke again into the cell phone. "I guess we're about five minutes away from the south end of the Strip. . . . What's that? . . . Okay, Lieutenant, I'll tell him. Good-bye."

Lucy folded up the phone. "He says he'll alert everybody. And he said for you to slow down."

Steve grinned. "I'll slow down when they catch Malloy, and not before.

In the meantime, anybody who doesn't like my driving is cordially invited to step out at the next traffic light."

She narrowed her eyes and folded her arms. "Never mind. I'm staying to help you catch this guy. After *that,* we'll talk about your driving—and certain other habits I've noticed."

"What the hell have I gotten myself into with this woman?" he asked the wind rhetorically.

"You haven't even scratched the surface yet, mister." She leaned over and nibbled his earlobe. "I can be very tough."

"I believe you. Could I get a little tongue with that?"

"Keep your mind on your driving."

Forrester nudged the powerful car up to seventy, then eighty miles an hour. The throaty roar of the engine and the rushing wind precluded easy conversation. Ahead, glowing neon and flaring taillights told them they were almost upon the Strip. Thickening traffic forced them to slow as the monstrous bulk of the Luxor pyramid loomed up on their left.

"Okay, Richard Petty," said Lucy, brushing the dark hair from her eyes. "We're here. Now what? What are we supposed to look for?"

Steve relaxed in the leather bucket seat, allowing his wrist to rest loosely on the steering wheel. "I think I know. Look, the caller said Malloy was quote, driving a twelve-thousand-pound bomb, unquote, right?"

"Right."

"And he also implied that Malloy was not driving a truck."

"Right."

"Well, if Malloy is not driving a truck, what other vehicle would be capable of hauling a load that size?"

"I don't know. A Winnebago? Some kind of RV?"

"Possible. But unlikely. If this bomb is made up of plastic drums like the one in Oklahoma City, and if each drum holds, say, two hundred pounds, we're talking sixty drums. There wouldn't be enough room for them in any RV I've ever seen. And their suspensions wouldn't take the weight."

"What about a van?"

"Same problem: not enough room. Besides, the cops are checking every size of truck from vans to semis. No, it has to be something else. Something big enough to carry all those drums, but ordinary enough not to attract suspicion. Something that would look perfectly natural parked in front of a hotel. And for my money, that can mean only one kind of vehicle."

"What's that?"

"A bus! A big one. You know—one of those intercity buses, a Grey-hound. It's so obvious, I'm annoyed I didn't think of it before. If they packed the passenger compartment and the underneath luggage area with drums, there'd be more than enough room."

"God, Steve, I think you're right. So, we look for a bus?"

"Yep. And we call Frank Marshall."

She picked up the phone and shook her head. "Sorry, Chief, no can do."

"Huh?"

"Battery's dead."

"Damn."

"So, Man of Steel, I guess it's up to us to save mankind." Lucy unfas-tened her seat belt. "Wow, I've always wanted to say that." She stood up-right in the convertible, holding on to the windshield frame for support. The extra height allowed her to look over the tops of other cars and into the courtyards of the big hotel-casinos.

"No buses anywhere that I can see," she reported after a few moments.

By the time they reached the palmy Moorish portico of the Aladdin, they were barely crawling. In front of Bally's chameleon candy-cane columns, they ground to a full stop, a hundred yards of three-lane traffic be-tween them and what had to be the world's slowest traffic light at Flamingo Road.

45 With a hiss of air brakes, Buster Malloy brought the giant double-decker Greyhound Americruiser smoothly to a halt beneath the cantilevered porte-cochère of the Roman Palladium.

He checked his reflection in the rearview mirror. Driver's cap at the correct angle, tie straight, sunglasses adjusted to hide the missing eye. He brushed off the short-sleeved gray shirt with the Greyhound logo on the pocket and rose from the driver's seat. Boosting the bus had been easy. Breaking into the locker room at the depot and stealing the uniform had been the tough part. But he'd pulled it off. For the last time, Buster glanced down the aisle at his "passengers"—white chemical drums looking like headless ghost riders obediently seated in pairs all the way to the back. In an uncharacteristic flash of black humor, Dan Shiller had christened the stolen bus their "portable boom box."

Malloy no longer noticed the pungent mixture of ammonium nitrate fertilizer and nitromethane that permeated the interior of the vehicle; during the long drive in from the desert his nostrils had become desensitized to the odor. All sixty-five drums were interconnected by detonator wires. If everything went according to Jurgen's calculations, the wires would simultaneously set off a blasting cap buried in each drum, which in turn would detonate the stick of dynamite to which it was attached. The resulting explosion would unleash almost three times the power of the fertilizer bomb that had destroyed the Alfred P. Murrah Federal Building in Oklahoma City.

A tangle of wires joined each drum to its neighbor. Other wiring harnesses disappeared through three roughly hacked holes in the floor to connect with the remaining drums in the three luggage compartments below.

Attached with duct tape to the wall beside the driver's seat, an electronic timer with a green LED readout was frozen at twelve minutes. Malloy reached over and turned a key, starting the countdown. 11:59 . . . 11:58 . . . 11:57, it began, inexorably headed for zero and oblivion for hundreds, if not thousands, of human beings. As Jurgen had suggested, the big Irishman removed the timer key and tossed it to the back of the bus, where it disappeared into a thicket of wires. The precaution was redundant; a duplicate timer in the center luggage compartment, wired in parallel to the one beside the seat, would continue to run and would detonate the entire charge even if the first timer were disabled.

Satisfied with his preparations, Buster picked up a gray tote bag and casually stepped down from the bus, closing and locking the door behind him. An African-American doorman wearing a white jacket with gold braid trim intercepted Malloy as he ascended the wide marble steps leading up to the front doors.

"How long you gonna be, my man?"

The bogus bus driver stopped and smiled reassuringly. "Not more'n fifteen minutes, pal. I got a loada ol' ladies to pick up. I jus' need to go inside an' round 'em up."

"All right. But make it fast, I got a pile of traffic coming through here."

"Be right back, *bro*," Malloy retorted cynically, clutching his bag and disappearing through the smoked-glass doors of the Roman Palladium.

After sitting out three long reds at Flamingo Road, Steve Forrester was finally able to inch the Mercedes-Benz convertible across the intersection.

Lucy Baker, standing up in the convertible like a politician in a St. Patrick's Day parade, scanned the hotel fronts anxiously. Nothing she had seen so far remotely resembled a Greyhound bus.

But wait! That familiar shape a quarter mile back from the road! The red, white, and blue livery, the big windows reflecting the overhead lights of the Roman Palladium—could it be? "Yes," she cried, answering her own question. She gripped Forrester's shoulder with her left hand and pointed excitedly with her right. "Look, Steve! At the entrance to the Palladium! It's definitely a bus!"

Forrester screeched to a halt and pulled on the hand brake, provoking an instant chorus of honks from the cars behind. Awkwardly, he pulled himself up by grasping the top of the windshield and stared in the direction she was pointing. "You're right." He squinted hard, shielding his eyes from the neon glare. "And look—somebody's just getting out of the bus. A big guy. I can't see his face from this distance—but I'd bet the ranch it's our friend Malloy!"

"Oh my God, Steve . . . but we're on the wrong side of the Strip . . . and we're hemmed in by traffic. How do we get there?"

"The hard way," he replied grimly, sliding back down into the bucket seat. "Fasten your seat belt."

He jammed the Mercedes into gear, released the brake, and popped the clutch. They were in the center lane on the northbound side of the Strip; they had to jump one lane in order to reach the median. Using the space that had opened up in front of them when he stopped a moment earlier, Forrester accelerated and cut the wheel hard to the left. In a hopelessly optimistic turn signal, he pointed his arm at the tiny space in front of the Yellow Cab that occupied the lane he needed to cross. As he had fully expected, the taxi driver was not moved. The man indignantly blew his horn, determined not to allow any fancy sports car to cut in front of *him*. It had been a tough day.

"Sorry, fella," Steve muttered. "This is going to hurt my car more than it's gonna hurt yours."

Forrester gripped the wheel and relentlessly pursued his course, crunching his left front fender into the right front bumper of the cab. As he angled across the other car's path, its bumper scraped an ugly groove all down the left side of the Mercedes. The taxi driver slammed on his brakes, but it was too late. The Mercedes's left rear wheel well caught the taxi's bumper, ripping it completely off. Enraged, the cabbie leaned on his horn and uttered Arabic imprecations at this crazy man in the silver convertible who had just despoiled his beautiful car! Forrester ignored the yelling; he was already steering his front wheels up and over the concrete lip of the median. As the rear wheels reached the steep curb, they spun wildly, momentarily losing traction. Then they grabbed, and the big sports car scraped over, ripping off one of its twin stainless-steel mufflers in the process.

"What's that noise?" Lucy yelled.

"We just lost a muffler," Steve shouted back. "Hang on now!"

He accelerated hard off the other side of the median, landing directly in the path of a knot of oncoming traffic. Brakes squealed and horns blasted as startled motorists desperately attempted to avoid this unexpected shot across their bow. One car slid sideways and was rammed broadside by the vehicle behind, causing a chain reaction of rear-end collisions. Another driver did not see the Mercedes coming until he was virtually upon it. Frantically he turned his wheel to the right, barely managing to avoid T-boning the silver convertible but nevertheless sharply clipping its front right side.

Lucy screamed and Forrester fought the wheel as the force of impact lifted the right side of their car and threatened to tip it over. But the heavy convertible held its ground and bounced back down with a spine-jarring crash. Forrester regained control and pointed it toward the Palladium's main entrance—the famous triumphal arch topped with the gilded charioteer sculpture. A high-pitched squeal now emanated from his right front wheel as the tire rubbed noisily against the crumpled fender, but Steve was beyond caring about the car. Somehow they had to reach that bus, to warn people, to disarm the bomb before it was too late.

He accelerated up to the gate and swung the wheel hard right. Almost there—but damn it all! Traffic on the carriageway leading up to the hotel's main entrance was jammed right back to the sidewalk. A virtual parking lot of private cars, limousines, and taxis completely blocked access to the Roman Palladium.

"Now what do we do?" an ashen-faced Lucy Baker asked.

"Only one other way in," Forrester replied matter-of-factly, slamming the car into reverse, roaring out backward as far as he could, then screeching forward across the sidewalk, knocking over a trash can and scattering terrified pedestrians.

The car bounced back down onto the blacktop of the Strip and squealed off rapidly in a southbound direction. A hundred feet farther along, he jammed on the brakes and executed a sliding right turn—into the exit gate.

With smoke now pouring out of the right front wheel well as a result of the friction of metal against rubber and a loud roar emanating from beneath the partially disemboweled vehicle, Forrester once more floored the Mercedes, racing in the wrong direction up the Palladium's one-way exit driveway.

Suddenly a small red car appeared directly in his path. Forrester squeezed right to let the other vehicle pass on his left, but its driver panicked—instead of turning right himself in order to get by, he braked hard and slid directly into the path of the big convertible. Steve frantically jerked the wheel back to the left, but it was too late. The crumpled right front fender of the heavy Mercedes caught the hapless subcompact and lifted it like a toy, pushing it over the marble retaining wall and into the reflecting pool surrounding the fountains.

Grimly, Steve Forrester drove on. Lucy glanced back to witness a sodden but apparently unhurt driver climbing out of the window of the little red car.

"Almost there!" Steve shouted—when a big yellow-and-black sign loomed up ahead of them. DO NOT ENTER! it read. SEVERE TIRE DAMAGE! BACK UP NOW!

"All I can say is, this better be the right bus," Forrester muttered through gritted teeth, maintaining speed as they approached the angled spikes that protruded ominously from the roadbed. Four loud bangs rocked the car as each of its tires exploded in turn.

But they were there! He skidded the Mercedes sideways on its shredded tires, finally grinding to a halt at a skewed angle in front of the bus, less than a foot from its massive bumper. Not surprisingly, the Mercedes's driver's door was jammed shut. Steve vaulted over the side, noting with resignation as he did so that the car's bodywork now more closely resembled a demolition derby loser than the pride of the German automotive industry.

Lucy jumped out through the still-functioning passenger door and raced around to join him.

The gold-braided doorman planted himself in front of the couple. "Are you crazy?" he yelled. "What in hell do you think you're—"

Forrester held up his hand. "Sorry. I'm Steve Forrester, Vice President of the Galaxy. This is an emergency. Where's the driver of that bus?"

"He went inside a couple of minutes ago. To get his passengers. Look, Mr. Forrester, what's going on here?"

"To make a long story short, we believe there's a bomb aboard that bus."

"Motherfucker." The man's eyes widened. "Why didn't you say so?"

Forrester ran to the Greyhound bus and attempted to open the door. It was locked. "You got anything I could pry this open with?" he called out to the doorman. But the man had gone. Steve just caught a glimpse of a gilt-edged figure disappearing rapidly past the taxi stand toward the gates.

"There must be another way in," said Lucy, scanning the bus.

"Hey, you'd better get out of here," Forrester said with a worried frown. "This thing could go off at any time."

He watched as she swallowed hard and set her jaw stubbornly. "Well, I'm not leaving. You know, you're not the only one involved here. This is *my* town, too. And I don't intend to let these bastards destroy it."

Forrester hesitated, admiring her courage but still dubious about exposing her to such danger. "No use both of us risking our lives—"

"Why? Because I'm a weak, defenseless female? Get real, mister. There's no time to argue . . . and you could probably use my help." She pointed to a window halfway down the bus that was slightly raised. "Look, that window's open. I'm small. If you boosted me, I could get inside and open the door."

"But—"

"Hey, we're in this thing together."

"Okay, let's do it." He clasped her around the thighs from behind and lifted her easily. She reached up and grasped the frame of the open window. With a wiggle and a final boost from Forrester, she managed to insinuate her slim body through the opening, scraping a shin painfully on the way in and landing awkwardly atop a pair of plastic chemical drums. The pungent stench inside the darkened bus caused her to blink and gasp for breath. With difficulty, she half rolled, half fell off the drums and into the aisle. Then, holding on to seat backs, she pulled herself to her feet and headed up the aisle—only to immediately trip over a tangle of wires. As she fell, she smashed her left elbow on a plastic armrest.

God, it hurt. But there was no time for self-pity. Somehow, squeezing back tears of pain, she stumbled to her feet and reached the front of the bus. Now, how did you open the door? She looked around quickly.

There—above the door. A little lever with a knob at the end marked EMERGENCY OPEN. She pulled down hard on it. There was a click and a hiss of compressed air, and the door swung wide.

Forrester bounded up the four steps two at a time. One glance down the aisle at the wired-up plastic drums told him that his hunch had been correct. And unless they did something about it, the Roman Palladium would suffer the same terrible end as the Alfred P. Murrah Federal Building in Oklahoma City.

"Are you all right?" he asked Lucy.

She bit her lip and nodded. "There's some kind of clock there taped under the window. It says less than seven minutes—"

"It must be the timer for the bomb."

"Can you disarm it? You know, cut the wires . . . or stop the clock?"

Steve peered closely at it. "I don't think so. There's no key. And I wouldn't know which wires to cut—even if I had something to cut them with."

"Maybe we should wait for the police."

He glanced again at the LED readout on the clock—06:47. "Look, if that thing's accurate, there's no time. We've got to get this bus out of here—now!"

Fortunately, Malloy had left the big diesel engine running. Forrester slid behind the wheel and dumbly scrutinized the myriad instruments, the serried ranks of switches and blinking lights. "Hey, lady—you got any idea how to drive this thing?" he asked hopefully.

"No . . . but isn't that a gearshift by your right arm? The doodad that says 'R-N-D'?"

"I believe you're right! We're in business!"

He jerked the lever into D and simultaneously pressed down on the accelerator pedal. With a hiss of compressed air, the bus lurched ahead. There was a grinding crash.

"Steve! Watch out for your car!"

"Oh, shit. Well, it's too late now. *Auf wiedersehen,* old friend." As the bus gathered speed, its massive rubber-faced bumper lifted the battered Mercedes-Benz convertible, pushing it on its side and finally flipping it completely over like a child's toy.

Buster Malloy hurried through the elegant lobby, past the imposing marble statue of Julius Caesar and into the men's restroom.

The bomb's timer was set for twelve minutes; Malloy had allowed himself five minutes to change into the biker's outfit, then another seven to get well clear of the building.

Inside the cubicle, he stuffed the bus driver's uniform into the tote bag and crammed the bag behind the toilet. Tucking the helmet under his arm, he adjusted the wraparound sunglasses to conceal his deformity. Buster was certain that porch monkey of a doorman would not recognize him without the uniform. But even if he did, so what?

Buster strode confidently back out through the front doors of the Roman Palladium. Oddly, there was no sign of the doorman. But what was this? The door of the bus was open! And it was starting to move!

With a roar of indignation, Malloy dropped his helmet and raced for the bus. As he neared it, the big vehicle casually pushed a silver Mercedes convertible over onto its back and out of the way. Gradually, it gathered speed. Malloy's legs pounded like pistons as he raced for the bus; he just managed to seize the grab bar mounted on the open door. For a moment, he ran beside the bus, legs windmilling, pulled along by the grab bar, breathing hard, his face purple from anger and exertion. Finally, with a monumental effort, he heaved his bulky body up onto the bottom step.

"Well . . . if it ain't . . . the big boss . . . Steve Forrester," he gasped. "I shoulda . . . known . . . it was you."

Startled, Forrester glanced at his new passenger. "Get off this bus, Malloy!"

"No way . . . *Mister* Forrester." Chest heaving, the big man slowly climbed to the second step and paused. "Now you just . . . put them brakes on an' back right up."

"Go fuck yourself."

Still breathing heavily, Buster Malloy deliberately pulled himself up to the next step. He spotted the woman standing back in the shadows and squinted in her direction. "Miss Baker, ain't it?" he panted. "What are you supposed to be, then . . . Mr. Forrester's shotgun rider?"

"Get back, Malloy," Lucy cried, her voice unsteady. She looked around desperately for a weapon, anything to stop this madman from coming any closer. Her eye fell upon a solid-looking brass fire extinguisher suspended from the wall behind the driver's seat. She lunged for it and fumbled frantically with the clip. But Buster was too fast; rising cobralike from the stairwell, he swung a beefy closed fist in a wide backhand arc and smashed Lucy across the upper chest, knocking her back between the seats.

"Enjoy your trip, bitch," Malloy sneered.

Lucy fell hard, the wind knocked out of her. The fire extinguisher clattered to the floor and rolled from side to side in the aisle as Steve frantically accelerated.

The clock read 04:53.

With no further obstacles between him and his target, Malloy launched himself directly at Forrester. Steve tried to fend off his attacker with a straight-arm, but succeeded only in knocking Buster's sunglasses off, revealing one bloodshot green eye and one ghastly empty socket the color and texture of chewed bubble gum.

"So that bastard Druperman didn't think we'd do it," Malloy snarled, struggling to oust his opponent from the driver's seat.

"You stupid son of a bitch," Forrester panted, managing an elbow to Malloy's midsection. "We *did* pay the money. Your pal screwed you."

For a second, Buster froze. Then he began to laugh, a rising, humorless cackle with an undertone of pure madness. "Well, then, fuck him," he screamed. "Fuck Druperman. Fuck you. And *fuck this town!*"

With his left hand, Malloy roughly seized the collar of Forrester's jacket and yanked him half out of the driver's seat; with the other, he grabbed the big flat steering wheel and tried to force it around to the left, attempting to scrape the bus to a halt along the marble retaining wall of the reflecting pool.

Determined to keep the vehicle moving away from the building, Forrester held the pedal to the floor and tried valiantly to resist Malloy's pressure on the wheel. But from his awkward position half on and half off the seat, half sitting and half lying, he was unable to obtain the leverage he needed to overcome the larger man's brute strength.

Inexorably, the bus veered left, but instead of grinding to a stop as Malloy had hoped, it smashed through the retaining wall of the Palladium's reflecting pool at thirty miles an hour as if the wall were made of glass. The impact blasted a great spray of chipped stone and water, causing an outrushing deluge at the spot where the big vehicle had breached the wall. Like a dam burst in a Hollywood disaster epic, a wall of water cascaded out onto the manicured lawns and concrete forecourt. Still moving ahead, powering through the two-foot-deep pool, the mighty Greyhound's speed raised a huge sheeted bow wave on each side, while its momentum caused it to snap off in turn each of the fountainhead statues as easily as a bowler would knock down tenpins. Behind the great vehicle, high-pressure jets of water spurted unchecked from broken mains.

Awkwardly splayed across the driver's seat, Forrester nevertheless managed to keep his foot pressed down on the accelerator. He knew that the farther away from the Palladium he managed to push the bus, the more lives would be spared. He squirmed and twisted, unable to obtain the advantage over his stronger, heavier opponent. As a former amateur wrestler, Steve could have given a respectable account of himself in a fair fight, but now, arched backward across the seat, he knew he was losing the battle for control of the Greyhound. His head rocked as Malloy landed a glancing blow to his temple; he felt a massive hand grab his belt and begin to haul him bodily off the seat and away from the controls. With a triumphant roar, the bitter, deranged ex-Marine raised a giant hamhock of a fist above his head.

The green LED readout on the clock timer read 04:02.

Guns drawn, two Metro cops burst out of the front doors of the Roman Palladium just in time to witness the Greyhound's voyage of destruction through the reflecting pool.

As they watched in fascinated horror, the vehicle began mowing down fountains. It smashed into the little red car, the subcompact that had been forced into the water only moments ago during Forrester's wild inbound charge, and tossed it skyward in a shower of flying fenders and shattered glass.

"What the hell's going on?" one of the policemen asked a valet parker.

"This crazy guy roars up in that Mercedes." The attendant indicated the inverted wreck of Forrester's car. "There's a woman with him. Then they break into that bus and drive off. Another guy jumps on board just as they're leaving. What a fuckin' mess. There's gonna be hell to pay when the bosses see this."

"Did these people say anything?" the other cop said, switching on his shoulder mike.

"I'm not sure. I thought I heard the guy from the Mercedes say there was a bomb on the bus."

46 **Lucy Baker** grimaced in pain. Everything hurt.

Agonizingly she raised her head. What was going on? The bus was moving—but nobody was holding the wheel. Sheets of water were cascading over the windshield. And Steve—Steve was in trouble! Malloy had him pinned helplessly across the driver's seat and his fist was raised in the air, preparing to strike his adversary a crushing blow.

She had to do something fast! As the bus rocked, the fire extinguisher rolled against her leg. She grabbed for it, stumbled to her feet, and, with all the force she could muster, brought the heavy brass cylinder down two-handed on Buster's skull—just in time to prevent him from administering the coup de grâce he had aimed at Forrester.

Buster Malloy's single eye rolled up, and he collapsed in a heap.

Steve lurched back to a sitting position in the driver's seat. Without his foot on the accelerator, the bus had begun to lose momentum. He grabbed the wheel and pushed the pedal back down to the metal. The Greyhound surged forward through the final reaches of the pool and smashed its way out through the retaining wall at the end as easily as it had smashed its way in.

03:49 remained on the clock.

Forrester accelerated the bus back toward the outbound driveway, plowing furrows in the lawn and shearing off half a dozen decorative cypress trees en route.

"Are you all right, Lucy?" he asked anxiously, glancing up at this beautiful, brave woman who had stopped Buster Malloy in his tracks—and probably saved his life, at least temporarily.

"I . . . think so," she replied. She was hanging on for dear life to the vertical support pole next to the driver's seat. Behind her, Malloy lay sprawled in the aisle. "Can I ask a question?"

"You bet." Forrester peered through the windshield, now cracked in several places and spattered with wet grass and leaves. For some reason, there appeared to be no traffic directly ahead of them on the southbound side of Las Vegas Boulevard.

"Where are we going?"

"There's a demolition site just north of here on the far side of the Strip."

She peered anxiously at the clock timer on the wall. "Can we make it there in three minutes and twenty-seven seconds?"

"No sweat—just relax and enjoy the ride."

As the bus rocketed through the exit gates onto the black asphalt of the Strip, Steve suddenly realized why there was no traffic in his path. A multi-vehicle pileup, the result of his previous unconventional crossing in the Mercedes, was blocking all three southbound lanes. Mangled cars and trucks, steam pouring from broken radiators, were strewn all over the road.

With an apologetic wave to the cluster of stunned motorists, Forrester banged the low-slung Greyhound across the empty lanes and over the median, creating a shower of sparks as its undercarriage scraped the raised concrete.

He pressed the horn for the benefit of the northbound traffic. But it was too little warning, too late, for the hapless oncoming motorists. With virtually no time to react, they cringed helplessly in their vehicles as the huge bus suddenly materialized in front of them. It plowed into the front end of a minivan, spinning it around like a top. Unable to stop, two other cars slammed into the van, sending it spinning again in the opposite direction. Steve wrenched the steering wheel hard left to head north; the big bus heeled over and its rear end momentarily slid out, smashing into the same Yellow cab from which Steve's late Mercedes-Benz SL 500 had ripped the front bumper minutes earlier.

The apoplectic Arab taxi driver leapt back just in time to avoid being crushed between the two vehicles. Waving both fists in the air as the bus fishtailed off down the Strip, he called down the death curse of Allah upon both the demented infidels who had conspired to destroy his brand-new cab—the evil driver of the Mercedes-Benz convertible *and* the satanic chauffeur of the Greyhound Americruiser.

For years, the Drifts Hotel and Casino had enjoyed a place of honor on the Las Vegas Strip. Its golf course was world-renowned. In its fabled showroom many of the world's best-known entertainers had launched their careers. The famous and near famous had stayed and played at the Drifts.

But finally, the old girl's time had come.

Her demise was slated for two days hence.

The building had been gutted. Work crews had purposely weakened the hotel's supporting columns in preparation for the scheduled implosion; it only remained to place dynamite charges at strategic points and detonate them. Like the blowup of the Dunes several years earlier, the Drifts implosion was to be a photo op—a media event to capture even the most jaded Las Vegan's attention, if only momentarily.

To conform with local regulations and to discourage trespassers, an eight-foot-high plywood construction fence had been erected around the site.

Steve Forrester fervently hoped that no overzealous demolition worker was inside that fence at ten minutes before midnight on a Friday.

02:43 and counting, said the clock timer at Forrester's elbow.

"This horn just isn't loud enough to catch people's attention," Forrester complained. "Where the hell is the high-beam switch? If I could flash my lights, it'd give cars a chance to get out—"

"Maybe it's that button on the floor by your left foot," Lucy suggested.

"Let's find out." He stepped on the smooth, round button. A tremendous blast from the Greyhound's powerful air horn caused them both to jump. "Fantastic!" he exclaimed. "This'll wake 'em up!"

With his left foot now firmly planted on the air-horn button, Steve threaded the big bus through traffic at forty-five miles an hour. Some motorists reacted to the blaring noise and pulled aside. Others refused to move over, forcing Forrester regretfully but relentlessly to push them out of the way with the mighty Greyhound. An angry crescendo of horns and a swath of damaged and wrecked vehicles marked his desperate drive toward the Drifts implosion site.

"Half a block to go," Steve announced to Lucy. "Just past that traffic light. If it stays green, we might just make it!"

"Stay green," she implored the light. "Please stay green . . . oh, please stay green . . . oh, shit."

As the light perversely changed to red, three lanes of unsuspecting traffic in front of them obediently braked to a halt.

The clock read 02:06.

With no driving room ahead on the road, Forrester desperately opted for the only alternative left to him. Without slowing, he hauled the wheel to the right and bounced the bus up onto the sidewalk, praying that the air horn would clear people out of the way. The continuous blast did alert two pedestrians in his path—they dove to safety with just a fraction of a second to spare.

Steve flinched and Lucy ducked instinctively as a streetlamp loomed in their path. Smash! The metal structure snapped off and flew back over the roof of the bus. A pole-mounted traffic light was next; Forrester simply drove straight through it. This last assault on the battered windshield's integrity caused it finally to implode, showering Forrester and Lucy with a million crystals of safety glass.

"I can't see 'round this corner—better hope there's nothing coming," Steve said earnestly as the Greyhound left the sidewalk and entered the intersection without slowing. He glanced left, then quickly right, and his heart stopped! Bearing down on them less than fifty feet away was a huge transport truck!

Fortunately for Steve and Lucy, the quick reflexes of the trucker saved them from a broadside ramming. In a cloud of blue smoke and screaming tires, the monstrous semitrailer skidded sideways, jackknifing to a shuddering halt inches from the side of the speeding bus.

"Thank you, Lord," said Steve Forrester.

01:55, the clock read.

"Watch out for the fence!" cried Lucy Baker.

Through the knocked-out windshield, they could see the plywood fence that surrounded the Drifts rapidly looming closer. "Cover your face!" Forrester commanded, squeezing his own eyes shut as they smashed through the fence in a cloud of splinters, knocking plywood panels and four-by-four fence posts aside like jackstraws. Inside the compound, Steve maintained speed. The heavy vehicle rocked alarmingly as it bumped and jounced over piles of rubble, scraping the Greyhound's underbelly and causing the explosive-filled plastic barrels to lurch ominously in their seats.

Straight ahead, the headlights picked out a marble staircase, half a dozen steps high, leading up to the black hole where the Drifts' main lobby had once welcomed visitors from around the world. Now the famous hotel was merely a pile of steel and concrete awaiting its final indignity—an event Steve Forrester had reluctantly been obliged to reschedule.

He pushed his foot hard to the floor, hoping to power the bus up the stairs and bury it in the gutted lobby.

"Hold on tight, Lucy!" Steve yelled.

She hugged the vertical metal pole in a death grip.

A hundred feet to go. Speed fifty miles an hour . . . fifty-five . . . then—*wham!*—ahead of the wheels, the low-slung front bumper struck the staircase first, jarring the entire frame of the bus. The impact lifted Steve out of his seat and almost sent him flying across the steering wheel and through the glassless windshield. Somehow he held on. Lucy's feet slid out from under her, but with a superhuman effort she managed to keep a grip on the pole.

Despite the initial impact, the combination of mass and velocity did the trick; the Greyhound's remaining momentum shot it up the staircase and propelled it into the dark, deserted lobby.

Its odyssey ended when the eleven-foot-high bus wedged itself under a ten-foot section of ceiling, bringing the big vehicle to a rapid, grinding halt. The headlights cut a swath through an acrid dust cloud, illuminating the ghostly skeleton of the once-proud establishment. Only naked columns remained to divide the vast empty space; shards of broken glass and chunks of rubble littered the bare concrete floor.

When the call came in describing the chaos at the Roman Palladium, LVMPD Lieutenant Frank Marshall and Sergeant Morris Jaworski were parked outside the Galaxy in an unmarked Crown Victoria sedan.

Marshall quickly realized what was happening.

He switched to the patrol-car frequency and thumbed the mike button. "All units near Las Vegas Boulevard." With his free hand he unfolded a street map onto the dashboard. "Clear civilian traffic immediately from the vicinity of the Drifts demolition site. Code 445. Set up roadblocks at the following locations: Flamingo Road and the Strip. Desert Inn Road and the Strip. Spring Mountain Road and I-Fifteen. Spring Mountain and Paradise Road. Do not acknowledge. Code 3."

"You know, I haven't patrolled in a black-and-white for years. I know Code 3 means 'Emergency Radio Traffic Only,' " Jaworski said. "But what's a Code 445?"

Marshall flipped a switch activating the siren and the blue grille-mounted flashers. "It means 'Explosive Device,' Moe." He slammed the car into gear and sped off down the Strip.

"I get it. There's a bomb on that bus. And Steve's driving it away from the Palladium." The scruffy police scientist tightened his seat belt. "But why the Drifts, Frank? What makes you think Steve's headed there?"

"Put yourself in his position. You've got twelve thousand pounds of live explosives on board. Probably set to go off with some kind of timer. You wouldn't risk driving the bus away if you thought the bomb could be disarmed. But you figure it can't. So you head for the only spot within a mile where it can explode with a minimum of damage. Steve turned north on the Strip—"

"In the direction of the Drifts."

"Let's just hope the crazy bastard makes it in time."

Dust filled the gutted lobby of the Drifts Hotel and Casino. Steve Forrester pulled himself stiffly from the driver's seat of the battered Greyhound Americruiser and staggered to his feet. He checked the timer: 01:20 . . . 01:19 . . . 01:18 . . .

"Feel like setting a new record for the hundred-yard dash?" he asked Lucy breathlessly.

"I guess so."

"Then let's go for it!" Steve leaped into the stairwell and gallantly extended a hand to assist her down the steps.

She began to move toward him.

Suddenly, without warning, her ankle was seized from behind in an iron grip!

She screamed in surprise and fright.

"You ain't . . . goin' nowhere . . . pretty lady," Buster Malloy croaked. Holding on to Lucy's ankle with his right hand, he hauled himself to his knees. Still kneeling, quick as lightning, the big man reached up and locked his left forearm around her neck.

Forrester rushed back up the steps. "Let her go, you sick son of a bitch!" he said.

"Stay back, or I'll snap 'er neck like a fuckin' matchstick!" Malloy hissed. Forrester froze. Buster Malloy rose from his kneeling position, keeping the headlock on Lucy; as he drew himself upright, he dragged her up with him so that her feet left the floor. She struggled to twist free, but her captor's animal strength was overwhelming.

Steve was paralyzed by indecision. Every fiber in his body ached to charge wildly at Malloy, to crush the life out of the murdering son of a bitch and free Lucy. On one hand, he knew the big man would not hesitate for a second to carry out his threat. But on the other hand, what choice did Forrester have? He glanced frantically at the clock: 00:56. They'd all be blown sky-high in less than a minute anyway. He had to do *something*. And he had to do it fast.

The reflected glow of the headlights shone in through the windows upon Buster Malloy's ruined countenance. It revealed a visage from a horror movie, the bogeyman's face out of a child's worst nightmare. Gore from the deep gash in his scalp matted his hair; blood coursed down his forehead and into the dreadful puckered hollow where his left eye had once been. It dripped from his nose and ran between his crooked teeth, lending a vampirish aspect to his twisted grin. Pure evil shone from Buster's blood-shot good right eye.

"Go ahead, Mr. Steve Fuckin' Forrester," he sneered. "You can leave. You jus' get outta here now an' save your arse. But Lucy an' me, we're stayin' for the fireworks. Ain't we, lover?" He tightened his arm around her slim neck and fondled her breast with his free hand; she clawed ineffectually at the massive bear paw. "Oh baby, what a fuckin' turn-on. Gettin' snuffed with you—I'm gettin' horny just thinkin' about it." Malloy laughed insanely, uproariously.

"Steve . . ." Lucy cried weakly, gasping for breath, "Get away . . . save yourself . . ."

Forrester knew that the psychotic killer was now over the top—beyond reasoning, beyond talk. Frozen on the top step of the stairwell, he looked about wildly for some instrument of deliverance, some miraculous machination that would permit him to release Lucy from Malloy's clutches before twelve thousand pounds of explosive released all of them from the bonds of Earth.

He looked to his left. Flashes of red and blue from outside the condemned building told him that the cops had arrived—too late.

He looked to his right. The clock read 00:33.

He looked down. The detonator wires! Malloy had somehow gotten his right foot snarled in a loop of wire! A chance—a slim one at best, but it was all he had!

In a flash, before his bloodied adversary could react, Steve reached down, grabbed a double handful of wire and pulled with all his strength. The loop tightened and jerked Malloy's foot forward. It skidded out from under him. Instinctively, he flailed his arms for balance, freeing his captive. With a roar of fury and frustration, the murderous Irishman toppled over backward as Lucy Baker stumbled forward.

00:24 showed on the timer.

Badly shaken and barely conscious as a result of Malloy's cruel choke hold, she collapsed in Forrester's arms. He threw her over his shoulder fireman-style and leapt from the doomed bus. With a strength and speed born of pure adrenaline, he raced for safety. In the darkened ruin of the Drifts's lobby, he tripped over a loose piece of concrete, almost losing his balance. Somehow he recovered. Hardly noticing the weight of his precious cargo, Steve burst out of the entrance. He plunged down the stairs without breaking stride. Across the moonlit courtyard he ran, zigzagging around piles of rubble, streaking for the only shelter there was: the plywood fence.

A hundred feet to the fence—and maybe twelve seconds to go before the Greyhound Americruiser became ground zero in the biggest blast Nevada had experienced since the fifties.

With a final burst of speed, Forrester dashed through the shattered fence. He spun around and gently placed a still-dazed Lucy in the lee of the closest intact section of fence. All they could do now was pray. He dropped to all fours and protectively straddled her body.

A uniformed metro cop stepped casually out of his patrol car and approached the prone couple.

"Excuse me, sir—," he began.

Steve raised his head unbelievingly. "Get down, you idiot!" he shouted at the young policeman. "There's a bomb—"

He never finished the sentence.

47 **If the implosion** of the Drifts Hotel and Casino had proceeded as planned, no more than fifty pounds of dynamite would have been required to bring it tumbling down.

The secret was the location of the charges. By placing them next to a few deliberately weakened support pillars in strategic locations, those pillars would have given way simultaneously, causing each floor to collapse in turn. With gravity doing most of the work, the entire structure would have tumbled like a house of cards.

Because there would have been no significant outward explosive force, the building would have fallen straight down, collapsing in upon itself, or imploding. Flying debris would have been minimized, the risk of damage to nearby structures negligible.

But Steve Forrester's unscheduled destruction of the building achieved quite the opposite effect. Instead of a neat implosion resulting in a compact, easy-to-scoop pile of rubble, the twelve thousand pounds of high explosives generated a violent, unconfined blast that scattered fragments of concrete and steel for over half a mile in all directions.

First came the flash. Brilliant, blinding, nova-bright.

A millisecond later, the roar. Thunderous, deafening, pure sound.

Then the shock wave. Irresistible, crushing, a giant invisible steamroller.

Huge chunks of concrete and steel rose skyward, tumbling in slow motion through the roiling orange-red fireball. Smaller pieces of debris flew wildly. Flaming embers arced through the night sky like wayward tracer bullets.

Some of the blast's energy was absorbed in the instantaneous creation of a fifty-foot-deep crater. But at ground level, the outbound shock wave still packed enough punch to flatten anything in its path for a considerable distance—including the construction fence around the site, which folded down and outward as if it had been fixed to the ground by giant piano hinges. Deafened by the roar and stunned by the shock wave, Steve Forrester hardly felt the impact of the fence as it collapsed upon him, striking the back of his head and knocking the breath from his body. Valiantly, he tried to hold on to consciousness, to stay awake for Lucy, but it was futile.

With only three-quarters of an inch of plywood to shield him and Lucy from the debris that was raining down like massive hailstones, Forrester's world faded to black.

"**Unit 3-16.** Request ambulances at intersection of Twain and Las Vegas Boulevard. Code 401B."

"Acknowledged, 3-16."

"Dispatcher, we have a Code 438 in front of Day's Inn. Disabled vehicles blocking access to explosion site. Request wreckers. Repeat, request wreckers at Day's Inn."

"This is Unit 2-31. Code 422 on south side of explosion site. Officer down . . ."

Impatiently, Lieutenant Frank Marshall shut off the radio. Let someone else coordinate the cleanup; despite the rancor he felt toward his ex-partner, there was no way he was going to abandon Steve Forrester. With siren wailing, he floored the unmarked Ford into the dust storm that was rolling outward from the explosion.

"This is worse than driving through L.A. smog," he remarked to Morris Jaworski as he slowed down because of the rapidly decreasing visibility. Ghostly outlines of the Strip's big neon signs glimmered down weakly through the haze. Smoldering chunks of debris littered the roadway, becoming more numerous as the two lawmen neared the explosion site. In the distance, faint pockets of flame flickered through the fog, marking ground zero. Damaged vehicles littered the road.

"I haven't seen so many wrecked cars since my ex-wife took her driving test," Jaworski noted. "Steve must have smashed through them like a snowplow. God, I hope he made it out of the bus in time. Before it blew, I mean."

"I do, too, Moe. Believe it or not."

"What is it with you guys, anyway?"

"Steve and me? Well, we may not . . . see eye-to-eye about some matters, but right now that doesn't seem so important. What he did took incredible guts. Let's just do our damnedest to find him."

"What about the people who were with him on the bus? Didn't the radio call mention a woman with him? And some guy who jumped on board just as he drove off?"

"I assume the woman is Lucy Baker. She had called me earlier from Steve's car. And I suspect the man might be Buster Malloy. We just have to hope that Lucy's okay, too. As for Malloy, I don't really give a shit." He paused. "No, scratch that. I hope the bastard's *dead*."

They drove north until they could go no farther. Traffic was completely stalled. Still a fair way down the Strip, the pale red-blue flashes of Marshall's hastily deployed roadblocks were just visible through the miasma

"Come on, Moe," said the LVMPD lieutenant, braking to a halt. "No way we're gonna get any closer by car."

The two men stepped out of the unmarked unit and began to run toward the blast site. When they reached the roadblock, Marshall stopped and asked one of the officers for a quick assessment of the damage.

"I don't know what happened at the other roadblocks, Lieutenant," the patrolman replied. "But I do know we kept a lot of vehicles from getting caught up in the explosion. And we cleared most of the traffic out of the area before the blast. If we'd'a had more than just a couple of minutes' warning . . ."

"Yeah. Well, we didn't. What about casualties?"

"Some civilians were hurt by flying debris. That's all I can tell you right now. We requested ambulances."

"All right. See if you can get these cars turned around and out of here. Let the ambulances through."

"We're on it."

The black-and-white squad car sat forlornly amid the scattered chunks of broken concrete and twisted metal like an abandoned junker awaiting its final journey to the crusher. The left side of the vehicle was severely dented. Its hood and trunk lid were gone. The candy-bar roof flasher was history. All four tires were flat. Except for a jagged crust around the frames, there was not a square inch of glass remaining in any of its windows.

The surviving member of the two-man patrol team sat facing out on the passenger seat of the battered car, his heels resting on the door sill. Blood oozed from dozens of tiny puncture wounds on the left side of his face and neck. A white-coated emergency medical technician squatted next to him, dabbing at the cuts and carefully tweezing crystals of safety glass from his patient's skin.

On the driver's side, between the car and the remains of the Drifts's construction fence, a motionless form, covered by a red blanket, lay on the asphalt. Another EMT had wheeled a gurney next to it and was unzipping a rubber body bag just as Frank Marshall and Morris Jaworski arrived breathlessly on the scene.

Marshall flashed his badge at the EMT with the body bag. "What the hell happened here?" he asked bluntly.

"I'm afraid this officer's dead, Lieutenant," the technician replied, indicating the still form at his feet.

"I'd like to know who it is. May I look under the blanket?"

"You don't want to see him. His head is completely severed. Must have been a piece of flying debris."

"Poor bastard," said Morris Jaworski.

"Why don't you talk to the other officer?" the ambulance man suggested. "He's over there in the car—being treated for cuts."

Shaking his head sadly, Frank walked around to where the surviving policeman was being ministered to by the EMT. Despite the blood, he recognized the man immediately. Greg Foster, a fifteen-year veteran of the LVMPD. And that meant his partner, the dead man, had to be Jerry Stern. A rookie, married with a couple of young kids, if Marshall recalled correctly. *Goddamn it,* the police lieutenant mused bitterly, *why is it always the ones with the most to live for who have to die?*

Aloud, he said gently to the bleeding cop: "How are you feeling, Greg?"

The policeman's voice quavered and he trembled visibly. "Oh God, Lieutenant . . . it-it was awful. One minute Jerry's s-standin' there . . . the next minute his . . . his f-f-fuckin' head's gone. He'd just g-gotten out of the car . . . to talk to this guy—"

"What guy, Greg?"

"I-I dunno. Some guy . . . ran out of the b-building just before it blew. Looked like . . . looked like he was carryin' somebody on his shoulder. He ducked down . . . behind the fence—"

"Where, Greg? What part of the fence?"

"Take it easy on him, Lieutenant," the EMT cut in. "He's still in shock. . . ."

Marshall ignored the medic and persisted. "This is important, Greg. *Exactly where did you see this man run to?*"

Foster waved off the EMT's ministrations and rose unsteadily to his feet. He pointed to the flattened construction fence. "Just . . . just over there, Lieutenant. See that sheet of plywood . . . with the big chunk of concrete on top of it?"

"He's under there?"

The injured officer nodded weakly and sank back onto the passenger seat of the ruined police car. "How'm I gonna . . . tell Jerry's wife?" he muttered.

"Hey, you! Give us a hand over here. Quick!"

The EMT caught the urgency in Frank Marshall's voice. He immediately abandoned the body bag and ran over to join the two policemen at the remains of the fence. "What's up, Lieutenant?"

"Somebody's trapped under this collapsed fence." Marshall indicated a sheet of plywood, reinforced with a frame of two-by-fours, one of hundreds surrounding the blast site that had been blown flat by the shock wave. The end of the sheet was pinned under a large jagged piece of concrete bristling with rusty rebar stumps. "If you two guys could roll that cement back just a little, I think I can lift this end."

Using the protruding rebar as handles, Morris Jaworski and the medic strained to move the heavy lump of concrete. Gradually, agonizingly, they rolled it back, an inch, two inches. The faces of both men shone red with exertion and dripped with sweat. Another inch—but it was enough for Frank Marshall. With a Herculean heave, he lifted his end of the fence panel knee-high. Then, using a weightlifter's clean-and-jerk motion, he reversed his grip and dropped to a crouch. With every ounce of sinew he possessed, the big policeman slowly straightened his legs and raised the end of the plywood sheet to shoulder height.

Jaworski and the EMT quickly ran to share Marshall's burden. Between them, the three men managed to slide the plywood out from under the chunk of concrete and toss it to one side. It had covered a slight depression in the ground. In the depression lay the dusty, dark-jacketed body of a man.

"Hey, hero!" The lieutenant crouched next to the prostrate body and frantically shook its shoulder. "Is that you?"

Steve Forrester stirred and groaned.

He rolled off the prone form of Lucy Baker, who coughed and blinked her eyes open.

"You guys all right?" said Frank.

Lucy lifted her head and nodded weakly. Forrester raised himself on one elbow. He spat out a mouthful of grit and bestowed a twisted grin upon his rescuer. "Chrissake, Frank," he croaked, "don't you ever knock?"

In the police lab at the Southwest Area Command, Morris Jaworski nodded his thanks to the fingerprint specialist. "Good work, Chuck. I guess that confirms it."

"The perps weren't so smart after all," the specialist observed. "Those thermite devices were loaded with prints."

"Obviously, they expected them all to burn up with the Obelisk. They figured you can't lift prints from ashes." Jaworski scanned the printout on his desk. "Daniel K. Shiller. Con man, card cheat, grifter. Last collar at Diamond Lil's for hand mucking. He was in the Spring Mountain lockup at the same time as Jurgen Voss. And Buster Malloy drove Voss to the jail that day. It all fits."

"What are the chances of nailing this Shiller?"

"Pretty slim. We've got a statewide APB out. And the feds are putting him on their Ten Most Wanted list. But I'd bet my badge he's out of the country by now."

"With fifty million U.S. dollars in his pocket."

"I know. But money doesn't always buy happiness."

The specialist sighed. "You're probably right, Sarge. All the same, I'd like to give it a try someday."

"Here's a late-breaking bulletin from News Thirteen Inside Las Vegas. I'm Debbie Blake."

The attractive blond newsreader's face dissolved to a helicopter shot of a deep crater surrounded by a sea of rubble. Tendrils of smoke still rose from the scattered wreckage as fire trucks hosed down the area. She continued her voice-over: "Searchers have found another body near yesterday's massive explosion at the Drifts's demolition site, estimated by authorities to be three times as powerful as the Oklahoma City blast. The body of an elderly man was discovered beneath the wreckage of a nearby collapsed wall. Officials have not yet released his identity.

"This brings to eight the number of known fatalities in the blast, including the bomber himself, whose body investigators say will probably never be found. Two passing motorists died when their vehicles were crushed by large pieces of concrete thrown out by the explosion. Three pedestrians were killed, either by the shock wave or from injuries caused by flying debris. A Las Vegas police officer died instantly when he stepped out of his patrol car just as the explosive was detonated. And a female visitor to Las Vegas was fatally wounded by flying glass when the window in her motel room across the street was shattered by the blast.

"Scores of injured people have been treated at area hospitals and clinics. Injuries range from cuts caused by flying glass to broken bones and internal injuries resulting from automobile accidents. Many collisions occurred when motorists lost control of their vehicles at the moment of the explosion.

"Damage to neighboring properties is estimated in the hundreds of millions of dollars. Acres of broken glass and damaged neon signs are the most visible results of the disaster, the worst to hit Las Vegas since the MGM Grand fire of nineteen eighty.

"A police spokesman credits the quick thinking of a casino executive for saving thousands of lives in what could have been the most terrible man-made catastrophe in U.S. history, eclipsing even the destruction of the World Trade Center." Footage of Steve Forrester and Lucy Baker being helped into the back of an ambulance appeared on-screen. "Steven Forrester, a vice president of the Galaxy Hotel and Casino, commandeered the Greyhound bus into which the twelve-thousand-pound bomb had been loaded by a gang of extortionists. He drove it away from the Roman Palladium, where it had been timed to explode within minutes, to the relative safety of the Drifts Hotel, scheduled for demolition tomorrow.

"With the help of Lucy Baker, a colleague at the Galaxy, Forrester subdued the bomber, Francis Marion Malloy, an ex-employee of the same hotel, who is believed to have died in the blast. One of his accomplices, Jurgen Voss, had previously committed suicide in police custody. A third gang member, identified as Daniel K. Shiller, is still at large, and a warrant has been issued for his arrest. Investigators have confirmed—"

Lucy pressed the MUTE button as the now-familiar images of the explosion's aftermath continued to flicker silently across the picture tube. "Been there. Done that," she murmured dreamily, snuggling closer to Steve Forrester on the Ethan Allen couch. "Why are we watching this, anyway?"

"I dunno. Must be something better on."

"Anything strike your fancy?"

"How about a cigarette?"

"Uh-uh. You promised. I meant, is there anything you want to watch?"

He flexed his sore muscles and thought for a moment. "How about one of those *I Love Lucy* reruns?" he suggested casually, cupping her breast in his bandaged right hand.

NORTH AFRICA, OCTOBER

PART V

48 In a vain attempt to alleviate the oppressive heat, Dan Shiller removed the Panama hat and fanned his face with it.

By the time the bus reached Zarzis, a sun-bleached Tunisian town on the coastal road to Libya, Shiller had removed his custom-tailored camel-hair jacket and abandoned his pure silk tie. The North African sun beat mercilessly upon the roof of the primitive vehicle, more of a truck with seats than a proper bus. Dust poured in through glassless windows. Most of the passengers spoke Arabic; a few conversed in Italian. About half wore Western garb of some description, while the rest were dressed in what looked to Shiller like soiled bedsheets. His fellow travelers were mostly men. Two heavily veiled women, one small child, and a malodorous goat completed the manifest.

The bus rattled steadily on through the blistering heat, stopping occasionally to pick up and discharge passengers. Dan unfolded a linen handkerchief and wiped his sweating forehead, instantly transforming the handkerchief from pure white to gray-beige.

Finally, after the longest four hours Shiller had ever spent on any public conveyance, the bus came to a halt at the Libyan border town of Abu Kammash. Two swarthy olive-uniformed Libyan soldiers with AK-47s slung over their shoulders climbed aboard. In Arabic, Italian, and French they demanded passports.

By the time the border guards reached Dan's seat, the fugitive from American justice had his passport ready—complete with the Libyan visa he had purchased two weeks earlier for a thousand dollars cash from a clerk at the Tunisian consulate in L.A.

"Americano?" the soldier whistled in surprise. He flipped open the blue-covered passport, then a smile of recognition lit up his unshaven face.

"Ah, Signor Shiller!" With gestures and a few words of broken English, the man indicated that Shiller should accompany him off the bus. "Signor Barrouhi . . . he wait for you in automobile. You come. Bring all weeth you!"

Dan needed no further urging. The people from the bank had promised that he'd be met at the border, but until this moment the con man/mass murderer had wondered whether that appointment would actually be kept. He picked up his jacket and his carry-on bag and followed the soldier out into the blazing African afternoon.

Shiller breathed a sigh of relief when he spotted the big Mercedes-Benz stretch limo with the tinted windows. Thank God for air-conditioning. And thank God he didn't have to travel the rest of the way to Tripoli in that fucking cattle car. It was about time these wogs started showing him a little respect.

The guard opened the back door of the limousine, and Dan ducked quickly inside. A heavyset man impeccably attired in a pin-striped double-breasted suit half rose from his seat and extended a manicured hand to his guest.

"Mr. Shiller! How delightful to meet you," the man said cordially in a mellifluous Oxford drawl. "My name is Sadok Barrouhi. I am a director of the Libyan Arab Foreign Bank."

"Glad to meet you."

"I do hope your trip from Jerba was not too uncomfortable," Barrouhi continued. "And I apologize for the inconvenience. It is unfortunate that the Western nations have seen fit to prohibit air travel to and from our poor country."

"Look, Mr. Barrouhi, it was a long, hot trip. But I'm here now. I just need a little sleep and I'll be as good as new."

"That is no problem, Mr. Shiller, your accommodations are all arranged. Meanwhile, may I offer you a drink? Scotch? Vodka?"

"Why sure—a scotch would be great. But I thought you . . . Moslems didn't drink."

The banker laughed. "That is the public custom. However, we are now in private. And I am afraid your decadent Western ways have quite seduced me."

Somewhere between Az Zawiyah and Tripoli, twenty-one hours of travel caught up with Dan Shiller and he fell asleep in the cushioned comfort of the Mercedes limousine.

He awoke with a start as Barrouhi gently shook his shoulder. Rubbing the sleep from his eyes, he became aware that the car had stopped. He looked out of the window; they appeared to be parked in some kind of enclosed courtyard. Armed soldiers, several grades more clean-cut and smartly turned out than those at the border crossing, stood at attention around the perimeter of the compound.

"Where the hell are we?" said Shiller. "This doesn't look like any hotel."

"You are right, Mr. Shiller. This is not a hotel. In fact, it is one of the residences of Colonel Mu'ammar Qaddafi."

"Colonel Qaddafi? You mean the president? Why bring me here?"

"The colonel has expressed an interest in meeting this mysterious multimillionaire. It is an honor that is rarely accorded to foreign visitors, particularly Americans."

"What does he want?"

"Why not let him tell you himself? In the meantime, perhaps you would care to refresh yourself in the guest room that has been prepared for you."

"Look, I don't know what's going on here." Shiller's sensitive antennae detected unwelcome vibrations. "The deal was, you'd put me up in a hotel, and tomorrow we'd discuss where the money was to be transferred. For which I'm paying you five million American dollars. Now if it's all the same to you, Mr. Barrouhi, I'd just as soon stick to the script."

The banker smiled apologetically. "I do sympathize with your position, Mr. Shiller. But one does not refuse an audience with the president of the Great Socialist People's Libyan Arab Jamahiriya. Perhaps if I came by your room in half an hour . . . ?"

49 **Colonel Mu'ammar Qaddafi** indicated a comfortable armchair next to his own in the big, green-draped salon. "Please be seated, Mr. Shiller."

Qaddafi exuded power. Physically, he was considerably shorter than Shiller had visualized, but there was no question that he naturally dominated his surroundings. His English was good, although heavily accented. He wore an olive-green military uniform and carried a sidearm. Dan wondered why he needed the pistol, surrounded as he was by guards carrying as much firepower as a small army. Probably a question of image, the grifter decided.

"We trust you had a comfortable journey."

"Ah, yes, thank you, Colonel."

"Is there anything we can do to make your stay with us more pleasant?"

"Well, sir, now that you mention it, I would very much appreciate being allowed to check in to my hotel. Not that it isn't a real honor to meet you—"

"We understand completely, Mr. Shiller. You must be tired."

"Yes. Well, it's been a real pleasure—"

"Tell us about the money, Mr. Shiller."

"What?"

"The money. Where did you get it? And why did you send it here?"

Dan Shiller felt a cold chill creep down his spine. "Ah, well, Colonel, since you ask, let me put it this way. The money is, quite frankly, from certain . . . activities that the authorities back home do not exactly . . . approve of. And the reason I had it temporarily transferred to Libya was because I knew that with . . . relations between our two countries the way they are, you know, I didn't think you'd be too eager to return the money. Or have me extradited."

"You are quite correct about that, Mr. Shiller. So, let us summarize. The money is the proceeds of criminal activity—we wonder if it has any connection with the recent events in Las Vegas?—and you want us to launder it for you through the Libyan Arab Foreign Bank."

"Yes, Colonel. And I'm paying them five million dollars for the privilege."

"It may not be possible."

Shiller's heart skipped a beat. "What do you mean?"

Qaddafi smiled, but his eyes were hard. "Have you considered staying here with us in Libya?"

"I-I don't think so." There was no way on earth Dan wanted to spend a single day longer than he had to in this desert rathole.

"That is too bad. Because, unfortunately, we cannot release the money to you at this time."

Shiller's shoulders slumped. "Why not, Colonel?" he asked dejectedly, not really caring what the bullshit answer was, knowing that he'd been royally screwed by this slimy little asshole. And there was probably going to be fuck all he could do about it.

"Our executive council has decided to hold the money in exactly the same way your own government has frozen our deposits in the United States."

"For how long?" Dan asked miserably.

"Until the U.S. government releases Libyan assets."

Or until hell freezes over, thought Shiller. "This is just fuckin' robbery," he muttered.

Colonel Qaddafi's eyes blazed. "What was that, Mr. Shiller? You dare accuse us of robbery? You, who have robbed and murdered your own countrymen?" He slammed his fist angrily on the arm of his chair and barked orders to the two soldiers who stood by the double doors to the great room. "Perhaps you will see the error of your ways after a few years of spiritual cleansing in the Al Baraq Detention Center."

"Oh God, no," Shiller wailed as the soldiers moved in to flank him. "Look, Colonel. I'll pay double what we agreed on! I'll give you half! Just let me go!"

Qaddafi smiled. "Why should we settle for half, Mr. Shiller, when we have it all? And we have you, too? Surely you can see the logic of it."

Epilogue

Through a series of credit notes and refund checks, Jack Wilson returned every cent he had expropriated from Defcon. The illicit transactions were never discovered.

Once he had accomplished this task, he tendered his resignation to chairman Bill Swinden. Swinden was cordial and appropriately sympathetic but made no attempt to persuade Wilson to stay on. "Good luck, Jack," he said piously. "I wish you all the best and I trust we'll meet again."

"I sincerely doubt that," replied Wilson coolly.

Thousands of mourners thronged the streets around the Roman Catholic cathedral in Jersey City where Tony Francisco's funeral services were held. Telegrams and phone calls poured in from around the world. Movie stars and entertainers, politicians and royalty arrived in stretch limousines and joined the late singer's grieving family in the packed church. It was like a star-studded Hollywood premiere. Francisco would have approved.

When the circumstances surrounding his death were revealed, family and business associates launched a series of massive lawsuits against the Galaxy and its corporate masters, Summit Enterprises. In the end, the courts held that the Galaxy was not liable for Francisco's death.

Gloria Latorella mourned Tony's death for almost a year. Eventually she and Solly Greenspan were married in a quiet ceremony.

Sales of Tony Francisco's albums skyrocketed.

Barney Leopold's family slowly recovered from the shock of his death by poisoning. His wife, Shirley, was surprised at the magnitude of her late husband's debts—and even more so by the nature of the people to whom he owed the money. But she managed to cover the debts with the proceeds of his life insurance. Upon the advice of her attorneys, she sued the Galaxy for negligence and settled out of court for a little over $3 million. Uncharacteristically, Emmett Druperman approved the settlement without a qualm.

Because the original receipt for Leopold's dice winnings had disappeared, however, Druperman adamantly refused to pay any part of them to his widow.

Bulk seasonings and unsealed condiments were henceforth banned from all Galaxy restaurants.

It was generally assumed that Buster Malloy's body had been vaporized in the Drifts blast. Helga Johanssen's body was never discovered.

Attempts to extradite Dan Shiller from Libya met with no success.

Torn between admiration for Steve Forrester's heroic act and resentment at his ex-partner's perceived insensitivity to his personal advancement, LVMPD Lieutenant Frank Marshall remained ambivalent in his attitude toward Forrester.

Emmett Druperman settled the strike against the Galaxy on his own terms, which amounted to giving the unions nothing. Within a few months, the megaresort was again posting record profits.

"Gamblers have short memories," rasped the CEO, shifting uncomfortably in his leather chair.

Amid speeches and flashing cameras, Steve Forrester and his fiancée, Lucy Baker, were honored for their heroism with a presentation of symbolic keys to the city by Las Vegas mayor Oscar Fairchild.

During the hourlong ceremony at City Hall, Lucy managed to maintain an appropriately modest demeanor, while Forrester squirmed with embarrassment and profoundly wished he were somewhere else.